For Nan and Bob,
Great neighbors, friends al
Jillian Methodists.
Jo

CALLING

Joe Samuel Starnes

Joe Samuel Sta

9-21-2005
Montclair, N.J.

jefferson press

ISBN 0–97189–745–X
Library of Congress Catalog Card Number: 2005929154

Whiskey River
Words and Music by J.B. Shin III and Paul Stroud
© 1972 (Renewed 2000) FULL NELSON MUSIC, INC.
All Rights Controlled and Administered by EMI LONGITUDE MUSIC
All Rights Reserved International Copyright Secured
Used by Permission

I Can Get Off On You
Words and Music by Waylon Jennings and Willie Nelson
© 1978 FULL NELSON MUSIC and WAYLON JENNINGS MUSIC
All Rights for FULL NELSON MUSIC Controlled and Administered by
EMI LONGITUDE MUSIC. All Rights for WAYLON
JENNINGS MUSIC Controlled and Administered by IRVING MUSIC INC.
All Rights Reserved International Copyright Secured
Used by Permission

Editing by Arlene Prunkl
Book Design by Fiona Raven

First Printing September 2005
Printed in Canada

Published by Jefferson Press

jefferson press
P.O. Box 115
Lookout Mountain, TN 37350

*In memory of Larry Brown, a great Mississippi author
whose fiction and essays inspired me to keep writing.
He left us much too soon.*

CONTENTS

"But you, son of man, hear what I say to you. Do not be rebellious like that rebellious house; open your mouth and eat what I give you."

Now when I looked, there was a hand stretched out to me; and behold, a scroll of a book *was* in it.

Then He spread it before me; and *there was* writing on the inside and on the outside, and written on it *were* lamentations and mourning and woe.

Moreover He said to me, "Son of man, eat what you find; eat this scroll, and go, speak to the house of Israel."

So I opened my mouth, and He caused me to eat that scroll.

And He said to me, "Son of man, feed your belly and fill your stomach with this scroll that I give you." So I ate, and it was in my mouth like honey in sweetness.

—*Ezekiel 2:8-3:3*

IF YOU GOT EARS

Timber Goodman hung his head. He was tired of looking through the dusty Greyhound bus window at the northeast reaches of the Mojave Desert, fifty miles from Las Vegas and all the money he'd lost. Everything in the early Sunday morning sun had seemed small and tacky, even the huge hotels that glowed at night, the strip so glittering that it had made his heart leap up when he pulled into town a few days before, only to turn his stomach as he took one last glimpse before heading back home through the hulking red and brown Nevada mountains that dwarfed the Crystal City in the light of day.

The sun was searing but dimmed by the tinted windows of the bus. Timber tried to sleep but was too hungover to get comfortable and his head hurt too much to read, so he just sat with his eyes closed, trying not to listen to the hum of the big engine and trying not to feel the steady vibration of the radials running along the hot asphalt of the road beneath his seat. The smells of coffee spilled on worn nylon carpet and bare feet and exhaust fumes and the sharp blue water in the bus toilet mingled and swirled in the dry air in the back of the Greyhound cabin. His mouth was dry and sour but it would be hours before he would have a chance to get something to drink.

He opened his eyes when the bus slowed down and pulled into the Valley of Fire Motel & Casino, a stop smack in the middle of nowhere. Close to his window he saw a lone man waiting to board, a real shitkicker in cowboy boots carrying a suitcase and a briefcase that must have belonged to someone during World War II. He was tall and thin, dressed in a dingy white dress shirt and a tattered blue suit missing a button, his slacks wrinkled and dirty like maybe he had slept in the desert in his clothes. He was sunburned and had greasy hair and scratches on his face, a gauze bandage taped clumsily on the left side of his neck.

Timber—the nickname came from his trademark deep-voiced shout of *"Timmmm–berrrrrr!"* when belittling fallen politicians on his past morning radio shows—leaned back in his seat and resumed his Louis L'Amour paperback and cursed riding the bus with rednecks, freaks, mumbling old people, Mexicans and assorted speakers of other languages. There had been a time in his late twenties when he was damn near a celebrity and flew first class when he traveled to Vegas for broadcasting conventions. He'd had a morning drive-time slot on Houston's biggest country station in the oil boom days, a time when people threw $100 bills around Texas like floppy tortillas. It had been more than twenty years; it seemed like another lifetime.

The ride back to South Dakota would take at least twenty-four hours. The bus was less than half full with most passengers spaced far from others. Timber, a heavy man with long legs and thick forearms, had been thrilled to find a row near the back of the bus that was empty all the way across. He hated it when someone sat beside him and he had to withdraw into a single seat, competing for the armrest. He had a bad ankle that he liked to stretch out, sometimes into the adjoining seat, flexing it often to try to keep it loose. Timber scratched his grizzled beard and ran his hand through his collar-length graying brown hair, a Kris Kristofferson-like style he had worn since the seventies.

The man with the worn luggage climbed onto the bus and was surveying the seats from the front. Timber hoped the man wouldn't sit close to him. At least he could sit across the aisle in one of the open seats and not in the next seat. The man stood up stiff as a board and lurched forward when the bus driver dropped the big silver bullet into gear and pulled off. Timber could see that the man had a light mustache, the skimpy kind that a high school boy might keep in hopes that it will start growing and fill in any day.

The man stopped about halfway down the aisle. He stared at the seats in the back of the bus, his face scrunched up like he was trying to read a name on a weathered gravestone. He didn't blink. He had wrinkles around his eyes like an old dirt farmer and loose skin below his jawbone—a look like he'd weathered fast but at one time had been fat and happy with fleshy jowls. He appeared to be scowling, with his teeth clenched and his lips pulled tight in one corner, but as he got closer, Timber saw he had a curious welcoming expression: half smirk, half smile. The scratches on his face looked fresh and he had a small blue bruise on his left cheek. His pupils were abnormally large and the color around them was a fierce pale blue, almost silver; his right eye was severely bloodshot, as though he'd been poked.

Timber had a lifelong habit of imagining what people he encountered were like at home, listening to the radio; he visualized the man tuning in to the farm and ranch report, the most followed news in Pierre, or the sports updates. This man would lie in a single bed with dingy sheets late into the morning listening to the radio and nursing a hangover and sometimes wounds from a bar fight, half dressed in his clothes from the night before; at night, he would tune into a country station and sip liquor while driving around in an old pickup truck listening to country songs about either drinking and cheating or love of family and freedom and God.

The man inched closer and Timber opened the book again, pretending to read. Timber watched from the corner of his eye as the man stopped at his row and set his briefcase down into a seat across the aisle. He lifted the battered blue hard-shell suitcase into the rack above the seats, jamming it onto the narrow shelf. It barely fit, wedged in as though it were a steel spike driven into a block of wood. The man stood for several long moments, nervously staring at the suitcase in the rack. He tapped it with his hand to make sure it wouldn't budge. Timber could see bruises and scrapes on his knuckles and his right wrist, a black fingernail on his left hand.

The man sat down in the opposite window seat and held his briefcase flat on his lap, sitting stock still. Timber stole glances at the man, guessing him to be just out of prison, a problem gambler and drinker. Timber figured he could relate to him about the gambling and drinking troubles but he was reluctant to talk to strangers on the bus, particularly the characters that boarded outside of Las Vegas. He imagined he and the man shared woman problems too; the wounds indicated he was most likely an angry drunk.

After a long spell the man moved, setting the briefcase on the aisle seat next to him. He clicked the two metal latches, opening the briefcase to reveal its contents: a black leather New King James Holy Bible, a liter of Jim Beam and a foot-long hunting knife of the sort Jim Bowie had died with at the Alamo. Timber stifled a laugh, letting out a little grunt he had intended to be inaudible. The man's eyes went straight to him and he had a slight smile on his face, as though he had been addressed.

"Hello there, my brother," the man said, his voice hoarse, a strong Southern voice with a hick twang. "How're you doin'?"

Timber nodded, avoiding eye contact. He looked down at his book and pretended to read again. He cursed himself for getting caught spying on the man. He was afraid he might not be able to shake him.

The man lifted the large bottle of bourbon from the briefcase.

"It's dry out there today. Hard to believe that we had a big thunderstorm here last night. The desert just soaks that rain up."

The man pointed to him with the top of the almost full bottle.

"Would you like a snort?"

Timber didn't answer.

"You sure?"

Timber shook his head without looking, turning a page as though he were reading.

"Well…all right, then," the man said.

He watched from the corner of his eye as the man uncapped the Jim Beam and took a pull. Before he recapped it, he held it across the aisle toward Timber and tipped it slightly, again offering him a drink with the gesture. Timber got a whiff of the red liquor but again shook his head without looking up from his book.

"That's all right, boy, it's still a little early," he said in a friendly voice. "You lemmee know if you want a snort later."

The man recapped the bourbon and put it into the open briefcase. He picked up the knife and examined the worn sheath where the name ZEKE had been pounded into the dark leather in block letters. He fingered the indentations in the cowhide. He then slid the knife out of the cover and wet his index finger on his tongue. He slowly ran his finger down the blade, glinted from the muted sunlight shining through the dark glass bus windows.

"Boy, this is some knife. It'll cut. It'll saw. It'll do 'bout anything you want. Good Christian men like Jim Bowie and Davy Crockett knew what they was doing with these knives."

The man put the knife back into the leather sheath and lifted the Bible from the briefcase. He closed it, clicking the latches. He put the briefcase under the window seat and moved over one seat closer to Timber but still across the aisle. He crossed his right leg over his left and turned to face him, his hand with the Bible resting on his knee.

"How you doing today, brother?"

Timber ignored him, hoping maybe he'd go look for another person for conversation. Timber calculated that it would take eight hours to get to Salt Lake City where he would change buses. He had never run into anybody like this back in the days when he flew on an airplane.

"Yes, my brother, that's fine," the man said. "Keep reading your book. I'm the Reverend Ezekiel Blizzard Jr., by the way, but you can call me Zeke. And don't let nobody tell you I ain't a preacher no more, just 'cause I'm out here rambling 'round the desert with a knife and a bottle of liquor. I *am* washed in the blood of the lamb."

Timber watched the preacher stretch out his arm and look at his watch, a weathered silver Timex that slid from under the cuff of the worn blue suit jacket.

"Son, we've got a long way to go. I want you to hear my story. It's all about how I got off on the wrong track, how I got lost from God's word right here."

He held the Bible in his right hand and slapped it with his left like a quarterback does a football.

"I think my story will do you some good, son. If you got ears, you're gonna hear my story...

"My story starts way before I ended up out here in the desert," the preacher continued, as though starting a sermon. "It starts back home. Home is Georgia. I lived just a few hours outside Atlanta...By the way, where you from, boy?"

Timber knew he was going to have to either answer or move. He wanted desperately to find a seat near someone quiet and sink down into his book until he got home to his dingy one-room apartment, but he was hesitant to be rude. Maybe the preacher would get off somewhere soon.

"Louisiana," Timber said without looking at him, still pretending to read.

"A *coonass* Cajun? I didn't take you for a Southerner at all, boy."

"It has been a long time," Timber said, still not looking up. "I've lived all over the Midwest and West since I left back in the early eighties."

"You don't sound like you from *Lose-ee-anna.*"

"Yeah. Well, I've worked in radio a long time and that causes you to lose your accent—*'specially* when you are not in the South."

The way 'specially came out of his own mouth echoed in Timber's head, the old drawl of home coming back up in his tongue.

"Well, I'll be," the preacher said. "We got that in common too. I was on the radio a few years myself. I wasn't a deejay. I had my own gospel hour. People all over North Georgia tuned in to hear me. I set 'em straight every Sunday."

Timber imagined the preacher on the air, his voice worked up to a fever pitch about Jesus and the Devil and the never-ending struggle for rural men's troubled, no good, sinful souls. Timber hoped now that they had spoken, he could go back to his book, eventually drift into a nap, and that would be the end of it. He knew he was only kidding himself.

"But I fell...I fell *hard*," the preacher said. "I lost my radio show, my church, my wife, my kids, my money, my house, my car, my dog—*my soul.* You name it, I done lost it. I did everything wrong I could do wrong. Cheating, stealing, conniving, lying, womanizing, drinking, drugging, gambling. I don't think Moses made but one or two rules that I didn't break. I was on the highway to hell in a hand basket, boy, I'm telling you what."

The preacher's voice had the rhythmic, evenly measured sentences with the dramatic flourishes Timber was accustomed to from Baptist ministers back home. Timber had grown up in a Baptist church, and one of his first jobs in radio had been to run the soundboard on Sunday, playing gospel music and monitoring the levels while preachers and their flocks from all along the pockmarked asphalt roads winding along the river between Baton Rouge and New Orleans came into the studio to preach and sing. It had been a long time since he'd heard the passionate voice of a Southern Baptist minister.

"Coming out here to *Las Vegas* didn't do me no good at first," the preacher continued. "It is *sumpin'* else. All the sins of man packed into one long flat street. It ain't no coincidence that Caesar's Palace was one of the first big hotels on the strip. You know, Christians blame the Jews and forget it was the Romans who nailed Jesus to the cross. I figure that hotel was one way Satan honored the Roman Empire for what they done to his adversary."

The preacher shook his head in a slow side-to-side motion, smiling like he'd heard a good joke.

"D'ya ever see on TV when Evel Knievel jumped his motor*sickle* over the fountains at Caesar's? That *sumbitch* was sure 'nuff crazy. One of the first things I did in Vegas was to go over there and walk off that jump, replay it in my mind. You know Jesus was on his side when he flew 123 feet in the air, bounced on the asphalt like a basketball and lived to tell about it.

"Nowadays, Vegas has got everything: Hollywood, New York, Paris, Venice *It-lee*, pirate ships, the South Pacific, desert palaces and medieval castles. All *right* there in one spot! Ain't no reason to travel the country or see the rest of the world—all the original stuff is old—you can see anything you want, brand new in Las Vegas right today."

Timber couldn't help but chuckle. Vegas *was* something else. He'd been going out there for a long time. He winced, guessing at how much money he'd gambled away over the years, 'specially this last trip. The money lost on baseball (*goddamn the Astros' bullpen!*) and blackjack over the weekend was a fortune considering he earned only $16,500 a year—before taxes. He'd made five times that much money in Houston in 1979. He'd gone to Vegas this time to scout out a new job at the broadcasting convention, but instead the trip turned into a drunken gambling binge that hung over his conscience like a black thundercloud. He'd won $1,000 the first night but lost it all the next night. The final night had been a disaster, money pouring out of his wallet like it was a bucket with a hole in it. A touch of nausea came over him when he pictured his next credit card bill.

The shifting gears of the bus along the highway roused Timber from his troubles. The bus was quiet except for the preacher's continuing monologue. Timber looked out the window to see the beginning of a jagged outcropping of rocks and, in the far distance, snow-capped mountains. The bus sped on toward Salt Lake City. Timber rested the book in his lap and looked at the preacher.

"You may wonder how I got the money to afford Vegas," the preacher said, his eyes intense, the pupils still large, an angry look with the one bloodshot. "I had all the money one man could ever need. But I'll tell you all that soon enough."

Timber glanced at the hard-shell blue suitcase above the seats.

"Yeah, boy," the preacher said, reaching over his head and thumping the case with his left hand. "I had cold hard cash all packed in there with my clothes. It don't take up as much space as you'd think when it's fifties and hundreds. But there ain't no more money there now. I'll tell you what I got in there soon enough…but I ain't to that part of the story yet. My hour has not yet come."

The preacher continued, leaning closer to Timber and making direct eye contact, his voice dropping to an impassioned whisper.

"I will tell you this: women *love* the money. It don't matter who they are. They love it and will do *anything* for it." He winked at Timber. "Yes, son, I guarantee you that they will…If I'm lyin' I'm dyin'."

He turned his head to look down the aisle and then behind him as if to see if anyone was listening. The rest of the bus was quiet as a tomb except for the constant thrum of the engine. He turned back to Timber, his pupils round as saucers, a sly smile on his scratched face.

"The Devil is the Devil but he do have some flash…I am telling you I have been there and seen it *and* done it all." He smiled and looked down as though recalling past glories. He then took a deep breath, the fresh-looking bandage rising with the inhalation, his face serious again.

"I know back home preachers whisper about me to each other over the phone in the late afternoon when their church offices clear out," he said, his voice lower, an angry tone. "They talk about me over bad coffee in Styrofoam cups at Baptist conferences all the way from Pensacola to Memphis. I can hear 'em now in their low voices, speculating on the weakness of my character and the void in my soul. Those old sons of bitches don't know half of what really happened or why it happened. They ain't never been to Vegas…Hell, they ain't been much of anywhere for that matter. No, those preachers who gossip about me don't understand, they don't know the half of it. They've never seen the strip glowing on a hot summer night. They are scared to death at the thought of coming out here and what might happen to them. Maybe it's good they know the truth about how weak they are inside. 'Bout all they are good for is telling silly jokes that make the old people giggle and load up the offering plates with their retirement money. Vegas would chew those preachers up and spit 'em out."

He continued his speech as if he were in the pulpit, his voice becoming triumphant.

"But Vegas didn't take me down in the end. I looked the seven-headed dragon in the eye and pulled on all ten of his horns. It was quite a battle and I didn't think I was gonna make it, but I did."

His voice rose higher, a fiery pitch, deep breaths punctuating his sentences.

"I *won* the war out here in the Valley of Fire. People ain't gonna understand what I did…*why* I did it. They gonna think I'm crazy and violent…sick and mean. But a prophet ain't a prophet in his *own* backyard."

Timber pondered the scratches and bruises on the preacher's face and neck, recalling the Bowie knife in the briefcase. He hoped the driver might help him if things got ugly. He wished he'd sat up front. He knew that most bus drivers carried pistols to protect against the instability of the traveling clientele. He diverted his eyes from the preacher and reached under his seat for his blue canvas duffel bag, stuffed with wadded dirty clothes and toiletries. The preacher kept preaching.

"John the Baptist didn't go out easy. I don't care, 'cause I did what Jesus would've wanted me to do…what He asked me to do. I'm just a lone voice crying in the wilderness, a lone voice that you are gonna hear."

Timber decided to make a break. He folded the paperback, put it into his duffel bag and began to stand. The preacher rose and moved across the aisle and pressed a firm hand on his shoulder, squeezing the top of Timber's fleshy arm. His fingers were bony and dry and strong. His bloodshot eye and huge pupils looked sinister and crazy up close.

"Naw, boy," he said, his voice soft but threatening as he pushed Timber back down. Timber dropped to his seat without resisting. His bad ankle wasn't strong enough for him to push back with any power. "Have you a seat. I ain't done with my story. You need ta hear it."

The preacher sat down in the seat right next to him, leaving the two seats on the other side of the aisle vacant. His breath smelled of bourbon and his hair of grease and his body of bandages. Timber looked out the window at the rocky desert going by and weighed his options. He was much heavier than this man. He should be able to bull his way out and down the aisle toward the driver, even with a weak ankle. But he didn't want to make a scene. And he was soft and weak while this liquor-drinking lunatic—the last kind of man he wanted to fight—toted a hunting knife.

Timber closed his eyes and leaned back. He tilted his head onto his left shoulder and turned away, feigning sleep.

"I got one question for you, boy," the preacher said. "What would you want more than any other thing on this earth?…If you could ask for any single thing, what would it be?"

Timber felt a nudge on his arm. The bony fingers gave him a friendly poke.

"C'mon boy, you got to have an answer for that one, don't you?"

Timber didn't budge.

"Aw, well, I can tell you the answer: *peace of mind*. And the best part of my story is that I've got *peace of mind*. And it ain't easy to come by, *by God*. You can only get it if you know you done the right thing by Jesus…and I have.

"And I can tell by the look in your eyes before you closed 'em, my brother, that *peace of mind* is something you are searching for. Maybe I can help you. So go on, sit back and gitcha some rest…If you got ears, you're gonna hear my story."

SHALL WE GATHER AT THE RIVER

And the preacher kept talking without pause. Try as he might, Timber could not tune his story out. The man talked a blue streak. Timber, unable to keep the stream of sound waves from his ears, listened, eyes closed. Like anyone caught in the crossfire of a rambling monologue, he heard the preacher's speech and reassembled it in his own way, imagining a vision of this cracker's rough South, painting a picture from the amorphous fireball that was the man's language, a nonstop sermon fresh out of the backwoods...

Ezekiel John Blizzard Jr. was born December 1952 in Armstrong, a muddy little town near the center of Georgia that held the state record for the hottest day (109 degrees, August 2, 1961). It was only about forty miles from Macon, the industrial hub of Middle Georgia, a town where almost one hundred thousand lived and most kept to themselves, unlike the egotistical, troublemaking big city of Atlanta up the road.

Reverend Blizzard was an only child, although his mama had several miscarriages before and after his birth. They lived in a shotgun shack out in the woods west of town. "They called 'em that 'cause the house was so narrow you could fire one buckshot shell at it and hit everything in there." The house was a quarter mile from the tracks and the rumble of the trains rocked the land, slightly shaking the earth as the boxcars passed through on the way to Atlanta. His daddy, Ezekiel John Blizzard Sr., was a country preacher who at one time or another held about every odd job Armstrong had to offer.

Everyone called them "Big Zeke" and "Little Zeke." If he set foot in Armstrong today, some of the old-timers would still call him Little Zeke, even though Big Zeke had died. Most people in town, however, had cautiously called his daddy "Pastor," even though very few had ever stepped foot in his modest church.

Little Zeke had long believed that a man's earliest memories were the key to what his life would be like. It was God's way of foreshadowing what was to come. His first memory was of being four years old on a crisp fall morning when the smell of sausage sizzling and buttermilk biscuits baking had permeated the small kitchen. His mama, "bless her heart," had opened the window over the sink, letting the scent of the flaky biscuits, peppery gravy and scrambled eggs waft into the dirt yard, attracting the dogs to the back stoop. The dogs had slept under the house for the first time that fall, abandoning the grassy spot down near the creek where they slept in the heat of the summer. Zeke had heard the pack the night before, scratching and growling as they negotiated their winter sleeping spots below the pine floor in his bedroom.

His daddy stomped into the kitchen that morning in the heavy wool coat he would wear the rest of the winter and poured a cup of coffee. Steam rose from the cup. His daddy's head bobbled slightly and his eyes were glazed, white lightning from the night before still coursing through his veins. He smelled like moonshine. The sun was up only an hour, the rays dancing on the wet grass blades only a few degrees shy of frost, the still green land hoping for a last burst of Indian summer. His daddy walked outside into the yard. Little Zeke, done with his breakfast and dressed for nursery school, followed to the porch and watched him.

The sky was brilliantly clear with white cirrus clouds the shape of corncobs drifting to the pink horizon. His daddy sat on the open gate of his pickup truck, sipping coffee, waiting with his long rifle resting over his left leg. When the runt dog waddled out from under the house, he took a piece of sausage from his pocket and side-armed it near the puppy. The scrawny brown dog with tired ears ran over to the sausage, his tongue flopping. Big Zeke sighted his rifle and pulled the trigger. The thirty-ought-six Springfield exploded. The dog lurched violently and fell still.

"Damn runt," Big Zeke said. "Don't see why the older pups didn't take care of 'im themselves. There oughta be a thinning of the pack. Sorry *dumb*ass dogs."

The other pups scattered when the rifle fired, hightailing it into the woods or under the house. The older dogs had made themselves scarce the minute they'd seen the gun—they'd heard the old Springfield before and knew it held nothing good for them. Big Zeke set the rifle down in the back of the truck and took a burlap bag with a brick in it and moved slowly toward the carcass, lying in a dark puddle of blood in the red dirt. He lifted the dead pup by a floppy ear and dropped it into the bag and spun it, closing it tight.

Little Zeke followed his daddy, trailing him about fifty yards, down the dirt path through the stand of pine trees, afraid to get any closer. The path descended to a muddy cowpond where Little Zeke caught tadpoles and frogs in summer. The water was the color of chocolate milk. He hid behind a pine tree while his daddy went down and tossed the bag with the puppy and the brick into the murky water, slinging it underhanded into the middle of the brown pond. The bag splashed, sinking fast with the weight of the brick. His daddy stood there, calmly watching the ripples fade. He lit a cigarette and shot a stream of smoke into the pale morning sky. A few final air bubbles rose to the top of the pond. Then the water was still again like before. Little Zeke stood there in a daze, half expecting the pup to rise from the water and run up to him. He watched the pond while his daddy smoked a cigarette. Eventually Big Zeke came along and grabbed him by the ear and dragged him back to the house.

Little Zeke couldn't sleep at all that night. His bedroom was in the front of the home that sat about fifty yards off a sharp curve in the road. He lay in bed listening as souped-up engines first became audible in the distance, a whining high roar and then gradually louder as the vehicle got nearer, rising to a loud growl in the turn. Headlights would shine toward the front of the house and then dart away as drivers careened in the other direction, the roar of their engines fading in the distance like the ripples in the pond after the splash.

The only steady job his daddy ever held was preaching at his own church, a job that earned him next to nothing. He worked odd jobs as a janitor in the mill or running mules on a farm or as a mechanic, but in his heart he was a preacher. He ran moonshine too, never his own stills, but helping his older brother Jesse haul it around. They had some cousins across the Alabama line who were deep in the white lightning trade. The fifties wasn't a bad time economically but Big Zeke always had a rough time of it; small country preachers who hadn't finished high school and didn't have a prominent church of their own always struggled. He had been stubborn and refused to succumb to the politics and compromises a career in organized religion required, but preaching was the only occupation he ever gave a damn about. When Big Zeke would go to Macon and meet a man in a store who would ask him what he did, he would answer, "Brother, I'm a lieutenant in the Lord's Army. I've been preaching for Jesus all my life."

Somewhere along the line Daddy befriended Luke Slicker, a Christian businessman who was a big donor to Armstrong Baptist Church, the largest and best funded of the churches in town. Slicker owned a stand of warehouses where coils of wire, lumber and sewing machine parts were stored. Impressed with Big Zeke's devotion, Slicker let him set up in a road-front warehouse near the crooked creek that was Armstrong's only body of water. It wasn't anything but a glorified garage that seated a maximum of forty people. It was always far from full, but it became a house of worship that he would occupy for most of his days, casting out Satan and explaining the Bible in his own red-dirt terms.

His daddy didn't mind the shabbiness of the old warehouse with the tin roof that passed for a church. He had his own body of holy water. Elbow Creek weaved its way through the neighborhoods of Armstrong, between the ruddy hills dotted with three-bedroom, two-bath homes and down to the mud flats of shotgun shacks and trailer parks. The creek was often tainted with garbage: a steady flow of beer cans and liquor bottles and paper; bald tires ranging in size from economy car to tractor; discarded household items such as broken chairs, washing machines and stoves. The creek did its best to cleanse the trash, carrying the lighter items on down to the Flint River. It submerged the larger pieces, household appliances mainly, that sometimes only partially sank in the murky brown water, jutting out above the surface here and there.

His daddy named the warehouse the Church on the River and worked the Baptist river hymns into every service. He had a strong, nasal voice that pierced the small sanctuary.

> Yes, we'll gather at the river,
> The beautiful, beautiful river;
> Gather with the saints at the river,
> That flows by the throne of God.

It was on a bend in this modest river that men and women and children were dipped, washed of their sins. His daddy's church sat across the road from the creek, near the mattress factory and the mill. Etched in Little Zeke's brain were the Sunday mornings when the small congregation, often as few as eight or ten, would finish the service with a baptism on the banks of Elbow Creek.

His daddy had dipped him in the creek on a dry October day, not long after his sixth birthday. He vividly remembered his daddy grabbing the scruff of his neck, his strong fingers squeezing him, his other hand pointed skyward, as he blessed him and dunked him into the cool water. It had been a sunny day, the kind of day Georgia was prone to have in October, not a cloud in the sky and bright as the day was long. It had been a dry summer and the water level was low. Zeke recalled a pile of old tires across the creek from where he was baptized, the round shapes emerging from the water in dark circles. He remembered the water, the color of coffee with heavy cream, warm and dirty, flowing up his nose and depositing silt in his ears when he went below its muddy opaque surface.

God did not call Little Zeke to his baptism. It was fear of his daddy. The same hand that had baptized him often smacked him, sometimes as punishment for a childish misdeed but other times for no good reason at all. Little Zeke often felt the wrath of Big Zeke's belt on his back and legs. Sometimes his daddy beat him with a pine board, a greasy bicycle chain, sometimes his bare hands.

Big Zeke's moods were the worst when he'd been drinking moonshine—it was a dry county back then but the white lightning flowed like the creek after a big rain. The clear liquor brought on his nasty spells with glazed eyes and a scowl that would frighten the Devil.

His daddy shared his rage on Little Zeke's mama, "bless her heart," a thin-lipped woman who cooked and cleaned and said or did little else. Her slight frame was ravaged from unsuccessful attempts to have more children but Big Zeke showed her no sympathy. Little Zeke often heard strained voices and shifting of furniture behind their door late at night, the creaking of the old pine floors under heavy steps. He could remember his mama, bruised and limping on many mornings, dark circles under her eyes. Twice he'd noticed a tooth missing.

"When I was young, a little boy even, I wanted to kill my daddy. Wasn't a day didn't go by that I didn't study on killin' him. I had a plan to shoot him and bury him back in the woods. Wouldn't nobody have found him if I put him in the ground deep, deep enough where the dogs wouldn't sniff him out.

"I got over it, though. He calmed down some when I got on up into my teens. I think maybe he saw how big I was getting and figured I might be able to take him down. I'da done it too."

Big Zeke was what the women around those parts used to call a "pretty man." He was tall and had long, muscular arms and light blue eyes and sandy brown hair. He had a swarthy complexion with a weathered face, the lines cut by the wind and sun adding a ruggedness that appealed to the ladies. And he had an eye for the women.

Many nights Little Zeke was the man of the house. At an early age he was aware of his daddy's running around drinking moonshine with women that had a reputation for sharing the fruits of their bodies about anywhere they saw fit. Word travels fast around small towns about such questionable liaisons and backroad rendezvous, even in the elementary school playgrounds.

Ricky Tompkins, a schoolmate in the third grade, said, "My daddy tells it that your daddy'll plug any hole that moves. Daddy said this town ain't got no dogcatcher but your daddy thinks he's the cat catcher. Every time some lady throws the cat, he's there to catch it."

Zeke laughed at the recollection.

"Daddy loved the women, all right, and that blood he passed on to me. I tried to fight it, said I wouldn't get into the same trouble, and for all my righteous talking as a young man, sure as hell if I didn't end up with the same weakness for 'em. When sumpin's in your blood, I don't guess there's much you can do about it. It's gonna git you sooner or later."

He said Zeke Sr. was known to run with women both black and white—"that was a big deal in them days, brother"—and it sullied his already rough reputation.

"Luke Slicker even came to see Daddy, who denied fooling around with them 'colored women' as the old men used to put it, but defended his right to have 'em in his church. Daddy's church was the only one in all of Middle Georgia that had blacks and whites worshipping together, although it wasn't that often. Anybody he could get his hands around their throat to baptize, he'd be happy about it: black, white, red, yeller, *green*—didn't make no difference to him. There wasn't a race he wouldn't baptize—or a woman he wouldn't put the moves on, either.

"Daddy loved baptizing people as much as he liked screwing women. I didn't have no choice in the matter when I got baptized. He choked me down in the water soon as he could. It didn't do nothing for me at the time. It was later—much later—when I got my calling."

It was Sally Claxton's baptism, more than ten years later, that turned Little Zeke's life around and set him on his path toward heaven. She was a lean young girl whose lanky fifteen-year-old frame was bursting into a woman's body. She had coal-black hair and radiant skin, a naturally dark complexion that was tanned from working outside. Many darker-skinned country people speciously claimed Indian ancestry but nobody ever doubted that Sally Claxton's grandfather was full-blooded Cherokee. She had eyes that were almost black.

She and her mama were among the transient population that rolled through Armstrong in a steady trickle, staying only long enough to gather a few paychecks here or there and attend about half of a school year. Landlords were never surprised to find a house empty when the rent was past due. Other times landlords would evict a family like the Claxtons with a simple command of "y'all gonna have to git on outta here now."

Sally Claxton and her mama showed up to church one cool spring morning in 1968 when Little Zeke was in high school. Her mama sent her down front at the end of the service. She told Zeke's daddy, repeating some of his words back to him, that, "I want to accept the Lord Jesus Christ as my only savior and be baptized in the river, there across the road, this morning." Reverend Blizzard, taking note of Sally's mama in a pastel blue dress with no bra and sandals and hair down past her waist, squeezed Sally's hand and prayed with her. Tears ran down his face. He told Sally he needed to speak with her mama, privately, in his "office" (the warehouse had an old trailer in the back where he stored hymnals and hid moonshine) to pray a little more and set up a time for the baptism. Every few months a family would come around like the Claxtons and want to be baptized that day—"with no more thought than if they was buyin' a can opener"—but Zeke's daddy always held out and made them come to church at least three or four more times, except when a child's daddy was a particularly large and threatening roughneck who insisted on baptizing his baby right then and there.

The morning of Sally Claxton's baptism was a sunny late April day that followed a rainy week. The white dogwoods along the streets of downtown Armstrong were near the end of their blooms; white petals had covered the sidewalks the week before. The previous Friday, county sanitation workers had swept the street, pushing the fallen blooms out with an old road grader, down to the bottom of the small hill, the metal blade shooting sparks as it scraped against the asphalt. A rain had come along that night and washed the dogwood flowers into Elbow Creek. When Big Zeke put one hand around the nape of Sally Claxton's neck and the other on her lower back and dipped her into the healing waters, she was amongst a patch of white dogwood blooms that came floating downstream, the creek higher than usual after a rainy few days. Little Zeke had been just another sixteen-year-old small-town country boy until Sally Claxton went under that water in a flowing, white robe. When she came up—her drenched black hair pulled back, her opalescent skin moist, her dark eyes illuminated by a glint of sunlight, the wet robe clinging tight to her thin waist and long slender legs, her dark nipples stiff and visible through the linen—he knew he would go into the water and baptize her kind one day.

"At that moment, my life changed. I got a purpose. Something sparked in me and woke me up."

He wanted to speak to Sally Claxton after her baptism, waiting outside the church door while she changed back into her jeans and blouse in the hallway. He could see through the window where a flimsy white curtain covered only about two-thirds of the glass, and he watched her slip off wet pink panties and slide into her jeans, wiggling her shapely hips a little to fit into the tight denim.

He was ready to preach, to minister to her, to save her soul. He waited by the door for her to come out but when she finally did (stopping to ring the excess water from her underwear) he couldn't summon up the words. He knew he was the man to save Sally Claxton from a life of demons and pain, to show her the way to an uncloudy day. He never got the chance. She moved on from Armstrong two weeks later when her mama got a job waiting tables at a new hotel down on Tybee Island near Savannah.

"But I can't never forget that girl." He shook his head and smiled. "Ever since that fine young thang went under the water for Jesus I knew I wanted to be a preacher. I said 'Lord, sign me up!' I can *still* see Sally Claxton coming up out of that creek, those dark eyes looking right at me…those wet pink panties."

A few weeks later Luke Slicker invited Little Zeke to attend the Armstrong Baptist Church as his guest. The big church was a world away from his daddy's tiny ramshackle chapel. It stood at the most manicured intersection in town, just off the business district, amidst dogwoods and azaleas and lush green grass. Across the street was the Methodist church and catty corner was the town's well-to-do funeral home, where a handful of cars was always parked. "The home," as it was known, always had a pot of coffee going for city officials, church deacons and others who gathered there and talked politics and rumor. City Hall was right down the street.

Zeke Blizzard got a gleam in his eye when he talked about Armstrong Baptist Church, what everybody called simply the "Big Church." He never forgot that first morning he attended. Zeke got there forty-five minutes early and sat near the back in the stillness. The huge sanctuary had a cream-colored ceiling, a gentle rolling arch with six brass chandeliers, three on each side. Sunlight flowed in through the large frosted glass windows. Four doors, two in the back and two in the front, opened onto the church floor. The congregation gathered slowly, taking their seats, the blue-haired ladies wobbling in, knobby hands and flabby jowls and thick glasses, flowing loose dresses, pastels of every color. The men wore blazers, some green like they had just won the Masters, and others maroon. Their ties were either much too short above the belt or much too long. They sat in family packs of fours and fives. They filtered in and waved at familiar faces, women bending and unbending their fingers, the men occasionally reaching out for a handshake and a *"How you doin', boy?"* or the more devout "Hello, Brother Luke." Luke Slicker was one of these men. He shook Little Zeke's hand before moving to a seat down front with his family.

Only a few minutes before the service was to begin, Zeke saw a rush of familiar faces: the high school football coach, the mayor, a well-known attorney and an insurance man whose photo he'd seen in the newspaper. They strode in the front doors with their shoulders back and confident smiles, guiding towheaded children with a firm hand. The image Zeke remembered most clearly was a group of teenage girls, including several members of the high school cheerleading squad, gliding through the front door clad in dresses clinging to their slim hips and tight sweaters that made their breasts stand out like plump tomatoes in a rainy summer hanging gently on the vine.

The girls took turns flipping their long hair, tossing it at the most opportune moments when it was obvious all eyes were upon them, an almost synchronized timing. The boys and men in the crowd watched from the corners of their eyes, darting glances the direction of the girls and consciously reminding themselves not to leer in church. They knew that this feminine show was the peak of the morning, the highlight of their day and most likely their weekend.

"I watched 'em girls and said to myself, 'I'm gonna get me some of that.' Sure enough, it wouldn't be too long."

The signal that the service was about to begin was when the assistant preachers and choir director filed in with perfectly blow-dried hair and smiles like they had been turned on by flicking a switch. They took seats along the back of the podium. When the pastor, Reverend John Daniels, approached the dais, the already hushed whispers fell silent. He was tall, a stout but fit man in a tailored suit with neat gray hair receding from his tanned face. He had perfect posture.

Daniels held the congregation's rapt attention. The pastor's graceful use of the language, his flowing sentences, smooth at times but dramatic and ending with flourishes at others, mesmerized Zeke. Zeke soon was a regular for Sunday school, Sunday morning and evening services, Wednesday night services, Saturday morning work groups. His daddy let him go to the Sunday morning service at the big church instead of his own church, as though he knew it would lead to something bigger for his son. Zeke figured, looking back, that his daddy had hoped he would become a great preacher and return to the little Church on the River and make something of it. "Daddy never did say exactly what he meant, but that's what he wanted. He wanted a bigger church for me. He wasn't all the way crazy."

Zeke would lie in his bed at night reciting lines from Reverend Daniels' sermons, echoing the phrases of the great man. He was powerful but graceful, unlike his daddy's labored, sweaty preaching.

About a year after his first visit, when it came time for someone to preach the youth sermon at the big church, Zeke was the only one who volunteered. (The popular boys, athletes with large foreheads topping off their expressionless faces, were interested only in football and girls' titties.)

Zeke chose the evils of adultery as his topic and prepared like nothing else he'd ever done in his life. He scripted out the sermon carefully, using as many of the flourishes from the Reverend Daniels as he could, memorizing it. He had gone into his daddy's church and practiced it there for hours, over and over and over.

It was a Sunday night when he stood in the Armstrong Baptist Church pulpit for the first time. He was surprised how different the sanctuary looked from up on the dais. High above the congregation, he looked down on the faces, all gazing up to him in rapt attention as he began his sermon.

"My dear friends, please bow your heads in prayer and in respect of the words of Jesus Christ. I'm sure you will all recognize Matthew 5:27 through 30:

You have heard that it was said to those of old 'You shall not commit adultery.' But I say to you that whoever looks at a woman to lust for her has already committed adultery with her in his heart. If your right eye causes you to sin, pluck it out and cast it from you; for it is more profitable for you that one of your members perish, than for your whole body to be cast into hell.

He paused and said, "Amen," then asked the congregation to lift their heads. His sermon went on almost a full twenty minutes.

"I told 'em 'God gave you a body, a sacred trust, and you shouldn't be throwing it around anywhere you see fit. You owe it to God to treat your body as His sacred temple.'"

Zeke recalled the congregation sitting still and attentive that Sunday evening, particularly the band of teenage cheerleaders that included Reverend Daniels' blonde granddaughter, Cindy. He could see her eyes, blue as hydrangea bushes, watching him.

The minute it was over and he lifted his head from his final prayer, the Reverend Daniels embraced him, holding him in front of the entire congregation. He said into his ear loud enough for the first few rows to hear, "That was a fine sermon, my son."

Luke Slicker was soon down front, suggesting that Little Zeke should go to the Bible college seminary over in Alabama where many Southern Baptist preachers were educated.

"Luke told me, 'Son, that was some sermon, I'm telling you. I'm sorry your daddy couldn't be here to see it, but I know he's got his own flock to tend to and he is too stubborn to set foot in any church other than that small one of his. But I see big things for you boy, big things in the ministry.'"

A whole line of well-wishers followed, including several old women who hugged him tight. The men—the football coach, the mayor and the insurance man leading the way—grabbed his hand in strong grips and looked right into his eyes, slapping him on the back as they left. It took him at least twenty minutes to get through the receiving line.

After he was done, Reverend Daniels shook his hand, a strong squeeze with his big, warm grip, and invited Zeke to dinner Tuesday night.

"It'll be good to break bread together, my son," the Reverend Daniels said. "The whole family'll be there. My granddaughter is about your age."

He and the preacher were the last to leave the sanctuary, shaking hands one last time and parting through doors on opposite ends of the church floor.

When Zeke stepped outside, he saw Cindy Daniels waiting in a shadow by one of the large white columns at the entrance to the church.

"Hey," she said. She tossed her hair back to one side and moved toward him, stepping into the circle formed by one of the floodlights that cast a milky white glow on the front of the church at night. She had on a skirt that ended just above her knees.

"Hey," he said back, grinning sheepishly.

"You need a ride?" she said, standing with all of her weight on her left foot. She slipped her right sandal off and glided her foot, toes pointed, an inch above the cement floor, effortlessly, like a ballerina. She finished the movement by touching the sole of her foot gently to her slender left calf and holding the pose.

Zeke had planned to call his daddy to come pick him up from the gas station down the block.

"Sure," he said.

"My car's around here," she said. "Come on."

Zeke had seen Cindy Daniels, or "Cin Cin," her cheerleading nickname, many times before. She had long blonde hair and watery blue eyes—the similarity to her handsome grandfather was striking—and smooth alabaster skin. She was lean and athletic. Cindy had never spoken two words to Zeke, even though he'd had a class with her one time. He'd moved in and out of the class silently and avoided attention, afraid even to make eye contact with her.

Cindy drove Zeke out of town the opposite direction from his home, her

Corvette Stingray flying along the two-lane road through the more affluent neighborhood in the hillier section of Armstrong. She didn't talk, driving beyond the large homes and onto a dirt road that dropped down from a hilltop into a deep forest of hardwoods, thick with green leaves in the spring. She pulled off the dirt road and parked on a grassy spot that had only the faint indentations of tires, the front of the car looking over a small creek, really nothing but a trickle in a ditch that flowed over mossy rocks. She flicked off the car lights—it was full dark—and leaned over Zeke and kissed him, letting her hair fall down over his face and neck.

"She smelled like gardenias and was softer than anything I'd ever laid my hands on, I tell you that's for sure. I ain't never gonna forget that girl, *or* her car. She was lean and smooth and soft. And that car was a *bad* ride...

"She didn't say much, just stripped down and straddled me in the leather passenger's seat and pushed that seat all the way back. I'm telling you, boy, at that point I was saved, a new man."

Zeke had been terrified to enter the Reverend Daniels' house Tuesday night. He wore the same suit in which he had preached his sermon. Cindy answered the door and gave him a deep look in the eyes—he thought he saw a twinkle—and then put on a formal, detached manner, announcing, "Granddaddy, the young preacher is here." The home was like something out of a television show about perfect families, except Cindy's father, a missionary, was in Mexico, ministering to sick and needy heathens. Cindy and her sisters all had Reverend Daniels' healthy skin and blue eyes, blonde hair and erect posture. Even his wife and daughter-in-law, Cindy's mom, looked like him. Zeke sat up straight, terribly conscious that he had no training in table manners, and surreptitiously watched the great preacher eat, copying his every move with knife and fork and napkin. He was worried that Cindy might rub her foot against his leg under the table, but she never dropped her guard. He was trying not to think about being naked with her in the bucket seats of her Corvette.

"You know, I can't even remember what we talked about, if we talked at all. I was so caught up in how good-lookin' they all were, how clean and charming and warm the house was, I can't remember what was said. I guess we talked about school and plans and things. I was as nervous as a chicken in a thunderstorm, I remember that."

After the pot roast and potatoes and carrots and green beans, Cindy told her granddaddy that she would drive Zeke home. She said she was ready to go, that they had some homework to go over before school tomorrow. The Reverend Daniels shook Zeke's hand at the door and paused, staring straight at him, and patted him on the shoulder. He gave a warm, affirming nod and said, "Son, you can make a great preacher one day. Just remember that."

Ten minutes later in the car, the Corvette engine turned off but still warm from the ride to the creek, Cindy smiled, her eyes twinkled. "He likes you so much," she said. She pulled off her skirt and top and went for Zeke's zipper with her mouth. Zeke leaned his head back and closed his eyes.

Cindy began giving Zeke a ride home every Sunday morning and night and Wednesday night, always stopping by the wooded spot near the tiny creek that she called a river. People had started to notice them leaving together. Zeke went on with his anonymity at the high school, although occasionally he'd see some hint of recognition from students who attended Armstrong Baptist. She didn't speak to him or spend time with him at school. She kept to her crowd, and he'd see her laughing or talking with friends or even flirting with football players, flipping her long hair back. He hadn't cared. He knew what he was getting and didn't bother about the rest. He had been worried at first that he might have to spend hours talking to her on the phone like some of the high school girls he had pursued had wanted to do. All they had wanted to do was jabber.

"I like to talk now, especially when I can get a drink or two in me," Reverend Blizzard said. "But when I was a young man, I didn't like to talk worth a damn. I got that from my daddy. He didn't say much at all to me. He let his swagger and his preaching do the talking. One of the best things about Cindy Daniels was she didn't give a damn for talking much either."

He and Cindy had been going to the creek regularly for about six weeks when he worried that they'd been found out. He had gotten out of the car without his shirt one Wednesday night before they were about to leave and walked to the edge of the stream and was taking a leak into it, watching his urine splash in the creek water, when he saw a pickup truck pull down the dirt road and shine a flashlight at him from about a hundred yards away. The light then shone on Cindy's car, and then flipped off. The truck slowly backed down the road. Zeke was concerned but Cindy told him not to worry about it.

Two days later Zeke was called to the principal's office just before lunch. He walked in to find Luke Slicker there waiting on him.

"Son, come with me," Slicker said, smiling. "The Reverend Daniels and I want to see you." Slicker winked at the principal and parted with a "see you later, brother."

Zeke obliged. He sat nervously in the front seat of Slicker's brand new Lincoln

Town Car, the big black automobile wide as a boat, cruising down the street toward the church so smooth it hardly seemed like they were moving at all. The dogwood and azalea blooms were long gone as it was late May and summer was almost there. Slicker had gospel music playing low, an eight-track tape he said was from a big church over in Louisiana. He smiled at Zeke, warmly but sternly. The music eased Zeke's mind except for the *cha-chunk* sound the tape made when it shifted in mid-song from one track to the next, right in the middle of "Amazing Grace."

Slicker parked next to the Reverend Daniels' blue Cadillac in the spot that was reserved for him next to the office door.

"Come on in, son," Slicker said. "We got some news for you."

Slicker led Zeke into the pastor's office, a massive room with a huge desk and white shag carpet. Zeke had never stepped on a carpet so thick. Fresh cut flowers filled several vases. Sunlight drifted in softly through the frosted glass windowpanes.

Reverend Daniels sat behind the desk reading the Bible, a black leather-bound New King James edition. It looked to Zeke like he was in the New Testament, in one of the gospels. Slicker gestured to Zeke to sit down in one of the stuffed armchairs that sat before the desk. He and Luke Slicker sat down. The pastor continued to read, not looking up, not acknowledging even Slicker.

Zeke couldn't figure out what it was but the Reverend Daniels looked different, more wrinkled and whiter, thinner and frailer than when he stood. His normally blue eyes looked gray, the color of wet sidewalks. He read for a few more minutes—what seemed like hours, Zeke recalled—until he raised his head and looked him straight in the eyes.

"Son, it says here that someone assaults you, you should turn the other cheek, and love your enemy." He poked his finger stiffly into a page. "That ain't easy to do. I'm a preacher, but I'm also a man. Some little nitshit molests my granddaughter, then I want to do something about it. Lash out and strangle the little son of a bitch who would preach in my pulpit, eat at my table and then take pleasure in the loins of my young'un. It's a good thing her daddy ain't around, 'cause he would kick your ass into tomorrow. Luke and I here would make sure he got away with it too."

Reverend Daniels' voice was low, scratchy, threatening, nothing like the warm baritone Zeke knew.

"But, boy, you are lucky. That ain't what I'm gonna do, although I'm tempted. Lord knows I'm tempted. But I been tempted before a lot of times and a lot of ways. I heard you preach that night and you got a gift. You got a *gift* that God gave you."

His voice was returning to its normal strength and warmth.

"You got to take that gift and develop it, share it with the world. Men of God ain't perfect, but you got to try. You are young and strong and have your life ahead of you. Don't take what Jesus gave you and flush it down the drain. Don't throw it all away just 'cause a little pussy feels good."

He picked up a folder on his desk and reached forward and handed it to Zeke.

"Luke and I have gotten you into the Bible college over there near Birmingham in the summer session, starting next week. You can go right on through into the seminary. You need to get your stuff together and be over there on Sunday. They got dorms and food for you, everything you'll need."

Zeke was a few weeks shy of graduating high school. He narrowed his eyes in thought.

"Don't worry about your diploma, son," Slicker said. "That's taken care of. And I done told your daddy what we are gonna do. He's proud of you."

The Reverend Daniels scowled at Slicker, who stopped talking. He then looked at Zeke like he was a doctor examining him.

"Son, I got two pieces of advice for you. The first is this: read your Bible hard and pray, every day and often." He reached onto the desk and touched his open palm to the Bible. "The word of God right here will show you the way."

He leaned back in his chair and steepled his fingers.

"The second part of my advice is this: keep your ass over in Alabama and don't be coming back around here." His voice was lower, angry again. "You stay the hell out of Armstrong, away from my family and this church. Remember that I done turned my cheek once. If I catch you screwing my granddaughter again, I'll go Old Testament on your sorry white ass. Now get the hell out of here."

GOD'S ROAD MAP

The bus began to climb. Timber watched the path of the Virgin River, parallel to Interstate 15, as it crossed the state line into the northwest corner of Arizona, leaving the Nevada desert behind. The stream trickled south as the bus traveled north, chugging up a deep gorge in the red rocks where signs advertised Grand Canyon attractions an hour away. Telephone poles on the side of the highway looked like rugged crosses loosely wound together by heavy black thread.

"So that's the story of how I got into the seminary," Reverend Blizzard said, his voice friendly. "Coulda turned out a lot worse. Old Reverend Daniels was tempted to skin me alive."

Timber broke into a deep chuckle, his gut shaking as the preacher laughed with him.

"You 'bout ready for a drink?" Reverend Blizzard asked. "I'm gonna have me another one."

"A little snort might be good."

"That's more like it." Reverend Blizzard reached under his seat and opened his briefcase. He handed Timber the bottle of Jim Beam. "Here you go, boy. I'm gonna go back here and take me a leak." He stood and walked down the aisle to the back of the bus.

Timber uncapped the bottle and took a pull, the liquor burning in his throat and warming his chest. The preacher's story—it was so vivid, so clear to him. He hearkened back to his childhood when he and his mama were in the church every time the doors were open. It had been a long time. He'd left the Baptist church behind when he moved to Houston in the midseventies and made it in big-time radio. Broke his mama's heart once when he told her he hadn't been to church, not even for Easter or Christmas, for years. He took another, longer drink, the old familiar taste of liquor strong but soothing…relaxing going down. Timber looked out the window and then down into the preacher's open briefcase to the worn black leather cover of the Bible. He could feel his mama's religion shifting around inside him, like a sleepy old dog stirring from a nap.

Timber put the cap on the bottle and handed it back to the Reverend Blizzard when he returned from the bathroom.

"Damn, that shitter stinks. But I been out in the desert for a few days. Wide open, dry air, those cool breezes at night. That big rain last night was a helluva storm. But it came and went right quick. It's nice out there, boy, I'm telling you, God's country."

He twisted the cap off the bottle and took another sip. Timber eyed him, the scratches and bruises on his face and hands, the bandage on his neck, the big pupils and the bloodshot eye. The skin on his forehead was beginning to peel from sunburn. His greasy brown hair was freshly slicked back but had not been washed for days.

"Where was it you got on—the Valley of Fire?" Timber asked, loosened up by the liquor.

"Yeah, that's right. I didn't think you was payin' any attention to me."

"How could I not?" Timber said. "You sat down right next to me and started talking."

"Boy, I'm trying to tell you how I ended up out here in the desert and what I done to get peace of mind. But you've got to hear it in the right order."

"Well, give me that bottle back. If this is a long story, I might as well catch a little buzz."

"Wouldn't hurt you none, that's for sure." The Reverend Blizzard handed the bottle back to Timber.

"The day I left home," the preacher continued, "I went to my daddy's church one last time. Daddy had a faraway look in his eye, like he was looking both into the past at my childhood but also deep into the future, into the life I would lead. He could see the man I would become. He was quiet, almost gentle.

"Mama went to church with us, something she almost never did, but she was there. For once, we were like a family. Daddy had always discouraged her from coming to his church—usually 'cause he might have a girlfriend or a woman he was interested in there—but he didn't that morning.

"I sat with Mama while Daddy preached and led the singing. We sang 'Jesus is Tenderly Calling.' Sang it twice, matter of fact."

The Reverend Blizzard lifted his head and softly sang, his singing voice rising higher than his speaking.

Jesus is tenderly calling you home,
call–ing today, call–ing today;
They who believe his name shall rejoice,
Quickly arise and away;
call–ing today, call–ing today,
Jesus is calling, is tenderly calling today.

Timber hadn't heard the hymn in years. He had been tempted to sing the backup refrain that accompanied the chorus, but he wasn't nearly drunk enough to start singing on a bus.

"For lunch that day," the preacher said, "Mama cooked a ham, deviled eggs, biscuits, coleslaw and potato salad. We ate quietly together in the little house where I'd lived the first eighteen years of my life, the last time I'd eat there. I remember how neat the twelve deviled eggs looked, lined up in that fancy red plate. The deviled egg plate had twelve slots, one for each egg. That plate was used for the one and only purpose of serving deviled eggs. I always figured the twelve eggs represented the twelve disciples. Daddy and I ate five apiece, while Mama nibbled on two eggs. Mama never ate much, she only nibbled.

"After lunch, Mama started to cry, weeping uncontrollably. She, Daddy and me got into the pickup truck to drive me to the bus station, all three of us in the front with Mama in the middle. Mama's face was streaked with tears by the time we got there. I hugged her when I went to get onto the bus and she howled, almost like a wounded animal of some kind. I didn't know then but I realize now that she was scared to be alone with my daddy. He hadn't been hurting her none since I got big—I growed up pretty quick when I was about fourteen, big as I am now—and he knew, I guess, 'bout my aim to kill him if he kept beating me or Mama. I threatened him once when I was about fourteen or fifteen. He laid off then. I don't know why I didn't worry about Mama when I left. I guess my mind was studying on Cindy Daniels, her grandfather and my new life at college. I wish I'd worried about Mama a little more, 'cause that was the last time…the last time…I ever saw her."

His voice trailed off, weak and trembling. His expression was blank, his head down, staring at his feet. Timber waited, wanting the preacher to resume, to tell what happened to his mama, the quiet woman who cooked and cleaned for him and struggled through life with his daddy. But he remained silent.

"Zeke," Timber said, "take you a drink."

He took the bottle from Timber without looking up. He held it for a few moments before twisting off the cap and taking a long draft. He handed the bottle back to Timber without putting on the cap.

Timber thought about toasting, "To mamas," but instead said nothing and chugged down two big gulps. His throat and chest burned, but then loosened up with a warm feeling, that familiar rush of blood. Every time he drank liquor there was that moment when the alcohol began to take hold, a surging warmth inside. It always made him feel better.

The Reverend Blizzard shifted in his seat, handed Timber the bottle cap and began talking again, lower this time. Timber screwed the cap on and listened.

"I wasn't a good son, not worth a damn to my mama anyway," the preacher continued, "and I hope the good Lord'll forgive me for it. I headed off to school and didn't hardly ever call home. Mama wasn't the kind to talk on the phone much and never had that much to say, so the times I called and only Daddy got on the line, I didn't think much about it. I told him about my studies and sermons I'd heard and told him to say hello to Mama.

"When I went home that Christmas, Daddy met me at the bus station. I figured Mama had stayed home to cook. But when I got back, the house seemed different, colder, even from the outside. There weren't no Christmas decorations around and I didn't smell food cooking. I said, 'Daddy, where's Mama?' and he said, 'She's dead, son. I didn't want to bother you with it and distract you from your Bible study. She died about three weeks ago.' He said, 'Her heart plumb give out on her. She dropped dead right here in the kitchen. I buried her myself down there by the church. We can go see her grave after we eat. I hadn't done a proper service yet. You and I can do it together.'"

"You *mean*…he…he didn't even get in touch with you when your own mama died?" Timber asked. "What'd you say to him? I'd have wanted to kill him."

"Yeah, I thought about it. I figured he was the reason that she was dead. I thought of killing him then and there and burying him out deep in the woods like I'd planned to do a thousand times. But we'd been studying the Gospels, how you've got to try to live your life like Jesus and all, so I turned my cheek—my *ass* cheeks that is—and walked out the door and back to town and caught the bus straight back to Alabama. I prayed all the way back on the bus for my mama's soul to get into heaven and for my daddy's to get into hell. I'm sure that's what happened. Daddy's burnin' and Mama's sittin' up on a big fluffy cloud. Mama'll be the first person I want to see once I get through those pearly gates. I'm gonna tell her I'm sorry for going off and leaving her."

Timber, emboldened by the liquor, smiled at the Reverend Blizzard's return to a preaching tone.

"You sure you getting into heaven?"

"I have no doubts, my brother. I am saved, *born* again…bound for the pearly gates."

Timber looked out the window at the approaching Rocky Mountains, the bus veering through big winding curves. The Reverend Blizzard's eyes reflected in the window.

"What about you?" Reverend Blizzard asked in his preacherly voice. "Will you be going along with me to that mansion in the sky?"

Timber turned from the window and looked down into his lap. All those images of heaven and hell that preachers had carried on about on those long Sunday mornings, his mama's arm around him, on his shoulder, rubbing his back, smoothing his hair. He unscrewed the cap and turned up the bottle for one more sip before responding.

"Not a chance," Timber said, his voice low. "Not a chance in hell."

Timber shrugged his shoulders and smirked like he did when he lost a hand of blackjack. He lifted his voice, a few bars higher and spoke in a rhythm imitative of an impassioned reverend in a pulpit.

"But enough about me and my *damned*-to-hell, *no*-peace-of-mind, good-for-*nothing* soul. Tell me how you became a preacher."

✦ ✦ ✦

The Bible college was unlike any place Zeke Blizzard Jr. had ever been. It had a long lawn surrounded by red brick buildings with elegant white trim and a large sanctuary that loomed over the campus. To Zeke it was a holy place, a place of inspiration, a place where something special would happen to him, a place where God lived and breathed and prepared His preachers to spread the word of the Gospel.

"I stood there on the steps of that church and stared, in awe, for hours, that first night I was there." It had been a sunny day with only a slight breeze and wisps of clouds drifting in the sky. He stood in the gloaming and watched the clouds transform from white to pink to dark stains on the heavens as the sky faded from brilliant azure to a deep blue and the stars gently lit up.

"I prayed. I asked forgiveness for my sins and trespasses with Cindy Daniels. I asked forgiveness for my impure thoughts about Sally Claxton. I asked forgiveness for not being a better son to my mama. And I vowed, by God, I vowed to make up for it and show people the way of the Lord, to lead them to Jesus. I didn't sweat blood but I was close to it, I tell you, boy, I damn near did."

He fell right into the rigid routine. Six hours each day in class, about that much homework. A rigid schedule of breakfast, lunch and dinner. There were eighty students, all white men from states ranging from Texas to Florida and a few from as far north as Ohio and Iowa. The campus sat out in the woods west of Birmingham, not too far from Tuscaloosa. Every day the preachers who taught at the school reminded the young men how lucky they were, how fortunate they were to be the chosen ones of God, to receive His calling, and how they had better get up early and read their Bibles and not waste this precious, mysterious gift of being the front men for Jesus, His sales representatives, His marketing team, lieutenants in Christ's army.

Zeke was as devout as anyone. He read the Bible all the way through twice that first year, the Gospels three times. He prayed over and over, apologizing for his sins and begging the Lord's forgiveness. He would go through all eternity burning in hell if he had to in order to show the Lord how devoted he was. He quit masturbating altogether, although he did wake up sticky one morning after having a dream about Cindy Daniels in a University of Alabama cheerleading outfit, her short red loose skirt flapping in the wind with no underwear. He prayed extra hard that day, worried that the Devil, Satan himself, was invading his mind when he was sleeping, putting pornographic images in his head. He had the dream a time or two again but soon, after a few months, vanquished Satan from his mind, once and for all, he believed at the time.

The Bible college, he soon learned, had a caste system. He had learned about caste systems in a world religions class where the preacher who taught it began by saying things like: "Okay, y'all, today we are going to see how all those towelheads in the Middle East got the words of the Lord wrong."

The caste system at this seminary resembled what he'd later learn the caste system about everywhere in the world was like, involving who your daddy was and how much money he had. One day at breakfast in the beginning of his junior year, the school dean—the venerable Dean Green—sat down with Zeke and began asking him questions about his daddy's church. The dean was a big man with an even bigger head, almost pink skin and dark hair. They were all questions to which Dean Green seemed to know the answers.

"Your daddy has that Campbellite church over there in Armstrong, doesn't he, son?"

"No sir, it's not Church of Christ, it's a Baptist church. He's just not affiliated."

"Well, son, just because you call yourself a Baptist preacher don't mean you are one. Having your own church requires more than just access to riverfront property."

Zeke was surprised at Dean Green's directness. Defending his daddy might make him look bad; speaking against his own daddy, regardless of how questionable the old man had been, wasn't good either. Family is family after all.

"What are your plans, boy, if you get through here and get ordained?" Dean Green had on a big smile but Zeke knew it was his smile of attack, a smile too big and insincere for anyone to believe, a smile that said *I'm gonna kick your little ass back in time if you don't straighten up and fly right.*

"You gonna go back to Armstrong and take over your daddy's *church down by the river?*" The dean's smile grew even larger, almost bigger than his face, bigger than life, like the hot sun bearing down on Zeke. His eyes looked like the eyes of a snake or a wild dog, crazed, ready to pounce.

"No sir." Zeke took a deep breath. "I've got no plans to go back to Armstrong unless Reverend Daniels would hire me in his church. My daddy started me out in the Bible and baptized me, but it was the Reverend Daniels who showed me that Jesus really loved me, that he died for our sins. I didn't get my calling till I heard the Reverend Daniels preach. He's my role model and what I want to be one day. I don't know if I could ever live up to him, but I'd like to try."

The dean's smile toned down about fifty degrees to a sincere, happy grin, a look that was natural, unforced. He put his arm on Zeke's shoulder.

"Son, that's just what I wanted to hear, just what I wanted to hear. The Lord has spoken to you and you have listened. You come on by my office this afternoon at four."

That afternoon, Zeke waited fifteen minutes before he was silently ushered into the dean's office by a thin woman who reminded him of his mama with her slight build, thin hair and defeated posture. But then again, every woman in her fifties of small build made him think of Mama, his poor dead mama.

The dean's office was remarkably like that of Reverend Daniels, as though many of the fixtures had come from the same Christian office catalogue. Only the windows were distinctly different, large and clear, overlooking the campus lawn. It was a sunny bright day but the quad was desperately empty.

"Have a seat, son," the dean said, gesturing to Zeke with a big smile. Zeke couldn't tell if the smile was one of the dean's fake smiles to cover over a nasty intent, or a sincere grin of warmth.

The dean handed Zeke a postcard-sized piece of paper with an address to a church over in Tuscaloosa and the name of Mary Huggins. Zeke studied the card and the dean watched him until he finished reading it.

"Zeke, I want you to speak to the young ladies' Sunday school class over there this week, teach their Bible lesson for them. I think they are reading in Acts. Give this young lady a call. She's a sweetheart of a girl. I know her mama and daddy, down in Eufaula. She's studying to be a teacher."

"Yes sir."

"Now boy, you behave yourself over there. When you go out and speak to people, you represent this school. I chose you for this group, this girl, 'cause you're devoted. You work as hard as anyone here. You got potential for great things."

The dean's smile grew outrageous. Zeke sat up straight.

"I ain't gonna lie to you, though. We did some checking around on your daddy. Your background worries me. You know you look just like him. I saw pictures of him when he was about your age."

Zeke nodded. The dean blinked repetitively.

"There's quite a few stories floating around over there, son. I guess you heard most of 'em and know which is true and which ain't. Well, the thing is, it don't matter what is true and what ain't, it's what people believe—that's something important to remember with your preaching too—it's what they *think* and *say* about your daddy. The *truth* don't matter. You've got to avoid the very implication of impropriety and sin. The Bible tells us to 'abstain from all appearance of evil.'

"What I want to know, son, is this…" the dean paused, as though letting the weight and impact of his question soak in to the air. "Do you, and son, I don't mean to offend you, I've got to do my job—the *Lord's* job—do you have…*sorry* blood?"

He paused and stared at Zeke, the smile in full spread.

"'Cause, son, something's in your blood, you cain't shake it no matter how hard you try."

A million images of his daddy passed before his eyes but Zeke couldn't make himself hate the man, he couldn't summon up the anger for his daddy that he'd had in the past. Something about him, sorry as he was, he was his daddy, he had his blood, he had his mannerisms and his skin and his teeth and the way he walked and the high-pitched nasal voice and the gift for seducing women and the calling from God to minister to people. Zeke sat, probably longer than he should, resenting the dean and the insinuation of his allegedly sorry blood, his hardscrabble upbringing out in the country on a gravel road where the yards did not have big green lawns and fancy cars. When the dean's smile had grown large and sinister, like a clown at the circus, Zeke answered.

"No sir, I'm washed in the blood of the lamb. I want to do the Lord's work, spread the word of Jesus, and cast off my sinful past."

But he felt the presence of Jesus slip away just as he said it. He knew he didn't mean it, that he was doing what he had to do, just going through the motions to get from point A to point B, a game of checkers in which he controlled his team, his moves, and was trying to beat the other team down. He'd prayed and prayed and prayed but God had played no part in his affairs.

Mary Huggins greeted Zeke at the door of the Sunday school room as though she had been waiting there for all eternity, had been sitting in that metal folding chair with her Bible in her lap as a writing board and her Sunday school lesson open, scribbling notes and thoughts in the margins until she saw him come up the stairs at the end of the hall. She practically jumped out of the chair and ran to greet him, at first as though to hug him before she paused and gracefully stuck out her thin white hand to welcome him to the Second Baptist Church of Tuscaloosa.

She had light brown hair that she curled a little tighter than necessary and blue eye shadow and a flowing loose skirt that stopped between her ankles and her knees. Her legs were covered in white stockings and she had a pair of white shoes to match the white belt that cinched the skirt around her waist, although not tightly. It was topped off with a baggy red cotton sweater. It was hard to get any idea at all what kind of shapes were under her clothes but he tried not to think about that; he thought about the reason he was there and that he wanted the reports back to Dean Green to be good ones. It was all politics. They were watching him and he would perform. He would pray over The Acts of the Apostles and they'd be touched if they chose to be, which most of them, being impressionable college girls who could have otherwise stayed home, would be.

There was something about Mary Huggins' plainness, a lack of threatening features, that attracted him. She didn't have gorgeous shapely legs and a long dramatic mane of golden hair. This was a woman he could live with, a woman who wouldn't eat into his brain and cause his loins to tingle and burn at just the very sight of her, like the very *thought* of Cindy Daniels had done to him; like Sally Claxton would have done if she'd stuck around town; like Sally Claxton's mama had done to his daddy. This was a woman who would not haunt him at night while he tried to sleep, a woman whose mind and body was pure and was devoted to cooking and cleaning and taking care of children. A woman devoted to God. He decided on her then and there, the moment she introduced him to the group and called him *Reverend*. "The good *Reverend* from the seminary…the young *Reverend* who grew up in Georgia…the *Reverend* who is going to share his Bible studies with us this morning." He chose to avoid the green-eyed gaze of a young blonde girl in a white linen dress—was it that warm outside already?—a lean girl with curves and circles that spun and ambled together forming her walk, shapes that moved slowly when she shifted in her chair and ignored him, her mind drifting off to the Devil knows what. He ignored her and instead focused on the devoutness of Mary Huggins, the soft chin that she held up, the hands squeezed tight in prayer, hands that had already done a fair share of washing and cooking although she was only eighteen.

He and Mary Huggins walked through the Tuscaloosa campus that afternoon and had lunch at the small house that she shared with three other co-ed teaching students from South Alabama. The tidy little house with azaleas and daffodils and a small green lawn and a porch to sit on was on the edge of town, just within an old neighborhood before the countryside spread out. She fixed pimento cheese sandwiches on white, lightly toasted bread and sweetened iced tea and pickles, all the time apologizing for not having a better meal.

"I'm so sorry, but I just didn't think we'd have lunch together today and this is all I can get together right now. You have to come back next week and let me fix you a better meal, something nice and hot and nourishing."

Zeke stared into her eyes, a grayish, almost hazel, and knew that he would be back next Sunday and the Sunday after that and the Sunday after that. They would have many Sunday dinners together. She had this look on her face that said she would do anything he wanted her to, absolutely anything—whether it be to go back in the bedroom and let him ravage her or sit on the steps and read the Bible with him, she wanted to do it.

He chose reading the Bible.

+ + +

The Greyhound bus plowed on through the sunny day, the weather cooling as the elevation increased. They passed from Arizona into Utah, white-capped mountains getting closer. The landscape grayed to the color of slate, replacing the red rocks of the painted desert.

"I'm telling you, boy, that woman was mine the minute I laid eyes on her. It was like she had been made just for me, to cook my meals and raise my young'uns and be the perfect church wife. She and I both knew it the minute I saw her standing in the doorway with her Sunday school lesson in her hand."

Timber always had been curious about seminaries, what the preachers did there, how they always came out of the seminary, with a diploma and a wife, ready to be ordained.

"So old Dean Green practically runs a matchmaking service?" Timber was feeling good, the first rush of liquor having shed his inhibitions and quieted his doubts. He was happy to be alive and have someone interesting to talk with. His hangover was gone, washed away by the morning bourbon.

"Yeah," the Reverend Blizzard said, "you are right about that. I think much of his work was searching out girls to marry off to the boys at the seminary. You ain't nobody as a preacher if you ain't married. You won't never get you a church if you single. Everybody's worried you'll be screwing all the women, and nowadays, I guess, they got to worry that you'll be after the little boys. But that seems to be a Catholic problem. All I ever hear about with the Baptist preachers is they can't keep their hands off the young women."

Timber smiled and nodded. He was catching a buzz and his voice boomed.

"My Baptist church always had all the hottest young women in town." A bevy of Louisiana teenagers from years past glided through his mind, their skirts blowing up in the wind at church picnics or sticky blouses clinging to them on windless days. "There's something about those Baptist women when they are young, in high school."

"Lord knows, they was my problem," the preacher said. "What's a warm-blooded man s'posed to do when girls from sixteen to forty-six are throwing themselves at him, inviting him over to minister during the day if they were married? Or in the evening for dinner when they were single? And the high school girls come round to the office after school in their short shorts and tight T-shirts? I ain't but flesh and bone.

"But I knew that my sermon, that first sermon about lust and sex and sin was the truth, the only way, and staying out of young girls' pants would in the long run be the best thing to do. And you see, I'd done had anything I wanted to with Cindy Daniels. Once you've had the deluxe rib platter the rest of the items on the menu don't look that appetizing. But it wasn't the Father or the Son or the Holy Spirit talking to me that time. I was being practical. I was doubting then, doubting heavy in my last two years in the seminary. Something 'bout the Honorable Reverend Dean Green's talk with me that day cast a shadow in my mind about why we was all here. Naw, it was good ole common sense. I could get pussy, or I could get me a good job at a good church and have a good honest devoted wife. I couldn't have both.

"So I went to lunch the next week with Mary Huggins. We read the Bible on her porch and talked about the weather and her garden. I knew that if I'd laid down with her then she'd been pregnant the moment I stuck it in—that I was sure of. It was meant to be. So I waited and waited till I put on that graduation cap and gown and walked down the aisle on that clear sunny Alabama afternoon and got my diploma, soon to be ordained as a minister in the Southern Baptist way. It was a lot like my baptism when I was six years old and Daddy held me down in the water. I didn't have no other choice and didn't feel nothing about it."

"If you had lost your faith," Timber asked, "why didn't you just leave the seminary and go get a regular job? Something where you could chase women and drink liquor and nobody would think a thing about it?"

"You know, my brother, that was never an option, 'cause God had a plan for me, He was calling me to work for Him. The believing would come later."

"So you mean you didn't believe, but you still followed God's plan?" Timber eyed the Reverend Blizzard suspiciously. "How does that work out?"

"Well, Dean Green was more than a matchmaker. He also found jobs for all of his graduates. I didn't have but a week before I set out for my first job."

"Where'd he send you off to?"

"Back to Georgia, but this time up north of Atlanta, where the hills start to turn into the Blue Ridge Mountains, a little town called Piney. I became the youth minister and assistant pastor at Piney Baptist Church, the biggest church in town. He said he tried to get me on with Reverend Daniels but the Armstrong church didn't have an opening. I guess he didn't know that I'd already filled one of Reverend Daniels' *openings* in my past."

Reverend Blizzard winked at Timber.

"The week after I got my diploma and my license to preach," he continued, "I went down to Eufaula and took me a bride. The Honorable Reverend Dean Green conducted the service. A few of my fellow students-turned-ministers served as groomsmen, and a few more attended to put a few bodies in the pews on my side of the church. I didn't even tell my daddy about it. He might not have come anyway. I figured he could have seen in my face that I was going through the motions. He could tell I was just doing it because I didn't know what else to do, not because I was feeling the faith, but because I felt like a piece in some big game of checkers. I didn't admit it to myself, but I didn't feel God at the time."

Timber shrugged. He'd never believed any of the preaching he'd heard about

God's plan for him, about God's role in the world. He doubted that God intended for him to work a downward spiral of low-paying jobs, most of them in miserable towns for not much money, doing the same thing over and over and over. He doubted that God had sent the phalanx of women over the years who had run roughshod over him and left him suffering in their wakes. God played no active part in the world, he was pretty sure of that. Certainly God wasn't as cruel to plan Timber's life the way it had turned out. His life should have been better than to be almost fifty, broke, alone and on a Greyhound bus listening to a fallen preacher.

Timber took another drink of Jim Beam, shifted in his seat and looked straight at the preacher, the first time he'd looked square at him. The blood-red mark was bright in the white of his right eye, but dark crimson where it colored over the blue ring circling the wide black pupil. His brown hair was slick and unmoving, his face red with sun.

"So, are you a believer, or you just following God's plans?" Timber said.

The Reverend Blizzard's face took on a sober look. He looked straight at Timber, half smiling, half glaring.

"Son, I'm both. I'm a believer, through and through. And I'm old enough to know that even if you ain't a believer and are lost from God's word, you—we— are all following God's road map—whether you know it or not... You ain't got no choice in the matter."

IN HIS MIND HE BEGAN TO PRAY

A reverend and a husband, June 1974, Zeke Blizzard Jr. pulled into Piney, driving a station wagon, his new wife by his side. The town sat along the blurry line where the Appalachian foothills began to turn into the Blue Ridge Mountains, about eighty miles northeast of Atlanta. Piney and Armstrong, Zeke's hometown, were very much alike in some ways: each had a selection of Protestant churches, mom-and-pop stores lining downtown streets and junk-yards on the fringes. It was the mountains that set Piney apart, looming just to the north of town, misty hulking green and gray shapes ever-present in the northern horizon, bathed in pink light in the early morning and evening, a black mass at night and a green forest with patches of gray slate illuminated by sun-light during the day. The mountains and the smaller population of blacks were Piney's main distinctions from Armstrong, a town marked by its heavily mixed population and gently rolling hills. Piney, the afternoon Zeke and Mary arrived, was green and lush with the warmth and moisture of summer that had settled into the town of ten thousand.

The town should have seemed familiar to Zeke, but moving somewhere that he did not know a soul, except for his new bride, was a frightening proposition. On the drive from Alabama to Piney he became scared, scared of the unknown, of what he was getting himself into, of having a wife he was responsible for, of making a name for himself in the church. He clenched the steering wheel and took deep breaths, sighing sporadically. He hadn't prayed sincerely all year. "I was tore up and didn't know what to expect. Hell, I guess I realized I didn't know nothing. I wasn't but twenty-two years old."

What he first noticed about Piney, something he remembered vividly years later, was the mill's work whistle, audible to every home in town, a languorous whine that lasted for ten seconds but seemed much longer, echoing through the houses and schools and churches and gas stations and row of downtown stores. It blew at eight, noon, four and midnight. It was a sound that people in Piney heard in their bones and to which the newcomers there quickly became accustomed. "That whistle always reminded you where you were, what time it was. It set your bearings for you."

Then he noticed the preaching on the radio. He had flipped along the AM dial until he came to the local station down near the right knob and heard the panting and shouting of a breathless preacher, declaring the righteousness of Jesus and the sacrifices He made. Each sentence was punctuated with an exhalation, a cross between a passionate moan and a grunt. "Gaspers," some people called such preachers. He turned the radio up.

"*Jesus* is going to come back down to the earth one day—*unh!* And he's going to look *around* and pull out a list of names—*unh!* And those that have been *saved* he's going to take with him up to heaven—*unh!* And those that have not come forth and officially and sanctimoniously given their lives to *God* will feel the fires and sulfur of hell—*unh!*"

He listened for a while, comforted to hear another man of God on the town's only radio station on a Wednesday afternoon. He waited to hear the name of the church and the preacher, but it was not announced at the end of the broadcast. The station instead went straight to the local news: a couple had been killed in a car wreck south of town; City Hall was having a chicken barbecue and tickets were two dollars each; the weather was warming up, almost ninety, but no rain was forecast. He clicked the radio off and looked at Mary. She smiled at him.

Their new station wagon, a five-year-old Ford with eighty thousand miles, was filled with all they owned in the world: a box of dishes and clothes, including two new dark preaching suits, white dress shirts and conservative ties, wide but without the kaleidoscope of colors of the seventies. Zeke also had a pair of blue jeans and a pair of khaki work pants, two denim shirts for around the house. Mary had a pile of dresses and sweaters and aprons. Zeke's parents had dressed the same way in the fifties.

He drove down the sloping main street lined with modest storefronts: a five and dime, a hardware store, a seed and feed, a pharmacy with a lunch counter, a Belk's and JC Penny, a sporting goods store and a Christian bookstore. He drove on past downtown, slowing as they went past the Piney Baptist Church where he would work, and on through the neighborhoods of homes, growing ever smaller. He stopped at a realtor's home to pick up the keys to half of a small duplex apartment on the edge of town, not far from the mill that made rubber for tires.

Zeke had made a down payment on the station wagon with a small bonus the church paid him when he accepted the job. The duplex where they would live was owned by a wealthy church deacon who let assistant pastors live in his rental property for reduced rates. A taciturn loom repairman who worked at the mill and his family would be their neighbors.

His fear escalated as they approached their soon-to-be home at the bottom of a muddy hill. The cinder-block duplex's yard was patchy, the landscaping sparse. Zeke parked and led his new bride to the door. As the screen door opened, she was filled with anticipation, he with dread. He put in the key and turned the knob.

"Home sweet home," Mary said, smiling. She put her hand in Zeke's as they stepped into the furnished living room. He forced a smile at her but was filled with trepidation.

"Oh, Zeke, our first home. It's so cute. We are going to be happy here."

"Yeah," he mumbled. He looked around at the pine furniture in the small living and dining room. He walked to the bedroom and then the kitchen, a dingy white linoleum floor, the same in the bathroom. He looked out the bathroom window at the small, muddy backyard enclosed by a rusty chain link fence. Beyond the fence, there was the back wall of a dingy white warehouse, also cinder block.

"It sure was nice of them to find us a furnished place," Mary said from the kitchen. She had a wet paper towel and was wiping out the cabinets.

Zeke, still staring out the bathroom window, had a sense that what was alien and strange would become like the back of his hand.

"That little town would be my home for the next twenty-three years."

Mary, "bless her heart," had been glowing since their wedding only days before, followed by a short honeymoon in Gatlinburg. She was thrilled to be a bride and took to decorating and cooking right away, intoxicated with her role of preacher's wife.

The first week she bought a collection of ceramic sugar bowls and spice jars, lining them up in the modest kitchen. Armed with dishes from the wedding, she had the house in order in no time.

She had been a virgin until their wedding night. The first time, in the darkness of the small hotel room in the Smoky Mountains, she undressed and got into bed.

He moved on top of her and into her. She cried in pain, sobbing quietly, reservedly. Tentatively was the way she did everything, Zeke soon learned. She had, however, an innate understanding of his need for sex, eventually even enjoying it herself, if only a little. She knew her role and was ready to fulfill it whatever it took. She never resisted.

"It wasn't Cindy Daniels, mind you…but it was good. And I could get it anytime I wanted. Practically, any time. And I didn't have to do it in a car or be on the look out for someone shooting my ass."

They established a routine that first night in their home that they would follow every night. At bedtime, like clockwork, always in the dark. As consistent and steady as the town's loud whistle, the rickety double bed would rock back and forth until he finished, trembling, spreading his seed inside her.

They did it without speaking and then slept soundly.

Zeke's first day on the job was Sunday. All he had to do was sit on the stage with the minister of music and the assistant preacher during the morning service and then stick around to meet and greet the congregation afterward.

The pastor, Reverend Norman Slatkins, had been there fifteen years. He was a little wrinkled man who had an impressive resumé of churches he had pastored throughout the Southeast. Prior to that, he'd worked as a missionary in Africa and India. His demeanor bespoke none of his accomplishments, however. He was small and quiet and hunched.

Zeke was shocked the first time he heard him preach. Reverend Slatkins slouched in the pulpit and rarely made eye contact with the parishioners, reading the sermon, typed in all caps and double-spaced, shuffling the paper when he moved forward to the next page. He was a robot in a slightly wrinkled suit going through the motions. Zeke knew enough to keep a smile on his face before his new flock but inside he was in pain, at least a daze, listening to the little man drone along through the prayers and mumbling through his sermons.

Zeke looked around the sanctuary. It was not as large as Armstrong Baptist Church but still had a good crowd, about two hundred or more, mainly families and old folks like in Armstrong and the other churches in Alabama he had visited. No one was listening. Mothers glared at their children to keep them still. The men gazed forward and daydreamed, a few looking to where a group of long-haired teenage girls gathered. Everyone here was marking time, doing what they had been raised to do but not believing, only waiting until the end of the sermon when they could go home and eat fried chicken or ham or a pot roast with biscuits and perhaps fresh vegetables, if any of the gardens had come in yet.

Zeke struggled to keep from frowning. It shouldn't be this way. He had seen people moved by the power and the glory of the Lord, by the message and the stories of Jesus, by the indescribable presence of the Holy Spirit. He hadn't been moved in almost two years since Dean Green sat him down and categorized him like a box of vegetables on a farm, ready to be shipped out. But he knew that time and fate were much stronger than Dean Green's flippancy. He was being called to inspire people, to bring meaning to the time they spent each Sunday morning. Unlike his daddy, he knew that it would take some time, a little posturing, a little playing of the game, but he would get his own church, he would inspire people, he would give sermons from his heart and not paper, sermons that were not read but preached. The Lord had come back to him.

Reverend Slatkins finished the sermon and introduced Zeke to the congregation.

"This fine young man comes to us from the seminary over there in Alabama and will minister to our young people," Slatkins said, droning. "Please stay around after the service to greet him and his lovely wife, Mary."

Zeke put on his preacher's smile for the first time, a big toothy grin with all his face muscles pressed into action. He had learned it from watching the assistant preachers in Armstrong and then in the churches throughout Alabama he had attended as a seminary student. The older pastors, the established reverends, didn't have to resort to such an effort-filled smile, but it was expected of the up-and-coming preachers. The smile and a big strong handshake was their trademark, their most effective tool. Zeke greeted the handful of parishioners who came down front afterward, mainly old women who welcomed him and said they were so glad to have him in their church. Zeke thought he noticed two of the teenage girls in the back, looking his way and whispering. He put them out of his mind and looked to Mary, beside him, glowing with the pride of a man of God's wife.

The job of Piney youth minister was an easy one, hardly a job at all when Zeke compared it to the odd jobs his daddy had held cleaning up in factories or running a tractor across a farm. All he had to do was coordinate the youth Sunday school program, host a Wednesday evening prayer session and give a short children's sermon in the first part of the Sunday service before kids six and under were ushered off to the nursery, their attention spans too short to follow the sermon. He was expected to attend the Sunday night services although he had no official role to perform. He also was on-call to visit parishioners in the hospital or conduct their funerals in case the assistant preacher was double-booked.

Zeke hoped after he had been there awhile that he would be able to preach a sermon on Sunday night but the Reverend Slatkins didn't volunteer it and Zeke didn't ask. Zeke sensed tension between the Reverend Slatkins and the assistant pastor, Reverend Buddy Sharpe. Buddy never got to give a sermon either.

Zeke had a cramped office in the church, three doors down from the Reverend Slatkins' large corner office. The old man was never in the office except for early Sunday mornings when he typed out his sermon in all caps and reviewed it. Outside the pastor's office sat Carolyn, the church secretary, a quiet woman in her midsixties with dark, dyed hair and thick glasses. She only spoke when she was spoken to or the phone rang.

Zeke started out his first work week reporting at nine every morning and staying a full business day. He soon realized that ninety percent of the time it would be only him and Carolyn, waiting in the stillness. She tended to a phone that hardly ever rang. When it did ring, she snatched it up and answered before it got through the first full bell. Zeke passed the time reading the Bible, a collection of Baptist sermons and other religious books. He idled for several weeks in the office, waiting for something to happen, expecting the Reverend Slatkins or Buddy or the minister of music to drop in on him and visit. But aside from Sundays and Wednesday evenings, no one appeared at the church. He asked Carolyn how often Reverend Slatkins and the other staff were in the office. She said most of their time was out visiting parishioners. Zeke suspected that they were out fishing or taking naps. Slatkins, in his brief instructions, told Zeke not to do any visitations until he'd been there six months and people got to know him.

He'd had only two discussions with the Reverend Slatkins: on the phone, after Dean Green arranged the job for him, to work out the details of his first day and his living arrangements, and, in person, the pastor had briefed him on his first Sunday about his duties as youth minister. The coolness baffled Zeke. He was accustomed to the warmth of church families. He had expected to be invited into their homes, served hot meals followed by dessert and coffee in the living room. That's how he had been treated by Reverend Daniels and in many of the small churches throughout Alabama when he was a seminary student. The Piney congregation also was surprisingly aloof, cordial at church but not inviting him into their homes, their lives. He'd heard that mountain people were different. Maybe that's what it was.

It went on like that all summer. Zeke told himself to be patient, his time would come.

One late Monday afternoon in August he was driving out in the country, listening to a sermon on the radio and looking for a fishing spot, when he saw a huge banner proclaiming a week-long revival with services beginning that evening at the Church of the Rock. Zeke found the little church on a backroad, a quaint red brick sanctuary with a gravel parking lot surrounded by a stand of pine trees and one lone live oak tree near the front door. "I got me a feeling right then and there, that this would one day be my church."

Zeke and Mary attended the service that night. The small church was about three-fourths full, about seventy-five people, and had a warmth to it, a family feel. People smiled kindly at him. The old preacher, Reverend Walter Thomas, was colorful, emotional, calling for lost souls to repent and be reborn, panting like the preacher Zeke had heard on the radio, panting like Zeke's daddy did when he preached, the old-time religion, promising salvation to anyone who knelt down before Jesus. The pastor mentioned several times during his sermon that he was retiring and the church was looking for guest ministers until a new pastor was called to take over. He prayed, "Lord, send us a brilliant new preacher here. We can't pay him much money, but Lord, he will be a rich man in love and kindness, surrounded by men and women and children who love Jesus like no one else. Can't no Christians anywhere compete with the fine folks here in the Church of the Rock."

Zeke and Mary went down after the service and introduced themselves to the Reverend Thomas and the deacons gathered there. Zeke said he'd be glad to preach anytime they would have him. They greeted him with warm smiles and firm handshakes. When the pastor learned of Zeke's position at Piney Baptist, he invited him to give the revival sermon Wednesday night. Zeke paused for only a second. He could arrange for someone else to lead the prayer meeting. This was an opportunity to preach. He suspected he was starting to feel the Lord's call.

Reverend Slatkins was curt on the phone when Zeke called him at home the next morning to tell him of his plans for Wednesday night. Zeke had recruited an able substitute amongst the Piney Baptist deacons.

"Well, son, I don't guess there's much I can do about it now," Slatkins said. "You told those people out there you'd preach, so you've got to do it. But you've hurt your chances of standing in my pulpit."

Zeke had ruled out his chances of that already.

The Wednesday night Zeke was to preach was a sticky evening, one of the hottest of the summer, with little breeze until a heavy cloud cover bubbled up into the sky. The clouds had been building up all afternoon, a gray roiling mass by the time the service was about to start. The air cooled off rapidly when people began coming into the church, dodging the intermittent precipitation of the impending thunderstorm, big fat drops of water splashing against the car windshields and the church roof that would build to a hard rain. Lightning flashes and thunder rumbles began to slowly creep in from the distance. Zeke sat proudly on the podium with the Reverend Thomas. "I wished that my mama, bless her heart, and my daddy, even though he was a son of a bitch, could've seen me then."

The congregation sang several of the old-time hymns, "The Old Rugged Cross" and "Send a Great Revival." The simple, small sanctuary with an A-frame roof and rough, dark beams across it had beautiful acoustics, unlike Piney Baptist. The bigger church in town had a stillness in the air, almost like a moisture that sapped up the music and singing, taking the life out of it. Perhaps it was only Reverend Slatkins' demeanor that threw cold water on everything. In the little country church Zeke felt at home. The chorus of voices, although scratchy drawls of laymen and women, comforted him with the old hymns, hymns he could hear his daddy singing. Soon he was introduced.

"I'm telling you, when I took that pulpit, the Holy Spirit came over me and God gave that sermon to those folks. I told them about Jesus and how He died for our sins. How He gave Himself instead of others. How He put Himself in our place on that cross.

"I told 'em, 'Imagine hanging there on a cross with nails in your hands, a crown of thorns around your *head*, dying *slowly*, suffocating, dying criminals on each side of you. But no matter how bad it got, Jesus still had the faith. Faith in His Father who created him, faith in His Father that He would be saved.' Someone in the congregation, near full that night, shouted *amen*."

Zeke had spoken adequately to many Sunday school groups, youth functions and practiced dozens of sermons at the seminary. For the Sunday school and youth groups encircling him in chairs or his classmates in the little chapel at the seminary, he'd never felt the inspiration he did in the pulpit, the *call* of God. He had spoken before as though the words weren't his and he was a puppet reading from a prepared text about Jesus. In the pulpit that night, however, God was leading him on through the sermon. Although he'd drafted it, he didn't refer to the sheets of paper before him, but looked the parishioners straight in the eye and told them how it was, what Jesus wanted them to do, what they had to do to be saved.

He wasn't a gasper but his high tone took on a fever pitch, a rhythm not unlike the screamers and the panters. He had a passion, an edge that rang out, sonorously and rhythmically, a steady plea from the mouth of God. Every sentence had an urgency, an undertone that said "you'd better listen to this or else you'll burn in the fires of hell." The rhythm of each sentence begged for an *amen* to be added at the end. His daddy had been a screamer, ending almost every sentence with the trademark *"unh!"* that punctuated the speech and rhythms of so many Baptist preachers. Zeke had grown up listening to his daddy's sermons, a man with no formal training. His daddy had learned from listening to the hard-core Pentecostal preachers at Middle Georgia tent revivals and tiny churches tucked away on backroads, men who would holler ruination and damnation and salvation, pounding car hoods and rolling on the ground, speaking in angry tongues.

At the seminary Zeke had listened to audio tapes of hundreds of other preachers throughout the South. Those from the smaller, country churches tended to scream, while the preachers with larger congregations at the well-heeled churches tended to imbue fire and brimstone without losing their breath and panting like the backwater preachers did. He had done a lot of thinking and had made all sorts of plans in his mind as to what style preacher he would be, how he would sound when he finally stepped into the pulpit and met the gaze of hundreds of eyes. When he stood in front of a congregation for the first time since giving the youth sermon in high school, it flowed from him, the same way it had then in Armstrong Baptist. He was unconscious…God was talking through him as though he were a mouthpiece for Jesus. He recounted the story of the crucifixion and miraculous rise from the tomb. Then he rolled into his conclusion.

"Some of you, God bless you all, may *not* make it home safely tonight. Ain't nothing sure or safe in this world. Some of you may make it home but that don't mean *you* are safe either. Some of your souls may be *freed* from your body tonight in your sleep. I don't mean to scare you, but *that's* a fact. We are going around on this here earth like *passengers* in a car and we've all got to get out sooner or later. But I do know one thing: If you are *saved*, if you dedicate your soul to Jesus, you are going to that mansion in the sky where there ain't no clouds and the water is pure and cool, the sun shines warmly and soft breezes blow."

There were several shouts of *amen* following this statement. Zeke continued, his tone more somber.

"If you are not saved, if you've held onto your *soul* like it's tucked away in a safety deposit box down there at First National Bank, then you won't be so lucky if your time on earth ends tonight. Those of you who are not saved will *taste* the noxious sulfur in your mouths and noses and *feel* the fires of hell burning on your skin for all eternity. And remember: *eternity* is a very, *very* long time."

No one in the church stirred. All eyes were transfixed on him: the youngest children that often squirmed and squealed during sermons; men in work clothes and scraggly beards who often were dragged to church by their wives and stared at their feet; teenagers who usually gazed listlessly at the walls or the ceiling. He was getting through to all of them.

His serious expression transformed to a smile—warm, glowing almost, a kind wrinkle in his brow. The rapid rhythm of his speech calmed down. He spoke more softly, the pitch in his voice dropping gently.

"But if you come on down tonight and profess your love and devotion to our Lord, Jesus Christ of Nazareth, you can change your other-worldly travel plans to the mansion in the sky. Please *won't* you come? Won't *you* come?"

"*Amen*, brother," someone shouted.

"*Jesus* gave His life for you. Jesus hung on the cross for *you*. Won't *you* come down tonight and accept Him as your Lord and savior?"

"*Amen.*"

"Jesus didn't have to go up on that cross. He didn't have to die for your sins. He could have gotten out of it. But He did it. He went through with it the hard way. Won't you come down tonight and let Him know He *didn't* die there in vain? That His rising from the dead wasn't for nothing?"

Two very elderly women in the second row tottered forward. Zeke stepped down from the pulpit to the first row and hugged each of them. He led another chorus of *amens*, standing on the floor, and continued to preach.

"Some of you, I'm sure, have made this walk down front before, giving your souls to Jesus. But maybe that's been awhile. Maybe you've done some things since then that you ain't proud of. Maybe it's time to rededicate your life to Christ. He will accept you and forgive you of your sins. He's an all-knowing, all-loving God. Won't you *come down* for Him tonight?"

Zeke could see audience members fidgeting in their seats, almost pained expressions on their faces as they debated whether or not to come forward. He grabbed a hymnal and announced the page for "Tenderly Jesus is Calling."

"As we sing I want everyone to think about Jesus on that cross, calling softly to each of you to accept Him and His Father, the Lord our God Almighty, creator of the heaven and the earth. Jesus and I want you to come down tonight, come down and reserve your space in the Holy Kingdom."

Two verses into the song it was like a dam broke loose. At least ten people rushed forward. Three teenage girls. A man and wife and their eight-year-old. A lone workingman still in a blue shirt embossed with his name on it. A teenage boy. A single woman in her thirties. An older man there alone.

Zeke hugged them all, thanking them. "Welcome, sister. The Lord welcomes you into His house and with His love," or "Greetings, brother, Jesus is very proud of you for the choice you've made."

Zeke arranged the saved souls in a line across the front of the church parallel to the first row. He then turned to the congregation and finished leading the hymn.

"Let us pray. Lord, thank you for your presence in this room with us here tonight. Thank you for showing the light to these ten fine folks. Thank you for giving us your Son, who died for our lowly sins. Thank you for caring about us and keeping us. We love you, Lord. And I'm sure you know like I do that there are others here who want to come forward but they are shy or scared. Well, Lord, maybe we'll get them tomorrow night. There's two more nights in this revival. In the meantime, Lord, I ask that you keep them safe from car wrecks and fires and other disasters. Give them a chance to be saved, Lord, that's all I'm asking, just a chance. Thank you Lord and thank you Jesus. Amen."

He opened his eyes to the congregation, still transfixed, a few of the women with tears in their eyes. He heard Reverend Thomas step into the pulpit, behind and above Zeke's spot on the church floor.

"Let me add one more thing," the Reverend Thomas said. He smiled down at Zeke when he looked around. "Thank you Lord, for bringing this wonderful young man into our church, into my pulpit. This is a man I could turn my pulpit over to, Lord, so I hope you'll call him to do that."

Zeke closed his eyes again, as in prayer. *This* could be *his* church. The old man continued.

"I think I can see out there a few more souls who want to come forward. So let's sing the last verse again, just in case some of you want to come on down."

Reverend Thomas sang loudly and three more people moved forward, two women and a man, all the way from the back row. Their expressions were dazed, one of the women crying profusely. Zeke hugged them and squeezed them into the line with the other saved souls.

At the end of the verse, the Reverend Thomas proclaimed, "Thank you, Reverend Blizzard. Goodnight, everybody, and *hallelujah*."

Zeke was there for almost another hour shaking hands, greeting parishioners, hugging those who had been saved. Many others came down to meet him. Mary, whom he had practically forgotten was there, came and stood beside him. The parishioners were warm and genuine and kind, men in work clothes and women in print dresses of an older style, the sort to whom he could relate. Several told him they were very tempted to come down but they had been saved, or resaved, the preceding revival nights, the week before, the month before. A few even referred to him as "pastor" even though he hadn't even formerly talked to the Reverend Thomas about the job.

This *would* be his church.

After everyone had cleared out, the Reverend Thomas asked Zeke if he would go fishing with him on Saturday.

Zeke met the Reverend Thomas at the church half an hour before dawn. The old preacher, wearing a pair of blue coveralls, stood beside his light green Ford pickup truck packed with several fishing poles, a cooler and two quart-size plastic containers, one with Red Wigglers and one with catalpa worms. He sipped a steaming cup of coffee, pouring one for Zeke from an old red thermos that sat on the top of the truck's roof. He had thin white hair and glasses, his skin wrinkled but tight on his weathered face.

"Good morning, son," the preacher said. "Let's go catch us some of them *brim* and *crappie*...maybe even get us a bass or two."

Zeke got into the front seat of the preacher's truck, a three-year-old model with a very neat cab. Reverend Thomas dropped the clutch on the steering wheel column into drive and took off fast, crunching gravel and stirring up dust along the narrow roads that led into the woods behind the church. The old man smiled as though he was stifling laughter the whole time, chuckling when he made a sharp turn or when he stomped the accelerator and dust flew up, the fishing gear in the back sliding from side to side. They were deep down in the woods at the bottom of a steep hill, the leaf cover of August thick, the morning still dark black when he turned the wheel sharply onto a tiny side road, a grassy trail marked only by the tires that had run through before. The truck slid as the old preacher pressed the brake, stopping only about ten feet from the edge of a pond, its brown water illuminated by the truck's headlights. A small fishing boat with an oar was flipped over on the edge of the shoreline, tied to a tree with a rope.

"This here is the preacher's secret fishing hole. I'm out here 'bout every single day, 'cept Sunday of course. I hadn't brought anybody but my sons and wife out here—ever. And I don't bring them that often."

Zeke started to speak, to thank the preacher for his generous invitation, but he couldn't get a word in edgewise. The old man kept right on talking.

"Yes, son, I've been fishing in this lake for forty years. *Forty* years. That's as long as those Jews roamed the desert. Can you imagine that?" Again he gave Zeke no chance to answer. "Roaming around in that dry dusty desert for all that time. You believe every word of the Bible literally, son?"

"Well, sir, I—"

"No, me either. You can't take every word of it as factual truth. It's the gospel truth, but sometimes I think that's different from the *actual* truth. Now don't get me started in the pulpit on that. I don't want to have to try to explain myself to the laymen. The best thing about this church is the people here don't go off on some smart-aleck, *intellectual* bent trying to disprove stories in the Bible and convince everyone something or another ain't so. There's a reason preachers don't take questions. People around this church know that God works in mysterious ways and they are willing to cut the preacher man some slack on questions about the Bible. This has been a good church to have, boy, I'm telling you that. Good people. Good country people. The best forty years of my life."

The old preacher got out of the truck, slamming the door. He was spry, flipping the boat over and pushing it into the pond, holding the rope as it glided out. The dawn was beginning to break, but the horizon was not visible from the pond's edge. The pond was about five acres, a kidney shape. It was surrounded by hills that sloped down, its shorelines thick with pines on the far side and leafy hardwoods where Zeke and the preacher stood. Crickets that had been chirping faded as the light slowly grew brighter.

The old preacher grabbed four Zebco rods and reels from the back of his truck in one hand and his tackle box in the other. Zeke got the two containers of worms. The preacher set the reels down and pulled the boat to the side and he and Zeke unloaded the gear into it. Then he untied the rope, holding the boat by its edge.

"Get in here, son, and grab that paddle. I want you to do the steering."

"Yes sir."

With minimal conversation the old preacher directed him to a spot near the far shore of the pond where they dropped a small anchor, baited two hooks with Red Wigglers and two with catalpa worms, then cast out their lines. The sun was still not over the trees but the pond and its shorelines were visible, the sky a purple shade of blue except for the eastern horizon with pink, orange and red coming on. Zeke, who had done his fair share of fishing for bream and crappie when he was a boy, enjoyed the solitude of the early morning on the lake. He loved casting out, the reel spinning smooth in his hands, the fishing line racing away from him, shooting out the silver loops on the pole that harnessed it, the weights and the bait splashing into water thirty feet away. Soon he felt the familiar tap of a fish on the worm. He played it slow, waiting for the fish to take the hook, and then reeling it in to the boat. The bream were too small to put up much of a fight but gave a mild, somehow oddly comforting tug against the line. Zeke, as the old preacher did, preferred this to serious bass fishing. Catching bass required using lures or minnows and constant reeling in and casting out, over and over until the big bass came along. And how those fish fought like the dickens. Dropping lines in the water and waiting for the bream and crappie was all right with Zeke. It was nice to sit on the lake and take the fish that God gave you.

The old man pulled a pack of cigarettes from a pocket under his coveralls and offered one to Zeke. Zeke shook his head and the old man lighted up, softly exhaling the smoke from his lungs, letting it drift around him and over the pond in the windless air. Zeke liked the old man even more for having the courage to smoke in front of him, the confidence in who he was to enjoy a vice here and there. He wondered if he ever took a drink.

For two hours they sat together, quietly but not with the awkward pauses of two people trying to make conversation. It was the companionship of two men who understood one another, two men who valued solitude over pointless chatter. The old man smoked two more cigarettes. They caught twelve bream, two nice crappie, and one two-pound bass that hit a fresh catalpa worm. The only words spoken were compliments of the other's fish. "That's a nice one, son." "Pastor, that's a pretty fish." The sun had risen high up over the trees, shining hotly on the pond. The lack of breeze, standard for an August day, made it hot and sticky by midmorning.

"Son, let's leave some of these fish in the pond for the next time. I've got some sausage biscuits and coffee in the truck. We've got us a nice mess of fish for a good little fish fry. I was thinking about having you and Mary over to the house this evening. But first I got to ask you a few questions."

They put the fish in the cooler and flipped the boat over and tied it to its designated tree. The Reverend Thomas served Zeke a sausage biscuit and black coffee from his thermos. They sat on the bottom of the overturned boat and ate.

"D'ya meet Henry Walker when you preached the other night? He's got a hog farm not too far from here. He makes best sausage you ever put in your mouth. Some folks think it's a little spicy, but not for me."

"No sir, I don't recall if I did," Zeke said. "But this is some fine sausage. Good biscuits too."

There was a long pause. Reverend Thomas looked out across the pond and then back at Zeke. His eyes were a cloudy blue.

"Son, you talk much to your daddy down in Armstrong? I was surprised you didn't tell me your daddy was a preacher."

"No, uh, sir. I, uh, haven't talked to him in about four or five years. Not since my mama died."

"I knew him a long time ago, years ago. I'm a good twenty-five years older than he is—what's he, about fifty now? Anyway, preachers around this state get to know each other. He was a young man then, not much older than you are, I guess, when we tried to get started with a small Georgia Baptist group. Mainly it was country preachers whose churches didn't get recognized for one reason or another by the big Southern Baptist Convention.

"We had a meeting down in a motel in Macon, about fifty of us. I could smell liquor on his breath that second morning. His eyes were bloodshot. Rumor was he picked up some woman downtown and had her in his room that first night. He was wild.

"But he could preach. He was the best of that bunch. There was something about him I liked. I invited him up here to preach in our revival—that was about the early fifties, I guess—and he gave quite a sermon. He was quite a screamer, sort of like me, but wilder and louder. Your style is different, though, but I can still see some of your daddy in you when you preach. The tone of his voice—yours has it too—had something that gets into people's hearts, makes 'em believe. It's one of those things that you can't teach. You can't even describe it. It's a gift, and you got it, son, you got it."

Zeke didn't respond, but only gazed down at his feet. He had put his daddy out of his mind, a rough memory. But he was more than a memory. People knew who he was. He still walked the earth down in Armstrong, still preached every Sunday. Sooner or later Zeke would have to confront him, have to deal with him.

"Your daddy could've been a big-time preacher. He would have gone over great on the radio. But his womanizing and his drinking got the best of him. Once you get that label, son, you don't ever shake it. Has he still got that tiny little church of his down there?"

"Yes sir, but he's never got many people in it."

"You know, he lied to me when he was here. Told me he was single and went after this redheaded girl in my choir. Charmed her right out of her dress in the back of his car the night after he preached. She wasn't nothing but a teenager, a high school girl. Her father was a sheriff's deputy and came right up on them, parked on a back road not far from here. He pulled his gun on your daddy and chased him off through the woods. Your daddy naked as a buck. He showed up at my house, begged clothes off of me. I gave him an outfit and told him to get the hell out of Piney, not to show his face around here no more. I found out later he was married."

Zeke hung his head in shame. He felt sure he'd never get this church. He'd felt so good in its pulpit, so confident with the congregation, so comfortable out on the lake with Reverend Thomas. He'd had visions of going fishing regularly with the retired preacher, maybe even smoke some cigarettes with him. That was all lost. Maybe his daddy's infamous visit was why everyone was so cool to him at Piney Baptist. Surely someone remembered the story of his daddy. It was a small town. Things like that got around. Small-town people didn't forget a story like that no matter how long ago it was.

"But son, you ain't your daddy. I can tell by the look in your eye. Your wife is a good, honest woman. And, after I heard you preach the other night, I want you in this church. God wants you in this church, doesn't he? Have you gotten the call?"

"Yes sir," Zeke said, his voice weak. He kneeled down and placed his head on the overturned boat's bottom that they had been using as a seat. "Dear Lord, thank you for—"

"Naw, son." The old preacher cut him off, putting his hand on his shoulders. "Get up. You ain't got to pray to convince me. I heard you preach. All you got to do is let the old retired preacher use the lake. I'll support you. And don't worry. I ain't going to say nothing about what your father did that night. That was a long time ago. Nobody 'round here knows him. The old sheriff's deputy died about ten years ago. He was a good man and didn't never run his mouth. The daughter moved away, California, I think, and doesn't ever come back. They were as ashamed of it as your daddy was—probably a lot more embarrassed than him.

"You'll be fine here," the old preacher said, patting him on the shoulders. Zeke rose from his knees and sat back down on the boat. "You'll be just fine here, son, just fine."

Reverend Thomas stood up. "I almost forgot. I have a gift for you." He opened the door of his truck and retrieved a paper bag from behind his seat. "This is something to welcome you to our church, to our pond. You'll get some good use out of this."

He pulled a knife in a leather sheath with Zeke's name on it out of the bag and handed it to him. Zeke slid the knife out of its cover—revealing a big shiny blade.

"That's good for cleaning fish," Reverend Thomas said. "But a good knife like that will cut about anything you need to cut."

After his transition to pastor, which took a few months, Zeke and Mary moved in the parish house the first weekend of October. The pastor of the Church on the Rock made only $3,500 a year in 1974, but the house where the pastor lived free-of-charge made up for the meager salary. It was a spacious three-bedroom ranch on five secluded acres only a mile from the church, close to the fishing pond. Reverend Thomas and his wife had moved out in early September to a lake house north of Atlanta, their retirement home.

The house seemed gigantic with only the first sparse furnishings they had purchased on their limited credit: a bed, a dresser, a simple pine table and chairs, a bookshelf, a loveseat, a television and a battered coffee table. The kitchen cabinets swallowed up their modest collection of dishes. Zeke and Mary moved everything in three trips in the station wagon, the table tied precariously to the top on the final run. The dining room set was too small for the large room. Even after all the furniture was unloaded, both spare bedrooms remained empty.

The Reverend Thomas and his wife, Matilda, were their first guests in the parish house. Mary fixed country-fried steaks with mashed potatoes and butter beans. She fried a batch of okra and squash. She made flaky biscuits for sopping in the dark brown gravy. She cut slices of fresh tomatoes. They sat down around the small square table, jammed with hot dishes and plates. Reverend Thomas smiled warmly upon them, joining hands with both Mary and his wife to pray. Both women automatically reached to join hands with Zeke, completing the circle.

"Lord, thank you for sending this young man and his wife to our humble church, our simple but wonderful parish house. Father, I *know* you have great things planned for these young people and their life of worship and religious leadership here. Thank you Jesus, thank you Lord, for these *splendid* keepers of this church and this house. *Amen.*"

They ate together comfortably and heartily, the meat tender and the vegetables fresh from the garden of a parishioner, a layman's gift to the new preacher. Zeke had never felt so happy before. He could hardly believe this house and this church was his, so soon after finishing the seminary. Mary looked the best she ever had tonight, practically glowing. He took a bite of a gravy-soaked biscuit, a sip of sugary sweet tea, fully believing in the Lord's blessing.

After cake and coffee, Reverend Thomas and Matilda walked from room to room in the house and told Zeke and Mary their memories of each one: a son's toys, their daughter's last night before she went off to college, a wallpaper project in the bathroom. They talked about guests who had stayed with them. Reverend Thomas had built the house himself twenty-five years ago. His family was the only one who had ever lived in it. He and Matilda examined the sparse furnishings, glancing at each other, smiling gently, as they entered each room.

Before they left, Matilda wanted to show a few things to Mary in the kitchen, tips about the stove, the oven and such. Reverend Thomas and Zeke went into the backyard. Stars were beginning to appear in the early night sky. The weather was pleasant, if not slightly cool from a breeze that rustled the leaves of the trees. The elder preacher lit a cigarette and softly exhaled a long stream of smoke. They stood for a few minutes, the silence between them comfortable, looking at the sloping backyard and the forest beyond the fence at the bottom of the hill. Reverend Thomas exhaled again and turned to Zeke.

"Son, I'm proud of you. Don't let me down, now—you hear? Be strong. Be disciplined. The Lord has smiled on you. You've got it good. I know you'll be fine, I can feel your love for God in my bones. You love the Lord, don't you, son? And Jesus?"

Tears formed in Zeke's eyes, his voiced choked up.

"Yessir, I do. I do."

The following Friday, Mary had gone into town for a doctor's checkup. Zeke was sitting at the dining-room table preparing his sermon for Sunday, having a cup of coffee, gazing out the front window. A moving truck, driven by Reverend Thomas, pulled into the yard, the brakes sighing as he cut the engine. Two deacons were with him.

Reverend Thomas got out and met Zeke on the porch.

"Son, we've brought you enough furniture to fill up this fine house," he said. The two deacons began unloading a bed from the truck, carrying a mattress toward the front door. "The Lord and I want you to be comfortable here, so the church discretionary fund is going to fill it up for you. I felt bad for taking all my things with me when I left, leaving the house empty for a fledgling preacher like you."

Zeke, speechless, was flattered but embarrassed at the old man's generosity. He had been taught to take no charity of any kind. His daddy had always refused welfare or unemployment or food stamps, even in their leanest years.

A man's got to provide for his own. The Reverend and the deacons unloaded beds and furniture for the guest rooms, sitting chairs, rugs, lamps, a writing desk, patio furniture for the back porch, end tables for the living room, a recliner and matching couch.

Zeke joined in to help. He pulled the Reverend Thomas aside as the house filled up. It took some strength for him to muster up the words.

"Sir, I can't just *take* all this. Just let me know how much it cost and I'll pay you—the church—back for it."

"No, son, I won't hear of it. This is the church's house, and although I'm retired as pastor, I still feel responsible for it and can still write checks on the discretionary fund. If you want to pay somebody back, you pay it to the preacher who takes over here after you. But I hope that won't be for a long time. Doing your job for the Lord, for Jesus, will be paying it back."

Reverend Thomas and the men finished unloading in less than an hour. They shook hands with Zeke and drove off.

Zeke was sitting in the recliner in the fully furnished living room, a notebook in his lap, when Mary got home two hours later. He was working on a sermon about the Lord's love and generosity. She smiled and tears began to flow down her cheeks. She looked fuller, more womanly. He began to tell her about the furniture from Reverend Thomas, but she walked over to him and put her fingers to his lips.

"Zeke, honey. I've got some big news. The doctor says I'm pregnant."

Zeke stood and hugged her, a long, tight grip. He could feel her trembling. He held her, looking over her shoulder and into their big green yard, the October day sunny and warm, an Indian summer before the crisp North Georgia fall set in and the leaves changed and winter gusts blew down from the mountain. He thought of his daddy and his childhood.

In his mind he began to pray. *Lord, don't let me mess this up. Help me Jesus, I know it won't be easy. I'm weak and you are strong. I don't know what I've done to deserve all this, just don't let me throw it all away…*

The prayer worked. For a long while, anyway. They had three children. Zeke did well, making it almost twenty years until the Devil reared his ugly head.

GROWING TIMBER

Fishing. The Reverend Blizzard's stories called Timber back to his childhood, fishing on the Louisiana bayous all those years ago when Daddy had taken him out in his old motorboat, cruising along the winding waterways of the swamp.

"My daddy was a man who liked to fish," Timber said, filling in the silent gap after the preacher, drained from his long monologue, paused in the telling of his life story. Timber could see the preacher's fishing pond on an early morning, dew on the grass and mist rising off the water in the thick air, the sweet smell of honeysuckle in the summertime.

"I thought you said your daddy was a radio man?" Zeke woke from his daze, shifting in his seat. The bus motored deeper into the growing mountains of South Central Utah, snow-capped peaks idling in the distance.

"That was his profession," Timber said. "He owned the station. I grew up in radio. My earliest memories are of my daddy on the air, me playing in the lobby. Sometimes I'd even sit on his lap while he played records or made announcements. I learned early that when the red light is on, don't breathe a word. You had to be quiet when that red light flicked on."

Timber looked to the floor where Zeke had set the bottle.

"Hand me that bottle there, Reverend."

He uncapped it and took two big sips. He held the bottle, about half full now, and began to explain to Zeke how he had listened to the radio even before he could walk or talk. Told him he didn't get the nickname Timber until he was a grown man on the radio in Houston. His parents named him Thomas Luke Goodman Jr. but as a child, everyone called him Tommy, and family and close friends called him Tom-Tom. His daddy, Tom Sr., anchored the afternoon and evening air time. The only other news outlet in town was a weekly newspaper.

"At church, people would point, whispering, 'That's the radio man's son, Tom Goodman's boy.'"

He could still hear Daddy's deep, smooth speech, a voice as familiar to locals as the sticky humidity in the Louisiana lowland on the north bank of the Mississippi River, wide and winding before it ended, spilling dirty water into the Gulf of Mexico. New Orleans was only fifty miles away but a good two hours over the pothole-filled roads, roads breaking up and sinking into the sandy soil. He told Zeke most men around Whitcomb worked in one of the chemical plants or refineries between Baton Rouge and New Orleans. Going to the Big Easy was a trip the blue-collar families made only once or twice a year. Baton Rouge was closer, but there wasn't much reason to go there except for LSU football games. Most people in Whitcomb just stayed put.

"Daddy would take me down to the station with him all the time. I remember him sitting in the booth in front of the microphone, wearing a coat and tie and headphones, reading from those old dusty yellow sheets of paper." He told Zeke he could never forget that radio station's small lobby, the UPI printer clattering away, printing out stories onto one long roll that spooled out onto the floor.

Timber spoke, not looking at the preacher, but staring straight ahead at the back of the seat in front of him. Daddy was a handsome man, he recalled, when he wasn't carrying extra weight. About six feet three with light brown hair, he fluctuated from fat to medium. His eyebrows were brown, slightly darker than his hair. His forehead jutted out a little, the rural genes of many Mississippi country people, but he had a thin nose and round, smooth lips. He kept his hair and sideburns neat. When he turned forty, he grew a sandy brown mustache that had the effect of making him look tough and younger. Timber had the same complexion and hair color, although sloppier and starting to gray.

"My daddy always had the radio on, tuned to his station—in the car, at home, wherever. From morning to night. This deejay named Booger was on every morning. We ate breakfast listening to him every day."

Timber told the preacher he never knew Booger's real name, didn't know if anyone in town did. "For all I knew, Booger *was* his real name."

A Mississippi native like Timber's parents, Booger was in his early fifties when Timber was a baby. He was almost completely bald and wore thick glasses, a style that made him look about seventy. His voice was raspy and his country way of speaking made him sound older than he was. On the radio he went into a rhythmic rant, high-pitched, but endearing.

Timber explained how Booger would start out every morning screeching

"*Good morning, Whitcomb,*" before and after every song and newscast. "Are y'all having a good day? Okay? *Oh—kay?*" He dragged out the second *okay* to such a high pitch that even the laziest dogs within earshot would stiffen their floppy ears and dart their eyes in the direction of the Emerson sitting prominently in the living room. This was the early fifties when the radio was a centerpiece to be displayed, Timber said, before TV came along and diminished the standing of small-town radio men.

"I'm telling you, Zeke, Booger was a great salesman. No advertisers anywhere got as much for their dollar as those who bought time on Booger Johnson's time slot, from six to noon each day. He sang their praises to high heaven, mixing in the advertisements before and after every song. Even during the newscasts."

Timber could hear Booger's voice, that voice he had heard when he was still a baby in his crib.

"He sounded something like this," Timber said, and closed his eyes and concentrated, raising his voice high. "'I was down there at the Winn-Dixie the other day and don't you know that I wasn't *even* hungry? But they had these pork chops just a-sittin' out *there?* And I bought me four—only *forty-nine cents* a pound—can you *believe* that? And I fried them things *up?* With some *okra?* And some *taters?*'"

Timber laughed, the preacher did too.

"Yeah," Timber continued, returning to his deep drawl. "Booger made all of Whitcomb hungry when he got to talking about the specials at the grocery. The Winn-Dixie would have paid any amount of money for his ads."

Timber had tried to explain Booger's voice to big city people before—the insanely high pitch, the rising sentences, each statement phrased like a question—but they never got it. They couldn't understand how a man with such a voice could be on the radio, much less a local icon adored by listeners and advertisers alike.

And big city folks also refused to believe that Booger doubled as a Pentecostal pastor on Sunday, preaching to his own congregation in a backwater church in the swamp before driving into town to the radio station that afternoon to give the very same sermon over the air, the very same one he'd preached in church that morning, panting and screaming and gasping, stamping his feet, slapping his hands on his thighs and the desktop, not caring how close he was to the microphone, his audio rising and dropping in great volume throughout the broadcast but always finishing with a frenzied climax like he was finishing a marathon and had only enough breath left to give the news: "Christ has *risen*—He *died* for your sins," before collapsing, exhausted by this sinful, material-minded world.

Zeke shifted excitedly in his seat. He reached for the bottle, held it up as though making a toast.

"That's my kinda man—a hard-workin' preacher. The salt of the earth." He took a big drink, his Adam's apple bobbing in his throat.

"Yeah. Booger was something else," Timber said. "There was one other deejay: Hyatt. Hyatt Delacroix. The Cajun voice of WKAL-AM 1450. Remember, this was Louisiana."

Hyatt had been on the air in Whitcomb since 1930. He was in his early sixties when Timber was born but he sounded like he could be one hundred years old. His soft rhythmic French-Cajun accent contrasted with Daddy's big-city professional radio voice and Booger Johnson's ecstatic squeal.

"Hyatt never sounded excited about anything," Timber said. "He always sounded like he was about to fall asleep on the air. I fell asleep listening to him every night. Just thinking of him now makes me sleepy. But those old Cajuns around there'd listened to him all their lives. They loved him."

Hyatt played traditional Cajun music, heavy on the accordion and fiddles. Timber's daddy well knew the value of appealing to the old Cajuns, many long-time customers of the city's modest businesses. Nobody would complain about two Baptist Mississippi boys on the radio—Daddy and Booger—as long as Hyatt was around with his Cajun tongue.

"And Hyatt liked to fish," Timber said, "and drink beer with my daddy."

Timber paused, before continuing.

"Fishing was how I hurt my foot. On one of those trips with Daddy and Hyatt."

Zeke eyed Timber, examining him as though he'd learned he had a contagious disease.

"You hurt your foot? You look all right to me. You ain't a cripple, are you?"

"No, but I've got a slight limp. I don't need a cane or a wheelchair or anything like that, but it hurts like hell sometimes. I've told a lot of women over the years it was a football injury…but it was really fishing."

The preacher's inquisitive eyes with the big pupils asked for the story. Timber was glad to have someone to talk to, to share a drink with. He was getting a buzz, loosening up. And it was refreshing to tell the truth about his foot, abandoning the lie he'd been repeating for close to thirty years, a tale he'd told so many times he almost took it to be true. He would never see this crazy preacher again. He could tell him the truth, practically anonymously and without repercussion.

"It was a long time ago," Timber said. "I was only six years old. Daddy had this old motorboat he kept covered up in Hyatt's yard, down on the bayou where they fished. Catfish and bream mainly, but bass sometimes too.

"The boat was old, aluminum. The engine on that thing was small, but it was ornery and loud. It was a bitch to get started up. Daddy would pull and pull on that thing to get it cranked. He always looked proud of himself when it first got started, that engine screaming."

Timber drifted back into memory and the story poured from him, the truth as best he could recall. He opened a vault that had been closed for many years, the images rushing forth like bats flying out of a cave at dusk, darting through a dying sky. He condensed the desires and failures of his past to meager words, rich and heavy in his crisp baritone...

Grand cypress trees laced with Spanish moss hung over the water early that morning, the sun just beginning to come up when Daddy pulled the plastic tarp off the boat. Hyatt lived back in the swamp in an old one-story clapboard house, a far-flung community of Cajuns that preferred life tucked back in the woods, several miles away from town, connected to the world through a maze of crushed shell roads.

Daddy and Hyatt pulled the boat across the wet grass to the bayou, a few feet deep, that led to the larger spillways and canals, a labyrinth of water that flowed to the muddy Mississippi. They weren't going that far, just a mile or so to where the channel cats were known to bite.

Timber walked slowly behind them, the boat sweeping a path through the dew. They slid the boat down in the water, back first, the motor adjusted at an angle so it wouldn't scrape against the ground. Hyatt held the front and Daddy stepped into the back of the small boat, shifting the engine so the propellers dropped into the water.

"Come here, Tom-Tom." He held out his hand. Timber wore a jumpsuit and cowboy boots, the same fishing outfit he always wore. Mama wouldn't let him leave the house to go fishing any other way.

"You don't know what might get your little feet," she had said, putting the boots on him that morning. But once out in the boat Daddy usually let him take them off, especially when it got hot.

Timber took Daddy's hand and stepped into the boat and sat on the middle seat. Hyatt then handed Daddy the rods and reels, a container of bait and a cooler with sandwiches and beer—always beer.

Before Daddy and Hyatt could crack open the first beers, Daddy had to get the old boat started. He sat in the back and pulled on the worn rip cord, yanking for all he was worth.

It often took some time, as many as fifteen minutes of pulling. He would yank it hard, take a break, catch his breath and then yank again. The motor would spin, sputter a little and then fall silent.

"Dat was close dere, Big Tom," Hyatt would say, and chuckle. The old man got a kick out of watching Daddy struggle with the motor. He'd tease him good-naturedly, winking at Timber.

After a long struggle the motor always sputtered to life, and they were off. Daddy smiled big, holding the engine's rudder, gently guiding the old Evinrude outboard, his eyes bright in the morning sun. They were cruising, enjoying the soft breeze of muggy swamp air manufactured by the boat. He reached out and tousled Timber's hair, light brown, almost blonde at that age.

Daddy grinned at Hyatt. The old man nodded, reaching for the cooler. He pulled out two cans of Jax beer and opened both, handing one to Daddy. The red, gold and white cans were moist and shiny with drops of condensation reflecting the sun. Hyatt held his can up and Daddy raised his too, as Hyatt shouted, "Salut." They both took a swig.

The ride was always Timber's favorite part of the outing, cruising along the surface of the murky water, morning fog hanging in the air before the intense heat of the day settled over the swamp. Daddy always looked happy sipping beer and guiding his old boat. He wore a denim shirt and jeans, one of the only times Timber saw him without a tie.

It was a ten-minute ride to the spot where they cut the engine and dropped the small anchor. Daddy helped him bait a line with a stinky chicken gizzard.

"Daddy. What does *salut* mean?"

"Ha ha, boy," Hyatt said. Timber turned toward the front of the boat where the old man sat, smoking a cigarette. "Salut is French, a wish for health and good luck. Salut always to you, my son." Hyatt raised his beer and took a sip. Smoke drifted straight up from his cigarette on the windless morning.

Daddy reached into the cooler and got another beer, popped it open. He pulled Timber into his arms and placed the can into his hand, his little fingers barely big enough to hold it. He guided Timber's arm up in a gesture like he and Hyatt always made with their beers.

"Say it, son—*Salut!*"

"Salut," Timber said. He smiled, proud of the accomplishment, holding the can up in front of him.

"There you go, boy," he said. "Now take you a sip."

Timber knew, even at that age, that it wasn't right. After fishing trips, Daddy always said, "don't tell your mama Hyatt and I were drinking beer, all right son?" Timber held the can guiltily, thinking of Mama. There was never any beer in their house. He took a sip, his little fingers gripping the can tight. The beer was bitter in his mouth. He scrunched up his face, forcing himself to swallow instead of spitting it out.

Hyatt laughed, a slow steady chuckle. "That's the little Baptist boy I know. Now, come on, Tom, let's catch some fish."

Daddy and Hyatt baited their hooks and cast out their lines. Daddy guided his cast, the line zipping through the air before the slick black chicken liver plopped into the water. They sat smoking one cigarette after another, drinking beer. When a can was empty, Daddy or Hyatt would hold it casually over the side, filling it slowly until it sank. Timber watched the cans make the unceremonious plunge to the bottom, the Jax beer logo fading from view in the mud-colored water.

After awhile, Daddy handed him an empty. "You can sink this one, son." Timber pulled his cowboy boots off. The hard flat soles and plastic heels slid against the aluminum boat, but his bare feet gave him traction just fine. Daddy never cared if he was barefoot, only Mama. Her rule was that if you left the house you kept on your shoes. Mama and all her rules.

Timber leaned over the edge and held the beer can in the water, careful not to fall, letting water flow into the empty can, a *glub-glub* sound. When it was heavy enough he let it go, watching it plunge from sight.

Hyatt and Daddy continued to smoke and drink but caught no fish. The silence held on for long spells, broken by the pop of a fresh beer or of one of them reeling in their line to check their bait. The only steady sound was the cawing of crows and the occasional roar of a motorboat far off in the distance.

"When they going to start biting?" Daddy asked.

"Sooner or later," Hyatt answered, spitting in the water for punctuation.

Neither Hyatt nor Daddy seemed to mind that they didn't catch any fish. Two more cans were emptied and sunk in the water.

"Well, Tom," Hyatt said, "'bout time to head on back. We'll get these old cats next time."

"Yeah," Daddy said. "Don't want to take 'em all today. We'll be back."

They reeled in their lines and set the poles in the boat. Daddy pulled up the anchor, wound the rope around it and set it by his seat. He grabbed the starter cord in his right hand and balanced himself with his left hand on the top of the engine.

Timber sat in the middle seat, watching Daddy's arm, flexed to crank the old engine. He yanked the starter cord. Nothing. He yanked it again. A small sputter and then silence. Again. Nothing. He tried about ten times, getting only a sputter here or there. The movement of the propellers caused the water to rush a little before falling still.

Daddy paused to catch his breath. Timber had sunk the last beer can near the back-left side of the boat. He stood, stepping onto Daddy's seat, straining to see the can. Daddy's back was turned so that he faced the motor and could not see Timber standing behind him. Daddy reached quickly, yanking the starter cord. The engine roared to life. Standing barefoot on the seat, Timber tottered, trying to catch himself as the noisy boat lunged forward. He lost his footing and fell over the side, splashing hard onto the water's surface.

He flailed his arms, trying to swim, but the boat darted left, toward him. The side of the aluminum hull banged against his head, forcing him under. The boat raced over him and the propeller slashed his right ankle and foot. He saw red blood swirling in the water before he gulped a mouthful of the warm bayou.

"That's about all I remember," Timber told Zeke, conscious of the lingering ache in his foot as he said it, forty-three years later.

"The next thing I know is I woke up in the hospital, my mama praying over me, tears in her eyes. Daddy was in the room too, on the other side of the bed, but not as close. My leg was strapped down with my foot slightly elevated. From the shin down, it was wrapped in a huge bandage, the size of a cast. A bag of blood hung beside me, flowing into my arm. I had a knot on my head.

"I remember Mama talking to me. She said, 'You are going to be all right, little Tom-Tom.' She kissed my forehead. 'You will be all right. The Lord was with you. You are a lucky little boy. Jesus loves you.'"

The hospital room was small, permeated by the sterile smell of tile scrubbed with ammonia and starchy white sheets. Nurses in bleached uniforms wearing hats made of thick folded cloth came in and out, checking his temperature, refilling his I.V. bag, bringing him food and ice water.

Mama was always there. She babied him, held his hand, read to him, cut up his food for him. She ran out and got cookies for him after lunch. She prayed over every meal, holding his hand tight, her eyes clenched shut as she thanked the Lord "for saving my little boy's foot. Thank you Jesus, thank you Lord, for all you've done for us."

At night she prayed with him before she pulled the room's one armchair to the end of his bed and sat there, watching him sleep. Whenever he woke, she was there. She didn't take her eyes off him.

He slept in fits and starts. He would doze during the day, groggy from the pain-killers they gave him. He lay awake much of the night, a street light shining through the white metal shade, the fragmented light cut neatly into lines on the wall.

The pain in his foot came and went, hurting more and then sometimes less, but always hurting. Doctors stopped in daily to examine him and mark down notes on a chart hung at the end of his bed. He was strapped to the mattress like a dog that might try to run away.

Daddy visited every morning after breakfast. He didn't come by at night, Mama explaining that he had to work and needed a good night's sleep. The nurses let Timber play a small transistor radio in the afternoons. Hearing Daddy's voice on the air comforted him. He missed going down to the station with him. Timber listened, the volume low, until the late afternoon when Daddy passed the broadcast on to Hyatt. Mama didn't care for Cajun music and turned it off promptly at five o'clock.

Mama left the hospital for the first time on Sunday morning when she went to church. Daddy stayed with him, pulling the maroon upholstered armchair by the side of the bed and leaning back against the wall, the two front feet slightly raised off the tile floor.

"Son, how's the foot today?" He didn't give Timber time to answer. "They say you might be able to go home this week."

"It hurts, Daddy."

"I know it does, son. But you're tough. You'll be all right soon."

Timber grimaced. He missed Mama's babying.

Daddy leaned forward in the chair. He took a sterner tone.

"What did you tell your mama about the accident?"

Timber swallowed. Mama had asked him lots of questions, but he did not tell her about the beer. She had asked specifically if Daddy and Hyatt had been drinking. He lied, told her no. He had never lied to Mama before.

"I just…told her I stood up. That I fell when the boat started."

"Did she ask about drinking beer?"

Timber nodded.

"What did you tell her? You didn't tell her we had beer, did you?"

A queasy feeling came over him. "No, Daddy." He shook his head slowly. "No."

"That's a good boy, son. You're a good boy."

Daddy reached out to pat him on the leg, but then thought better of it and stood and tousled his hair like he'd done when the boat was motoring along. Timber whiffed the aftershave on him, cutting through the smell of bandages and ammonia.

A long silence passed between them. The radio was turned off. Daddy hated to listen to the preachers' sermons that filled the airwaves on Sunday. It was the only day of the week he didn't listen to his station.

"Daddy, when will I get to go home?"

"Soon, I think, son, soon." Daddy stood over him. "I know no man wants to spend the night in a hospital. And you know another thing no man wants to do?"

His tone was serious again. He sat back down in the chair. Timber shook his head.

"No man ever, *ever* wants to stand up in a boat...You hear me, son?"

Timber nodded, tears welling up in his eyes. He had known better than to stand up, especially while Daddy was cranking the engine. Daddy had taught him better than that.

He went home the following week. Every morning when he was first home from the hospital he waited in bed until Mama came to help him get into the wheelchair.

"How's your foot, darlin'?"

"It hurts, Mama. It hurts."

"Oh, my poor darling." She kissed him on the forehead.

Changing the bandage was torture. It was swollen twice as big as normal— crusty, black, a thousand stitches. He almost threw up the first time he saw it. Mama held his hand, saying sweet things to him.

After a few weeks, she began asking, "Do you want to try walking on it today? The doctors said you should try to walk on it pretty soon."

He concentrated on the pain. If the propellers had hit him at a different angle, doctors said it could have chopped his foot clean off. There was no way he was ready to walk on it.

"I can't, Mama. It hurts too much." She lifted him up and put him in the chair. He feigned lifelessness. "You little rag doll."

Daddy was home the Sunday after Timber's stitches had been taken out, before Mama left for church. He had overheard Timber's conversation with Mama about walking again. He came into the room, his eyes playful and feisty.

"C'mon now, son. It's never going to feel good, 'specially that first time you walk on it. You've been home several weeks. The doctors said you should walk on it as soon as you can. Let's give it a try."

Daddy came toward him and pulled down the sheet. He reached for Timber, lifting him by the armpits.

"*Tom,*" Mama said. "*Don't* hurt him."

"I'm not going to hurt him, Mabel," he said, holding Timber up, his feet dangling. "He needs to try this foot out. Make it stronger. You heard the doctors."

Daddy lowered him down to where his feet touched the floor.

"All right now, son. Try it, easy like."

"Careful, Tom-Tom," Mama said, her eyes wide.

He bent his knee and lifted the injured foot up, standing on one leg, but he was weak and had to put the bad foot down for balance. The pain shot through him and he fell toward the bed, screaming, reaching out to catch himself.

"Come on now, son." Daddy lifted him under the armpits again. "Don't give up that easy. I'll help hold you up. *Don't* be a *crybaby.*"

"*Tom.*"

"Hush, Mabel."

Daddy moved him along the floor slowly. He tested out the foot, touching down. It was painful, a sharp sensation, not the dull ache he was used to when he was in the wheelchair or the bed. He cried out, but Daddy kept moving him.

"That's good, son. Keep using it. You gotta use it to make it stronger. I know it doesn't feel good. But you want to walk again, don't you? You won't ever get anywhere being a crybaby."

Daddy did the same thing every morning that week. After a few days, Timber was walking without assistance, limping heavily on a small wooden crutch, an adult one that Daddy had sawed down to size for him.

The bus engine hummed low in the background. Timber told Zeke he never saw much of his daddy while he was recovering. Daddy would have breakfast with them, listening to Booger Johnson's morning show, and then he was off. Timber usually didn't see him the rest of the day.

"Daddy always worked late at the radio station or went to meetings: the Kiwanis Club, the Shriners, the county emergency management agency. He was into everything. I'd hear him come in after I went to bed, his car pull into the driveway, the back door slam shut, his footsteps in the hallway.

"I guess I missed seeing him, but I was happy, too, when it was just me and Mama."

Zeke had put the bottle of bourbon under the seat. Timber sighed, shook his head, a wistful smile on his face.

"Oh, *my mama*. When she was young, in her wedding pictures, she had straight, dark hair and thin shoulders. But in all my memories of her she looked much older, a lot heavier. She wore flowery dresses that in the summer had sleeves short enough to show her flabby arms. Her hair was graying. She looked a lot older than Daddy did, I guess."

He paused, then perked up a little.

"I'm telling you, she made sure I ate well. She'd fix chicken salad sandwiches, trimming the crust off toasted white bread. I loved her potato salad. She fished pickles out of a big jar for me. That first Sunday afternoon I was home from the hospital she boiled a huge pot of crawfish and sat next to me, shucking them, pulling out the slivers of meat and arranging them on my plate. She kept asking me 'Is that enough, baby?' I ate two helpings before she even began to eat."

Timber told Zeke he began reading children's books his mama bought for him while he was recuperating. His favorites were stories of cowboys and Indians. He read and then reread the books, lying in his bed, after the radio went off the air at nine, sometimes by flashlight when Mama insisted he turn off his lamp. "It's a habit I still have today." He gestured with the Louis L'Amour paperback.

"But my favorite thing, that summer, was listening to baseball games on the radio with Mama. This was before the Braves moved to Atlanta and the Texas teams came along. The Cardinals were our team."

Timber recalled the relaxing patter of the play-by-play on the radio. Mama would fix vanilla ice cream with chocolate syrup and they would sit on the porch, listening. When it was gone, he would stretch out on the couch in the living room while she tickled his feet. They followed each game to the end.

"But baseball or reading never took precedence over religion in my house. Mama listened to the white gospel station out of Baton Rouge, whenever baseball wasn't on the air. Church was her thing. Lots of nights she'd rub my back and hum, lulling me to sleep with hymns."

Timber began to sing, softly, almost a whisper, so as not to disturb others on the bus. He would show this Baptist preacher he knew a thing or two about religion.

What…a friend we have in Jee—sus,
All…our sins and griefs to—bear.
What…a privilege to care—ree,
Ev…'rything to God in pray—er.

"That's a good one, boy," Zeke said, nodding. "A good one. One of my favorite hymns."

After Timber turned seven and was walking more comfortably with the crutch, Daddy began picking him up in the afternoon and taking him to the radio station. He had missed going down there, basking in the red on-air light while Daddy was in the booth. He could read well for his age, so well that Daddy had him gather up the UPI stories from the printer and trim the roll into orderly sections with a pair of scissors. He followed stories about Soviets, Eisenhower and Nixon and closer to home, Governor Earl Long's shenanigans, civil rights marches in Alabama, Elvis Presley in the Army—all of it poured down the lines into the printer and was automatically typed out by the machine in the radio station's lobby. It soon became Timber's job in the evening to make sure the roll of paper was a good two inches thick before they left so the news stories could print out overnight.

He had not been out to play with the neighborhood kids since his accident. He was always in the radio station while they were playing baseball, pretending to have wars in the wooded wilds around the town, or going fishing and catching frogs and snakes in the ditches. He couldn't do any of that with his bad foot. But radio was his refuge and after awhile he didn't think much about what the other boys were doing. He was in the radio business, born into it. It seemed inherently normal to him that news stories came down from the sky or by phone lines to be read out onto the radio. The act of taking this news and reading over the air to the local residents was a divine rite, a religious, important act. Daddy was the informer of the people. News, weather, sports, the farm report—it was natural, in his blood.

Timber nodded, looking right at Zeke. "I was a radio man when I was just a boy."

When he was walking again without the crutch, Mama had him back in church. The only time Timber's mama made him do anything that he didn't want to do was on Sunday. *Every* Sunday. He and Mama never missed Sunday school, the morning service that followed, and then the evening service. Although the majority of local residents, most with French names such as Gautreaux and Devereux, were Catholic, Timber's mama was a devout Baptist. She believed in baptism and the literal word of the Bible and being born again and turning your life over to Christ. No drinking, no smoking and no dancing, a creed that ran contrary to the Cajun lifestyle. It occurred to Timber at a very young age how odd that so few of the Louisianans he knew were going to heaven; most, especially the Catholics, were bound for hell under the criteria the Baptist preacher spelled out every week.

Daddy went to church only on Easter and Christmas. He didn't seem to worship anything at all other than the mystery of the ionosphere.

Timber was uncomfortable on that first morning back in Sunday school, fending off other children's curiosity of his bandaged foot. He limped into the room and took a seat in the back. But he couldn't go unnoticed as he had hoped. The children gathered around him.

"I heard they had to rescue your foot from a big ole gator and sew that thing back on," Dickie Simmons said, examining the bandaged foot. "I heard they shot that thing right between the eyes."

"No, that ain't true," his friend Billy Puckett said. "The motorboat chopped it off and they found it on the riverbank. Hyatt Delacroix sewed it back on with fishing line."

Timber was big for a seven-year-old. Before the accident he might have wrestled Dickie or Billy to the ground for making fun of him. All he could do now was to ignore them.

"Class! Take your seats," Miss Foster shouted. "Open your books. Leave poor little Tommy alone. No such thing happened to him."

The children slunk back to their desks but often peeked back to look at Timber during the lesson. After the class ended with Miss Foster praying and thanking Jesus for bringing Timber back to Sunday school, the children bolted out, running to the playground where they played in the swings before the church service began.

"See ya, *gimpy*-leg," Dickie yelled back to Timber, sparking peals of laughter.

Gimpy-leg. The name would stay with him through all of the second grade. He kept to himself all that year, quietly looking forward to afternoons at the radio station with Daddy and evenings and weekends with Mama.

The following spring he was baptized, earlier than most children went forward into salvation. He hobbled down the aisle one Sunday at Mama's urging, but he too was moved that day, a few weeks before Easter, when he answered the Lord's call, the preacher's pleas for lost souls to come down and dedicate themselves to Jesus. The old preacher, a feisty screamer from East Texas, pulled Timber's face close and welcomed him breathily into the "club of salvation and everlasting life." His breath smelled of coffee and sweat and rot, his light blue suit of mothballs.

A month later, after Easter, following a sermon, the congregation gathered in the parking lot around a large metal tub full of water, three feet deep and six feet long, roughly the shape of a huge coffin. The tub had a short stepladder leading up to it. Timber wore a robe over a T-shirt and underpants, the first of three people waiting to be baptized—totally immersed—into the love of Jesus Christ, the Father and the Holy Spirit. Behind him was Emily Jacks, a plump girl about twelve who was a good head taller than he was. She pushed at him and told him not to take too long, that she wanted to get it over with because her mother was fixing a big meal with her favorite dessert, strawberry shortcake.

Behind Emily, at the end of the line, was a sullen, thin man with bags under his eyes and a crew cut that appeared he had done it himself. Rumors around the church were that Pastor Roy, the preacher, had ministered to the man at Angola, the Louisiana state prison, and brought him to Whitcomb to rehabilitate him after his release. No one knew what he had done. Pastor Roy would only say that the crime was in the past, that he was a new man, and that he was being reborn into the world at the Whitcomb Baptist Church. Everyone figured it was something terrible, otherwise the pastor would have told them. Almost all of the church members were in attendance that morning, eager to see the ex-convict, known only as Rusty, takes the plunge. It wasn't often an ex-inmate got baptized.

It was a hot day and they all stood in the treeless gravel parking lot, sweating, squinting in the sun. Pastor Roy didn't hurry, though, but he held his Bible in his hand and read about the importance of baptism, about John the Baptist, about why Christians weren't truly Christians unless they took the all-consuming dip in the holy water of Jesus.

"I wish he'd hurry up," Emily Jacks said to Timber. "I don't see why he couldn't have said all this back *inside* the church. This sun's burning me up."

Timber gazed at the big tub of holy water. He didn't know what made it *holy*, having seen the church janitor filling it with a hose that morning as Mama parked the car.

Pastor Roy handed his Bible to a parishioner after another ten minutes of praising the Lord and explaining the baptism. He gestured to Timber to come forward. Timber didn't move, stricken with panic. The preacher said, "*Come on,* son—the Lord is waiting." Emily Jacks pushed him, a good hard shove, and he stumbled forward, limping with tentative steps.

He made his way up the three-step ladder, the preacher guiding him, and then stepped down into the water that came up to his chest. The water was chilly, the bottom of the tank ice cold, a sharp contrast to the heat. Pastor Roy took him firmly by the shoulders, a bright look in his eye, and shouted, "By the powers vested in me, I anoint you in the water of the Father, Son and the Holy Spirit," and dunked him. The force took Timber by surprise. He was daydreaming about the way the cold tank felt on his bare feet, and although he had been instructed to hold his breath, to pinch his nose if needed, he was open-mouthed and inhaling when Pastor Roy plunged him backward and held him down. He sucked in a nose and mouthful of water, choking as soon as he went under. He flailed his arms and kicked his feet but Pastor Roy gripped him stronger, holding him another ten seconds to make sure the baptism took. When Pastor Roy loosened his grip and pulled Timber back upright, he splashed the water madly. Pastor Roy put his arm firmly around his waist and lifted him over the back wall of the tank, dropping him in a heap on the loose gravel. Timber gasped and choked until he began to cough, spewing out water, and then vomited, shooting out chunks of three sausage biscuits he had eaten for breakfast. Mama rushed forward from the crowd to where he lay crumpled in the gravel and hugged him, running her fingers through his hair.

"My baby, oh my baby," she cried, oblivious to his brush with death. "You've been baptized! You've been baptized! Your soul will live in peace forever."

Emily Jacks sneered down at Timber as she ascended the ladder. "Excuse me, can you move? It's my turn." She turned to the preacher. "Don't worry, Pastor Roy, I'll hold my nose."

Timber, propped up by Mama, began to recapture his breath. Mama had her arms tight around him, kissing his forehead. His heart beat slowed down and his vision came back into focus as his tears stopped. He swallowed, the sour taste of vomit in his mouth, and looked under the tank to the other side of the parking lot. He could see the people gathered in a half circle, watching Emily Jacks take the plunge. They had forgotten him and were anxiously awaiting the ex-convict's baptism. He felt anything but saved. Mama helped him up and he limped off to the car, holding her hand tightly.

About a year later, when he was nine, came a Sunday Timber never forgot. Mama left the house that morning planning to fry up a chicken with biscuits and gravy and fresh-picked okra until a Sunday school teacher brought a big mess of fresh catfish. Mama took a bag full of the fish. She preferred to freeze the chicken and clean and cook the catfish—she said there was nothing better than fresh catfish right out of the water—but she had promised Tom Sr. fried chicken for lunch. He didn't like changes in the plan. She decided to stop by the radio station on her way home, a rare whim for her.

WKAL-AM was a little building, not much bigger than a Quonset hut, built of cinder blocks. It sat on a dusty lot in the industrial south part of town, between a trucking company and a lumberyard. The station's antenna, the highest structure in Whitcomb, towered above the grimy neighborhood. Mama was nervous driving her old black Dodge, gripping the wheel with both hands. She didn't like to drive and she particularly hated streets where the big trucks made up most of the traffic. Her eyes widened as a chemical tanker rumbled past them on a narrow avenue.

Timber turned the radio on, but she turned it back off.

"It makes me nervous to drive with the radio on, hon," she said, never taking her eyes off the road. She drove on, her mouth pursed tight, her eyes jumpy.

"Mama, you missed the turn," Timber said. He had been there so many times with Daddy that he knew the landmarks of the dusty back streets by heart: the Chicken Fried Chicken sign, a Jesus Saves bumper sticker on a creosote-covered post, the big metal gate to the trucking company lot right before the radio station. She stopped suddenly in the street, backing slowly into a gravel driveway, overcautiously. She headed back the other way and almost missed the turn again. Timber couldn't fathom that Mama didn't know the route to the radio station where Daddy spent most of his waking hours.

He turned the radio back on, much lower this time. Mama glanced disapprovingly but did not turn it off. The Sunday radio sermons began conservatively in the morning with Catholic masses, both in English and French, and then gradually worked up to the screamers like Booger Johnson later in the afternoon. A sermon by a Methodist preacher was droning on, the preacher rather reserved compared to the Pentecostals that would come later that day.

At the station Timber was surprised to see Daddy's Ford and the Oldsmobile of the new advertising woman, Delores Arceneaux, parked sideways in the small driveway. Mama parked in the street.

She got out and told him to wait in the car, that she'd be just a minute, but he ignored her and walked along behind. He knew she wouldn't scold him—she almost seemed relieved that he was with her. Her hands were shaking. She clutched her small black purse with both hands, as though she needed something to hold for support.

She opened the door, Timber at her hip, on her left side. He could see through the lobby and into the small office, the door half open. He got a good look at Delores Arceneaux, on her back on the desk, the skirt of her flowery dress pulled up to her waist and the top buttons loosened to reveal her huge bosoms, one of which Daddy was licking, his tongue extended. Her long black hair was flowing back, hanging down the side of the desk. Her eyes were closed and she was moaning on long exhalations following deep breaths. Daddy, shirt unbuttoned and pants in a bunch at his feet, was between her legs, straining, his face a look of rapture, until he turned his head toward the open door. His cheeks turned crimson, a vein in his forehead bulged, his eyes furious. He stormed up and slammed the door to his office.

After a few seconds of rustling and strained whispers, he came out, shut the door behind him, and yelled at Mama, still standing in the doorway.

"I thought I told you never to come down here…while *I'm working.*" His face was beet red. "I've got…*business* here." He glared at Mama but did not look down at Timber.

Her chin quivered. She began to speak but couldn't get the words out. Timber was frozen at her side. Daddy held his hand up and pointed to the car.

"Go…*now*. Get *out of here*, Mabel."

Mama tightened the grip on Timber's arm and led him to the car. Her eyes were angry and her chin trembled. He could not process what he had seen, could not make sense of it. They rode home in silence, the radio off. The image of Daddy with Delores flashed through his mind, but he didn't understand. He watched the street signs and houses going by, wondering about Daddy, his stomach tightening into a knot.

Mama marched into the kitchen and cut the heads off the catfish and gutted them, frying up the white filets, her face tired and cheerless over the popping grease in the skillet. She froze the chicken for another day. Daddy didn't come home for lunch. Timber, nervous and wanting to cheer up Mama, talked about his Sunday school lesson and the upcoming Cardinals game. She laughed tentatively at his stories, half smiling at him, patting him on the head. "You are a sweet boy, Tom-Tom," was all she said. She was not herself. He skipped his usual second helping of catfish and took a restless nap while the game droned on the radio. He was unable to focus his attention on it. His mama had gone into the bedroom and shut the door.

Later they went to the Sunday night service as they always did. They did not utter a word about Daddy.

He and Mama ate catfish leftovers and ice cream for supper after church. Later she kissed him goodnight and tucked him under his sheets.

He was anxious, fidgeting in his single bed. He turned on his small transistor radio on low and listened to Daddy up until the final nine o'clock newscast.

"And that concludes today's broadcast on Fourteen *Fifty*, WKAL-AM, Whitcomb, Louisiana." His voice was smooth and strong, unlike the high-pitch twangs or Cajun mumbles of most local men. "Thank you for listening, and we hope you'll join us tomorrow morning at five for the Reverend Billy Graham's program, *The Hour of Decision*. Good night, Whitcomb."

The station aired "Dixie" and then "The Star-Spangled Banner," the customary conclusion to each day's broadcast before signing off, fading to static as signals from far away bled into the airspace, a word or a phrase randomly tossed in with the garble of noise. Timber turned the radio off and rolled over and tried to sleep, picturing Delores Arceneaux, sweat on her brow, the top of her dress open, her moans. He could hear Daddy's car pull up and the door slam shut, the front door opening. He heard Mama weeping but no words.

He lay awake much of the night, his mind racing. He clenched his fists tight, wondering who his daddy was, what his daddy did when he was not at home—which was most of the time. He tried to remember things that Daddy and Hyatt had talked about on those fishing trips when he was little, until he hurt his foot and Mama wouldn't let him go anymore. But he couldn't remember. He had been too young to understand. There was still so much that didn't make sense. He didn't fall asleep until very late, just before the dawn when a neighbor's dog began to bark.

Six months later he and Daddy sat talking while Mama cleared the dishes away from the table on Sunday afternoon. There had been no subsequent incidents. His parents were getting along well. Daddy was in a cheerful mood and had been home more often than usual. Timber asked to be excused but Daddy put his hand on his shoulder.

"Stay here a minute, son. Your mama and I have something to tell you."

He feared the worst. Timber had heard about a few families that had been through divorces, daddies that were long gone. At the radio station he'd read wire stories about Hollywood separations like Marilyn Monroe and Joe DiMaggio. He suspected that things happened between these couples like he had seen with

Mama and Daddy and Delores Arceneaux. (Delores had left the station shortly after he and Mama had seen her with Daddy.) He fidgeted in his seat.

"No, Tom-Tom, don't you fret. It's *good* news," Mama said, kissing him on top of the head. She sat down.

"Your mama is having a baby, Tommy. You are going to be a big brother."

Timber was shocked. He knew he was supposed to smile but a million thoughts ran through his head. Wasn't his mama too old to have babies? Besides, he liked being the only child, spoiled and not having to share Mama's love with another sibling.

"I hope it's a girl," Mama said. "Cause I already got the sweetest little boy in the world."

Five months later she was born. Mama named her Beverly Beatrice Goodman, drawing on the name of her grandmothers, old Mississippi women born before the turn of the century, relatives Timber had been told existed but whose faces he'd never seen. They would call her Bev. Mama, almost forty, handled the pregnancy well, the doctors told Daddy, but she looked terrible to Timber when he went into the room to see her and his new sister for the first time. The smile on her lips belied her haggard, pale face. She held the baby high on her chest and kissed her on the top of the head, over and over.

"Oh Bev! You are *so* sweet. My sweet, *sweet* little girl. Isn't she *sweet* Tom-Tom? Isn't your sister the sweetest little baby you've *ever* laid eyes on?" Her voice, despite its thrilled spirit, was tired and cracked. Timber nodded and forced a smile at his mama and his new sister. Mama didn't let Timber or Daddy hold the baby. She resisted the nurse who came in to take Bev when visiting hours were over, a tear running down her cheek when she finally relented at Daddy's urging.

Soon Timber would be spending much more time at the radio station while Mama raised the baby. She doted on Bev night and day. For the first six months that Bev was an infant, Mama refused to leave the house with her except to go to the store.

Timber enjoyed not going to church. It was the one time in his life that he could say he was closer to Daddy than Mama, those first few years Bev was a child.

Everyone, especially Mama, said his sister was the prettiest little girl anyone around had ever seen. Unlike Timber, who had brownish hazel eyes and straight brown hair, Bev took after an aunt on Daddy's side with big blue eyes and blonde curly locks, white as cotton.

Mama spoiled Bev, much more so than she had Timber when he was younger. *Bev* this. *Bev* that. It irritated him to no end to watch Mama fuss over her.

It was clear even as early as her second birthday that Bev had a distinctive, rebellious personality, one to push as far as she could get away with. She tried to turn every doorknob she got near, squeezing with her tiny, moist fingers, crying until Mama came along and opened it for her. Mama would let her into every room she wanted to visit, watching the scampering blonde child attentively, rushing to her whenever she began to cry, often for no reason at all.

Timber grew to where he couldn't stand to be around his sister, avoiding the assignment of watching her while Mama ran an errand. The child was either ecstatically happy or ferociously sad and angry, an alternating dervish of laughing, shouting and foot stomping or sobbing in the fetal position. She would never just sit quietly. She was great motivation for Timber to stay at the radio station as late as he could.

Daddy gave him more challenging assignments, teaching him how to monitor the levels on the sound board, how to check the antenna signal, how to cue up records and play them, how to best segue into one song from another, how to operate different kinds of microphones.

While his mother's favorite sport was baseball, Daddy, like most Louisiana men, was a football man to the core. Friday nights and Saturday afternoons in the fall were sacred. The mighty Whitcomb Panthers were a perennial power and past state high school champions, and his daddy and Hyatt had been broadcasting the games live on the air since 1947, never missing one. Down the road in Baton Rouge the LSU Tigers commanded the following of the entire state, fielding great teams in the late fifties and early sixties, going undefeated in 1958 and claiming a national championship with a win in the Sugar Bowl in New Orleans. Daddy attended all of the LSU home games, occasionally taking Timber to the huge stadium filled with thousands of screaming Louisianans all decked out in purple and gold. To Timber, there was nothing to compare to the frenzied moment when the LSU Tigers exploded onto the field in the bright white and purple jerseys with gold britches and helmets to the screams of thousands packed into the stadium, led by the best-looking cheerleaders he'd ever seen, jumping and dancing and smiling to beat all, waving pom-poms like their lives depended on it. It sounded like everyone in the state of Louisiana was cheering at once.

The fall that Bev was born, Daddy began taking Timber on the road for all the high school games. It was the biggest event in town every week for ten weeks of the year, even longer if it was a good team and they went deep into the playoffs, which they usually did. Timber took on Daddy's love of following football, knowing the names, numbers, heights and weights of the players, their game stats in detail.

He was eleven when he began keeping a notebook of games. He threw himself into those football weeks, reading all the newspaper articles and stats on the opposing team he could get his hands on, and then writing statistical reports that his daddy taught him to do, reports that Daddy and Hyatt Delacroix could use on the radio. He soon could quote the Whitcomb High record book from memory. Timber and Daddy would go by the practice field once or twice a week to watch the team scrimmage and later huddle around and shout cheers, riling themselves into a frenzy of head-butting and butt-slapping and furious yells. The camaraderie of the team was contagious and Timber got an adrenalin rush every time he was around them, sometimes listening in on the coach's riveting pep talks. After practice and games, he would follow his daddy onto the field and then to the locker room, holding the tape machine for Daddy while he did interviews with the sweaty players and coaches, all of whom spoke of football as though they had been fighting in a war.

Two years later, when he was thirteen, Timber was at the first game of the season, an away game at a small town near Lafayette, a long way from home and deep into the Cajun swamp. Most every player on the opposing team had a name ending in *eaux*, unlike Whitcomb that was only about half Cajun. The early September night was as hot and muggy as summer days—fall in Southern Louisiana didn't take hold until about November. Timber had set up the telephone that they used to transmit the game from the tiny press booth, a white box made of plywood, where Daddy and Hyatt Delacroix sat while broadcasting the game. He'd tested the microphone levels and called the radio station, speaking to Booger Johnson, who stayed on the air until game time.

"You coming in loud and clear, Tom-Tom."

Timber wished he could lose the childhood nickname. Daddy had started calling him "Tommy." At least that was a start. And Daddy was beginning to treat him more like a man, trusting him to do his job without worry or double-checking him. He hoped one day soon people would call him "Tom" too. He was getting taller, his voice was changing and he began to imagine himself an adult. He was a radio man, after all, and each radio man has a point in his life, a time when he gets his calling.

For Timber, it was September 5, 1965, in Breaux Bridge, Louisiana. Daddy and Hyatt had begun the hour-long pre-game show, chatting about last season, the surprise loss in the playoffs, a "devastating, *gut*-wrenching, *heartbreaking* loss." They talked of the yet unspoiled hopes and dreams of the new season, always anxious and exciting, especially before the first game when no one knows for sure how the team is going to do, how they will gel together. Timber had heard Daddy talk about great players that did not work together as a *team*—he pressed the fingers of both hands in a gesture for emphasis—but he'd seen other teams of players with less talent but more heart and determination that made for great success. He said the legendary state championship team of 1948 played together like a *well-oiled machine.* Whitcomb had since fielded players with as much skill, certainly they'd had bigger and stronger players than the '48 team, but none ever approached it in heart and *team*work. He meshed his fingers together every time he said this.

Daddy and Hyatt traded stories about the state championship year—both had been much younger then, only their second season together on the radio—and as always, recalled the team with great nostalgia and reverential tones. A game never went by that they didn't recall a play or situation from that 1948 season, seventeen years prior, as though summoning lost youth.

They were about halfway through the pre-game show when Timber's daddy slid his microphone in front of Timber. Hyatt was talking about the '48 team's defensive line. Daddy put his hand on Timber's shoulder and shifted his headphones from his ears. "I'm gonna let you on the air, all right?" he whispered. Timber nodded ecstatically, wide-eyed. He had felt he was ready for air time since earlier in the year when Daddy began letting him practice reading news reports and introducing records after the station signed off.

Hyatt Delacroix wrapped up yet another remembrance of the great '48. "And now, I'm going to turn it over to you, Tom, to introduce a special guest."

Daddy, his headphones back on, leaned in front of Timber and spoke into his microphone.

"Thank you, Hyatt. This guest is a young man who knows as much about this Whitcomb Panthers team as anybody. He'd be dangerous if he shared everything he knows with the other squad, but he wouldn't do that for any amount of money, cause he is as loyal as the day is long. *Tom*, what do you expect from the Panthers this year?"

Timber realized that every day of his first thirteen years was in preparation for this moment. His daddy had called him a *man*.

"Yes sir, thank you for having me on," he said, his voice strong and steady, a tone well beyond his youth. He was nervous, but tried not to sound like it. "This team has great talent, especially on the offensive side of the ball, but they have to make sure to avoid turnovers. Sometimes the defense is susceptible to a big play, but if they hang tight as a unit, they could be one of the best groups of Whitcomb Panthers ever to step on the field."

Timber could see Hyatt and Daddy smiling at one another, nodding their heads, affirming Timber's talent on the air. He continued, strong and smooth, a voice better than most men.

He broke into a big smile, watching the green football field as the teams in bright gold and blue and red and white uniforms and shiny helmets warmed up before the game, the high school bands along the track brassy and loud with their drum cores. The stadium lights were turned on but the sky was still fairly bright in the early evening, the summer days beginning to shorten, a few wispy clouds colored pink by the beginning of the sunset. Everyone seemed happy, excited to be there, and he could picture the radio audience at home in Whitcomb, listening to the game, nodding their heads at his remarks. None of them could see his weak foot. No one could call him gimpy-leg.

After that first night on air, Timber began to grow like a weed, shooting up from a five-foot-tall pudgy boy to a stocky young man of almost six feet by the time he was fifteen. He had two seasons of football broadcasts under his belt and was hoping for studio air time. Although he still limped noticeably, his ankle was much stronger. He looked more like Daddy every day.

He was at the radio station one Saturday night when Daddy signed off the air and surprised him with an invitation to go see Hyatt Delacroix's band. Hyatt played in the Old Swamp Boys, the Saturday night regulars at an old Cajun dance hall down on a bayou, a good thirty miles south of Whitcomb. The Cajun men and women all loved to dance. Baptists, especially the devout ones like Timber's mama, believed dancing was evil, a celebration of the Devil.

The dance hall was like nothing Timber had ever seen before, one of the places Mama said was cursed, the patrons bound for hell. Daddy parked in the crushed shell parking lot and a cloud of dirt flew up, dusting the cars and pickup trucks parked there. The old hall was a rickety wooden structure with an open end, a cement floor and long bar stretching all the way down the right side, covered by a tin roof. A potpourri of peanut shells, dirt and sawdust formed a film across the floor, gritty underneath Timber's feet. At the end of the room, Hyatt Delacroix and three other men who looked like Hyatt were setting up a drum set, bass, accordion and microphones. Timber saw two fiddle cases propped up against the wall.

Most in the hall were speaking French, particularly the many older folks. Behind the long bar, Timber saw glittering liquor bottles, mostly gin and rum and some bourbon, and three large coolers from which the two old men tending bar kept pulling bottles of Dixie or Pearl beer. To the right of the alcohol, at the end of the bar, was a woman in her sixties selling boiled crabs dusted in cayenne pepper. Daddy told him to have a seat at the end of one of the long picnic tables in the back of the hall while he bought a Dixie beer and two plates of crabs.

"Son, they don't have any cokes," Daddy told him when he sat down. "You can have a sip of my beer to wash these down with."

Daddy showed him how to crack the claws and break the shell to get to the white-hot meat. The crab was spicy, much spicier than the dishes Mama cooked. Soon Timber was grasping for the bottle. The beer was very cold with a strong bite to it, sloshing in his mouth. He grimaced as he swallowed it down.

"Now you know not to tell your mama about this, don't you?"

Timber nodded cautiously. His memory of the old fishing trips popped into his head, sinking the cans into the water. It was something Daddy never spoke about.

"'Cause I'd hate to have to tell her I caught you down here *drinking* a Dixie beer." Daddy smiled and slapped him on the shoulder.

Even though Timber had grown much closer to Daddy since his sister was born five years back, they didn't keep secrets from Mama. Timber realized that there were probably many things Daddy, always taciturn when not on the radio, did that he and Mama knew nothing about. He was mighty comfortable with a bottle of beer.

Timber took another bite of the crab. He swallowed down the spicy meat and reached for another drink. This time it went down a little easier. There wasn't much left in the bottle. Daddy had been draining it in big gulps.

"Hang on there, *podnuh*," Daddy said. "Let me get us another round."

Daddy was soon back at the table with a Dixie and a Pearl beer. He slid the Pearl in front of Timber.

"Try this one, boy," he said. "It's a little easier going down. You also get a little puzzle under the bottle cap."

He thumped the cap across the table to Timber. "See if you can figure it out."

Timber picked up the cap and examined the black icons etched into the underside of it. The images of an eye, what looked like an ocean wave and some type of portable instrument like a screwdriver were printed on the inside of the cap, a plus sign between each picture. He shrugged.

"What you got to do is decipher the pictures into a saying, whatever it may be," Daddy said. "I've seen you with your puzzles and games. I bet you'll be good at these."

Timber looked again.

"The first one is an eye, so it must be as in *I*," he said, pointing to his chest to explain himself.

"Yeah, that's right," Daddy said. "What's that second thing, the ocean?"

Timber contemplated the wave. He gazed across the room at the bar and the band, still setting up. Something clicked.

"*Sea*—that's the sea. As in 'I see.'"

"Son, you got it. But I don't see what that little chisel thing is, what it means."

"What's a tool that looks like this?" Timber asked. "An ice pick? A needle? A screwdriver?"

"That doesn't make sense, does it?" Daddy took another sip. Timber set the bottle cap on the table, the puzzle facing up to him. He took the last bite of his crab, and followed it up with a sip of the cold Pearl beer. It was full and icy and flowed down his throat, much smoother than the Dixie beer. How strange it was to think that he was sitting with Daddy, drinking beer. He lost his concentration on the puzzle.

Daddy reached for the bottle cap and pulled it to his side of the table, examining it again.

"*Awl!*" Daddy shouted out. "That's it. It's an awl, those little tools that leather workers use. *Eye…Sea…Awl—I see all!* That makes perfect sense."

Daddy laughed loud, a strong guffaw Timber had not heard from him before. Timber smiled, taken aback at Daddy's effusiveness.

"Your mama would agree with that one," he said. "Too bad it ain't true. Ain't nobody can see everything."

Daddy, still holding the bottle cap, flicked it hard with his fingers and it shot over Timber's head and onto the dance floor. Timber flinched. He'd wanted to save the cap as a souvenir of his first beer. Instead he watched it fly, landing and rolling in larger circles that became smaller until it finally fell over. A large man in cowboy boots crossing the room stepped on it without so much as even noticing it. So much for the first piece of his bottle cap collection.

On the stage, Hyatt Delacroix stepped up to a microphone and began speaking in French. Most of the crowd moved on the floor as the accordion and fiddles started up. Timber watched their feet as they stepped round and round in circles, shuffling over his bottle cap.

The bass and the accordion chimed in and Hyatt began to sing. Timber had heard Cajun bands in person a few times at the county fair, but he'd never heard anything as good as Hyatt Delacroix's band sounded live, a pleasant mesh of accordion, fiddle, bass and drums. Dancers in the room swirled and stepped gracefully as Hyatt sang standard Cajun classics such as "Jolie Blonde" and the "Louisiana Waltz" in his high French voice.

Timber tapped his foot and nursed the Pearl beer. Daddy was smiling, a wider, looser smile than Timber was accustomed to, keeping time with his hands on the table top, slapping them along with the shuffling rhythm.

"Son, I'm gonna get me another beer—you all right?"

Timber nodded. He watched Daddy at the bar, standing next to a tall, dark-haired woman in a black dress who recognized him. She looked to be about thirty, resembling a lighter Delores Arceneaux with dark hair, a seductive olive complexion. Daddy bought her a drink and stood talking with her, smiling and easing his arm around her waist. Soon they were out on the dance floor. Timber was surprised to see that Daddy knew the moves, spinning the dark-haired woman, stepping to the rhythm and catching her. Timber slumped, self-conscious about being by himself. He and one very old lady propping her elbows on a walker were the only ones still sitting. But no one was paying him any mind.

After five songs, Daddy and the woman walked back to the bar. Daddy looked back to the table where Timber was sitting and made eye contact with him and nodded. He bought the woman another drink and patted sweat from her forehead with a napkin, and then picked up a placemat and fanned her. A sense of unease grew in Timber, a concern for Mama who was probably baking a cake or combing Bev's hair right this minute. He knew something wasn't right but he didn't know what to do about it. On the other hand, Mama was obsessed with nothing but the church and her little girl. The image of Delores Arceneaux from almost six years ago flashed in his mind. He was beginning to feel a little lightheaded from the beer…his seat seemed to be sinking under him.

Timber saw Daddy and the woman talking, closer than before, finishing their drinks. He put his arm around her waist and led her to the door. Timber wanted to follow but didn't dare. Daddy wouldn't leave him down here, would he? He sat for five minutes before Daddy rushed back in and came over to the table.

"Son, you sit tight," he said. "I've got some…er…business with this woman I need to take care of. I should not be more than an hour or two. Here's three dollars if you need anything."

He turned to leave, but then stopped after a step and turned back.

"Oh yeah, if you happen to meet her, you are my nephew? Okay?…*Okay.*"

Timber nodded slightly. His daddy turned and headed out the door quickly. Timber chafed, clenching his fists. He regretted he had come. He wished he had just gone home to Mama.

Timber sat there listening to Hyatt sing, the music jangling along, for thirty minutes until the band took a break. He watched Hyatt shuffle in old man steps over to the bar and pick up a clear drink that the bartender had set aside for him. Hyatt leaned back on the bar and, after wiping off his steamy glasses with a napkin, surveyed the dance hall. He looked surprised to see Timber sitting back there, and he walked toward him.

"Hey there, little *Tom-Tom*," he said. Timber winced. "Where's big Tom? I know he didn't give you the car keys tonight, even though you getting as big as a man can be."

"He said he had some business to take care of, but he'd be right back."

"Ah ha ha ha," Hyatt laughed, his familiar old man's cackle. "I bet he did. Well, son, you'll be all right. Hyatt will keep an eye out for you." He paused, focusing on Timber as though he was sizing him up.

"Son, how 'bout I get one of these young Cajun women to teach you how to dance? They did a fine job with your daddy, as you can tell. Probably too fine a job. I bet they can do the same with you, bad foot and all. You look like you've been moving around pretty good on that thing lately."

Hyatt reached out and took Timber's arm, between the elbow and shoulder, to lead him onto the dance floor. Timber tensed, gritted his teeth and snatched his arm from Hyatt's grasp. He pressed his butt onto the wooden bench and mashed his good foot firmly onto the floor. Mama wouldn't want him to dance. He wasn't about to try with his limp anyhow.

"*No*. I'm not dancing." His eyes stared holes into the table before him. His back was straight as a board and his fist and teeth were clenched.

Hyatt stepped back two steps.

"Suit yourself, son, suit yourself." He turned and walked off, muttering something in French; the only word that Timber understood was "Baptists."

Timber took a deep breath and relaxed. Mama would have been proud of him, but he still felt guilty for being there, for drinking the beer. He'd been having similar guilt after he masturbated, something he'd discovered recently, seeing fleeting visions of Delores Arceneaux.

Two hours and many accordion-driven Cajun medleys later, Daddy returned to find him at the table. Daddy had a relaxed look on his face, his shirt untucked.

"Let's go, boy. Sorry I left you here so long."

Timber didn't speak but followed dutifully.

He got in and leaned against the door of Daddy's Ford, his arm along the window, and rested his head on his elbow, feigning sleep as the car shot through the shell roads, shooting up plumes of dust in their wake. He was too upset to talk, angry at Daddy in a way he would never tell him. He imagined the shapes of twisted trees in the black swamp outside, flying by in the murky night. Daddy said nothing on the long ride home.

Daddy never apologized or explained and the evening at the Cajun dance hall was never mentioned. He made up to Timber for it, however, by giving him his first live studio air time, a newscast, the following weekend, on Sunday at noon. He bought him a new blue blazer and gold tie for the occasion. Mama didn't like it because it meant Timber would have to miss church, but radio always won out over Jesus in her protestations to Daddy.

Timber was nervous but handled the newscast like an old pro. Those who heard him remarked they couldn't tell him from his daddy. From then on, every Sunday from noon to nine, he was in charge of the radio station, running the soundboard for the preachers who came into the studio to do their sermons on air, or patching in to churches via phone lines. He also did the hourly newscasts, weather and read the obituaries if there were any. He relished the air time, the magic of his voice being splintered into sound waves that reappeared into the homes and automobiles of everyone for a fifteen-mile radius.

The last three years of high school passed like a breeze without any re-markable incidents or events. Timber had not missed a Sunday radio shift or a football game and had plodded his way through high school classes, doing just enough to fulfill the requirements to graduate. He was eighteen, six feet two and almost two hundred pounds, although not an athletic shape. He still had an air of awkwardness, the limp slight but ever present, goofy in the gold and blue graduation cap and gown on the first Saturday morning in June 1970. He walked as upright as he could on the foot and ankle that never had completely healed. He had been too shy to have a high school girlfriend, or even many close friends for that matter.

Timber looked to his family sitting together in the gymnasium during the pomp and circumstance and dull speeches, the first time they had been together as a group in public in at least five years, maybe more. Mama forced a smile at him. Her face looked gray and loose and sad. Daddy, on the other hand, looked slimmer than in past years, ever confident. He seemed to be staring off into space and not at the proceedings. Bev, tall for an eight-year-old, had long blonde hair framing her big blue eyes. She sat fidgeting.

After the ceremony, Mama hugged him and kissed his cheek. Daddy, in a distant mood that day, shook his hand calmly, firmly. Bev strayed along the edge of the crowd, causing Mama to chase after her. They all posed together for a picture, but Timber was anxious to get it over with and out of the robe. He held his high school diploma in his hands and wondered what it was good for. He had half-formed plans to go to a community college and then maybe LSU. But all he really wanted to do was to be on the radio.

That night Mama fixed a big dinner, Timber's favorite, to celebrate: country fried steaks in thick brown gravy with buttery mashed potatoes, biscuits and fresh snap beans from the farmers' market. She also made a chocolate cake with a thick fudge icing on the top, sprinkled with pecans.

They ate much later than usual, almost nine-thirty, because Mama had planned on Daddy being there. Timber had been at the kitchen table at eight *and* nine when she called the radio station, the evening deejay telling her both times that he had not seen him.

"Would you please tell him to come home if you see him? I've got a big dinner on for our son's graduation party. Tell him we are going to go ahead and eat…if you see him."

She finished cooking the meal, placing it out on the round oak dining-room table. She smiled at Timber, but he could see worry in her eyes, encircled in dark blue rings. He always knew when she was forcing a smile because she pulled her lips tight, almost a straight line.

Mama, despite her many hours in church, wasn't one to pray for a long time before meals. She didn't let a meal pass without a quick saying of grace, usually a short "thank you, Lord, for this food and the wonderful life you've given us, Amen." She had only slightly longer prayers for Christmas and Easter. But this time she sat at the table and gripped Timber's fingers tight. She reached for Bev with her other hand and clenched her eyes shut.

"Let us pray. *Dear* Jesus, thank you for sending me such a *wonderful* son, a gift from the Lord. I am so proud of him. Be with him in his journey in the world and make him a *good* man, an honest man, who loves and cares for his family and doesn't abandon them in times of need, but cares for and gives them all the love in his heart and does not go running around—" she paused. She took a deep breath. Timber pretended to keep his eyes closed but watched her. She labored, her eyes tight, sweat glistening in the lines scrunched on her forehead and brow. "He's a *good* boy, Jesus, a *good* boy, please watch over him."

Bev began to squirm in her seat, her chair creaking. She let out a low sound like a sigh, a small squeak from her throat. Mama did not open her eyes.

"Thank you Lord, too, for this most beautiful, *sweetest* daughter on earth, a wonderful little child, a gift from God. Lord, please look after her and keep her safe and in your light. Jesus, God, please watch over my babies—oh, *my babies*—and keep them safe on a straight and narrow path that leads to your everlasting love. Thank *you* Jesus, thank *you* Lord. Amen."

Her eyes opened and she smiled, a sincere smile this time, the first happy one Timber had seen all day. She passed him the serving bowl brimming with gravy, the thin cube steaks submerged in the brown steamy broth. The three of them ate quietly except for a rambling story from Bev about a black kitten she had seen down the street. Mama listened attentively but Timber ignored her, eating two helpings and a big piece of cake.

After dinner, slow and lazy and full as a tick, he went to his room and listened to the end of the Cardinals and Dodgers, a late game that lasted past midnight. Koufax threw a complete shutout. When it ended he read for a while from a new Louis L'Amour western, the book from a collection Mama had given him for graduation. He'd already read most of them, but enjoyed them just as much the second and third times around. He fell asleep about two. Daddy had not come home.

He slept late, until half past ten. He showered, shaved and put on his coat and tie in preparation for his shift. He was surprised when he came into the kitchen to see Mama, usually long gone by this hour for Sunday school, sitting at the table with sheriff's deputy Lieutenant Charlie Gibson. Timber knew him because he went to their church. Mama's head was hanging and her eyes were bleary.

"Hello, son," Lieutenant Gibson said somberly, standing. He was a big man with a flat-top haircut like a soldier. "Come out here and talk with me." Mama sobbed a little but didn't lift her head.

Timber and Lieutenant Gibson walked out the back door and stood in the yard under the oak tree. It was a steamy day, Louisiana hot even in the shade.

"Son, there ain't no easy way to tell you this…" He took a deep breath. "Your daddy was killed last night. Shot with a shotgun, down about fifteen miles south of here, down in the swamp. The man that did it also shot his own wife dead and then turned the gun on himself. A murder-suicide. Your daddy was in the wrong place at the wrong time."

He put his hand on Timber's shoulder. "I'm sorry, boy...I'm real sorry."

Timber looked down at his feet and sighed. He didn't have the urge to cry when he thought about Daddy. But when he turned to go back in and saw Mama, her head down on the table, tears started to well up. He fought them off and went to hug her.

WHAT WOULD JESUS DO?

Zeke Blizzard settled into the Church of the Rock and made it his home. He filled up twenty years with sermons, prayer meetings, revivals, weddings, funerals and fishing trips. The people of his church were good country people. He was the perfect preacher for them, cut from the same rough cloth.

Mary raised three children, doting on them. Ruth and Sarah, the two teen girls, were a little temperamental and independent, but were generally good kids. Zeke especially loved his little boy, eleven-year-old Zach.

Mary had been a good wife. She was not an excitable woman like many he knew in the church, women prone to gossip and chatter and complain. Her cooking was excellent and she still submitted to him in the bed, although she wouldn't fellate him, even after all these years. He had reasoned that every man had to give something up, a sacrifice in return for something else. That seemed to be how God worked.

He should have been perfectly happy with the use of a private fishing pond, the parish house rent-free, a family that loved him, a wife who cooked and cleaned and raised the kids and earned a steady income teaching school. Many men would have been willing to trade places in a second. But something was stirring deep inside him, a gnawing, a longing for something more, something deeper. He had read the Bible front to back and back again many times but didn't have an answer. Could a man's mission in life be all settled by the age of forty-two?

He volunteered for a prison ministry to break the monotony. Prisoners were a prime market for souls in need of salvation—a "captive market," preachers joked to each other. Several times a month he began visiting Alto, a big state prison about an hour from Piney. It was designated for young men locked up for drug-related charges, robberies and assaults.

There were many there in need of preaching. He found more than anything that he enjoyed the trips out of Piney, getting away from the little town, his home, Mary and the kids. So when the opportunity for a monthly trip to a federal prison in Florida arose, he jumped at the chance. It was a long drive, thirteen hours. He awoke at three in the morning to drive it straight through. The beginning of the trip excited him like nothing else had before, the anxiety and excitement and thrill of an adventure, going *somewhere*. He relished watching the dark sky turning to dawn, like a photograph in an illustrated Bible. He stopped his Oldsmobile along the interstate every so often for a cup of hot coffee that smelled as good as it tasted, sugary with heavy cream; with each stop farther south the land was flatter and the air was more humid and warmer, a climate so thick he could reach out and touch it.

In the past twenty years he had not left Georgia except for trips twice a year to see Mary's family in Alabama. He had not been back to Armstrong and had no contact with his daddy, although the old man was still alive as far as he knew.

The inmates at the federal prison in Florida were vastly different from the troubled young men to whom he'd ministered in Georgia prisons. Most of them were older, white men, many his age and above, serving time for a variety of sophisticated capital crimes: corporate theft, forgery, white-collar scams, insurance cons. They were a harder group to convert than the younger men. The old guys had been around the block, they had been preached to before, maybe even converted a time or two before backsliding. Some of them had been in for a very long time.

It was in the concrete penal compound tucked away in an isolated pasture surrounded by scrubby Florida pines that he met Arnie Putzel, an old man with an electronic voice box. Arnie sat near the window gazing out into the field while the preacher gave a short sermon about God's forgiveness—the favorite topic of inmates.

Arnie stuck around after Zeke's sermon and helped straighten up, moving the chairs back into place, putting the hymnals away. The old man shuffled around, his breath raspy and deep.

"Thank you, Brother Arnie," Zeke said. "I'm glad you join us each month. Are you saved, Brother Arnie?"

Arnie smiled, slyly. His face was crimson as though he'd just stepped out of a scalding shower and had a series of moles in the layout of the Hawaiian Islands that started on his forehead and drifted down to his chin, the largest on his right cheek. His thin white hair was cropped in a military-style buzz cut and he smelled of Old Spice.

"You know that part in the Bible where Jesus flips over the table of the money changers and runs them out of the temple?" Arnie asked, his robotic voice deep and measured. The machine-like speech came not from his mouth but a hole above the collar bone, startling Zeke.

"Yes, of course, Arnie. That's in all four Gospels."

"Well. Is it true a banker has as much chance getting into heaven as a camel through the eye of a needle?"

Zeke pondered the question before answering.

"Arnie, Jesus said that it's harder for *rich* men to get into heaven than it is a camel through the eye of a needle. Not just bankers."

"Yeah. But the banks is what I know best—I used to rob them."

"Oh," Zeke said. He was uncomfortable when the inmates talked about their crimes. Most of the time they never went into any detail, choosing to say only that they were sorry for what they'd done if they admitted to doing anything at all. Zeke always told them that Jesus knew the truth.

"I robbed eight banks before they caught me," Arnie said. "And I wanted them to catch me."

Zeke didn't know what to say to that. Arnie kept right on, pouring out his story, his voice box droning. He was a failed insurance salesman from Wisconsin who had retired to St. Petersburg, Florida. He had passed the time drinking Budweiser in the Golden Palm, a bar with a cement floor in the back part of a rundown strip mall near the Sunshine Skyway.

Arnie's only relative who had stayed in touch with him was a niece who worked as a bank teller in Orlando. She had visited him a few times a year and chattered endlessly. She said bank tellers were taught that whenever a robber approached them, they were to calmly clean out the drawers and hand over the money without resistance. The only tactic was to sneak a tiny, time-delayed explosive canister with purple dye into the bag, but only if the bank robber did not see it. Arnie said she told him the banks learned long ago that losing $10,000 or so to a robber was cheaper than paying the legal fees and medical bills when someone got hurt or killed, not to mention how bad it looked in the newspapers and on television. Banks were insured for the loss and wrote it off on their taxes. The offsetting tax benefits of robbery were so good for the bottom line that branch managers were usually upset if their bank didn't get robbed at least once or twice a year. Arnie's niece told him about a gag award for the "Most Robbed Bank" that Bank of America executives gave out at their regional conference. She said the bankers laughed so hard that some of them fell out of their chairs and spilled gin and tonics on their golf shirts and khaki slacks.

Arnie told Zeke that four years ago his Social Security checks had ceased without explanation. He spent hours on hold on the pay phone in the steamy black asphalt parking lot of the Golden Palm, unable to get anyone to help. It was then that he decided to rob a bank. He figured the prison care had to be pretty good for a World War II vet with a voice box. If he didn't get caught, he would have all the rent and beer money he needed. Either way, he wouldn't be homeless or have to take a job rounding up the carts at Wal-Mart. He took a bus to Tampa, hobbled into the first bank he saw and gave a teller a note that said he had a bomb and demanded money. She gave him a bag of cash and he thanked her. He netted $14,500 that afternoon.

He said he went on to rob eight banks in two weeks. Each time he gave the bank tellers a note, they willingly obliged. Only three tellers used the exploding dye packs. He always checked the bag as soon as he stepped out of the door and tossed the little metal canister into the bushes, where a few minutes later it would explode, emit a putrid smoke cloud and stain the azaleas purple.

He became more brazen with each heist. After his seventh robbery, he walked straight from the bank to a dive bar with a dirt parking lot and blue-collar clientele. He stayed long enough to buy six rounds of drinks for the house. He was certain that the police would come pick him up. They never did.

For his eighth robbery, Arnie hired a white limo that waited in the bank parking lot while he took $4,000, all twenties. He then went to a crowded upscale bar in the swanky Tampa neighborhood of Hyde Park. The tanned and neatly pressed young patrons of the bar looked at him like he was a leper until he bought four rounds for the packed house. He drank seven martinis himself at $18 a pop. At the end of the night he didn't have enough cash in hand to pay the $500 limo bill. He tried to get out of the car to go get cash from the approximately $60,000 accumulated under his bed, but the limo driver thought Arnie was planning to stiff him. The police were there right away.

Only after police booked Arnie for theft of services did one of them realize he matched the description of the bank robbery suspect. He confessed and was turned over to the FBI. Arnie demanded a jury trial, not to fight the charges, but because he wanted an opportunity to complain from the witness chair about Social Security. He fussed about them good. He was sent to the soft prison, where the very oldest of America's federal offenders convalesced. It was much more comfortable than his old trailer in the crowded mobile home park.

Zeke drove home that night with Arnie's story on his mind. He was not a politically minded man but on a subconscious level he'd always resented the power of banks, the control of the money, his money, his parishioner's money, their existence reduced to paper. It stuck in his craw. He didn't think it right that hard work and sweat could be quantified into dollar bills. If he had to choose between banks or a bank robber, he'd take the bank robber every time. He pictured Jesus flipping over tables, stacked high with coins, the change clattering on the marble floor, the bearded Jews scurrying to collect the money, their robes fluttering in the dry wind. What would Jesus do if He came to earth today? He might rob banks Himself, taking the money to feed hungry children, house the homeless, expand church ministries for alcoholics, drug addicts, prisoners and other troubled souls. So many people were hurting that needed His help. Yes, Arnie was in the right, Zeke nodded, gripping and regripping the steering wheel. He was in the right.

On his next visit to the prison, Arnie led Zeke to a fenced-in grassy lawn with benches that faced a green pasture edged by a stand of slash pine. He and Arnie looked across the verdant land, flat as a board. Arnie again did most of the talking. Zeke had become accustomed to his robotic voice.

Arnie said he had learned more about banks during his trial and later befriended several other "retired" bank robbers in the pen. He pointed out that the amount stolen is never reported in the news. The FBI always withholds that information. They don't want to encourage potential bank robbers who could see that sometimes a good robbery can net $25,000 or more.

"That's a lot in cold hard cash—no taxes," Arnie said.

Arnie went over the details of all eight of his robberies, talking nonstop for two hours until the dinner bell rang, signaling it was time for Zeke to go. Arnie looked at Zeke as the clanging rattle stopped.

"Are you going to rob one yourself, preacher?" His robotic voice had the hint of a laugh in it. A smile wrinkled onto his face. Zeke broke eye contact and looked away.

"Ah, um, no," he said. "Why would you think that?"

"Sounds to me like you are," Arnie said. "I've never talked with a preacher for so long without Jesus coming up once."

The idea of robbing a bank began to eat at Zeke, occupying all his waking thoughts, sometimes his dreams. His sermons began to take on a political tone, mildly attacking the great wealth of corporations, banks in particular. The anti-bank and big government references got most of the heads in the working class congregation nodding steadily.

Zeke began following any news he could about bank robberies. It was rare that police caught anyone. When they did catch someone, it usually was a person with a serious mental problem, such as a schizophrenic woman in Macon who robbed a bank with a note she scribbled over an old grocery list. Her note read: *GIVE ME THE – DORITOS ICE CREAM – MONEY PLEASE.* A teller loaded up her bag and she walked off. They didn't even try to stop her. She didn't get caught until she took off all her clothes and put the money, along with her clothes and a half gallon of bleach, in a washing machine in a Laundromat three blocks away. The newspaper said police found her sleeping naked on the sidewalk.

He began lingering in the bank in downtown Piney, waiting in the longest line, eyeing the tellers as they moved cash from the drawers to zippered bags to the safe. He would occasionally request a meeting with a customer service representative to go over the church's statement, pretending to want financial advice, asking questions about interest rates and construction loans.

He continued to visit Arnie in the Florida pen. But one late winter morning Zeke arrived at the prison to the news that Arnie had died of a heart attack. The next day Zeke gave the eulogy in the unmarked cemetery where they buried the inmates without family. He led two prison guards and two inmates in "Amazing Grace" and "Rock of Ages," their voices off key and tremulous under a gray sky. He spoke of Arnie as though he had been a revered citizen. As the pine coffin was lowered into the ground, Zeke sensed Arnie's spirit, rising above the pines on the edge of the field, bound for a resting place in heaven.

After Arnie's death, Zeke resigned from the prison ministry. He began reading newspapers and magazines late into the evening in his church office, a small room cluttered with hymnals, Bibles and prayer books. He told Mary he was writing sermons about Jesus. She never doubted him.

In the afternoons he began scouting out locations for his first heist. He decided that Anderson, South Carolina, right across the Georgia state line and on the interstate, about sixty miles from home, would be a good start. It was big enough to have several branch bank locations on its modest outskirts but it did not have heavy traffic that would tie him up when he made his getaway. He drove over to Anderson several times, studying a map of the roads, sitting in the parking lot of the Bank of America branch, noting the ebb and flow of customers. He watched the employees leaving at the end of the day to get a look at the tellers.

He picked out a meek-looking, fortyish woman with curly hair and glasses of a style that made her look much older.

He began to gather the tools he would need. In a junkyard he found South Carolina license plates to put on his car. From the church's collection of clothes for the needy, donated in a charity drive held every summer, he picked his disguise: a Clemson University baseball cap, a baggy flannel shirt and faded jeans, a pair of worn sneakers that wouldn't leave footprints.

One afternoon in the church he took a small black Bible from one of the front pews, the cover faded after years of sitting and weekly use, and went into his office, locking the door behind him. He ripped out a page from Matthew. In black magic marker he scrawled:

GIVE ME ALL THE MONEY
I'VE GOT A GUN AND DAMN SURE WILL
USE IT IF YOU SCREAM OR CAUSE TROUBLE
HAND IT OVER NOW

He held it, rereading it. It was what he was aiming for, to-the-point and threatening. Arnie had told him you want to get the teller's attention right quick, let them know you mean business. Below his crude message he underlined Jesus' words, "you have made it a den of thieves."

With each robbery he would use a specific verse, one pertinent to the ultimate message he meant for the banks. The *damn* banks! He'd read an article about the Bank of America CEO who was paid $45 million annually. He seethed, thinking of all the wealth and control that a few men and their giant corporations held over people, his people. Someone had to do something, someone had to take a little of it back for Jesus. He knew the impending rapture foretold in Revelation was coming and one day God would take care of the greed and demagoguery. Until then, he was going to do what he could.

It was deep into summer, July, when he drove to Anderson in his Oldsmobile. He had attached the fake South Carolina plates, his Georgia plates in the trunk. He also brought his second-best preaching suit with a black satchel for the money. With the baseball cap and dark sunglasses, he looked like most any working man, certainly not like a preacher. He recalled a class on behavior at the seminary that taught baseball caps weren't becoming on a man of God. With the flannel shirt and the old baggy jeans, he didn't even recognize himself.

His confidence was emboldened when he set out that Thursday afternoon. But when he got to the bank and found a spot in the far edge of the parking lot, he started doubting. He thought fondly of his family, his home, his biweekly fishing trips. Getting caught would mean giving it all up. He'd seen the inside of prisons and knew he didn't want to go, although there was something appealing about the simple, monkish prison life. He could run a good prison ministry if he was an inmate himself. He sat in his car thinking these things, watching the trickle of customers into and out of the bank. The sun beat down on his car, the engine near boiling after the sixty-mile ride. He had turned the motor off but started it up again as he began to get hot, cranking up the air conditioner. He unconsciously turned on the radio, somewhere in the AM dial. That's when he heard the Reverend Jerry Rodgers, an old Mississippi preacher he'd heard years ago. Reverend Rodgers was the best, he remembered, at raising the hair on your neck, inspiring you to take action for the cause of the Lord. The radio crackled alive.

"You can't sit back and let the Devil run roughshod over you, son, you gotta fight him *every* day," Reverend Rodgers exhorted. "The Lord God put you on this *earth* when He did for a reason…He gave you life *for* a reason…He gave you breath in your lungs and blood in your veins *for* a reason so you would do *His* work!…You gotta *take* what is rightfully yours, lest the Devil gets it for his *own*. Git out there, son, *do* the Lord your God's work. Take ole Satan by the ears and shake 'im up!"

He got out of the car and walked through the parking lot. A big white fluffy storm cloud on the horizon looked to him like a cherub angel resting on its side, smiling down. A breeze kicked up that very moment, dropping the temperature ten degrees, a cleansing wind, the kind in advance of a late afternoon thunderstorm. He picked up his pace and walked into the bank, the cap pulled down, sunglasses on, his chin tucked low against his neck.

The bookish teller he had seen before was there, on the end, quietly serving a customer. She had the shortest line. He waited behind a mother and daughter, about sixty and thirty respectively, as they made a transaction, something about their recently dead patriarch's estate. They moved along, the mother slowly counting her bills and rereading the receipt before putting it in her purse.

Zeke felt at peace. He stepped up to the teller and handed her his note. Her eyes widened as she read it, her skin turned ghostly pale. Zeke handed her his bag across the counter. She lifted half-inch stacks of bills bound with narrow bands of construction paper and dropped them into his satchel. She slowed for a second, almost losing her breath, when Zeke leaned close to her and said, "Git it all—*now*." She lifted the plastic tray lining the drawer and picked up two bulging envelopes, dropping both into the bag. Zeke knew then that he'd hit some sort of jackpot. He had a vision of a warm ray of sunshine upon his shoulders, God's smile across his back.

The other tellers and customers didn't notice a thing. She had made no effort to sneak a dye pack into his bag. Soon he was on a lonely dirt road outside of Anderson, changing into his preaching suit and putting his Georgia license plates back on his car, tossing the old clothes and Carolina plates into an overgrown ditch. He stuck the satchel under his spare tire in the trunk, fighting the urge to count it. There would be time for counting later. Although Jesus was with him, he sensed the presence of the Devil on the dusty roadside littered with crushed beer cans and used condoms. He knew Satan's playground when he saw it.

Back at the church there was not a soul in sight. He went into his office and locked the door. He opened the satchel and spread the money out in short stacks, the piles demarcated by the range of denominations, ones all the way up to fifties. The two envelopes stuffed with fifties accounted for most of the $12,000 spread on his desk. He sat gazing at the money surrounded by his Bible, family photos, a paperweight in the shape of a cross that had been a gift from his in-laws when he graduated the seminary. He clenched his hands and prayed, then he hid the money under some old blankets in an old trunk in the boiler room. He went home and enjoyed his family's company for the first time in several years.

Four months later he robbed a First Union branch in Chattanooga, easy as pie. In another three months he knocked off a bank in Tallahassee, then three months later one in Montgomery. Each time he wore the disguise of hat and sunglasses, handing the teller a holdup note on a Bible page. Each time his bag was filled with money, usually between $5,000 and $15,000 each, but in Montgomery he walked away with $24,000 because there was only one teller on duty and he made her clean out all three drawers. He'd headed off the exploding dye packs, twice catching tellers trying to sneak one in the bag, when he muttered, "*aw aw now*," in a low, threatening voice, a put-on deeper than his own. The very fact that they were willing to ruin the money with purple dye rather than let it go to the cause of the children of the Lord enraged him, emboldening him against the greed of the anti-Christian banks.

He had chosen banks just across the Georgia state line to ensure that he wouldn't be recognized. Going into a different police jurisdiction was a good idea, Arnie had told him, because the various police forces often didn't work closely together. Police in places like Chattanooga would be very unlikely to track down a Georgia country preacher. Crossing state lines often meant going into a different FBI district, the agency charged with investigating bank robberies. Lawmen were easy to confuse, Arnie had said. Zeke bought a radar detector to help avoid the police.

Driving the long distances in the car—he told his wife he was scouting out locations for more prison ministries—gave him time to get away from Piney and think. He turned the dial, scanning small-town radio stations, listening for sermons of the local preachers, men shouting their praises and damnations over the airwaves. He heard some good sermons, got some great ideas for sermons of his own. He began to imagine himself on the radio station in Piney, his sermon broadcast out across four counties.

Another year passed with four more robberies: Birmingham and Anniston, Alabama; Jacksonville, Florida; and North Augusta, South Carolina. All went without a hitch. But the novelty had begun to wear off. He was bored with the out-of-state scheme and had run out of mid-sized towns bordering Georgia, so he decided to hit a bank in the Atlanta suburbs. The city had grown exponentially in his lifetime to almost four million people.

He had never liked Atlanta, the *Olympic* city. It had always been full of itself, egotistical, the shameless boosterism of just how great a city it was. It was as if those doing the boasting had yet to convince themselves. He avoided Atlanta, going only once or twice a year for church business or a Braves game.

He watched the Atlanta preachers on television, taping their broadcasts. They were proud in their expansive pulpits, their fat faces beaming insincerely into the camera, begging in soft voices for viewers to send more money. None of them were able to rise above a citywide following. Billy Graham, Jimmy Swaggart—*those* were preachers, men to follow, men who made you believe. The Atlanta preachers—simply a pack of smiling, talking heads—paled drastically in comparison. Even Alabama, small as it was, had much better televangelists. Robbing Atlanta banks would be good revenge on the unholy, phony city. And Lord knows there were plenty of branch banks, one-story prefab structures thrown up overnight, dotting the landscape of the sprawling metropolis, serving the banking needs of the thousands who moved there every day from all over the country, all over the world. Why people flocked there he would never understand.

His first two bank robberies in Atlanta went smoothly. The aloof tellers and customers, most of them pressing cell phones to their heads like magic salves, were unruffled by the fact a bank robber was in their midst.

After those two robberies, Zeke's stash grew to more than $50,000 in the hidden trunk. He pushed it behind the old boiler that coughed and hissed in the winter in a valiant effort to keep the sanctuary warm. He padlocked the trunk's latch.

He got serious about a time slot on the local radio station, putting down a $500 deposit to get on the waiting list. The station owner said it looked promising that the hour held by the Methodist Church would open up because their new preacher wanted to cut expenses and save the $150 per week cost of the air time.

Each week Zeke began to imagine himself on the radio, his voice broadcast out to save lost souls. His preaching began to be fierier, more political and impassioned. He was more than a warm body to simply call out the hymn number and lead the prayers.

His plans, however, came dangerously close to unraveling during a heist in Marietta, an Atlanta suburb. It was only about sixty miles from Piney. He knew a few people who went there to go to the big mall or to see a highfalutin chiropractor. He thought it was too crowded to run across a Christian he knew amongst the hordes of heathens there. But he was walking through the bank parking lot after the robbery with his satchel full of money, wearing sunglasses and a baseball cap, when he heard Bobbie Jo Montgomery.

"Reverend Blizzard!" she screamed from the parking lot behind him. "Reverend Blizzard. What you doing over here in At-lanta?"

He never even saw her but he recognized her voice like she was calling to him in the pulpit from the third row. He had a vision that the world was a basketball the Devil was spinning on his finger. But then he felt God take the world in his hands and stop the spinning. Zeke caught his breath and took off running like a cat on fire.

He never looked back. She hadn't seen his face. He had on an old cap, overalls and a sweatshirt, an outfit he never wore in Piney. He had gotten too cocky and had let his guard down, walking like he did when he was preaching an emotional sermon. It amazed him that of the four million people running around Atlanta, she could pick him out from the back, by his walk and body language, and he could identify her loud squeal without even laying eyes on her.

His car was behind a strip mall nearby so she never got a look at it. He prayed out loud as he sped off, his tires spewing up pebbles of fresh asphalt.

"Oh Jesus, please be with me in these times of need, Lord. I'm sorry I got complacent and let Satan sneak up on me. Keep the Devil outta my path, Lord, keep him outta my path."

He didn't feel Satan's presence at all the rest of that afternoon. It was a smooth ride home. He scanned the radio, finding a Swaggart service. Zeke sang "The Old Rugged Cross" right along with him. He continued to sing back in his office while counting out $11,450, mostly tens and twenties.

Bobbie Jo caught up to him before church that next Sunday morning.

"Reverend Blizzard, I did the craziest thing the other day, just the craziest thing," she said. "I called out to a man in *At*-lanta I thought was you, but sure enough, this man had just robbed a bank."

He smiled his biggest smile, showing all of his teeth.

"Oh, Bobbie Jo. A bank robber?"

"Yes sir, he had just cleaned out the bank. He was carrying a tote bag on his shoulder and just strutting along."

She looked down at his shoes like she was picturing the way he walked when he called out for lost Christians to come on down and reclaim their souls.

"Well, I hope they caught him. Did he hurt anybody?"

"Naw, I don't think so. The *poe*-lice asked me to describe him, but they didn't seem to care that much."

"Well I'll be."

"The funniest thing was, after the robbery, the bank tellers were all laughing and joking in the parking lot. I think they got the rest of the day off."

"Well, I'll be." He turned to walk away.

But something occurred to him and he called back to her.

"Hey, Bobbie Jo," he said. "Did he have a gun, use a holdup note or something?"

"I don't know, Reverend Blizzard. I tried to ask more questions but the *poe*-lice put up a barricade and shooed me away."

He smiled a loving, Christian smile at her.

He was in great form in the pulpit later that morning, sweat pouring off his brow, tears down his cheeks. He told the story of Jesus that they all had heard so many times.

"All Jesus *ever* did was good," he shouted. "He was *always* in the right. But they crucified Him as a *criminal*…Jesus was on the *wrong* side of His country's laws. The *laws* of the land…the *laws* of those with power, money and *control* of the government."

He gripped the sides of the lectern, dropping his volume a notch, sometimes to an angry-sounding whisper.

"Ancient Rome is *still* considered one of the *greatest* societies of all mankind...They invented Latin, the language that the English we speak *today* is based on...They were great engineers, building roads and *grand* buildings everywhere they went...They were great warriors, putting much of the *world* under their rule...They were great legislators, forming governmental bodies that our *Congress* is based on today."

He took a long pause to catch his breath. He looked right at Bobbie Jo, sitting in her usual third-row spot with her sister and children. Then he put his head down and inhaled deeply. It was dead quiet. He threw his head back and shouted, clenching his fists and raising his arms like he was signaling a touchdown.

"But they killed...my...Jesus!"

He looked down at Bobbie Jo again and pointed his finger at her.

"They *killed your* Jesus, Bobbie Jo." He began to look around, making eye contact with the parishioners who never missed a Sunday, all sitting wide-eyed, transfixed on him.

"They *killed your* Jesus, Ricky! They *killed your* Jesus, Josephine! They *killed your* Jesus, Willie!

"This ancient Rome, the greatest society of history...*nailed our Jesus on a cross!*" Tears streamed down his cheeks and he broke into a sweat that stained his armpits. He lowered his voice, speaking breathlessly.

"And their brothers near 'em, the Greeks, another of our great societies, had *their* problems too. Some of the greatest Greek minds...the men who some say *taught* us how to *think*...the *philosophers*...they *lay down* with other men!"

He took another long pause for emphasis. References to homosexuals always riled up his congregation. He could tell by the way Bobbie Jo was biting her lip that she was deep in thought. Everybody in the church was listening intently, many with their faces scrunched. A few eyes were twitching. He smiled slightly and changed his tone of voice to a pleasant one.

"Most of us think about our country today as the greatest society...don't we?"

Most everyone nodded their heads, the older men most enthusiastically. A few smiled, as though they expected him to turn on a positive note. They looked relieved. He could see parishioners relaxing their posture and taking deep breaths. But he wasn't taking the easy way out.

"*Things* is happening here, right here in the good ole U.S. of A, like what happened in ancient Rome and ancient Greece thousands of years ago!

"People is crossing the Lord's will every day with the *blessing* of society…Look at how the *I-R-S* takes our money…Look at how our politicians take advantage of innocent young women…Look at what the bank wants to charge you next time you just want to buy a simple *home* for your family!

"Being part of the greatest country in the world don't make you right in the Lord's eyes!"

"Amen," Bobbie Jo blurted out in perfect rhythm with his sermon. He made quick eye contact with her to let her know he approved.

He steeled his expression and looked straight at his parishioners.

"This is the greatest country in the history of man. But that don't mean the good ole U.S. of A wouldn't crucify Jesus if He came along again."

He paused, scanning the faces of the congregation.

"*What* do you think our president, Mr. Bill Clinton, woulda done if he met Jesus?"

Many shook their heads and smirked at this suggestion. He continued.

"You got to try hard to tell *good* from *evil*." He picked up the pace. Bobbie Jo and several others chimed in with *amen*, punctuating his fast-moving sentences.

"It ain't as clear as our politicians, lawyers and bankers would like you to believe it is…"

"*Amen!*"

"The Devil is *on* the side of the government…"

"*Amen!*"

"He's on the *side* of these multinational corporations with their same-sex domestic partners you read more and more about in the newspapers…"

"*Amen!*"

"He is on the wrong side and you gotta *question* every day which side you are on, which side *our* institutions are on…*Satan's?*… Or the *Lord's?*"

"*The Lord's! Amen!*"

"Well…I'm gonna play for the *Lord's* team."

"*Amen!*"

"And I want *y'all* to join me."

"*Amen!*"

He smiled. "Come on down front here if you want to give your soul to Jesus."

"*Amen! Amen! Amen!*"

Seventeen people, the most ever, came forward that morning to rededicate themselves to Christ. He hugged them all, squeezing them tight. It was an inspiring sermon, he thought, one of radio broadcast quality.

RED STICK SUNDAYS

It seemed to Timber that everyone in Louisiana came by the house after the funeral with cakes, casseroles and condolences, talking about everything but the specifics of what happened to his daddy out on a backroad in the swamp, the gunshot wound so gruesome they were forced to have a closed-casket funeral, the undertaker urging his mama to remember him like he was.

Johnny Robelot, station manager of KKPX-AM in Baton Rouge and a long-time friend of Daddy's, brought a cool lemon meringue pie. He had a shiny bald head and thick horn-rimmed glasses. His wife was a short woman shaped like a duck. When Mr. Robelot learned that his mama had decided to sell the station and rid herself of the radio business altogether, he told Timber he would have a job for him at the end of the summer.

Two months later Timber waited in a folding chair at the Baton Rouge station. He figured every radio station lobby in Louisiana was the same: thin carpet, wood paneling, offices about the size of a walk-in closet decorated with gaudy plaques and framed photographs from the previous decade. The few stations he had visited with Daddy were all alike. Not much to see, just rundown little cinder-block huts on the wrong side of the tracks with a big antenna towering above, red lights blinking to warn away the crop dusters and low-flying New Orleans-bound jets. Timber thought it was a good thing people can't see what they were hearing on the radio. He nervously flexed his bad ankle, an attempt to relieve its stiffening. His foot had been hurting him more lately.

Timber's mama had sold the radio station to a big broadcasting company based in Dallas that shut down the local studio and replaced it with programming from a New Orleans affiliate. She had learned from the lawyers that the station had significant debt and that the transmitter and antenna were the only parts worth selling. Only $1,500 was left after the loans were paid off. That and a $1,000 life insurance policy was the only money his mama had in the world. She had never held a job in her life. But she had held herself together better than Timber thought she would.

After half an hour, Mr. Robelot waddled out. He shook Timber's hand, remarked how much he sounded like his daddy, and told him he could start the next night on the overnight shift.

Timber would have done the job almost for free—and that was close to what he was paid. His strong voice and willingness to work long hours for not much money without complaining got him promoted in his second month to the afternoon drive-time shift when it opened up. Only the morning slot was more prestigious, and with the high turnover rate at radio stations, he expected it would be available within a year or two.

He commuted forty miles between Whitcomb and Baton Rouge, setting out in mama's car about three every afternoon and not returning until the wee hours. It was a long drive over pockmarked roads busy with oil tankers and pulpwood trucks, more than an hour each way. He got excited every afternoon when the Baton Rouge skyline came into view, the ghost of Huey Long still in the air almost forty years after his death, palpable in the twenty-five-story capitol building, a skyscraper by Louisiana standards that loomed over the Mississippi River. Timber wanted to move to Baton Rouge but he couldn't leave Whitcomb so soon after Daddy's killing. The long commute and the ten- to twelve-hour-long work shifts left him no time free except to sleep and have an early afternoon breakfast with Mama. He saved his first few paychecks and bought a 1966 Dodge Dart so he wouldn't leave Mama without her car.

Timber had never seen so many young women in one place as Baton Rouge. They pranced all over the town, the very best looking of the university co-eds gravitating to internships at the capitol. The towering skyscraper also was the site of the professional women, clerks and stenographers and receptionists. Timber would walk around the grounds of the state house just to see the fine carriage of these women in their immaculate blouses and finely pressed skirts, running errands for Louisiana's most powerful men and doing it with a strut. Other girls were drawn to the football field where they cheered for the proud LSU Tigers, big flashes of purple and gold. This was a younger crowd of carefree co-eds, athletic and fickle. Timber watched the girls from the corner of his eye when he covered practices and games but he never had the nerve to speak to them. They wouldn't be interested in a gimpy-legged radio man who lived at home with his mama.

After a long year of commuting, he decided to move. He put a deposit down on a tiny apartment in Baton Rouge, about a mile from the radio station, equidistant to the chemical plant north of town. Mama seemed fine, wrapped up in church and Bev's life—she was ten and involved in the Girl Scouts—but he dreaded telling her. He had planned to break the news on Saturday, his off day, but he procrastinated, lying on the couch watching college football games, worrying about it. He decided he could do it on Sunday morning before he left.

She was at the table, reading the Bible and dressed for church, when he woke and went into the kitchen. "Good morning, darlin'," she said, barely looking up. She had put out a box of store-bought donuts, foregoing the big breakfasts she used to cook. She was focusing all her energy on the word of the Lord, studying and praying for hours every morning.

Timber poured a cup of coffee and sat at the table next to her, taking two donuts. She was moving her finger along the gilded pages, held by a worn brown leather backing. She touched his forearm with her hand—the way she had done in church a thousand times before when she wanted to make sure he paid attention—and read aloud to him. Her voice was tired but with conviction.

"'When *He* had turned around and looked on His disciples, He rebuked Peter, saying, Get thee behind me, *Satan*. For you are not mindful of the things of God, but the *things* that be of men.'"

She paused, scanning down the page. She looked up at him to make sure he was listening.

"'For what will it profit a man if he gains the whole world and *loses* his own soul? Or what will a man give in exchange for his soul? For whoever is ashamed of *Me* and My words in this adulterous and sinful generation, of him the *Son of Man* also will be ashamed when *He* comes in the glory of His Father with the Holy angels.'"

She paused for a minute but did not look up. Her lips moved as though she was saying a prayer to herself. She then turned the page and began to read another passage to him.

"Mama," he said interrupting, looking down at the table, not at her. "I've got something to tell you."

"In a minute, honey. There's something I want to read you from Matthew."

She began to read again but he did not follow the words. Her thick dark hair was graying fast, her double chin was more exaggerated, the skin on her face ashen. Large round circles drooped from her eyes. His daddy had been dead a year but his mama looked a decade older. He waited until she finished reading, something Jesus said about the evils of lust in one's heart.

"Mama," he said, touching his hand to her forearm. "I need to tell you something important."

"What is it, baby?" She lifted her head. Her hands still held the Bible as though she were reading it.

He almost decided not to tell her, considered even changing his plans to move to Baton Rouge. He hadn't moved any of his things yet. He would have to buy a bed, furniture, dishes and a TV for the new apartment, a piece or two at a time. He couldn't afford it all at once. But that wasn't his main concern. He was leaving his mother only a year after his daddy had been killed. But he would visit every weekend and call her every day. He had been a good son. He deserved to go out and have a life of his own.

"Mama, I've rented an apartment in Baton Rouge." Her face went still, as though she didn't understand. "I'm going to stay there during the week while I'm working. I'll be home every weekend though, to see you and Bev. And if you need anything, I can come over in the morning before work. But I want a place of my own. It's a little place, not too far from the station. I'll take you over there to see it, soon. Besides, it's dangerous driving those roads so late at night. You said so yourself."

Her chin trembled, quivering slightly. She didn't say anything. She loosened her grip on the Bible and it flattened out on the table, pages open. She turned from him and stared across the room at the far wall. Her eyes moistened. He didn't know what else to say. She dropped her head, letting it sag. She closed her eyes and sat that way for a few minutes.

"Mama, I don't want to hurt you." He put his hand on her shoulder. "I love you and I'll make sure I take care of you and Bev. I'm not going to abandon you. I'll take care of you. I'm not leaving you."

She straightened up and looked him in the eye, a piercing look. He pulled his hand away.

"Your daddy told me something like that one time." She closed the Bible and picked it up, hugging it to her chest. "I'll be okay. I've got something I can rely on."

It was almost a year later when Timber saw a girl he recognized in a smoky French Quarter doorway near the corner of Bourbon and Iberville streets, inhaling a cigarette, her dark eyes a little glazed, scanning the crowded street, packs of drunks ambling back and forth. She was a waitress in Baton Rouge, an Italian restaurant near the radio station. He imagined her Italian but remembered from her badge that her name was something Cajun. He had watched her dozens of times over his lasagna or fettuccine, foods that Mama had never cooked for him.

She was tall and her long dark hair was slightly curly, hanging around her face, falling down onto her shoulders. Her skin was moist, glistening in the humidity, her lips full and half open, the beginning of a smile as she recognized him. He liked the Italian place, often eating a late lunch there before going on the air. He had been full-time on the afternoon shift almost two years, deejaying, doing the news, the life in radio he'd always wanted, the life his daddy once had.

She stood like an apparition in the fluffy cloud of smoke wafting from the door, the live band inside the bar playing an Allman Brothers song. She smiled full, looser than her on-the-job smile. She had great dimples and brown eyes as dark as chicory coffee. He crossed the street and raised up his plastic beer cup to her in a toast. She smiled and stepped forward, raising her daiquiri, tapping it against his.

"Cheers," she said, laughing, leaning forward.

"Cheers," he responded, taking a sip of the beer, watching her over the rim of the cup.

She was drinking a hurricane, the red drink staining her lips and tongue. He was relieved his radio peers—desperate men more than twice his age—had stayed back in the strip club, stuffing dollar bills in the stretched-out garter belts of broken-down old whores. There was nothing worse to him than to be in a rundown strip club with no money.

He was twenty years old and had never been with a woman. This woman standing before him in the doorway was the reason he went to Capolinni's, but he never had gotten up the nerve to ask her out on a date. They'd never had much of a conversation even though the eye contact and smiles had always been there. He shifted his weight onto his good foot and tried not to let his limp show. She stepped away from the door and closer to him.

"I'm Sherry." She hugged him, talking into his ear. "It's so good to meet you, stranger."

"I'm Tom." Her arms on his back and her breath on his ear sobered him up, undoing the effect of four beers in the Bourbon Street Pussy Cat Club.

"I've got a joint in my car," she said. "You wanna go?"

"Yeah." He had never smoked pot before. She grabbed his hand and led him toward the east part of the Quarter, walking fast. He hustled to keep up, unable to hide his limp.

"You hurt your foot?"

"Yeah."

"How?"

He didn't want to get into it. He didn't want to mess this up. Then it came to him.

"Oh…it's an old high school football injury. I busted it up in a rough tackle against Breaux Bridge."

"I bet the boy you tackled got hurt more than you." Her voice lilted and she moved her thumb to caress the fat part of his hand.

The farther from Bourbon Street, the narrower and darker the side streets got, the acrid smell of stale beer and urine on the cobblestone sidewalks, an occasional drunk passed out on the curb. She seemed oblivious to the surroundings and looked at him coyly.

"You're the nighttime radio man, aren't you?"

"Uhm, yeah." She *knew* who he was.

"Why did you never ask me out?"

All that time sitting longingly eating lasagna, ordering a meal he could barely afford, she had *wanted* him to ask her out. He smiled, standing up straight.

"Why do you think I ate there so often? I wanted to—to ask you out—but I didn't think you would go."

"I don't see why someone on the radio would be intimidated by me, a lowly waitress." She raised a hand to brush her long dark hair behind her ear.

She stopped on the sidewalk. She moved to take his other hand, pressing herself to him, only a few inches shorter than he was. She tilted her hips toward him as they stood, the street dark and abandoned except for a lone car speeding down the one-lane street. Her jeans were tight and she put her thigh between his legs. He had his arms around her waist, letting his hands slide a little low, below her belt on the curve there. He had no idea what he should do next.

She batted her dark eyes again and kissed him. She stuck her tongue into his mouth and moved it gently, applying suction. It was a powerful kiss, unlike any of the few timid pecks on the lips he'd gotten from awkward girls in high school. She held him tight, kissing him, her head moving in a slight circular motion, the two alternating tendons of her neck flexing gently as she moved. Her hips had the same rotation, forward and back, powered by the slight shift onto her right knee and then back onto her left.

She pulled back from him and smiled. She gestured to the car behind her, a 1964 Chevy Impala. It was silver and had seen better days before the Louisiana sun and humidity took its toll, eating away the paint. She pulled her keys from the purse and unlocked the passenger's door. She pushed the front seat up and climbed into the back, looking at him the whole time with an impish grin. She reached for his left hand and pulled him in with her. He shut the door behind him and she pulled him on top of her, kissing him with all her might, her body moving under him, rubbing against him with almost every inch of her front side. He undid the buttons on her blouse and his fingers touched her satiny black bra. She squeezed his hand gently to slow him down and then reached for her purse on the floorboard.

She pulled out a cigarette-sized joint and a lighter, popping the spark wheel under her thumb. A flame crackled up. She lit the joint and inhaled, flat on her back under him. He was propped up on his arm, hovering over her. She blew a stream of the sweet smelling smoke up at him.

"Come here," she said, moving her face close. Her voice was throaty with smoke. "Open your mouth. Get ready to breath in."

She inhaled and then exhaled, pursing her lips to blow a narrow column of smoke as she pulled his face only an inch away. He inhaled the stream of cool smoke from her mouth and blew it out. She then held the joint, burning fast, to his lips, and he sucked in hard. This time it was much stronger. He felt the hot smoke penetrate deep into his lungs. He withheld the urge to cough. Almost immediately he could feel it slipping into his brain, through his shoulders like warm soup in his veins, relaxing him, making him warm and happy, at ease. He soon was very stoned. Sherry took one long last puff and put the joint out in the metal ashtray in the armrest behind her head, clicking the aluminum top of it shut. Her blouse had fallen all the way open, showing the smooth tanned skin of her stomach. She lifted up onto one side and reached behind her, and then back down again as she pulled her bra away. He stared at her bare tits. Delores Arceneaux crossed his mind.

"Come here, Mr. Tom…my radio man," Sherry said, sultry as could be, putting her hand behind his head, guiding him. He pressed his lips and tongue to a dark nipple, following her lead from there.

After their night in New Orleans, he began seeing Sherry Groveneaux once or twice a week, always on her schedule. She took to calling him on occasional mornings before she went to work, inviting herself over to his small room to get in his bed. He tried calling her often but rarely was able to reach her. She lived in an apartment with three other girls who never knew where she was or when she would be back. When he and Sherry lolled in his bed after midday sex, he would ask her if he could take her to dinner and a movie, to a Saints game in New Orleans, maybe spend the weekend in the French Quarter. But she was always busy, working, visiting her large extended family in Lafayette, or going out with her girlfriends. She had an active life outside his room but he was not part of it.

Having Sherry in his bed thrilled him like nothing else before, but he was lonely when she wasn't around. He wasn't part of the college crowd so he didn't have much opportunity to meet anyone his own age. The students were in class during the day when he was free, and at night he was working while they went out. He still went home to Mama every weekend on his one day off. His few co-workers were much older and either married with children or bitter, hard-drinking men who had worked at numerous radio stations across the country, never staying in one place for more than a year or two. The older deejays resented Timber, at the youthful age of twenty, ascending to their ranks. He saw very little of them. Only when he went on the air in the late afternoon was anyone else in the station. They would soon clear out and leave him alone. That was fine with him. He was happy with his hands on the knobs that controlled the airwaves, projecting his voice out to all of Baton Rouge. He sat in the dark radio booth, imagining Sherry listening to him or picturing LSU co-eds driving in their cars, on the way to fraternity parties, hearing his voice.

He tried to fight off the depressing spells with weekly visits home but his lonely bug traveled right along with him. Nothing at home brought him happiness. Mama was more church-obsessed than ever. She talked about little else.

Bev was still a pest. Her cottonlike platinum hair had grown long, well past her narrow shoulders. She had big blue eyes and a flawless complexion, a face symmetrical with delicate features. Timber's mama was worrying about her, worrying that she was only eleven but was already getting attention from older boys at the junior high, gawky boys who often called on the phone and slinked by the house, peering from the street. Bev spent most of her waking hours at home on the phone, his mama said, often late into the evening. Mama said she tried to make her hang up at nine but sometimes, when she couldn't sleep, she'd check and find Bev sitting on the corner of her bed, her knees pulled up to her chest, deep in conversation. On many of Timber's visits home Bev wouldn't be there, sleeping over at a friend's house on Saturday night, something Mama allowed only if she met up with her in church the next day. It was fine with him if he didn't see Bev at all.

Timber used his Sunday afternoon shift as an excuse to leave Whitcomb early without having to go to church. "I can't, Mama, I've got to work," he said, although he had plenty of time because he did not go on the air on Sunday until six at night.

Pangs of guilt crept up in him when he left and she hugged him at the door, her eyes moist, talking about how she wished he would go to Sunday school and the morning service. She stood in the doorway pleading with him, recalling his child-hood when they'd gone together, speaking of it as if it had been another lifetime, a million years ago. He'd tried to appease her with half-lies, promising that he'd go to church with her soon, "maybe next week" if he could get permission to go into work a little later. He knew he most likely wouldn't go, not next week, not until Christmas rolled around, and then not again until Easter. It was one of the very few times he'd ever been less than truthful with his mama. But there was a new woman in his life. Sherry Groveneaux was coming to see him after Sunday Mass.

The first time Sherry came over she'd brought gin, tonic, limes, ice and two heavy glasses to Timber's sparse apartment. She mixed up the highballs at his kitchen sink, talking the whole time about her co-workers at the restaurant, her family, her dog. He sat in his bed near the door of the kitchen and watched her as she worked, her quick hands, gracious but strong, splintering the ice with a butter knife, squeezing the lime with her slender fingers, stirring the drink and taking a girlish sip, and then an "ah, that's good, *baby*, that's *so* good. You are gonna like this."

Gin tasted to him like sap sucked out of a pine tree, the taste of green fresh pine needles on his tongue. He sipped it and scowled.

"What's wrong, *baby?*" she said, her dark-as-night orbs twinkling, a flash of the brilliant smile. "You don't like *gin?*" He took another sip to cover his distaste and then smiled at her, the lime and pine tree taste bubbling in his mouth.

"No, Sherry, you sweet thing," he said, low and deep, a voice he could tell she liked, that radio-strength timbre. "It's great. I like it very much."

She smiled and set her drink down on the nightstand. She took his glass from his hand and set it down too. She reached to his waist and pulled up his shirt, removing it over his head and tossing it to the floor. Her hands grazed his chest. She tugged at the waistband of his boxers, and he hurriedly slid them off. She stood by the bed and threw her blouse and skirt over a chair, slid her black panties down over her long olive legs, and then reached both hands behind her, pausing. Her eyes smoldered, watching his anticipation as she undid her bra and revealed herself to him.

She moved to him on the bed and they did what she had come to do. She was in control and on top for a start, on top of him until she rolled over and pulled him into her, wrapping her legs around behind him as she started to moan, bucking against him in a bear hug, shaking the mattress on its flimsy metal frame until he was sure it would collapse. She moaned until she began to scream, her screams always brought him to the finish as well, a swelling, shooting, a dream in his mind. He could feel her tremble from the inside out.

Afterward, they lay back and sipped their drinks. She said there was something about going to Mass that always made her want to have a drink and get laid.

"I mean—baby—I gotta have something to confess." She was sitting naked on his mattress, her back against the wall. Her laugh was lilting and soft, a sweet giggle drifting through his room.

The taste of gin was growing on him as he tried to put the image of his mama and sister in a church pew out of his mind. His past in Whitcomb was starting to fade out like a far-off radio station in the opposite direction from where he was driving, a fast-dying signal at his back.

Another year passed. He was alone in the station, about halfway through a set of hit songs—"Tie a Yellow Ribbon 'Round the Old Oak Tree," "Bad Bad Leroy Brown" and "Crocodile Rock"—when he got the call at midnight, a Friday in the summertime, 1973.

He was coming up on his three-year anniversary at KKPX-AM, most of that time on the long afternoon and evening shift that ran until midnight, playing the top forty hits, reading the news, running the tapes of talk shows and canned programming. Whatever Mr. Robelot put down on the play sheets he did. The old man occasionally told him, "that big voice of yours sounds great, Little Tom," but he hadn't offered him a raise yet. He was twenty-one years old and he was making only $88 per week, a salary far below what school teachers and policemen and secretaries made, despite the fact he was somewhat of a celebrity. Sherry continued to come see him twice a week, every Wednesday and Sunday before his shift, although that seemed as far as the relationship was ever going to go.

Most callers on Friday nights were kids requesting love songs. He answered the phone on the third ring.

"KKPX-AM."

An older man's voice, loud with a slight drawl, authoritative. "Tom Goodman?"

"Yessir."

"This is Ronald Fountaine. I own KWPT-FM in *Houston*, Texas." The words rolled off his tongue like he was introducing royalty. "We are the up-and-coming country station. I bought it last year and changed the format."

"Yessir." Timber did not know what to think. The second line began to ring and he ignored it.

"I've been over here visiting my in-laws and heard you. You gotcha a great radio voice, son, a strong one."

"Thank you, sir."

He paused.

"And I need me a new deejay. The demo tapes I've been getting ain't worth a pot of piss....You know anything about country music, son?"

His daddy had played some country, only the most popular stuff, but Timber was not the kind to buy records or follow bands. He preferred Cajun music or American rock 'n' roll like Elvis and Chuck Berry, much of which had fallen out of favor in the early seventies for hippie music and the Beatles.

"Yessir, a little," he said.

"What you don't know, I can teach you," Ronald Fountaine said. "You ever been to *Houston*, Texas?"

"No sir."

"Well, son, it's a sight to see. And you—I hope—are headed this way."

LOVE OFFERING

She sat in the sixth row on the right side, by the aisle, a redhead with long straight hair that fell past her shoulders and down her chest, trickling into her cleavage. She held her neck straight and her posture perfect—uncommon in Piney—a town of slumpers and slouchers, flabby jowls and beer guts.

Zeke had been sitting in his office, talking with the sound man, a volunteer from the congregation who helped with his radio broadcasts, when he first saw her through his window. She stepped out of her father's patrol car and was graceful enough to walk through the gravel like it was a red carpet. She had on high heels and a snug green knit dress with bare shoulders and a cut that exposed her thigh when she was at the longest point of her stride, a shape he could not forget even after one glance. He'd heard about Jolene Wiggins, the sheriff's only daughter. Reliable rumor had it that she'd run off with an older man to Los Angeles about eight years ago when she was only seventeen, a man with money who saw her in a mall in Atlanta, and talked her into auditioning for movies. She fell for it, and him. He ultimately died from an overdose of cocaine. She got drunk and crashed her car down a Hollywood hill but survived. Her father went out there and rescued her, bringing her back to Piney where she had been for about six months, recovering from a deep depression. Zeke had never seen her before. He couldn't see that anything was wrong with her.

The Church of the Rock was almost full. Ever since he had started broadcasting on the radio, the pews filled up, the regular congregation steady and new faces every week. Word of mouth had spread like crazy through Piney. He would need to expand the sanctuary within a year or two at the rate he was going. Nothing would be worse than to have to turn away souls from the house of the Lord. He *would* raise the money to do it.

The fact that the sheriff, previously a Piney Baptist man, would bring his daughter to his church was a sign of the rise of his credibility, the ascension of his ministry. Zeke understood that the sheriff probably didn't want to parade his troubled daughter in front of the leading social set at the *big* church, and it always would be the *big* church, just as every small town had its *big* church where those who had to be seen were seen. But the sheriff knew he had a daughter who needed religion. She needed Jesus at this time in her life to reach out to her and help heal deep wounds. Word was that she had been suicidal, the word coming from a good source, Janelle Harrison, the dispatcher at the jail who was a close confidante of the sheriff and a longtime member of the Church of the Rock.

Zeke could see how Jolene could be the kind of woman to get into trouble. She was about twenty-five and stood about five feet seven inches tall. She knew how to wear heels and a dress and how to fix her hair and carry herself in a package that caught men's eyes from a distance, a movement subtle and yet piercing, the kind of wiggle that drew him to the window during his conversation with the sound man about the morning service. He forgot what he'd been saying.

He stood in the pulpit that morning and looked right at her, meeting her green eyes staring back at him, her lips pursed slightly as she listened, watching him. Something bubbled up inside him. He had not had this kind of desire for a woman in a long time, all the way back to Cindy Daniels in high school. He was inspired to a great sermon, calling up the fires of hell but talking about the rough waves of the Red Sea parting, the cool water of salvation, the peace that passed understanding that only the good word of the Lord could bring. Jolene Wiggins was the first one down front that morning to be saved. It was as though the rest of the congregation had parted for her, expecting her to lead the way, to follow some sort of destiny. He stood on the church floor before the pulpit and greeted her. She held out her hand and bent to kneel, but he reached for her and hugged her, pulling her to him, speaking into her ear, through that long tangle of red hair, telling her that he would take care of her, that Jesus Christ was Lord and cared about her soul, and that she would be in His ministerial care. He hugged everyone that came forward, but she...she was different.

He had spoken the Lord's words to her but the passion was all his. He could feel the love—desire, lust, whatever it was—raging inside him. He knew it to be ridiculous, illogical, a dangerous freight train of desire and fears and anger and need yet he was powerless to it, unable to reason with the burning desire within him. He knew that he would have a devil of a time with this woman.

Six Sundays after Jolene Wiggins stepped down front and entrusted him with her soul, Zeke invited her to go fishing with him. He waited for her at the church on a Tuesday morning. He had never before taken anyone from his congregation fishing with him, reserving the mornings on the lake for himself alone, a private pleasure where he could sit and think without the common conversations or interrogations that marked all of his interaction with churchgoers. There was something peculiar in the way people approached a preacher, a look of suspicion in their eyes, as though they wanted to see him fall. He'd remembered teachers at the seminary talking about this, how everyone was doubtful, almost hoping for a failure or transgression, a weakness, a slip to reveal that he was a son of man, not just a man of God. He never completely relaxed or let his guard down with people. A few of his congregation he liked to chat with, but for the most part he kept to himself when he could. He certainly protected the solitude of his lake. There were times when he was younger he had sat in his boat and spoken aloud to Jesus, talking specifically about his own soul, his desires, his sins, his guilt at not being a better preacher, a better man, a better child of God. It had kept him on a straight path. He had occasionally taken his children with him and taught them how to fish but they were never eager to go back. They were content to stay home and play video games or go to the mall and walk around, talking to friends. He had taken Mary fishing a few times before but he didn't encourage it, nor did she act like she wanted to be there. Her last visit to the lake had been almost ten years ago, and it had been four years since the last time she said she'd like to go out there with him again. He knew it was just talk. They had no desire to be together on the lake or anywhere else for that matter. Married twenty-one years, they saw each other aplenty as it was. He had no passion for her, but her penchant for keeping her mouth shut and leaving him alone was a great asset in a wife. He wouldn't have lasted a year with a nagger.

Jolene was about an hour late. Zeke was sipping black coffee and gazing out the window where he could see the parking lot and the hills across the road stretching into the horizon. Fall was coming on strong in the leaves, red and brown and orange, and the high grass in the pasture and along the roads was thinning and drying, its summertime green fading to hay. She pulled up at nine, much later than he ever started out for a fishing trip. She drove her daddy's old GM pickup truck, his extra vehicle since he usually drove a big blue Ford Crown Victoria with his name and title painted in cursive on the side. She parked and got out of the truck. She had her long hair pulled back tight in a ponytail that reached almost to her waist. She wore tight jeans that ended just past her knees, revealing slender calves and a button-down shirt that she tied up about her belly to show her hips and navel. The shirt had a light green checkered pattern, a shade of green like her eyes, bringing out their emerald color as she crossed the parking lot and stepped into the church door.

He watched with rapt attention and, for the first time in awhile, thought of his daddy. Big Zeke would have liked this woman. He could remember the sparkle that would appear in his daddy's eyes when a lithesome woman would pass his way, a devilish half smile. He could feel that very same expression on his face right now—a carbon copy of his daddy's leer.

Zeke had gone back to Armstrong the previous year to identify the old man after he had suffered a heart attack and driven his car off a dirt road and down into a gully, slamming into a pine tree. Big Zeke had lost his church when Luke Slicker had died. Luke's son, who inherited everything, saw no need to support a crazy country preacher and shut down the Church on the River. Big Zeke didn't last a year until he passed. Zeke was surprised he made it that long without a church to call his own, no pulpit to preach from. He and Zeke had not spoken since that night twenty-seven years before when Zeke found out about his mama's death.

The loss of the Church by the River also meant the loss of the family graveyard behind it, a one-plot cemetery where only his mama had been buried. When he had gone to Armstrong to administer his daddy's will, he'd driven down to see her grave and found that it and the old ramshackle warehouse that had been the church was gone, replaced by a large gravel lot with a high chain link fence to protect an army of bulldozers, dump trucks and ditch witches. A fleet of heavy-duty machinery rested over his mama's grave, if she was even still in the ground. Most likely, she was still there, the only evidence left of his daddy's Church on the River. Elbow Creek hadn't changed much except for a concrete culvert up a little ways that poured rainwater out of it when the storms came up, but otherwise, it remained fairly low, trickling.

He had braced himself for the visit to the house. All those old memories, his mama's dark circles under her eyes and his daddy's bloodshot, the creaks and groans of all those long struggling nights, nights of hurt and anger that seemed they would never end, a million hours of darkness and suffering before the sun came up. But while it was interesting to see the old place, he was not upset or traumatized by the memories. He was a true man of God, confident in his work, in who he was, even to the point where he had no doubts about his robbing of the banks, his outside-the-law collection of money for the offering plates.

The house, home to his daddy for almost fifty years, was bleak and unkempt. Nothing had changed except that odds and ends were stacked everywhere on top of the old furnishings. Hymnals and Bibles from the church were scattered about the floor and several piles leaned precariously by the fireplace, gathering dust. Broken chairs were stacked about the room. Zeke's old room was full of metal folding chairs and tarnished candlesticks. The large desk Big Zeke had kept in the trailer by his church stood on its side. In his daddy's bedroom, the sheets were unmade, crumpled in a pile, yellow and dusty. The kitchen stunk of mold and mildew and rotten food, flies buzzing everywhere. It was littered with broken glass and beer cans and depleted bottles of Jack Daniels and Early Times. Empty dog food cans were all over the floor. A small garbage can in the corner overflowed. Chicken bones were strewn about. He looked around for five minutes before leaving.

It took Zeke only three hours to dispense of this dingy past. He paid Bryce and Son's Funeral Home to cremate the body and dispose of the ashes however they saw fit—knowing full well that Daddy would have adamantly wanted to be buried in the earth. He gave all the contents of the house to a local junk store owner on the condition that he agreed to take everything and throw out the trash. He signed his acceptance of the will, taking ownership of the house. He then hired a local realtor and signed over the power of attorney to him with instructions to get the best price he could and send him a check and a copy of the contract when it was done. He never set foot in Armstrong again.

He was quite surprised six weeks later to get a check for $40,000, twice what he had expected for the old homestead. He put it away in a savings account for himself—Mary didn't need to know about it. With the money in cash from the banks and the proceeds from the house, he was sitting on much more than $100,000. Surely Jolene Wiggins would be impressed with that.

She rapped on the church office door and brought him back to the present.

"Hey, how're you?" he said, greeting her, opening the door to the sanctuary.

"Hey. I'm doing great. Sorry I'm late." She stepped inside, looking toward the pulpit. The church was quiet and bathed in soft light through the eastern windows. "I hope those fish don't quit biting."

"We'll find out. Do you want some coffee? I'm going to get me a cup."

"No, I'm fine."

"I'll be right out. You can meet me at my truck and I'll lock up."

He held the truck door open and shut it behind her. He had packed it with fishing gear and a cooler of sandwiches and soft drinks. Zeke had bought the old light green truck from Reverend Thomas when he went in the nursing home in the eighties. It was old, a 1971 model, with a front license plate that said "Jesus Saves" emblazoned with a cross.

He could hardly believe she was sitting next to him and tried hard not to stare. Her movement and posture were delicate, like a praying mantis poised on the branch of a tree. She was quiet on the first stretch of road, sitting primly, politely responding to his small talk about the weather, fishing, the church. He hated small talk, although as a preacher he had become good at it. He let the silence rest between them for a minute. The morning was clear and the woods fresh with fall and redness in the hardwoods, a blue sky without the haze of summer. A light breeze gently ruffled the grass and crisp leaves. They passed a cleared pasture, the grass fading green, full of Holstein and Jersey cows, white and black and red, circling and chewing and pissing and shitting around a red barn on the edge of the sloping field.

"How's your daddy like having you back at home?"

"I know he's so happy to see me. He's so sweet to me. My daddy is just the sweetest man ever. He's been so good to take me in—to keep an eye on me there for the past four months. I had some hard times out West."

Zeke started to say that he'd heard something about that but she cut him off and kept right on talking.

"So I know Daddy wished things had worked out for me out there. Can you believe I was there eight years? Eight long years. I never dreamed I'd be back here. But I'm glad I am. I'm lucky I've got somewhere to come home to."

Zeke started the truck down the narrowing dirt road until he came to the pond. The woods had thickened and the pines were mature, tall.

"It's so pretty and peaceful out here," she said. "It's just beautiful. Gorgeously beautiful. Thank you so much for inviting me. I bet you bring lots of people from the church out here, don't you?"

"Well," he paused, "every now and then. But I can't bring everybody, so don't tell folks you came out here with me. People tend to get jealous, so I don't bring folks that often."

He parked and got out. He pulled out the fishing poles, the cooler and his tackle box, shifting the cumbersome load to keep it balanced until he set it on the ground by his fishing boat. He went back for the paper sack with a plastic container of Red Wigglers. He kept his boat near the same spot that Reverend Thomas had tied up his old rowboat. Zeke had bought a much bigger boat a few months back that he kept covered with a tarp and chained to a tree. It had three broad, benchlike seats.

She stepped out and watched him begin to remove the tarp and unlock the chain.

"Can I help?"

"No, I got it. We'll be on the water in a jiffy."

Soon they were on the pond, the boat drifting, he in the back, rowing gently, she sitting in the front but turned back to face him, the sun hitting down at her in an angle, illuminating her red hair, pulled back tight on her head. She smiled wide, teeth as white as new typing paper.

"Ah! It's so good to be back in *sweet old* Georgia. I hadn't been fishing since I was a little girl, probably twelve years old."

Zeke did the calculation in his mind that she was a little girl not that long ago. He thought about how much her life had changed and how little his had progressed in the same time span.

"You think you'll stay here, in Piney?" he asked.

"I don't know. I used to think I could plan and predict my life—I was going to be a star, you know—but now I try to take it day by day. That's what my counselor told me to do, my counselor back at the hospital in L.A., that is. I don't have anyone here to talk to."

"You can talk to me."

"Do you mind? My daddy says he's heard nothing but good things about you. He really agrees with your sermons too. He and I listened to all of them on the radio before we came. That's why we chose your church. He was hoping that I could tell you about my problems…I'm doing a lot better."

"Sure, please do. The Lord doesn't want us to keep things bottled up inside. He wants us to share with our brothers and sisters and ease our burdens."

Zeke stopped paddling and dropped the small anchor over the side. He picked up a fishing pole. She reached for the other pole.

"No, hold on, let me get that for you." He laid the pole across his lap and opened the container of Red Wigglers and pulled one out. He jabbed the hook through its tail, coiled it around and then jabbed it again near the head. A pus-like fluid oozed onto his fingers. He dipped his hand into the water to clean it. He glanced at her to see if she was going to be squeamish but instead she looked fascinated, like it was something she'd never seen before. She leaned forward, closer to him. She smelled like gardenias.

"Wow," she said. "My daddy used to do the worms for me. Let me do the next one. I don't mind getting my fingers dirty."

"Do you know how to cast?"

"Let me watch you. Maybe I'll remember."

"I tell you what. Sit on this middle seat here, next to me."

She moved. He put his hand on her shoulder to guide her. He held the reel in front of her with his left hand and moved behind, reaching around with his right hand to where he had both arms around her. He guided her, pressing the button on the reel and then released his thumb, casting the line out. The worm and the hook and a few small lead weights on the end of the line zipped through the air, sailing out of the coil inside the silver Zebco reel, splashing into the still water about twenty feet from the boat. Her ponytail had flicked up during the cast, tickling his chin. His forearm grazed her hips and chest in the motion. He was aroused but tried to act like touching her didn't faze him. He cast his line out and sat back on his seat across from Jolene. She sat poised, holding the line in front of her.

"Now, we wait," he said, "for 'em to start biting." He rested his fishing pole on a seat, the tip propped on the edge of the boat and the line drifting in the water. "Relax. You can set the line down. It might be awhile, if they bite at all."

"I don't care if they do or not. I'm having a great time like this. The only thing we might be missing is if we had a few cold beers."

He didn't respond. Her eyes widened, as though she realized she shouldn't suggest drinking to a Baptist preacher. He hadn't had anything to drink since high school, and even then he'd drunk very little. He wasn't one of those country reverends who constantly preached against the evils of drinking, although he had seen the damage it could do to many a man, his father foremost.

"Oh, I don't mean I wanted to," she said. "I meant it would be fun if it was the right thing to do, but I know it's not right. My counselor wants me to stay off all alcohol and drugs. I've been good every day of the six months I've been home. Daddy has even quit drinking himself because of me. He threw out his liquor and doesn't even buy beer anymore, something he always used to do to relax. He's lost some weight, if you hadn't noticed."

"I thought he was looking good last time I saw him," Zeke said. "No offense taken about the beer. A cold beer doesn't sound half bad." She gave him a sheepish smile. "Don't feel like you've got to hold back on anything you might say with me. Anything...*anything*...you want to say is just between you, me and the Lord. Tell me what you feel. Why don't you just start at the beginning when you first left Piney? How'd you end up out there?"

She paused, furrowing her groomed brow. The boat sat still in the placid water, the water more blue than brown with the sun overhead. The leaves on the hardwoods high on the hills surrounding the lake were deep red and orange, but the trees bordering the lake, lower down, were still hanging onto a touch of green. The stand of pines on the south shore didn't change with the seasons.

"Well…" She halted. "Let me see." She took a deep breath. "I met my husband in a mall in Atlanta when I was down there with some friends. He was so sweet and handsome and funny. He was older, I knew that, but I thought he was twenty-one. He turned out to be thirty but by the time I found that out I didn't care, I was so deep in love with him. He had been an extra in movies and said he was beginning to work as a producer and that he was scanning the mall for pretty faces. He was a smooth talker. But I loved him. I really did love him."

She sighed again and her shoulders, usually held in perfect posture, sagged. Zeke watched her as she spoke, but she kept her eyes down. She stopped speaking. He leaned over and put his hand on her shoulder.

"It's all right, Jolene, it's all right."

She smiled faintly and continued.

"Everyone around here tells the story like I ran off the day I met Michael. I didn't. He gave me his business card and I gave him my number. He told me to call him collect anytime. I did. We had the most *beautiful* conversations, late into the night after my daddy went to bed or when he was out working on a case. Michael was so sweet and understanding of me. He told such fantastic stories of the Hollywood nights, the deep blue California ocean, glittering hills. I fell for him *so so* strong, I'm telling you.

"I told my daddy about him—I didn't tell Daddy his name—but I told him I was in love with a man in California and I wanted to move there when I graduated. Daddy freaked out. He started monitoring my calls and took the phone out of my room. He also begged me to tell him Michael's name, but I wouldn't do it. I was afraid what Daddy might do, him being a police officer and all. I called Michael from pay phones at school and at the 7-Eleven near the house. I was really upset with my daddy because he didn't understand. He wanted to treat me like a five-year-old. I wish I'd listened to him. But I didn't.

"Anyway, the next thing I knew Michael bought me a one-way plane ticket. Two weeks after my seventeenth birthday, I was in his bed in Los Angeles. Things moved really fast then. He gave me champagne or vodka all the time, and introduced me to cocaine. I didn't know any better. I snorted it like it was going out of style. He talked like it was the best thing there ever was, and at the time I thought it was. It gives you *such* a rush. I'll be lying if I said I don't miss it—that thrill of my heart racing and all my nerves tingling. I don't think there's anything like it. I get so bored sometimes I want to scream…"

She lifted her head to look up at him, the green eyes inquisitive, a different tone.

"Have you ever been around anybody hooked on coke? A lot of people in L.A. do it. Have you ever been out there?"

He looked down, trying to imagine what doing cocaine and living in Los Angeles might be like. He'd seen L.A. on the TV but he couldn't get there in his mind.

"No, I've never even been close to California, never west of Alabama." He did not look up, feeling almost ashamed of his simple life. He started to speak but noticed a tug on her line. "Hey, you got a bite."

"Oooh," she said, snatching up the rod and reel. She took the rod in her hands and began turning the handle to reel it in quickly.

"Gentle now," he said. "Give him a little running room. Don't yank it. He's pulling on that thing. He's a *big* ole boy."

"Do you want it?" she said, panicked, gesturing to him with the rod. "Take it."

"No," he said, moving to her seat. "I'll help you with it. We can bring it in together."

He moved onto her seat, reached around her again. This time she leaned back, pressing against him. Her ponytail tickled his face, the nape of her neck white and soft and moist with a bead of perspiration. He smelled her again. *Gardenias.*

The fish gave a strong tug on the line.

"It's gotta be a big bass," he said, low and soft, into her ear, "to pull that hard. He's a big ole boy, that's for sure."

He let the fish take some more line. It swam away from the boat until it was almost halfway across the kidney-shaped pond, more than a hundred feet from the boat.

"He's running off." Her voice was breathless in the chase.

"Yeah, well let's let him get that hook set good and tight. There's a stump over that way the fish hide around sometimes. But I'm not going to let him get that far."

Zeke stopped the line from spiraling out, letting his thumb up on the button and flicking a lever to lock it. The fish gave a big tug. He guessed the bass to be a four or five pounder, a whale for this pond. Only two or three times had he caught a fish so big here, and that had been at least eight years since the last one. The great ones didn't come around that often.

He slowly began to reel the line in, his arms still wrapped around Jolene, her hands draped onto his hands holding the pole, his face inches from the back of her neck. The fish began to swim sideways, circling back, as he gradually moved it a few inches closer to the boat. The fish darted from side to side, one way then the other.

"Oh, we got him hooked good now," he said. "We got him good now." He tightened his grip around her and began to reel in hard. The fish fought back, struggling for all its might. He was always amazed at the power a bass could conjure up. It had been awhile since he had fought one with this much pull.

He reeled in a little more, the fish's fight lessening a bit, until it was only about fifteen feet from the boat. He was thinking of cleaning the bass and building a campfire by the lake for him and Jolene to cook it, maybe even making a run to town to pick up a six-pack of cold beer, when the fish dashed. It leaped out of the water in a streak of glimmering green and silver, about two feet out above the surface, flapping its fin in the air, twisting this way then that. Zeke swore to himself that the fish's cold dark eyes looked right at him, as though to say, "I know who you are, preacher," before splashing back under the white churned water, free from the hook almost as if it had spit it out in spite, leaving only a limp line and ripples rolling outward, slowly to the edges of the pond.

"Oh my *God*," Jolene said, "he got away. He got away. I thought we had him for sure."

"Yeah, he sure did. He sure did." Zeke set the rod down on the boat and moved back to the other seat, gazing out across the water, the line dangling loose. He was upset at losing the fish but he tried not to show it. He wished he could put his arms back around Jolene and hold her, nuzzling his face on her neck.

"It ain't the first one to get away. Sure as shootin', it won't be the last."

It was all he could think of to say, a line his daddy had used. Even that thought had been hard to come by with his arms around her and squeezing her the way he had, feeling her excited breathing in the chase, the brilliant red hair flicking against his neck and his chin. He sat in the boat looking across the water like he had never seen the pond before. It all looked so placid and lifeless, a vacant isolated hole in the ground filled with rainwater and slimy fish and surrounded by trees and leaves that died and came back again each spring, except for the infernal pine, a straight shot of wood that could withstand the wintry blows that came down out of the Appalachians and froze the trees but could not kill them, these thick-barked bastards that had surrounded him all of his life.

She was quiet, sitting in the boat watching the last few ripples of the fish's splash rolling into the bank. He tried to still his mind.

"Let me get another worm on there for you," he said. "We'll get him this time."

"Aw, I don't know. I could take a break and just sit here. I don't know if we'll have such excitement again. Once you have something so exciting, so good like that was—even though we didn't catch him—it's impossible to get it that good again. It's usually disappointing when you try to do something twice…It's never as good as the first time…Besides, I never got to tell you the rest of my story."

"Sure." He looked to his reel, the line still in the water. He tightened it with a turn of the handle.

"So. I told you about the drugs, the coke. I got into it right away. All I did was sleep, do drugs, *fu*—uh—have sex, with Michael. We'd go to the bars, dancing some. He had a friend who had a big house with a swimming pool. I would lie around by it with some of his girlfriends, these gorgeous blonde women with tan bodies you couldn't believe. I never really got to be friends with them. They would lie there nude and encourage me to take off my suit as well. I didn't the first few times but then I did one time after I had several glasses of champagne. It was fun, free. Swimming nude was awesome."

Zeke had to look away as she told the story. He tried not to picture her nude, in the sun, her red bush glistening with water and oil and sweat, her nipples in the sunlight. He tried to block it from his mind. He opened the container of Red Wigglers and stared into it, the tiny little creatures crawling and twisting in the black gooey dirt from the bait shop.

"I'm going to check my worm." He winced, realizing how ludicrous he sounded. She didn't seem to notice, wrapped up in her own tale. He began reeling in his line but gestured for her to continue.

"I'm all ears," he said.

He pulled the line in and rebaited the hook.

"A few nights before my eighteenth birthday, Michael took me to a club that turned out to be a strip club. I was nervous but he told me to relax and have a drink. The women dancing there were unreal—tall, sexy, with fantastic bodies. Most of them had fake boobs, but their legs were long and lean. Of course, there were lots of women in L.A. like that. Sure enough, after half an hour or so, two of the girls I swam with were dancing, swinging on brass poles, pulling off their underwear— panties that had snaps that came undone in the front. They were graceful and sexy while grinding themselves against the poles, sometimes against each other. Michael leaned over to me and said, 'you know how much they make doing that? Several thousand dollars a night, sometimes.' The next night, I was up there.

"It was fun—at first. I liked dancing and didn't mind dancing in front of men. I was doing a lot of coke, so I was wound up the whole time. But then it got to be no fun. The boss of the club pushed me to be dirtier in the lap dances in the private rooms, where I had to sit on their laps and let them touch me, although not on my breasts or between my legs. I told Michael I wanted to quit. He got angry, furious, and screamed at me. He even choked me one time. He said I could move to another club, but I couldn't quit. I didn't know what to do, or how to get away.

He scared me. I still loved him. He was cheating on me too. That really made me crazy. Still does something to me, even though he's dead, it makes me so angry to think that my first love, the love of my life, cheated on me."

Zeke nodded along, still holding onto the reel. Her eyes had a faraway look, a sad green-eyed remembrance. The sun was high in the sky. A light breeze hinted at fall and the coming winter.

"The new club he took me to was in Vegas. He said a change of scenery would do us both some good. Everyone here thinks I spent most of my time in Hollywood, but I was in Vegas about half of the time, four years or so.

"Vegas was worse. The men were pushier, older, drunker. The money was better—the work was awful. And then one day Michael pulled me off the stage and walked me across the street to the little apartment complex where we had been staying. He took me into a different apartment. He gave me a key to it and said, 'this is your room here. Men will give you $1,000 for an hour—sometimes even less time. We need the money. It's just a job. Nothing else. You know I love you and wouldn't let anything bad happen to you.' The room was stocked with paper towels, condoms, disposable sheets like in the doctor's office. It was lit with a red light like a darkroom. It was tiny, just a bed and a bathroom and that was it. The bed and a nightstand with shelves was all that was in there.

"A man was waiting there. He was Russian. Named Vladimir. Michael shook his hand. He wore gold chains and had a goatee."

She paused, hesitant. Her eyes were watering. Zeke could barely listen to the story. It was making him crazy with desire on one level—on another it was making him sick. She took a deep breath and resumed.

"Vladimir told me to undress. He inspected me like I was an animal or a piece of machinery, a new car." Her chin was quivering. She swallowed hard. "And then he did it to me right there. Hard, with Michael watching at the end of the bed. I sobbed and Vladimir slapped me. But he smiled back at Michael when he was doing it. 'She will be very good for customers,' he said."

She began to sob, slowly at first. Her eyes were teary, and she sounded like she was choking when she tried to speak.

"I—I haven't told…anybody that. Not even…my daddy, not even my counselor. Nobody. Oh *Jesus*, I'm so sorry, I'm so *sorry*."

She fell into his arms, bawling. He comforted her, squeezing her tight. After awhile, when the sobbing stopped, she lay down across the seat and he put a seat cushion under her head. He took her ponytail in his hand and smoothed it out. He dabbed her face with a Kleenex. She closed her eyes and reached for his hand.

She held his hand in hers, smooth and cool and soft, caressing his fingers. He just watched her, worrying that her smooth light skin might burn; even though it was October, the rays were strong. He'd let her rest for a while and then they could go in under the shade. Her chest rose and fell with heavy breathing. He sat directly over her. He could see how a man would pay a great deal of money to have something like that, even if for only an hour.

It took her a long time to compose herself. Once she did, he rowed the boat to the shore and helped her out. He flipped it over and they sat on it. He gave her one of his mini-sermons that dealt with forgiveness, one that he had perfected on the inmates. He felt weak and stupid for not being able to come up with one original thought, as individually interpreted for her. But who was he to come up with something original from the Bible? She was moved, holding his hand and squeezing it when they bowed their heads and prayed. After his final *amen*, she opened her eyes and turned right into him.

"Thank you, Reverend Blizzard, thank you so much," she said, hugging him. "I feel so much better, like a huge rock is off my shoulders."

The leaves rustled in the wind. The breeze picked up, a sound like light applause. It was all he could do not to kiss her cheek. There would be a next time. He could bring some beer, maybe a little bourbon. He could buy it on his next trip out of town, right before he robbed another bank.

Sins of the flesh. Lord, how he knew about sins of the flesh. The Bible had much to say about it; as a preacher, so did he. He'd warned many a man, from his pulpit or in counseling, to avoid the temptation of lust, the façade of physical beauty. Sexual attraction he knew to be the Devil at work, an illogical force of nature, a contradictory and cruel motivation that was as powerful as an earthquake, or, having never been to California or anywhere close to an earthquake, what he suspected one would be like: overwhelming, holding you in its grasp, causing you to question your very nature, pulsing through you, from your innermost regions where there normally was no feeling at all, a dull void until it hit and then, Lord have mercy, it was a fire inside, a personal hell, a terrible longing that swelled like a sickness on the mind and the heart, rendering all things meaningless in the universe except that one object of desire.

He lay in bed next to Mary and wondered if he would ever sleep again. Only after a full night of tossing and turning, his mind racing, did he come close to drifting off, but then Mary's alarm clock rang and she began getting ready for school. He could smell coffee brewing, so he crawled out of bed to get a cup and sat staring at the table top or the floor, unable to see anything but Jolene's red hair and green eyes and smooth white skin, lightly freckled up close. He tried to keep from imagining her in high heels and nothing else, dancing on stage before leering men, men who were probably once Christians but had fallen long and hard to Sin City, gambling away the family money, money they should have been saving for the children's college or giving to the church or a gift for their under-appreciated wives, if their wives were still even with them. The gambling bug had never bit him. The sins of the flesh, however, were another story. He was tore up.

The next week they planned to go fishing again. He'd driven up to Johnson City, Tennessee, the previous Friday and held up a local bank, a branch crouched in a valley where a suburb was being built, bulldozers grading night and day. He bought beer and bourbon before the robbery. It was odd, a guilty pleasure after all these teetotaling years. The beers were cold with dew on the cans. He got an urge to sip one on the ride home although he knew he shouldn't while driving. He waited until he was a good sixty miles from the bank he'd robbed before giving into temptation and reaching into the paper sack on the floorboard. He popped the top of a can with his thumb and took a sip. He hadn't had a drink of beer since high school, and even then he hadn't had much. It was somewhere between bitter and refreshing, and he took another sip, feeling the bite on the back of his throat.

Soon, the can was empty and he felt better about life, a relaxing peace. He was tempted to drink another one, he still had an hour to go to get home, plenty of time for another beer, but he knew he needed to go slow with it, not get drunk right away. Only one beer had affected him. He could feel his own blood running hot and fast, the capillaries shifted into another gear. He wanted a second can but he needed the beer for next Tuesday when he and Jolene would go fishing again. He hoped the beer would do the trick. She was all he could think about. Even during the robbery, when he was normally focused, his mind was wandering to thoughts of her, what she felt like inside, what the taste of her nipples might be. He'd handed over his holdup note but was thinking of her. He shook his head and thought of an analogy of adultery and fire he'd used so many times: a man sees a fire burn, can see the flicker of the flame, feels the heat—why would he stick his hand directly into fire? Why burn himself intentionally? The answer he gave was the Devil. The Devil. But he wasn't so sure anymore.

She was there again on Sunday, the same spot in the sixth row. The church was packed but to him she was the only one there, the only one person in the peaceful sanctuary, bright-eyed, sitting up straight, hanging on his every word. She was a bright light in an otherwise dim world, a dim world he had been living in all these years, his mind on cruise control, going through the motions of pretending to lead a full, happy life when in reality he had only been regurgitating the doctrine and catch phrases he had picked up at the seminary years ago. Even the bank robberies and his radio show struck him as dull, mundane, a banal attempt at something more than ordinary. His passion for her was the first real emotion to hit him in a long time, since Cindy Daniels. Even then it wasn't so strong, so consuming. He felt like he was preaching right to her that morning, talking of sin and redemption and about doing what the Lord has planned for you, that He is a forgiving God regardless of what you might have done, that tomorrow was another day, that today is the first day of the rest of your life, that Love, His Love, Jesus' Love, can conquer all. *It was the morning and evening star.* He watched her as he preached, poised in the pew, a ray of sunshine through the frosted glass window dancing in her eyes. He wanted to save her every Sunday, every day.

They fished again on Tuesday. This time he brought the beer in the cooler and had the pint of bourbon under the seat.

She was late again, but only half an hour this time, dressed in tight jeans, a white T-shirt and sneakers. It was unseasonably warm. She had pulled her red ponytail through the back of a baseball cap. They smiled at each other, and he thought this certainly was not her everyday regular smile. Her smile was enhanced by her eyes, green jewels almost trying to speak, the light in them sparkling, dancing. He wondered how she had smiled at the men she had danced for and slept with, if they had been in the glow of the same look. He imagined, no, she had not been as sincere with them, that she'd been hardened, embittered, and her smile then could not have been so warm. She liked him. She was drawn to him. He could tell.

She baited her own hook with a worm, grimacing, laughing, but getting it rigged up. He helped her again with the cast, comfortably this time, his arms around her easy, like it was natural. His hands brushed against the smooth skin of her arms, his elbows grazing a firm breast. They got their lines in the water and settled back on the seats of the boat. She again talked about the beauty of the lake, how nice the trees looked, the glory of the fall day and how warm it was. "Indian summer," she said, repeating herself, "It's an Indian summer." He let her talk, watching her lips part and reconnect, studying her tongue, moist and curved in her mouth. She should have been in the movies, on television.

"I got a little burned last week. This light skin and all, so today, I've got some sun screen." She pulled out a tube and squirted blobs onto her hands and began rubbing it on her arms, her face and her neck. It took every ounce of willpower he had not to stare—he watched the fishing lines, stealing glances at her out of the corner of his eyes.

"Do you want some?" She gestured with the tube.

"No, I'm fine. I've been sitting out on this lake so long without it, I believe I'll be all right. But…I've got a surprise for you."

He reached for the cooler in the middle of the boat and pulled off the Styrofoam top. He pulled out an icy cold Budweiser, beads of moisture glistening on the can as it hit the sunlight, and popped the top and handed it to her. He then got one for himself, popped it open and held it up, as though he was making a toast.

"What is it I've seen people say in the movies? Cheers? Baptist preachers don't do much drinking."

She smiled hesitantly. "That's right. Cheers." She clicked her can against his. He took a big gulp, the strong bite of beer flowing down into his throat. His first reaction was a slight revulsion at the taste. He'd heard of men who sometimes drank ten or more beers in one day—he didn't see how they could do it. But his second sip did go down more smoothly than the first.

She tentatively sipped her beer and looked out across the lake, pensively. She turned back to him, her eyes down.

"Reverend, I don't know how I feel about this, drinking and all with you. My daddy would have a fit. My counselor would say it is a bad idea. I'm not so sure I'd disagree. I know you are just being sweet and all,"—she raised her eyes to meet his—"but it doesn't feel right, although the beer is good. But I know what the Bible says about giving in to temptation. I've been reading it regular, the verses you told me to read."

He knew she was right, that they'd both be better off to pour the beers into the pond and talk about her recovery and the Lord's forgiveness of sin, Jesus' great love. But the fire inside Zeke was too strong. He'd lived a good life and done what he believed the Lord had wanted him to do all these years. But where had it gotten him? He hadn't felt as alive, ever, as when her body had grazed his, when she looked deep into him with those eyes, those curling lips smiling at him.

"It's okay." He gave her a reassuring look. "It's okay."

He reached over and took her hand. His eyes looked straight into hers.

"You know the Bible has good references to drinking sometimes too. In Psalms it gives thanks to God for 'Wine that maketh glad the heart of man.' I don't think drinking is as bad as we Baptist preachers make it out to be. I don't think a few little ole beers will hurt us."

He could hear the preacher inside him, using "little ole," a phrase he normally reserved for the elderly or children's Sunday school classes. It seemed to be working on Jolene.

"Yeah, that's true, isn't it? I was reading the other day—they had wine at the Last Supper, didn't they?"

"They sure did," he said. "But it doesn't have to be our last supper, I hope, to have a cold beer." He half winked at her and she laughed. She then took her first uninhibited swig. He watched her throat, bulging gently up and then back down.

"Ah, that's good," she said.

He took a sip himself. The beer was getting smoother with each taste.

The sun warmed the lake and they each had a second beer. He was feeling as relaxed and happy as he could ever remember, as close to drunk as he had ever been. Her smile was even more radiant. She was talking a mile a minute, not about Hollywood or Vegas, but about happy times when she was a little girl and her whole family would go fishing, or of the little club she and her girlfriends had, playing in her backyard and holding club "meetings" in her daddy's truck trailer. Her voice sounded much more Southern too, the tone rising high up the scale as she finished her sentences. She didn't always sound like a local girl. There was a hint of it in there behind the wearisome California speech, the monotone, a lack of enthusiasm that the Westerners spoke with. The beer had taken all that out of her voice—deep inside she was a Piney, Georgia girl.

"The fish ain't biting worth a flip," he said. He knew they wouldn't since they hadn't put on a fresh worm in more than an hour and a half. "You want to sit on the bank and have a sandwich? I've got some pimento cheese sandwiches in the truck."

"Yeah, I'm getting hungry. And these beers are getting to me, a little." She smiled, a new smile, slightly mischievous as she leaned over and touched his arm.

He pulled in the line and rowed the boat to the shore, holding her as she stepped out onto dry land. He wished he had more beer. Next time he would bring a twelve-pack.

"I've only got one beer left," he said, "so we can share it. I do have some bourbon if you'd like a sip of that."

"Oooh. I'd be lying if I said that didn't sound good, but I don't want to get drunk, and that stuff will make me good and drunk, so drunk that my daddy will notice. I...I...can't. I want to, mind you, but I can't. I better just stick to the beer."

He didn't say anything to that, but got the sandwiches Mary had made for him early that morning from another small cooler in his truck. They sat on a log at the shore and looked out across the pond, still and bluer in the bright sun, no wind, although it was cooler, quite comfortable in the shade of the trees. The sandwiches early that morning were cool and creamy, the pimento cheese soaked into the white bread, softening it to a perfect moistness. They passed the last can of beer back and forth.

"You finish it," he said, handing it to her, about a quarter left. She turned it up and downed it, her throat muscles rippling.

"Ah," she said, "That's good. Now I said I won't drink any bourbon, but a few more beers wouldn't kill me. When I was in high school, and before I fell in love with Michael, me and my friends, boyfriends mainly, we'd ride around country roads for hours, drinking beer, throwing bottles at signs. It was so much fun, listening to music, cruising. Sometimes we'd just go out into a field and dance."

He told her he would buy some more beer and they could ride around awhile. They packed up the fishing gear and left the pond. He drove to a 7-Eleven about fifteen minutes away. He gave her money and stayed in the truck when she went into the store to buy more beer. He had driven north of Piney, the opposite end from the church, but he was still nervous. It was a small town and people talked—gossip was the number one pastime. Lord, how a story of him and the sheriff's good-looking, troubled daughter buying beer together would travel around town. The news would move quicker than wheels. He hoped that not many people would recognize his old truck—he only used it for odd jobs and when he went fishing. He also had put on a baseball cap and sunglasses, his usual bank robbing attire, so no one would notice him.

He sat low in the seat while she bought the beer, watching her over the dashboard. The store clerk, a teenage boy, checked her out, staring at her ass as she skipped back to the truck.

He drove farther north, a beer between his legs, sipping on it when there were no other cars in sight. They passed few other vehicles as he had taken the winding dirt roads through Booger Hollow, a loosely defined crossroads that everyone pronounced Booger *Holler*. They cruised down the dusty roads, some freshly scraped by a road grader, but others narrow and rutted still from the summer rains, passing small old farms, a few with barns rotted and long in disrepair, collapsing under the weight of rusted tin roofs. At the old Stone family place, two silos, long abandoned, were beginning to sag and lean. Weeds had grown high in the summer, strangling the house.

Jolene was drinking her beer fast. She finished her first one from the store before he'd even drunk half of his. They were drinking from bottles, long-neck Budweisers. She rolled down her window and took the empty bottle in her hand, gripping it upside down, and leaned on the door, letting her arm hang out, intently watching the side of the road through the open window. As they approached a road sign with a large arrow indicating a fork in the road, she shouted, an excited voice.

"Don't slow down! Stay to the right."

He sped up and she reared back her arm and let the bottle fly right before they passed the sign. It shattered with a booming explosion against the metal marker, splintering into a thousand pieces of brown glass. He looked in the rear-view mirror and saw the sign wobbling mightily, from side to side, a punch-drunk soldier unsteady on its one leg. She raised her right hand out the window in a closed fist and put her left hand on his shoulder, squeezing him.

"That was *awesome!* A *perfect* shot. I hadn't done this in years. Did you hear that thing when it hit?"

Her hand stayed on his shoulder, her finger soft on his neck above his collar. He turned onto a gravel road and she shifted, moving her hand from his neck. She took another beer from the sack on the floor.

"You ready for another one?"

He lifted his beer to his lips and chugged down the remaining third and then shifted the bottle to his left hand, taking the wheel with his right. He sped up and cocked his arm, a railroad crossing sign in his sights. He awkwardly slung the bottle at the sign but it sailed wide left and flew end over end, landing into a ditch overgrown with dry grass.

"Aw!" she said. "That was a good shot too. It ain't easy to hit them, especially left-handed. We never did do this in California. That's a shame considering all the driving you do there, all the road signs."

"Well, at least I'm ready for another one now."

She laughed a throaty laugh and got another beer for him, opening the twist top with her T-shirt. When she did, the belly of the shirt bunched up and pulled out away from her, he could see all of her bare stomach and some of her bra—white lacy cups.

She handed him the beer and began to fiddle with the radio, tuning into a South Carolina country station that played old country—Waylon Jennings, Willie Nelson, Johnny Cash. She turned it up. Willie's "Whiskey River" came on. He tapped his hand on the steering wheel with the rhythm and she sang along with it:

Whiskey River take my mind,
don't let her memory torture me.
Whiskey River don't run dry,
you're all I've got, take care of me.

They drove all afternoon, drinking beers, throwing the bottles at signs, him getting drunk, driving slower, but feeling warm and happy and carefree as never before, enjoying the country music in a way he had never thought possible. She was out-drinking him, a beer or two ahead, talking fast when she wasn't singing, talking about her childhood again.

Soon the sunlight began to grow slanted on the earth as the day wound down. They were far northeast of Piney, almost into South Carolina, not too far from North Carolina as well, a good sixty miles or more from home. He looked down at the dashboard clock and was amazed to see it was almost five. It seemed the day had passed in only a few minutes. He knew they should head back, that Mary would soon, if she hadn't already, begin to wonder where he was. More importantly, Jolene's father would wonder about her. These thoughts of responsibility flickered in his mind for a few moments and he turned around to head toward home. But then he looked at her and all Christian reasoning passed from his mind. She was again reaching into the sack.

"Only two left," she said. "Maybe we'll need that bourbon after all." She cut her eyes at him. "But first, I got to pee."

He drove toward the interstate to find somewhere with a bathroom she could use. He had to go, too, and would have been fine pulling off to the side of the road and relieving himself behind a tree, but he didn't know how she would feel about it. He'd let her suggest it if that's what she wanted to do. He would've liked to see her pull down her jeans in the bushes, but she wanted indoor plumbing.

They were near the South Carolina state line, almost eighty miles from Piney. He hadn't put that many miles on his old truck in the past year combined. He got onto one of the state roads, slightly busy with cars at the end of the workday, and followed the signs toward Interstate 85. He was surprised how far north the winding trail of back roads had taken them, not too far from Anderson, the site of his very first bank robbery almost four years ago. They topped a hill and drove down into the valley where the big highway had been cut. A cluster of fast food restaurants cropped up when the interstate came into sight. He pulled into the Waffle House. She jumped out almost before he came to a complete stop, a half run to the ladies' bathroom, her gait stiff-legged.

He took his time going in. He'd had five or six beers and on his feet he felt very drunk. The people in the smoke-filled restaurant—two lone men sitting at the counter, smoking, and a couple with three young kids in a booth—were blurry around the edges to him, almost not real. A George Jones song wailed mournfully on the jukebox, something about somebody who stopped loving somebody today. He went into the bathroom and stood at the urinal, the acrid smell of stale piss strong in the air, and it took him a long time to get started, but once the stream began, it was like a fire hose, pouring out for what seemed like a very long time. It felt good, relaxing, to pee such a volume, releasing a pressure inside himself that he hadn't realized was so great until it was gone. He washed his hands and shook them dry because there were no paper towels and the hand-dryer machine, on which someone had scratched "push butt, rub hands under arm," did not work.

He stepped back into the restaurant. Jolene was not out yet. He walked outside, passing a woman on the way in who recognized him, widening her eyes and moving her head a little in recognition, a look of slight shock. She went inside the restaurant and he to his truck. He could see the woman through the plate glass window peering out at him. She looked pale, scared. She would look away when she saw him but in a minute or two she would look back again.

Then it hit him: *she* was the bank teller from his very first holdup, not far from here. She had recognized him. He hoped that Jolene would hurry. The relaxing buzz from the beer now pounded like a headache. His palms began to sweat and he felt a trickle of perspiration under his right arm, gliding down his side. The moments ticked by like hours, almost like time had stopped while he and the teller exchanged furtive glances through the Waffle House window.

Jolene finally emerged from the restaurant. She had let her hair down and brushed it out so that the red glowed in the late afternoon sunlight. She had freshened her makeup and put on lipstick. She looked so good that he was distracted from his worry for just a moment, soaking in her glow, but then he saw the teller watching him and the fear came right back.

Jolene was ambling slowly, a little unsteady, a lazy smile on her face. She got into his truck. Before she could get the door all the way shut, he had cranked the engine and was pulling off.

"We need to head on home. I'm going to take the interstate."

He backed up at an angle so it would be hard for the bank teller to read his license plate when he drove away. The truck bumper almost hit a pay phone booth and came within inches of a long-haired shirtless man covered in tattoos.

"Hey, mother fucker! *Goddammit!*" the tattooed man shouted, holding the phone like a weapon he would throw if a cord weren't attached to it. Zeke didn't acknowledge him, but dropped the truck into forward gear and sped off. He barreled from the parking lot onto the street, rushing to the interstate ramp where he pushed the truck up to sixty-five, the highest speed the old truck could travel without rattling uncontrollably.

He was nervous on the interstate, but glad to be heading for home.

"What's wrong?" Jolene said. "You okay?"

"I'm all right," he said, watching his rear-view mirror for anyone following him. He was certain the teller had called the cops.

"I just realized how late it is getting. I want to get on back into Piney."

"I'm hungry," she said. "I need to eat something before too long with all this beer in my stomach. I was kind of hoping we could eat at that Waffle House back there. I haven't eaten there in a long time."

"Oh, I'm sorry," Zeke said. "I can't turn back now. We can get something to eat once we get home. We'll get there pretty quick on the interstate."

Although he was driving sixty-five, sometimes up near seventy, quite a few cars zoomed by him at a faster clip. He thought about his first robbery four years ago, how nervous he had been before, the worried drive back home. He remembered the bank teller vividly. She was the first one, had always been the most clear in his mind. Memories of the more recent ones blended together.

He saw a South Carolina state trooper headed the other way across the median. He worried, but the cop sped past, looking straight ahead. Zeke breathed a sigh of relief. His nerves calmed as they got closer to Piney. The headache brought on by the beer and panic subsided. He couldn't believe a whole day had passed, his riding with Jolene. She was sitting stiffly, against the window, looking out, her elbow propped on the window sill and her hand running along the top of the glass, cracked open slightly. He looked at her and that feeling of longing roared back into him again.

"Hey, we got two more beers," he said. "And a little bourbon too. You want a sip?"

She looked at him coolly for a minute, her first look all day without smiling, but nodded her head, a faint glimpse of a grin rising. She looked like a coy young girl. She wasn't much more than a girl, almost twenty years younger than Zeke. He was about her age when she first came into the world.

She reached into the paper sack and pulled out the pint of Jim Beam. She broke the seal on the bottle and took a sip. She shivered slightly, and then opened a beer, taking a drink from it.

"*Whew!* Needed a chaser for that one...*Old Jimmy B!*"

She handed him the bottle. His left hand guided the steering wheel as he turned it up. The sharp red liquor, pungent and fiery, burned his mouth. He thought for a minute he would spit it out, but he forced himself to swallow, feeling the fluid down his throat and into his chest, warming him, before it traveled further south and sloshed in his belly, mixing uncomfortably with a day's worth of beer.

She watched him, laughing a little. She held the beer to him.

"Get you a chaser," she said.

He took the beer and sipped lightly, the small sips easing the burn of the bourbon on his palate.

"That," he said, "is some *strong* stuff."

"No doubt about it."

He turned his attention to the road. It occurred to him he had been driving sixty-five miles an hour all this time, his vision slightly blurred, and maybe that was dangerous. He slowed down a little.

After another five miles in which she took another shot but he declined, they came to an exit north of Piney. He got off and headed to a little country store. He told her to wait in the truck. He parked at the back, behind the old wooden-sided building, covered in cedar shingles, unpainted. It looked like it was going to collapse any minute. Will's Place was known for its cheeseburgers, served up in wax paper. He got two burgers and fries and some cokes, glad that the old man behind the counter didn't recognize him.

It was getting dark. The clocks had been moved back for daylight savings time the past weekend but it always, every year, took him by surprise when he looked down at his watch and saw dusk coming on well before six o'clock. It was only five-thirty, but the sun was shining flat across the land, the light golden in the hills and on westward signs and tops of buildings and houses not blocked by tree tops. Shadows were gray on the low ground and those surfaces not facing the sun. His truck was parked in the shadows. About twenty minutes of daylight left.

He reached to hand her the sack of food as he got in the truck, but she was screwing the cap back on the pint of Jim Beam, almost half gone. She smiled a big lazy smile at him, her eyes not as wide as they had been.

"Hello, reverend preacher," she said with a slight slur, and laughed. She reached over and touched the back of his neck, her hand warm and smooth, caressing the outcropping of short hair there. He turned, almost leaned forward to kiss her, but instead put his hand on her firm thigh. The bourbon was hot on her breath.

He drove back to the fishing pond. He parked near the edge of the lake, the woods dark but the sky across the pond pink and blue with the white clouds illuminated like floating neon signs. The water was dark and silvery and calm in the falling darkness.

He opened the sack and the smell of the burgers and fries wafted out, warm and moist and delicious. He pulled out the fries, wrapped in a small cardboard boat-shaped container, and offered one to her.

"I think I want another drink instead," she said, and opened the bottle and took another sip, a big one. Again he watched her throat, up and down, rising and falling, her neck thin and firm.

"You're due for another," she said, holding the bottle up to him.

He was sure after the first drink that he did not want another taste of bourbon but she was holding the bottle to him, smiling alluringly.

"Let me pour," she said.

She lifted the bottle and pressed it to his lips. The red liquor flowed fast, a fire in his mouth, and she lifted it still. He took in as much as he could before putting his hand to hers to put the bottle down but some spilled on his chin and dripped down onto his shirt. He swallowed hard. It burned like gasoline in his esophagus. He thought he would vomit, but it passed. She was sitting next to him, screwing the top back on the almost empty bottle. She tossed it to the floor. It clinked against the door. She was up against him, and still moving his way.

"Come here, preacher," she said, her voice low, the words loose in her mouth. "Let me give you a chaser."

And then she was on him. He put his arms around her and her tongue was in his mouth, and his in hers, and she moved against him like a form trying to overtake him and swallow him whole. Soon she pulled back for a second and, her head turned slightly to the side but her eyes still straight, locked on his, slipped off her T-shirt and tossed it on the floorboard. Then she reached around behind her back, and slowly, almost as if putting on a show, unhooked her bra, pausing a moment, her eyes locked on his, liking the way his eyes were looking down, watching her yet-to-be-revealed body. Later and for years after he would think back to that moment, that it was something she had learned in her strip show, how to work the moment of revelation for all it was worth, but in the moment he could only react, like a possum in headlights, soon to be crushed by the bumper of a fast-moving pickup truck.

She revealed herself to him in the faint light of the dashboard. Her skin was white, luminescent with a light of its own, dramatic against the dark black vinyl of the benchlike truck seat. She opened the pint of bourbon and poured a few drops on each of her nipples, the liquid running down, tracing the curves and onto her belly. She reached both of her hands to the back of his head and pulled his face to her chest.

Soon their clothes were all bunched up together on the floorboard and she was on her back, under him, one foot braced in the steering wheel, the other on the empty gun rack on the back window, her head up against the passenger's door.

He pushed against her. She was tight but very wet and he paused for a moment, thinking of where he was about to go, a place where once he'd been there he could never deny having gone. Once you went somewhere like that you couldn't take it back. He moved into her and she began to tremble and scream.

"*Oh* Jesus, oh *Jesus*, oh *Jesus!*" He was tight on top of her, feeling her squeeze him, a series of throbs. He was beginning to feel himself about to peak, a heat running along his nerves like somebody had turned on the electricity into a copper wire, when…a *blinding blue light*…shattered the darkness, a rapid-fire staccato light…on again, off again, on again, off again…a hundred times a second, a frenetic speed, lighting the trees and the pond and the inside of the truck like some crazy movie or a ride at the county fair.

A flashlight from the passenger's side shone into his face and the door was yanked open. He arched back, still inside and on top of her, to see the scowl of Sheriff Don Wiggins. His eyes flickered hate in the blue piercing light. He grabbed Jolene solidly by the hair and yanked her out from under Zeke. She was slick with a sheen of sweat on her back and slid across the vinyl, tumbling onto the ground outside the truck. She fell into the leaves and dirt.

"*Get* in the car," he said to her. She scrambled to her feet, scampering toward the blue light.

The sheriff flicked off his flashlight and hooked it on his belt. He pulled his pistol and pointed it at Zeke, and cocked it with his thumb. It was dead quiet and Zeke could hear a bullet go into the chamber, the barrel right in his face. He then aimed the gun down between Zeke's legs. He was still hard and could smell her scent, a musky whisky gardenia. He backed up against the driver's side door and tried to cover his throbbing slick member. The sheriff held the gun on him for a second before quickly pointing it away and shooting out the windshield, shattering it, the explosion of the gun almost deafening at that range. Powdered smoke drifted into Zeke's face.

"You goddamn lucky I didn't kill you right then, preacher." The sheriff looked onto the floorboard. He gathered Jolene's clothes and shoes.

"I got some things to talk to you about. More than one thing. Be at your house in two hours."

He pointed the gun at him again, this time straight into his face. He leaned forward, touching the barrel to Zeke's forehead, before jerking it to the left this time and shooting out the back window. He turned and stomped off, flicking off the blue light and driving away, leaving Zeke by the lake, naked in his truck, millions of pieces of glass softly glittering by the dashboard light. The shot echoed deafeningly in his ears.

It was in that moment that he lost his religion, the first time he made a life-changing decision without looking inside himself and asking God what to do. Fear and drunkenness and lust had overtaken him. He reacted like an animal, moving only on instinct. He had only one choice: take his money and leave town. He knew the sheriff would ruin him. He suspected the bank teller's sighting would link him back to his truck and the robberies. He had an urge to vomit but fought it, shivering, until it passed.

He gathered his clothes and stepped out of the truck gingerly to avoid getting cut on the broken glass. He put on his shoes and pulled on his jeans and shirt. He wadded his left hand in a rag from the back of his truck and swept away the glass from the truck seat, and then pushed away the remaining shards hanging in the window frames so he could see to get the truck home.

He took a long last look at the pond where he had first fished with the Reverend Thomas those many years ago. It was shiny and black, a flat glistening sheen. He could hear a chorus of crickets and a bullfrog croaking in the night.

He drove until he was almost home and parked his truck way back in the dirt driveway of an old trailer that had long been abandoned. He took the knife Reverend Thomas had given him and he walked the last few hundred yards to his house. It was all lit up inside and he could see Mary moving back and forth in the front of the kitchen window and their daughters, Sarah and Ruth, sitting at the table, talking with her. He wanted to tell them goodbye, but he couldn't. Maybe he could explain things once he got settled, wherever he was going.

He got into his car and slipped it into neutral and let off the parking brake. It rolled back down the incline that was their driveway, toward the road. He was about to turn the key and start the engine when Mary came to the door, backlit by the light of the hallway, in her denim dress. All he could do was wave meekly, with his right hand. She waved back and gave him an inquisitive smile. She looked to the spot where he normally parked his truck, and then back over at him. He turned the key, the engine started and he turned around and sped out onto the road, wheels meeting pavement, making the transition from gravel to smooth surface, leaving the house behind him. He drove in the dark and didn't flip on his headlights until he was several hundred yards away from his home.

He was at the church in two minutes. Jolene's father's truck was still there where she had left it that morning. He kept the engine running and ran into the boiler room, retrieving the old blue hard-shell suitcase stuffed into the trunk, approximately $100,000 in cash in it. He grabbed an extra suit he kept in his office and his Bible. He put the suitcase in the trunk of the car and looked at his watch. Still an hour and a half before the sheriff would go to his house, looking for him. He could go a long way in that time, maybe across Atlanta and close to Alabama by then.

He mashed the gas pedal down and pulled out. He wasn't sure where he was going, but west, toward Vegas, seemed right.

H-TOWN!

At twenty-seven, Timber was a drinker. The bright lights of Houston, Texas, a world away from Whitcomb, Louisiana, summer 1979, another party, this one a celebration of KIX 97 FM's new status as the number one country station in Texas, automatically making it number one in the U.S., number one in the world. He'd grown into a big man, six feet two inches tall, 220 pounds, with broad shoulders and thick forearms. The boyish baby fat that he'd always carried had faded away. He wore his nondescript brown hair blown straight back and down past his collar. Except for the long hair, he looked just like Daddy, something he tried not to think about.

He ordered two tequila shots, sliding one in front of a girl he just met. She was from Corpus Christi, eighteen, moved to Houston fresh out of high school to try out for the Derrick Dolls, the Houston Oilers cheerleaders. She said her last name was Thompson, or something like that, hard to hear at the bar, but her first name was Maria and she said it with a slight accent, explaining that her mother was Mexican, maiden name of Rodriguez. She had long dark hair brushed straight back, falling down around her waist, flicking her bare midriff below the blue tube top, tight white pants hugging her hips, her ass shaped like two bubbles resting on the bar stool. Every man that walked by ogled her, eyes roaming down.

Timber ignored the gawkers and guided her in the tequila shot. He licked the salt off the back of her hand, downed the shot glass and bit the lime. She followed him eagerly, licking the salt off his hand, tossing back the glass and twisting up her face as she took a bite of the lime wedge. She was drunk, clinging onto his arm as she told stories, her breath hot in his ear, the music loud, Lynyrd Skynyrd, tunes he couldn't play on a country format but songs he liked to hear when he was getting a buzz on, even if it was a Monday night and he had to be on the air at six o'clock Tuesday morning.

A tall man in denim and a white cowboy hat with long dark hair jutting out from under it sidled up to him and stuck out his hand, said he was Bobby-Ray-Larry, something like that. Timber couldn't hear with the music blaring, the boisterous chatter of radio personalities, sales people and all sorts of hangers-on carrying on about one thing or another, half an hour past midnight, tequila flowing. Bobby-Ray-Larry had a firm handshake and was in a band from Nashville that had played earlier at a small club on the outskirts of town. Timber had not seen the show but thought he'd heard of the group, a decent sound but maybe a little predictable. The faux cowboy singer gave Timber a cassette, an advance copy of a record due out later in the fall, and asked him to listen. If he liked it would he give it some air time? Timber put the tape in his pocket and said he'd see what he could do.

Bobby-Ray-Larry had two tagalong blondes in tow, the second one giving Timber some serious eye, but half-Mexican Maria was hanging on him like a scarf, her arm around his neck, her body against him like she was his Siamese twin connected at the ribs. The second blonde looked familiar, like he'd seen her somewhere before, maybe in a group that had come back to his condo last summer, after the Hank Jr. show, to do some coke, or maybe he'd met her during one of the rodeo parties in February, the all-night bashes that followed the month of concerts in the Astrodome.

Before he had a chance to ask her a question, half-Mexican Maria said she wanted to go home with him, wanted to go *right now*, and he never passed up the chance at new blood, certainly not Derrick Doll potential. He shook hands again with Bobby-Ray-Larry and led half-Mexican Maria out to his car, a shiny red Karmann Ghia convertible parked in the street, top down. She didn't even notice his limp, slighter these days, his foot not bothering him as much. He shifted his weight onto his stronger leg and picked her up, dropping her in the passenger's side, her laugh loud and long, then a cheer, "all right, Timber," when she hit the seat. She wiggled her ass into the bucket Naugahyde, turning his way. He cranked up the car and they were off to his place, the Volkswagen-engineered motor purring in the compartment behind the seats.

They zoomed through the River Oaks neighborhood where excess oil money flowed, soaked up by the designer stores and artfully lit restaurants and luxury car dealers. Money in the Oil Patch ran deep and thick, pouring from the mansions and streaming down the wide, flat streets to the pockets of anyone willing to lap it up. Half-Mexican Maria had told him she was routinely tipped $100 a night for babysitting.

Timber's condo had plush white shag carpet, two inches thick with a heavy pad underneath. His large feet sank down into it, the cottony strands covering his toes. Half-Mexican Maria had passed out drunk, naked, on her back in his den. He had been hoping to get her into his bed, had eased her out of her clothes, kissing her by his bar when she collapsed, falling back onto the carpet with a thud before he could catch her. At least the carpet was thick.

She looked great naked. He threw a blanket over her and stepped out onto his deck, opening the sliding glass door and letting the warm Houston air float in the window, steamy and soft even in the middle of the night. The buildings in the distance glowed in the muggy air, the oil company skyscrapers glittering silver, shiny black and glassy green.

Timber had quite a view from his condo, the one he bought after taking over the morning drive-time slot on KIX 97 FM. He'd been in Houston six years, having left Baton Rouge in 1973. He'd been promoted at every station he'd worked for, and others tried to hire him away with regularity, even offering him new cars if he would take their jobs. Mr. Perdue, KIX 97 FM's station manager who was known for firing and hiring deejays with flash, gave him the vintage Karmann Ghia as a bonus for taking the job and a salary of $80,000 annually.

Maria was not one of his regulars. She was much more innocent than the usual honky-tonk angels he came across. There was no telling what he'd bring home when he went down to Gilley's in Pasadena. They treated him like a rock star down there, letting him on stage every Wednesday to introduce the bands or to poke a little fun at the shitkickers riding the mechanical bull. They gave him free liquor drinks. Mickey even let him park his car in the fenced-in lot where country stars would park their tour buses along with other VIPs. Hank Jr. was frequently on stage when he was in town.

He checked his watch, a Rolex, given to him by a jewelry storeowner who advertised on his show. He had to be at the station in a few hours to go on the air. The downside of the radio business had always been the getting up so early in the morning, but after two years in Houston he had come up with a routine. He stayed up all night, sleeping after his morning show ended. It was only four hours, and by ten-thirty in the morning he'd be laid up in his waterbed on cotton sheets and fat pillows, sleeping until dusk.

He fixed a pot of coffee. He took it black, drinking it all morning, right up to the end of his show. Sometimes before going on the air he took an occasional hit of speed if it had been a particularly wild night. He didn't mind going on the air with a lingering buzz from the night before. He could hold his liquor.

The red on-air light glowed, illuminating the booth, a low-hung ceiling covered with foam shaped like the inside of an egg crate, a small room designed for ideal acoustics. The overnight deejay, Andy Ray, gave him a dramatic introduction every morning precisely at six: "Get ready, Houston, it's *Timber* time!"

"Good morning, *H-town!*" he said, loudly, louder than most people could shout, but it wasn't a shout at all, just the deep powerful lungs inside him, an effortless voice that reverberated from down in his belly and chest in heavy tones, a baritone that traveled through the radio waves until it filled commuters' cars, enveloping them on their ride to work, his voice deep enough to drown out the air conditioner and the ambient road noise of eighteen-wheelers rumbling by.

"I hope everybody out there is having a good morning…whether you are up in the morning and off to school…heading for the gates of the refinery or an oil rig out in the Gulf…bound to shuffle some papers in one of the glowing glass office towers downtown…Timber is here to play some music for you. Who knows? We might even have us a little fun in between. Here's a new one by George Strait to get us started off right. Take it away, George."

As the jaunty Texas rhythm filled the booth, Timber tapped his foot and drummed his fingers on the desk. He looked through the clear glass window to the adjacent control room to see Andy Ray dancing a two-step with Linda Jean Wanamaker, the morning news girl. He was spinning her in the tight confines, both of them grinning big at six in the morning. Timber liked to think them emblematic of all his listeners out there enjoying his show. He imagined others doing the same all across Southeast Texas.

Timber wished that he could two-step with Linda Jean but his limp kept him from dancing. She was a looker—tall, blonde, filling out her tan slacks and silky white blouse, wearing pearls despite the early hour. He watched her move all over the tiny room, letting her Farrah Fawcett locks fall about her shoulders, bouncing along, Andy Ray dipping her. She and Timber were a team on the air, their patter back and forth the spiciest part of the show. They had met on the evening shift four years ago at another Houston station. Their voices and their chemistry clicked. Her smooth voice, deep for a woman but still laced with femininity—powerful and newsy when she read the headlines, but girlish and delicate when she and Timber cut up. Her infectious laugh made almost anything sound funny.

She was from Fort Worth, had a law degree from Baylor and was married to an Exxon executive. Her husband, she told Timber, wanted her to stay home and have babies and tend house, which for a River Oaks woman meant managing the maids. But she said she had always loved radio, having studied journalism as an undergrad at the University of Texas where she worked for the student radio station.

Linda Jean was the one who'd given him his on-air name, Timber Goodeneaux, shortly after they started working together when he was still going by Tom Goodman. Timber was making fun of a Texas congressman who'd resigned after a scandal involving road construction bribes, the third legislator from the Houston area to do so in a month.

"Linda Jean, can you hear that sound out there? That sound out in the woods, up toward Austin?"

"Nnnn—oh," she drawled the word out and giggled, girlish and husky all at the same time. "*What* sound is that, Tommy?" She instinctively called him Tommy when everyone else called him Tom.

"It's the sound of the big trees falling—can you hear them, up in Austin, shouting *Timmmm—bbberrrrrr!*" He did it again. The beginning T of the word rolled off his tongue and then he shut his lips and the "*mmmm*" sound rumbled through them like a heavy truck or low-flying jet plane that shakes small houses until the M ran its course and he dropped lower to the "*berr*" sound, dropping off, the R's fading away slowly like a chainsaw in the distance winding down. "*Timmmmm—BBBBERRRRRrrrrr!*"

Linda Jean laughed hard, and Timber watched how she moved, her chest and shoulders shaking. She caught her breath and said: "*Timber*…that should be your name, Timber *Goodeneaux*, the Cajun comedian."

He nodded enthusiastically, smiling at her. Yes, Tom Goodman was too plain, too simple. He liked the ring of Goodeneaux. He wanted to capitalize on his Louisiana-*ness*—Cajuns were hot stuff in Texas—even if he was English in ancestry, he'd grown up in Cajun country.

"Ladies and gentlemen," Linda Jean said, "I introduce you to Mr. Timber Goodeneaux."

Timber thought back to Hyatt Delacroix and put on his best Cajun accent. "Why, hey dere, Miss Linda Jean, I do tank ya very much."

She laughed again in a way that got to him, a laugh that he thought about late at night.

Timber was getting a cup of coffee near the end of his morning shift, ready for it to end, hoping half-Mexican Maria was gone from his home when he heard the new receptionist shouting out to the ad sales director.

"Some old country-sounding woman has called *four* times, asking for a Tom Goodman." Her voice was West Texas flat. "She said he's a deejay. I couldn't find that name on the roster. She swears he works here. Is there somebody by that name who used to work here or something?"

Timber had only a minute until the next song ended. He dashed over to the receptionist (the fifth one Mr. Perdue had to hire that year, a buxom redhead with too much eye shadow and curly hair piled on top of her head like a stack of burnt corn cobs) and snatched the note from her. He didn't know her name yet but was sure she knew that he was Timber Goodeneaux. Everyone knew him.

"I'm Tom Goodman," he said, curtly. "In case anyone calls here by that name. But do *not* use it otherwise."

He rushed back to the booth and got into the chair as the last few bars of a song played out on a mournful note, the black disc spinning evenly on the turntable. He clicked a button as the song ended. The red light above the door glowed on.

"That was George Jones with 'He Stopped Loving Her Today.'" He read out the names of a few other songs, and then handed it off to Linda Jean, skipping their usual chatter. He waited as she read the news, fingering the note in his pocket. His mama had called *four* times that morning. He did not call home often. Since moving to Houston he talked to her maybe once every two weeks, if that. Every time he talked to her and told her about how his job was going, about his new condo, his new car, or a famous person he met, she would wait, almost as if she wasn't listening, always responding the same way. "That's nice," she would say in a tiny voice as she waited to get in her one question for him, the one she always asked him, even though the answer was always the same. He hated the question, wished she wouldn't be so small-minded to persistently ask but their infrequent conversations featured it every time, usually near the end of the phone call. Hearing it always made Timber want to hang up.

"Have you been to church?"

"No, ma'am."

And then she would start. "You need to find you a good church home over there, Tommy, with good Christian people who will care about you. I'm worried about your spiritual life, about your soul. You need to give thanks to Jesus, to get right with God. That's the most important thing. Life on this earth is short but the afterlife is forever. Eternity is a very long time."

"Yes, ma'am," he said, biting his tongue. Didn't she think if he had been to church he would tell her first? It angered him that nothing else mattered in his life to her than if he went to church or not. She didn't care about the great success he was having, that his show was number one, that his and Linda Jean's faces were plastered on billboards all over town, in high-profile places along the interstate where thousands every day looked at his picture while listening to him on the radio. He'd been sending her $200 a month to help with her expenses since he got his first big job in Houston, although she probably gave it all to the church. Regardless of how much she irritated him, he always finished with an "I love you, Mama."

He rarely had visited home since moving to Houston. The times he had—short trips for Thanksgiving, Christmas, his mama's birthday in early July, and once for Easter—were unpleasant. Each time Mama had insisted that he go to Sunday school. It wasn't too bad because the attendees in the young adult class were impressed with his success, although they seemed intimidated by him. He was shocked how many of his schoolmates whom he had once looked up to had grown up to be unpolished, awkward adults. He was a stranger among them.

Sunday with Mama involved about six hours of worship: After Sunday school was church, both morning and evening services. The church had a new preacher, another East Texan, but this one much more fundamentalist than the last, prone to two-hour sermons. The congregation had seemed much changed each time Timber had attended, more blue collar and informal, some folks driving from deep in the piney woods north of Whitcomb, where the Cajuns faded out and the crackers lived. Timber noticed that a few of the more respected Baptist families that had worshipped there—the local druggist and Lieutenant Charlie Gibson from the sheriff's office—no longer attended, but were replaced by lean, hard-looking families from the pinelands, men in gray work shirts and pants, women in denim dresses, all with leathery skin, home-done haircuts and beady, dark, desperate eyes. They were the first to roll in the aisles and speak in tongues.

The last time he had visited was more than six months ago, at Christmas. He had reluctantly gone to church with Mama to make her happy. Bev, seventeen by now, had refused to go and spent the night away at a friend's house.

He and Mama settled into their usual seats for the service after Sunday school. Everything was normal until about halfway through the preacher's sermon, a mother and son sitting right in front of them began babbling. The son, ten years old, fell into the aisle, kicking his feet and writhing his hands out above his head, shouting, "JEE-JEE-JEE-JEE-JEE-*JEEZ—ZUS!*" It was almost a moan, almost a joke, a sound a ten-year-old would make just to be annoying. The mother then lay flat in the pew, shouting at the top of her lungs, drowning out her son and the preacher, yelling, "Lor—Lor—Lor—*LA—LA—LA—LA!!*" Each babble got louder and louder as it rose to the end. Timber just hung his head at the outrageous display, longing for the days of the peaceful services when everyone sang hymns, perhaps chiming in a modest *amen* at the end, and then listened gracefully to the preacher. He noticed, however, Mama's legs and hands beginning to twitch. He looked at her face. He had never seen such an intense look, her eyeballs bulging and bloodshot, her jaw locked tight, her brow furrowed, looking straight ahead to the preacher. Her fists were clenched and she was beating them on her knees in the rhythm of the chant of the wailing woman. Timber had a sinking feeling in his stomach. There was no way he could stop her. She blurted out a noise that sounded like an attempt at the word *hallelujah* as yelped by a dog that had been run over by a car. She leaned back in the seat, her legs and body straight as a board in her flowery blue print dress. Mama reached out and grabbed Timber's shoulder, her grip tighter than he ever imagined it could be, her thick short fingers digging into his skin.

"*Haalllllllaeejelajdljuh! Haalllllllaeejelajdljuh! Haalllllllaeejelajdljuh!*"

Her wail did not sound human. It overpowered the mother and son before them, both beginning to lose steam. They turned around to watch Timber's mama. Everyone in the small church focused on her, watching the sound coming from her lips. She turned to him between bellows, her sad angry eyes fixed on his, as though to ask, "Why aren't you joining me, son? Didn't you see the mother and son before us, the little boy supporting his mother, his mother who brought him into the world and gave him life so he could revel in the glory of the Lord? Do you not love your mama?" That was what Timber read in her eyes. He turned away, looking at the rest of the congregation, their gazes transfixed upon him, asking the same question, "Why are you not a better son?" But there was no way he could bring himself to speak in tongues. He did not feel it. He loved Mama, but he could not roll in the aisle for her blabbering nonsense. He was a respected deejay in Houston, Texas. He was semi-famous, after all.

He'd talked to Mama briefly, twice a month, since. He missed her birthday for Willie Nelson's annual Fourth of July picnic at the Texas World Speedway in College Station where he was invited to be an emcee, hanging out with a gaggle of drunken college girls backstage. He sent Mama flowers, a bouquet of red roses, and called her from a pay phone. She said they were "nice" before asking him if he'd been to church. He had been meaning to visit her but hadn't gotten around to it. The radio station had begun scheduling many special appearances for him, mostly weekend gigs broadcasting from the Mercedes and Cadillac dealerships. Sometimes the dealers let him take a car for the weekend when business was good, which it almost always was in Houston in 1979.

He sat with her phone messages, waiting on his shift to end. He knew what the problem was without asking.

Bev was seventeen going on twenty-five—one look at her could tell him that. She had long blonde hair down to her waist and she wore tight bell-bottom jeans with small tube tops that showed off her belly and accentuated the fact that she never wore a bra. She had boyfriends well into their twenties, long-haired men who drove all the way from New Orleans or Baton Rouge to pick her up, taking her away for the weekend, Timber's mama said. Bev told Mama she stayed at her friend Julie McKimble's house, but Mama said no one ever answered the phone there. And Bev hadn't gone to church with Mama in almost a year. Timber didn't know if he could blame her for that.

He called home the minute his shift was over.

"Hey, Mama, this is Tommy." She was the only one with whom he ever referred to himself as Tommy.

"Oh, Tommy, I couldn't get ahold of you. I called about half the radio stations in Houston and nobody knew who you were. I—"

"Mama, I told you. I have a different name on the air. It's Timber Goodeneaux. That's what everyone here knows me as. I've told you that ten times at least. I don't know how many times I have to tell you."

Every time he had told her about his radio name, she'd responded, "that's nice."

"Oh. That's right. I forgot."

"Mama," he said. "What's wrong?"

There was a long pause.

"Bev is gone. She didn't come home all weekend. I finally got in touch with Julie McKimble. She said she hasn't seen her since school last week. Doesn't have any idea where she is."

It was *Tuesday* morning.

"Did you call the police?"

"No, I wanted to talk to you first." Mama's voice was weak, raspy. The preacher said I should wait and not call them, but I wanted to see what you'd say."

"Yes, ma'am. We should definitely call the police. I'll come home this evening. I'll get a flight right away."

"You don't have to, Tommy. I'll be all right. The preacher and folks at the church are looking after me, praying with me. I'll be okay."

He was surprised she discouraged him.

"OK, well…I can come later in the week if she doesn't come home. I'll call the police for you. They'll probably come by to talk to you. Do you have a photo you can give them? Do you remember what she was wearing?"

Timber was sure she had been wearing something skimpy, probably something like half-Mexican Maria the night before. Bev probably was just laid up in bed with a boy somewhere. He figured it wasn't the first time either.

But the pull of home was strong. Mama was all alone except for that crazy pastor from East Texas. He was from somewhere up near Nacogdoches, a little town called Diboll, a few hours north of Houston, one of those little towns where the preachers scream and holler. Timber did not want to leave Mama completely in the charge of a man like that. He and the church were all she had left. He thought back to when he was little and it was just he and Mama in the house most nights, his foot barely strong enough for him to walk.

He was on a noon flight to Baton Rouge out of Houston Hobby Airport. On the plane exhaustion came over him and he slept soundly on the one-hour flight, waking to a dry mouth and a crick in his neck, a hangover settling in as the numerous cups of coffee had worn off, leaving his stomach churning and his nerves jittery. He rented a car at the airport and headed straight home.

The yard was overgrown, the St. Augustine lawn thick and choked with weeds, the fast-growing grass overtaking the curbs and the dirt driveway, little patches of growth in the lawn clumped and gnarly, like a relief model of an Amazon rainforest. The house was falling into disrepair. A gutter hung loose on one side and the white paint was beginning to peel away in big chunks. The shingles on the roof were beginning to curl, the once slate black sheets baked to a charcoal gray by the sun.

There was a strange car in the driveway, a newer model Thunderbird, dark green. It had a bumper sticker that asked, "Have your read your Bible today?" and a decal in the shape of a fish. It had to belong to the Reverend Shaver, Whitcomb Baptist Church's preacher.

Timber rang the doorbell, a strange thing to do at the house he'd lived in most of his life, but he didn't want to be rude and barge in on company. Reverend

Shaver answered the door. A man in his early thirties, not much older than Timber, he had a severely short haircut and wore a dark blue suit with a wide purplish tie.

"Hello, Tommy, welcome home." The preacher shook his hand firmly, covering their handshake with his left hand, a move Timber was sure he used for funerals and family tragedies.

Timber's mama was sitting on the couch, her Bible open on the coffee table. She had aged even more since he'd seen her last. Her hair was gray and thin. She had gained weight in her middle and her face sagged, her skin dry and pale.

Timber had a hard time getting out of the preacher's grasp and to his mama. She did not get up and greet him at the door like she always did. The first few years he'd lived away, she would wait on the porch and be at his car to hug him as soon as he pulled up, wrapping her arms around him the minute he opened the car door. She always had a hot big meal waiting for him.

There was no food today, and Timber realized he had not eaten anything in almost twenty-four hours. He had slept only an hour. He moved past the preacher and to Mama, putting his arm around her in a sitting hug, a gesture she reciprocated passively. He took one of her hands. It was deathly cold.

"Hey, Tommy." Her voice sounded far off, as though from another room.

"Hey, Mama. Any news?"

"News?"

"From Bev."

"Oh—oh no. Reverend Shaver and I have been praying for her though."

The preacher, standing over them like they were teenagers and he was their chaperone, shook his head ruefully.

"Yes, we have," he said, his voice much too loud for the small living room. "Your mother and I summoned up the great eternal spirit of Jesus. We could feel Him in the room, right here with us. He is going to reach out to Bev and bring her straight back to us, safe and sound. I think," he paused, dropped his preaching voice and spoke more like an East Texas man sitting on a bar stool, "that Jesus is the only one who can get through to that crazy girl—she's wild as a buck."

Timber glared at him and turned back to Mama.

"So, Reverend, thank you for coming by. I can take care of things now."

"Son," Reverend Shaver said. "I wouldn't run off and leave y'all. The Lord's work here is unfinished. Ms. Goodman, do you want me here?"

"Yes, yes, please pastor. Please stay." Her enthusiasm for the preacher was much stronger than her greeting of Timber. She reached her hand out to the preacher and he took it.

"Thank you, ma'am," Reverend Shaver said. "Me and Jesus'll be right here... Son, I'll do whatever I can to help y'all."

Timber cringed at being called *son* by a man only five years older and making less than twenty percent of what he did in a year. He tried to ignore the preacher and watched Mama, her gaze distant across the room. The look she had on her face was the same expression she'd had after he she spoke in tongues. He imagined her squirming on the couch, howling at the ceiling, the preacher egging her on.

"Mama, have y'all called the police?"

She looked to the preacher, who answered for her.

"No, son. We don't want to get your sister in trouble with the law. I feel confident she has just run out on a drinking binge, cavorting with the Devil. She'll be home soon."

Timber bolted up, most of his weight on his good foot, towering over the preacher, a short man.

"What the *hell* are you talking about? What if she's been raped or killed? Who knows what could have happened to her? She's a seventeen-year-old girl who's been missing for *five* days. We've got to call the cops. They'll at least have a chance to track her down. Jesus—" he almost said, "ain't going to bring her home" but caught himself. He knew there was no arguing with his mama about this. He paused, took a deep breath, and finished his sentence, "Jesus," he said more calmly, "I think, would call upon and work through the fine Christians in the police department. He will help them to help us bring her home."

His mama lifted her head, a trace of a smile at him.

"Oh, Tommy." Her voice was coming back stronger. "That sounds more like you." She stood, shakily, and hugged him full this time.

"Okay. I'm going to go see Lieutenant Gibson at the sheriff's office and file a report. Mama, do you want to go with me?"

"Son, I don't think that's a good idea," the Reverend Shaver said. His mama had told Timber the last time he was home that Lieutenant Gibson did not like this new preacher and had pulled his family out of the church and gone to the Methodists—his mama said the word like she was spitting it—and several other longtime members had followed. Lieutenant Gibson had even tried to recruit his mama. She refused and had not spoken to the Gibson family since.

"No," she said, slightly harsh, looking to the preacher. "I will not go down there."

"Okay, that's fine," Timber said, simply happy to have her consent to go to the police. "Maybe I'll talk to a different cop, whoever is there. Do you remember what Bev was wearing when you saw her last?"

"I can't remember. I don't think I saw her leave."

"Something tight, I bet, letting it all hang out—like every time I ever saw her," the Reverend Shaver said, rough East Texas once again. Timber eyed him angrily. "The clothes of the Devil," he said, back to his preacher tone.

"Mama, do you have a recent photo of her?"

"I don't," she sighed. "But there might be one in her room."

Bev's room wasn't what he expected for a teenage girl. It was like that of a ten-year-old after the room was cleaned and the toys put away. It had light blue trim, a matching chest of drawers and nightstand, a white fur teddy bear sitting in a small rocking chair in the corner. There was one framed picture of her on the chest, a photo that was at least four years old of Bev and two friends, soaking wet in bikini swimsuits by the side of a river, apparently at camp. Even in the photo, young and skinny, her sexuality shone through. Timber could see the woman she would become in her young body even then. He lingered on the photo. He needed a newer one. He opened the door to the closet to find a collection of silky halter tops, slinky dresses, short skirts, a pile of leather boots and high heels.

He dug around in the pile of fancy footwear. Where had she gotten all these? Nowhere in Whitcomb—New Orleans most likely. He saw the edge of a worn shoebox at the bottom of the pile. He reached for it. It was heavy, full of photos and notes.

He shut the door to the bedroom, listening for Mama or the preacher. All he could hear was Reverend Shaver reading aloud from the Bible. Timber sat on the edge of the bed and put the box next to him. He grabbed a handful of the photos. The first one in the stack was of Bev, taken from above her head, naked on her back on a kitchen table, a woman's face pressed between her legs, only a dark head of brunette hair visible. Bev was grabbing onto the woman's hair, arching her neck back to see the photographer, her mouth open as though she were screaming. The next was a photo of her in the shower, smiling sexily, her blue eyes locked on the camera lens, her body like those of the Houston Oilers cheerleaders. In the next she was on her knees in the shower, sticking her tongue out erotically. The final one in the series was taken by a naked man looking straight down his chest, she swallowing him in her mouth, her blue eyes looking up at him through a tangle of wet blonde hair.

There were maybe two hundred photos in the box, most of them of her naked and many involving the man or the dark-haired woman, sometimes both, but Bev's face was the only one that could be seen. The man had long brown hair that sometimes hung down into the edge of the photographs. His genitals, feet, legs, hands and stomach often slid into and out of the frames, but Bev was always at the center of the snapshots, her eyes serious and blue and deep, locked on the camera.

Timber stared down at the floor. His hands were shaking. He could never let Mama see these. It would put her over the edge, possibly into a permanent psychobabble of tongues.

Amongst the photos were notes, written in a flowing script on typing paper folded into the size of small index cards. He unfolded the pages and read, hopeful for a name or address or number that could lead them to Bev, but they contained nothing but poems, lyrics about drugs and sex. The pages were decorated with swirling cartoons of sinister characters, monkeylike men and unicorns mating with buxom women and animals. He shuddered, remembering she always drew well. One poem read:

> My pink blonde angel
> Dancing in your white boots
> I am the dangerous stranger
> Coming for you in a leather suit
> Take me inside you
> I know that you will see
> All the things we can do
> All the things that we can be
> My pink blonde angel
> Come with me you'll see

All of the notes were odes to Bev, most with references to snorting cocaine and drinking and sex. He stuck the most innocuous note he could find, a nongraphic one about having sex in the woods, in his pocket. Maybe the police could use it. He thumbed back through the photos, pulling out two or three of her in a tight T-shirt, smiling into the camera—before the shirt came off and she moved forward, overtaking the photographer, the usual theme of the sessions. He closed the box and hid it back deep in the crammed closet. At some point he would destroy the collection to prevent Mama from stumbling across it. Nor did he want the police to see these pictures of his sister.

Lieutenant Charlie Gibson didn't recognize Timber at first. Even when he did remember him, he wasn't friendly as Timber expected. "Chollie," as everyone pronounced it, was a big man, six feet four inches, with a military-style buzz cut of hair that had been jet black but was now speckled with gray. He had the erect posture of the Marine Corps sergeant in Vietnam he had once been. He was very official in his brown sheriff's uniform, trousers stuffed into calf-high black boots, unlike the casual demeanor he wore in church.

Lieutenant Gibson sat behind a desk and asked the questions Timber expected when he reported Bev missing, studying the photo and the note, raising an eyebrow as he read the short poem.

"Well…son. We'll see what we can do. My experience is that once somebody runs off, it's really up to them if they want to come back home or not. I hope she'll come on home to y'all soon.

"How's your mama? I know she must be a wreck." He was beginning to sound less official, a little more like Timber remembered.

"She's a wreck all right, distraught. And that preacher—"

"Yeah, I know him. We had a falling out not long after he came to town. I miss that little church. I grew up there. But we are happy with the Methodists. I wish your mama would have come over with us. But she was mad as a hornet at me. Still is, I guess."

"She hasn't said so, but, yeah, she does resent you for that. She didn't want me to come down here."

"Where are you these days, son? I hadn't seen you around since…I can't remember when."

"I'm in Houston, working for a big country station there. Doing well."

"Houston, huh? That city is too big for me. I've been twice. That was enough."

"You know," Lieutenant Gibson continued, "I remember back in the days when your daddy was here, somebody turned up missing, he'd announce it over the radio for us. Sure enough, soon as he did, whoever had run off would usually come on home pretty soon.

"It's a shame. The radio station here being gone and all. It's all New Orleans news. It ain't like it used to be. I guess your mama told you that Hyatt Delacroix died. Just didn't wake up one Sunday morning. Had played in his band the night before. Now, Booger Johnson's still around, alive and kicking as much as ever. He's got a job at the new grocery store west of town, rounding up the carts in the parking lot. Of course he's still got his little church."

Lieutenant Gibson didn't seem to be in much of a hurry to get to work on Bev's case. He asked few questions about it.

"Well...what about Bev, my sister? When do you think you'll know something?"

"Son, there ain't no telling." Lieutenant Gibson shook his head. "There ain't no telling. I'll let you and your mama know if we hear anything. I'll send the photo around, to the state police."

He stood and Timber followed his lead. He stuck his hand out for a shake. Lieutenant Gibson's grip was firm and strong. He looked Timber up and down.

"How's your foot, Tommy? Looks like you still have that limp after all these years. I still remember that day out on the bayou when you was little. You are lucky you didn't lose that foot."

Timber shrugged, said it was fine.

He thanked him and went to leave but stopped in the door. Lieutenant Gibson sat down and began filling out a form.

"What about a reward?" Timber asked. "Would that help?"

"Sometimes, yeah." He didn't lift his head. "It can't hurt none."

"All right, then," Timber said. "I'll put up five-thousand, cash."

Lieutenant Gibson stopped writing and looked up at Timber.

"Five thousand?"

"Yes sir."

"That's a lot of money, son."

"Well, I want to find her. And I can afford it."

Lieutenant Gibson let out a low, long whistle.

"I guess Houston's been good to you, all right. I'll make a note of the reward. You ought to send something to the Baton Rouge paper, and the local paper, get that photo in there. Have anyone with information contact the sheriff's office here. Use the main phone number. That kind of money, she just might turn up quick. Lots of people don't make that in a year."

Timber shook his hand again and left. His grip didn't feel as strong this time.

Timber stayed on in Whitcomb the whole week but there was no sign of Bev, although many church people called to check on his mama when the photo and the reward ran in the papers. Timber desperately missed going on the air every morning. Radio made him feel alive. Being in Whitcomb made him feel dead, especially when he turned to the old familiar spot on the dial and heard the New Orleans news, no mention whatsoever of Whitcomb. Timber longed to hear KIX 97 FM, Linda Jean's sultry laugh.

He called her one morning after their shift. He told her—omitting the graphic details—about the photos and notes he found, and how he was worried about Mama, about how he distrusted the preacher who came to the house every day and prayed with her. He told Linda Jean about the reward money he'd put up but that he thought Bev might be gone for good.

"You poor, poor thing," she said. She made him feel better. He missed her. "Your mother is lucky to have you."

The Reverend Shaver and Mama saw him off from the house that Sunday night. It had been a full week of trying to talk to her about something, anything, but religion. To hear her tell it, Jesus, Moses and Elijah were her personal friends. Timber went to both church services. At least Mama hadn't spoken in tongues. She told Timber on the drive to church that evening that whatever happened, it was God's will, that God knew what was best and all she could do was pray and God would make the choices. She was content with that, her voice stronger and her eyes clear. She seemed sane enough for him to leave her alone if she wouldn't come to Houston, something he had suggested but she would never do. He couldn't stay. And even if the preacher was a phony—Timber was certain he was a charlatan—Mama liked him and he checked on her and encouraged church members to look out for her. His evening sermon was reasonable, less scream- ing and more about the do-unto-others-as-you-would-have-them-do-unto-you spiel, Jesus' Golden Rule that made much sense to Timber. It was a message he wished preachers spent more time on, even though he had his great doubts about Christianity. He didn't know what he believed about God anymore. East Texas preachers and those who spoke in tongues were almost enough to turn him against religion.

He was glad to be back in H-town, a nickname he had popularized on his radio show. He put his convertible top down at the airport and cruised up I-45, the skyscrapers gleaming in the muggy air. He spun west of downtown and onto Allen Parkway, becoming Kirby Drive around a bend as it cut through River Oaks, and then a right on Westheimer Road, the wide flat street that stretched out as far west as Houston went, a long way into the plains toward Katy, a sub- urb that unfolded into the cow-filled range that was the rest of Texas. Moist air blew through his hair and he breathed deep, not minding the mild smell of the refinery and chemical plant that drifted north on the windless night. He watched the cars, tail lights by the thousands, scooting along the road. He checked out women in Mercedes and Porsches, long hair almost too big to believe.

Timber knew one brunette who had hair down past her ass and carried a brush in her large purse that was the size of a small rake. On occasional mornings she would stand before the mirror on his dresser and bend over, letting that long dark mane fall forward over her head and almost touch the floor, reaching back to the nape of her neck and brushing down. She stood so he could see her ass, the smooth firm curves, her legs spread slightly, her feet shoulder width apart. The delicate muscles in her back rippled, her arms slender and tight, taut from brushing her hair so vigorously twice a day. This girl had once fooled around with Willie himself and had been Kristofferson's regular for a short time a few years back, even living with him in Hollywood for a few months. She ended up in Timber's bed maybe once or twice a week. He badly wanted to see her tonight. He pulled off to a pay phone and called her number but she was not home.

He went to the Rusty Horseshoe, a place she frequented, and ordered a whiskey sour. It was a slow night, so he chatted with the bartender about the Astros' mediocre season and the upcoming Oilers' exhibition game. He was ready for football. Every weekend from September to November he'd go to Austin or College Station for a college game on Saturday, and when the Oilers were home, back to Houston for the tailgate party at the Astrodome. The announcers would invite him into the booth for the pre-game shows and he'd show off his football knowledge learned on the air in Whitcomb, remembering how he'd wowed his daddy that very first time on the air. The games were enjoyable—the crowds were big and went wild like nowhere else he'd seen—but the parties, cooking out in the parking lot, drinking bourbon and cokes, and then the after-game chaos in the bars, were something else. Texas girls went wild, breaking out their tightest jeans, getting fixed up like they hadn't all year. Every primped-up woman he met he told the story of his football injury, how he badly broke his ankle tackling a fullback, cursing him with a limp that never healed.

The brunette did not show, but three women rolled in and sat next to him, the closest to him a blonde with brown eyes and a deep summer tan. He'd seen her before down at Gilley's, running with a moneyed crowd. He thought she'd had a wedding ring on the last time he saw her, but tonight her ring finger was bare. The women he met on Sunday nights were desperate, ones that hadn't gotten any all weekend and were ready to give it one last try "to sling the cat," as his radio buddies said.

He turned to talk to her, but something about the way her hair was pulled back tight on her head reminded him of the photos of his sister. The notes and pictures he had thrown into a trash bag, pouring in a can of paint to ruin them before tossing them into a deep hole at the Whitcomb landfill. Normally he'd have dropped names and invited her back to his place, but now he just felt sick. He called it a night and headed home.

The blonde also reminded him of Linda Jean, whom he lay in bed that night thinking about. He'd tried many times before to get her out alone for drinks, but with no luck. She was the stay-at-home-with-the-wealthy-husband type. If she did go out, her husband always met her. They'd have two drinks at most, and then they were gone, usually on the way home before eight. She was different when her husband was around: quiet, subdued, particularly to Timber.

But on those mornings when they were on the air together, their voices swirling, playing off one another, laughing, the spark was unmistakable. Timber had met many Houston radio listeners who believed they were a couple. She was flirty in the station with him too, sitting close, joking with him, those big expressive brown eyes looking directly into his. He'd seen how women acted when they wanted a man; he had been fortunate to be on the receiving end of it fairly often the past few years. He was sure he saw that from Linda Jean. But he couldn't get her to take the next step. He even tried to kiss her once when they were in the record library and she brushed up against him.

"Timber! I can't! I'm married." She held up her ring finger, the rock glittering under the fluorescent lights of the hallway. *"Remember?"*

She cut her eyes at him, lively brown lights that had a language of their own.

"How about lunch, then, today?"

"I've told you before, I work out in the middle of the day. I don't eat lunch. And you've got to get some sleep—you and your staying awake all night long. You might fall asleep on your plate. I'll see you tomorrow."

And so it went, usually once a week when he had worked up the nerve to ask her out, to try to set up a liaison. Only a few years before he would never have been so bold. He tried everything.

But nothing worked. Each week she shot him down, as summer drifted slowly into late October and the stifling humidity let up.

There was still no news of his missing sister, not a single clue. His mama resigned herself to the fact that she probably never was coming back. She had been through such a loss before. He had been meaning to visit but hadn't gotten around to it, although he was calling at least twice a week. His mama kept asking him if he'd been to church and he kept asking her if she would visit Houston. He hadn't and she wouldn't.

Fall settled into Houston like a welcome breeze. Every night he went somewhere the liquor flowed. More and more of the country bands playing around town asked him to their shows, enlisting him to do the introduction, letting him hang around backstage. Mickey Gilley gave him the regular Wednesday night emcee gig, introducing the bands, the songs, chatting it up for KIX 97 FM. The promotion department loved him, booking him one special event after another. The more his celebrity grew, the more the women threw themselves at him.

And football season was as big a party as ever. He began doing more than drinking to get through those hardcore party nights. Most of the music business was deep into cocaine, noses mashed into mirrors in backrooms, behind locked doors everywhere. The coke wound him up so much that it required huge doses of liquor or a joint to bring him down when the coke ran out or he simply could not snort anymore, the inside of his nose burned and raw. He stayed away from the blow on nights before his radio show after one bad morning a sore throat caused him to have such a high pitch that listeners didn't recognize him, mistaking him for Jimmy Gentry, the afternoon drive-time personality.

He saw Linda Jean and her husband, Dickie, at the Oilers-Steelers pre-game party in the radio station's luxury box, a buffet of BBQ ribs and chicken and all the beer, bourbon and margaritas they could drink. She had on light blue slacks, Oilers' colors, and a low-cut silky white blouse. Timber watched her as she went through the food line, revealing more of herself than she intended as she bent over to inspect the steaming trays. He spied on her during the game, sitting by her husband, a man with almost no personality. She sat behind Mr. Perdue, the station manager, and jumped up and cheered like the cheerleader she had once been, screaming for the Oilers, for Earl Campbell, for Coach Bum Phillips, striding the sidelines in his boots and white cowboy hat. Timber sat next to Jimmy Gentry, doing shots of Jack Daniels and chasing it with Budweiser, the *King of Beers and the Official Beer of the Houston Oilers and KIX 97 FM*, a banner proclaimed in front of the luxury box.

At halftime he and Jimmy snuck into a small closet off the hallway and snorted the rest of their weekend's coke off a small pocket mirror a drunken blonde had left with Timber the night before. They were crowded close together with brooms and cleaning supplies beneath a bare light bulb.

"Man, this is going to get me through the second half, and then I'm going to crash," Jimmy said, sniffling. He was short and skinny and had long hair.

"Naw, we are going out," Timber said. "Don't be a big pussy. We can get some more. I'm going to try to get Linda Jean out with us." He snorted the last line.

"Shit, you're crazy man. That husband of hers has been scowling at you, boy. You better be careful."

"Don't worry about that. She's got a thing for me. I know it."

"Son, you're a damn legend in your own mind," Jimmy said.

By the end of the game, Jimmy was falling asleep in his seat. Timber didn't feel so energetic anymore either. He hadn't slept since Friday night; about forty-eight hours of drinking and snorting coke had worn him out. He planned to catch Linda Jean and her husband on the way out of the game, offer to take them to dinner. Maybe he could kick her husband's ass right then and there, and take Linda Jean home with him. But when the end of the game neared, the Oilers down two touchdowns, he noticed that she and her husband were gone. He had taken his eyes off her to watch the Derrick Dolls dance. He was pleased to see half-Mexican Maria kicking her white boots up high, strutting in those short baby blue skirts, shaking her pom-poms for all she was worth. Maybe he could hook up with her after the game, take her back to his place and this time keep her awake, finish what he had started earlier in the summer.

He left Jimmy asleep in his seat and wandered out into the hallway of the Astrodome and down a back staircase toward the dressing rooms. He thought maybe he could catch up to half-Mexican Maria. He flashed his press pass to the security guard who smiled and gave him a friendly slap on the back. He stepped out into the hallway as the game ended and soon was overrun with the Steelers, giants in yellow britches and black helmets, swarming toward the dressing room. He tried to run out of the way, his foot hurting him, and he stumbled and fell, scrambling back to his feet before Mean Joe Green almost stepped on him. He stood off to the side while the mob passed by. When he finally got out onto the field, the cheerleaders were long gone, as were most of the players and referees.

He limped to the fifty-yard line. He had been dead tired on his feet, but standing in the middle of the eighth wonder of the world rejuvenated him. He was living the *life*. He wished Linda Jean were standing there with him. He had to have her, one way or another. After a few beers with the announcers, their usual post-game wind down, he would go by her house and set things straight.

He wobbled out into the parking lot about ten, his car one of the last in the Gold lot, right next to the stadium entrance where the players and coaches parked. It had been one of those dry, temperate days in Houston that made it a shame the football team played indoors, unlike the September games when it was so hot that the preacher giving the invocation thanked God for air conditioning.

The top on his car was down and fresh night air blew on his face. He could handle a car after drinking more liquor than most men could hold down. He drove toward River Oaks where Linda Jean and her husband lived. He thought he knew the house from a picture she had once shown him, but after disturbing two aristocratic elderly couples, the second one threatening to call the police, he gave up.

He went home and called, dialing wrong numbers the first two times. He took his time, concentrating, and got through to her house on the third try. It rang four times before her husband answered, a weak and tinny hello. How could a woman with such great vocal cords live with such a puny voice?

"Linda Jean, please," Timber said.

"Who is this?" her husband said snottily, a grown-up prep-school whine.

"This is Timber *Goodeneaux*...lemmee talk to Linda Jean."

"What do you want?" the exasperated man-child said. "She's asleep."

"I want to talk to Linda Jean."

"About what? It's midnight. You'll see her in the morning, you drunk ass."

"You *sonuhva bitch!*"

The line went dead.

He redialed several times, sitting on his couch with a cold Shiner Bock in his hand, getting either a busy signal or more wrong numbers.

He woke in his clothes, on the couch, to pounding on his door. His eyes went to the clock on the wall: six-fifteen.

"Shit."

He had never been late to a shift before, despite many long nights. That was bad news for deejays. But he was a big-time deejay, the number one show. He could get away with it.

The pounding outside continued.

"Timber! Timber!"

He stood and let Jack Swindall, the advertising sales director who was also a neighbor, into his condo.

"Timber. You all right? Andy called me when he said your line was ringing busy. You better get down there, boy, before Mr. Perdue hears about this."

He splashed water on his face and hurried to the parking deck. In fifteen minutes he was in the booth, taking over from Andy Ray, thanking him for covering for him. His voice was a little scratchy, the back of his throat still numb from the coke, but he was fine once he got warmed up and had a cup of coffee. He played "A Boy Named Sue," a long Johnny Cash song, followed by one of his favorites by Waylon and Willie.

Andy Ray brought him a cup of black coffee and a hit of speed. He took a sip and dropped the pill down his throat. Linda Jean gave him an icy stare from the news booth and looked away when he smiled.

He went in the booth and said good morning to her but she pretended not to hear him, reading closely over her copy, making edit marks with a pencil. Willie Nelson's tenor filled the silence:

Take back the weed, take back the cocaine, baby,
Take back the pills, take back the whiskey too.
I don't need them now, your love was all I was after,
I'll make it now, I can get off on you.

He went back into the deejay booth. The song played out and Timber took the microphone, his voice resonating, the speed beginning to wake him up. He still had a buzz.

"That was Willie with a song I picked out special today, for a little princess named Linda Jean." Her eyes widened in the booth and she pursed her lips tight. "If you all could see her now, see how cute she looks with a pencil behind her ear, ready to read you all the news, you would see why I'm in love with her. She's just a doll, I'm telling you what. A walkin'…talkin'…Texas doll, that's for sure. Aren't you, Linda Jean?"

He turned on her microphone. She looked ready to kill him, but then forced a happier expression, looking down.

"Aw, now, Timber, aren't you silly this Monday morning? What got into you this weekend?—Don't answer that, I've got a lot of news to get through." She sounded shaky, nervous.

"Now hold on," he said. "You know I've been in love with you all these years, ever since that first time we shared microphones. I think everyone knows that—can hear it. Hell, half the people I run across in this town think we are married."

He was no longer speaking on the pretense of entertaining the audience. He was looking straight at her. She glared at him. She started to read the news again, the first story about President Carter meeting with the Soviets.

"Hold on now, sugar," he cut in, "what about us? Can we go to a romantic lunch later, say at Maxim's or Café Annie?"

"Now Timber," she said, gritting her teeth to put on a light voice, but death in her eyes. "You know I'm a happily married woman, to a man, an oil man, I love and cherish. You came along a little too late—and a dollar short to boot."

She smiled derisively at him, crinkling her eyes. She started the news again but again he talked over her.

"He's a lawyer—a *lawyer*—for Exxon, right? Not a *real* oil man."

"He's got a law degree, but he is a real oil man, overseeing exploration in South America."

"For Exxon, right?"

She nodded, but said nothing over the air.

"Don't nobody get their hands dirty, shuffling paper for Exxon. I bet he ain't never had any oil under those pretty manicured fingernails of his."

Linda Jean tried to start the news again but Timber turned off her microphone.

"*Exxon*...They've got that stupid tiger for a mascot. That thing ain't nothing but a big hairy pussy...like your husband."

He turned her microphone back on and said, "now for the news."

Her face was red. She shook her head, took a deep breath, her shoulders trembling, and began tentatively reading the stories. She mispronounced several Russian names. It was the worst she'd ever sounded on the air.

As soon as her broadcast was over and he started a song, the red light went off and Mr. Perdue charged in the booth, Andy Ray right behind. The old man's face was crimson, his eyes bulging, his neck tense in his collar and tie. He gritted his teeth as he spoke.

"*Goddamn*, Timber. In my office—Andy Ray is taking over this shift."

"Aw, c'mon, now, I'm just getting warmed up. Look at the phones." The lines were all lit up. Timber did not get up from his chair.

Mr. Perdue looked like he was going to spit. He raised his hand up and pointed a finger in Timber's face.

"No," he shouted. "In my office or I'll fire your ass right here."

He turned sharply to leave and then stopped. Andy Ray cowered in the corner. Both of Mr. Perdue's fists were clenched at his side. He swiveled back around and toward Timber as though he was going to punch him. A vein showed in his neck.

"*Hell* boy, as I a matter of fact, *I am* firing you right here. This ain't no fraternity party, boy, this is big-time radio.

"You got a hell of a voice, a hell of a radio presence, but for one, it's illegal to say *pussy* on the air. The FCC is going to be all over my ass. Two, you are drunk." He gestured wildly, shouting at Timber, who sat motionless in the chair. "And three—and most important of all—the lesson you better learn if you *ever* want to work in radio again: you don't ever—*ever*—piss off an advertiser. Exxon is the biggest damn oil company in the world. They spend more money with us than almost anybody. Who in *thee hell* you think pays your salary?"

Mr. Perdue stopped shouting and turned as though to leave. He took a long deep breath. He moved to the door and held it open, but turned his head back to speak to Timber again.

"Get your stuff and get out of here in ten minutes or I'm calling the cops to throw your ass out. You might as well hightail it back to the swamps of Louisiana, you dumb *coonass*."

VIVA LAS VEGAS

The sky ahead of Zeke was cloudy and black. Interstate 20 rolled through the gentle hills of West Georgia, softly up and down, the road a straight shot, wide open, about midnight. He was driving almost a hundred—the radar detector quiet, not a single light flashing red—but it seemed like he was hardly moving, the car not a car but a rowboat or a gondola, a gondola like he had seen in movies and travel shows about Venice except he was gliding gently through hills of pine trees. Vegas had a casino hotel with canals, men in striped shirts and straw hats standing on the narrow boats, navigating the waterways with long wooden poles. Maybe he'd stay there a night or two, learn to play blackjack, roulette. Billboards for the Waffle House, Exxon and Jesus supplied the rare flashes of light along the road, sporadic beacons in the muggy dark.

He had changed into his number two preaching suit but he wouldn't be preaching anymore. He could afford new clothes when he got to Vegas. Maybe he would even stop along the way and buy a slick new suit in Texas. He'd always wanted to head west. As a child he'd pretended to be a cowboy, riding horses in the painted desert and sleeping on the ground, campfires smoldering deep into the night. He had never been north or west of Alabama.

He could go on to Vegas, L.A., Mexico, any of these places would be good for his purpose—a new life, a new name. It didn't matter where he went, as long as it wasn't Georgia or Alabama. There was a whole world full of places where nobody knew him.

He was in Louisiana by the dawn, zooming through the Mississippi twilight. He was near exhaustion, the sun at his back, the morning cooler, a light frost on the land, trimming the pine trees and light brown grass in silvery dew. He needed sleep. Two giant cups of coffee had helped to sober him, along with the fear of going to jail, the fear of dying, a bullet shattering in his brain. His head was hurting, stiff and heavy as a brick. His eyelids began to droop. His arms were like lead, hard to hold up.

He drove until he could barely keep his hands on the steering wheel. He pulled into a motel behind a truck stop after crossing the Louisiana line, near Monroe. A sour old man with a face like a prune said check-out time was eleven but he still had to pay the full rate, $29 for the night, if he checked in. Zeke asked for two nights. He paid with a $100 bill.

He lay in the motel bed thinking of how dark it had been when he and Jolene were parked in his truck by the fishing pond, her long tangle of red hair falling down over her face, pinned between their chests, her body hot under his, a slick sheen of sweat on her skin, her smell like a damp gardenia as she moved and moaned until the blue lights screamed, the light shining into the car and directly into his face, blinding him.

Goddamn, what was wrong with him to push things so far, screwing the sheriff's daughter? But then the sway a preacher man holds over some women is a powerful thing, stronger than both the woman *and* the man, almost as strong as religion itself over all of God's hapless children.

He had feared a bullet to the head or between the legs, in the gut. He imagined how he would die a thousand ways. And then a peace had come over him. He was ready to go if his time had come. Jesus would accept him into His house with honor and the good Lord would understand that he was, as all men are, simply tempted by desires of the flesh, a pawn of the Devil as much as of the Lord. He wasn't the first preacher to succumb to sexual indiscretions.

And he knew that God was on his side in the bank robberies. He hadn't hurt a fly and the banks didn't need—at least they could get by without—the piddling amounts of money he had stolen in the past few years. Much of that money had gone to the Lord's cause, putting his sermon on the radio, expanding the outreach of his church, saving souls and bringing sinners to salvation. Twenty-three years he'd been preaching. The Lord knew what he had done. The banks would have done worse with that money. He decided to have a good time with the cash that was left.

And he could never go home. He would be locked up for years, his wife would be shamed and his children would see him in jail. The parishioners he'd ministered to all of these years would be heartbroken, might lose their faith. It would be hell on earth for all of them if he returned to Piney.

He slept well past dusk. Later that night he drove through Northern Louisiana and on to Texas. He bought a car in Dallas, a three-year-old red Firebird, from a small used car lot, trading in his Oldsmobile for next to nothing. When the old man doing the paperwork asked for identification, Zeke gave him $11,000 cash—the asking price had been only $9,000. He took the money into his trailer office, counted it right quick, came out and handed Zeke the title and said, "get the hell on out of here."

He drove across Texas for a night and a day thinking about a new name for himself. The harder he tried to come up with something, the more elusive it was, until he crossed the New Mexico state line and he saw it on a billboard. It was like a vision. He'd been working the name Johnny around in his mind, different variations, until he saw huge red letters advertising vacations to a Mexican resort called the Sands. He'd be *Johnny Sands*. Zeke Blizzard was a goner.

◆　　◆　　◆

The Greyhound bus continued ascending the Rocky Mountains. Snow covered the valley where the highway passed, mountain peaks in view on each side. Signs advertised scenic lookouts in the Black Mountains and camping in the Dixie National Forest.

"How 'bout that?" Zeke said to Timber. "Didn't think they'd have anything *Dixie* out this far."

Timber couldn't believe what he was hearing. This redneck Georgia preacher was sure enough crazy. He took another glance at the old hard-shell suitcase in the overhead rack and thought about Zeke's alleged bank-robbing money, wondering what was in his scuffed piece of dusty luggage.

The Reverend Blizzard continued his monologue unabated.

"And I knew, by God, that what I was doing was right, what Jesus and the angels wanted, what the Holy Ghost and the Good Lord had planned for me.

"See, not everybody understands *that*, not everybody *knows* their plan. It's all about that peace which is a long way down the road past understanding, if you know what I mean."

Timber looked at his watch. Two o'clock. The bus was four hours from Salt Lake City. He'd been listening to this raving reverend for about four hours already. He hoped the preacher would get off before Salt Lake but he seemed to have no particular destination, no goal other than to tell his story. At least Timber could lose him in Salt Lake. He considered getting off in one of the small Utah towns to escape the preacher, but something, the urge to look when good sense says to turn away, tugged on him, kept him in his seat, involved in the preacher's story. He was determined to finish out this wild parable unraveling before him.

Timber figured the bank robbery stories were made up, at the very least exaggerated, but he didn't know for sure. This Georgia cracker preacher came across as brutally sincere and honest, answering Timber's questions without hesitation, not afraid to look Timber in the eyes with his oversized pupils.

"Why, again, are you telling me all this?" Timber asked him during a break in the detailed narrative.

"'Cause, son, you were selected to hear it. You are the chosen one, so to speak."

"Who chose me?"

"The Lord. He chooses everything."

"Why me? I haven't been to church in years."

"Mysterious ways, boy, mysterious ways. But I do know the Lord expects you to do something with this story. I don't know what. I just know I've got to tell it to you."

"*Unh* uh…you just sat down and started talking."

"Whether you believe or not, son, it'll hit you one day—whether you are ready for it or not. It don't matter how much time you've squandered, only what you do when the time comes."

Timber was growing a little tired of the preaching but he wanted to hear how the man's story ended.

"Where you headed?" Timber asked. "You getting off in Salt Lake?"

"Yes, I'm stopping there. But I'll go as far as Jesus wants me to go. I'm following the Lord's plan, son. I have no schedule of my own. Wherever He leads, I'll go."

Snow-capped mountain peaks formed the horizon, the side of the road dusty with black, crumbled slate. The cooler air outside had seeped into the bus. Timber reached into his duffel bag below his seat and pulled out a comfortable old gray sweatshirt, tattered along the collar and sleeves from repeat washings.

"You ain't got any liquor in there, do you boy?" Reverend Blizzard asked. "We 'bout killed this old bottle of mine."

Timber had taken ten or twelve big swigs from the preacher's bottle but had only a mild buzz, far from drunk. At least his hangover was gone. The long weekend of drinking, a heavy breakfast and twenty-five years of regular alcohol had built up his tolerance, made it hard for him to get drunk, even when sipping straight bourbon.

"No, don't carry a bottle with me. You can finish off what you got left. I'm good."

"Aw, there are six or eight good shots left in here. It's getting colder up here in these mountains. I ain't never been up this far north. I'll take a little sip to keep me warm."

The Reverend Blizzard took a pull and capped the bottle and put it away. The knife handle clinked against the glass as he shut the briefcase.

Timber had mixed emotions about everything he had told the preacher. He had needed the drinks when he talked about his childhood and Bev's disappearance. She was still gone, as far as he knew, twenty-three years later. She would be forty this year if she was even still alive. The stories of home saddened him. It was so long ago. The Houston firing angered him, yet again, like it did every time. Mostly he was angry at himself, but also at the circumstances. He had never spoken to Linda Jean again. He had been so high up the ladder at one time, only to fall so far and so fast. The worst part was that he'd never recovered, never regained that fleeting glory that had come to him so young. The rest of his life since then wasn't worth telling, although some of it could be entertaining over a few drinks. It had felt good to get some of it out. He'd told this crazy preacher things he'd been carrying around inside for years. He knew the liquor had loosened him up, but something about the wild-eyed reverend was sincere. He had made Timber want to talk.

But now Timber was sick to death of his own damn story. He wanted Zeke to finish his.

"So, what'd you think of Sin City the first time you saw it?"

"Man, I'm telling you what, those glitterin' lights in the desert were something else. Made me want to get a drink right then and there. Those casinos just glowed like fire in the desert, like the Wizard of Oz was waiting on me. I thought right off how foolish and silly I'd been, living the simple life—of course, I know I'm a simple man but I'm telling you what I thought at the time. I didn't know then what I know now.

"I thought, 'I'm almost forty-five years old and I ain't seen a damn thing.' Well, I decided to see it all, right off the bat. I took a look at the Mirage, those fiery volcanoes out front burning and bubbling. But then I saw that big pyramid, the Luxor, at the end of the strip and headed for it. I got me a room up near the top with giant windows. That view was something else, the desert wide open—flat, spreading out to the mountains as far as the eye could see. At night, the strip glimmered and flashed. It was beautiful, by God."

✦   ✦   ✦

The Luxor was unlike any building Zeke had seen. Its glass pyramid shone, a blazing beam of light firing up into the sky out of sight. A huge sphinx fronted the pyramid, staring solemnly down the strip. A sign proclaimed it was larger than the original built by the Pharaoh ages ago.

Inside the pyramid opened up to a huge cavern, large enough for seven airplanes, more signs boasted. People milled about amongst the noisy bells of slot machines and spinning wheels, chattering over smoke and drinks. A band played in a distant corner, rhythm and blues floating around the giant space.

Zeke signed in as Johnny Sands. A clerk asked for a credit card and I.D. Zeke instead slid a two-inch stack of bills totaling $10,000 across the counter.

"How's this for a deposit?"

The clerk, a young man neatly groomed and impeccably dressed, said that would do just fine. He picked up the phone and made a three-word call. Soon a security guard with a metal lock box, a .9 millimeter on his hip, the kind Sheriff Wiggins had fired, showed up and took the money from the clerk and gave Zeke a receipt. A moment thereafter a heavyset older man in a suit with a big smile arrived and shook hands with Zeke, welcoming him.

He gave him a gold-embossed business card that said *Billy Irwin, Director of Luxury Accommodations.* He said that if Zeke wanted anything, *anything* at all, he should not to hesitate to call him "twenty-four/seven." He shook hands again, his grip firm and warm, and re-emphasized his around-the-clock availability.

Zeke took a long hot shower to wash the weariness of the road off of him. It had taken him three days of driving across country. He shaved and put on his suit. He was glad the hotel room, costing him $200 per night, had a safe with a key in it. He took a one-inch stack of $100 bills, worth $10,000, and stuck it in his breast pocket. The rest of the money, about $80,000, he wrapped in a towel and locked in the safe.

He went down to the casino, the money a lump in his jacket. He liked the feel of the cash against his chest, knowing how hard he had worked to get it, practically risking his life. He should have shown his money to Jolene, should have taken her with him on a bank robbery. They could have been a team, like Bonnie and Clyde. She would have liked that. Her face was like a presence haunting him, an image burned into his brain, always with him. He imagined her in the casino or driving down the strip or by the pool he could see from the window in his room. He could see her turning tricks for lonely men like him. He wanted to invite her out here once things settled down for him, once he had time to truly become someone else.

The casino floor was vast, tables of busy gamblers as far as he could see. He knew nothing about gambling. He had only touched a deck of cards maybe two or three times in his life. His daddy had preached against the evils of gambling, believing that kings and jacks and aces were the Devil's calling cards, an invitation to sin and hellfire for all eternity. But here he was surrounded by cards thrown down in endless combinations, trying to add up to twenty-one on the blackjack table, or who knows what combination at baccarat. Velvety ropes cordoned off the high-limit tables populated mainly by Asians with stacks of chips of a grander color—purple, deep navy blue, chartreuse. He watched a Japanese man with silver glasses decorated with diamonds, focused and unyielding in his concentration on the never stalling movement of the cards.

The games had intricate rules, unspoken guidelines that everyone playing understood. He watched the cards and the money move back and forth, a never-ending tide, in and out, ebb and flow, the sun rising and setting only to rise again, just like the offering plates go out empty and come back full, then go out again, the cycles never ending, not unlike the operation of a church. The maroon carpet under his feet reminded him of the feel of the sanctuary floor he had walked on for so many years while preaching, the green felt of the poker and blackjack tables like the soft felt of the seat cushions, the little shelves on the back of the pews padded with such felt. The air in the casino was surprisingly clean and fresh and light, just like the sanctuary on a sunny spring morning. He heard they pumped in oxygen to keep the gamblers awake. And there were no clocks on the wall—time had no meaning in the church or the casino. These were rooms of eternity.

Except church had no cocktail waitresses.

A buxom blonde whisked by him, young, tanned, her hair pulled back into a flaxen ponytail that fanned out along her back in fiery points. Her eyebrows were dark and dramatically lined, a sharp cover over her brown eyes that had a light of their own. He watched her in awe. Her skin sparkled with specks of glitter.

She strutted by the blackjack tables like she was Cleopatra, flipping that platinum hair back every chance she got. The girls at the Luxor wore sexy little getups the casino claimed were Egyptian style: black velvet leotards decorated in gold embroidery and trimmed in silk bands of hieroglyphics. She wore a gold choker necklace, a strand of two-inch-high gold bars, looped tight above her collar bone that poked up against her smooth tanned skin. Her neckline plunged well below the choker, cleavage tanned and magnificent. Store-bought tits, of course, but he guessed those babies paid for themselves in two weeks. Some of the older waitresses wore little black skirts over the tight leotardlike costume, but not her. The stretch velvet hugged tight on her little ass, moving like a sack of cats heading for the river when she was hurrying back to the bar, a stack of chips on her tray. Her legs were long and thin and looked even more tanned than they were through those gold hose, propped up on four-inch heels. She probably made more in tips in one night than most men did in a week.

"Can I get you anything?" she said, startling him. She didn't seem real.

"Ahm, yeah," he mumbled, hunting for words.

"Would you like a beer, a drink, what?" She was impatient, her voice tired, distant.

"A Jim Beam."

"You want some ice in it, right?"

He nodded.

She wrote it down on a pad and hurried on, taking orders from a blackjack table behind him.

He stared at the cards again, the endless shuffle, trying to fathom all the card playing that had gone on before this very day, all the games he had missed. People had been sitting right here playing cards even while he was preaching, even while he was robbing a bank, someone was sitting here, ordering liquor drinks, choosing cards in some sort of system he didn't understand. Somewhere there was a reverend preaching about God's love while he was standing here at this very moment, watching the money move back and forth.

He waited until the cocktail waitress came around, dropping off drinks at the table. He watched how everyone tipped her with a few dollars or a poker chip.

He reached into his pocket and slid a $100 bill loose from the stack, dropping it on her tray when she handed him his plastic cup of bourbon and ice. Her eyes lit up, twinkling almost, and she leaned close to him, her breasts flattening out against him, and touched his shoulders affectionately.

"Thank you, so much." Her voice was warmer, throaty, marked by cigarettes. She smiled at him, looking right into his eyes. "I'll take care of you tonight, don't worry. Let me know if that drink isn't strong enough. I'll make them as strong as you want."

She moved on past, smiling back at him, a solicitous look.

"So how are you, sir?" The voice of Billy Irwin, director of luxury accommodations, boomed in his ear. He slapped a hand on his shoulder. "You want me to set you up on a spot at the baccarat table? I can set you up with a private dealer if you like."

"No, I'm fine, I'm going to wander around a little. I'll play some later."

Zeke was embarrassed for not knowing what to do, how to play. A hick in the big time. Billy Irwin, however, put him at ease with a friendly smile.

"Anything you need, you just call me or my staff. *Twenty-four/seven*. We'll take good care of you. Good luck at the tables." He winked and hustled away.

Zeke strolled through the casino until he came to a roulette wheel. The game appeared easy enough. He watched the inlaid wooden wheel spin, the white ball bouncing, no control over its fate other than gravity and the fickle slickness of the wheel, the little ball clacking and clicking as it bounced, a prisoner to fate, shackled to good luck or bad luck or both. Good luck for one man could be bad luck for someone else. The ball bounced and bounced, landing on thirty-three. No one had chosen that number. That would have been the one he would have taken. He sat down and slid $1,000 to the dealer.

"Tens all right?" the dealer asked.

"That's fine," Zeke said.

Two stacks of fifty red chips came his way. The dealer, a man of about sixty with white cottony hair, was welcoming, his false-teeth smile surprisingly endearing. He picked up the small white plastic ball and held it as though he were a magician and wanted everyone to see it before he made it disappear. He put the ball in the arc of the wheel and gave it a spin, starting it rolling around the mahogany rim. The ball shot around three spins, rushing against the direction of the wooden circle, before it began to wane. Two other players slid their chips onto the table—Zeke noticed how they played corners or bet on the lines between numbers. He hesitated with his bet, until he saw the ball slowing ever still, and the players next to him, an old man and a long-haired college kid, rushing down more bets. He slid $100 worth of chips out onto the number thirty-three. The college kid looked at him like he was crazy. The dealer, as the ball slowed down and began to bounce, clacking on the numbers of the wheel, waved his hand, smoothly and evenly over the table. In a voice steady, bored almost, he said "no more bets" just in time as the little round plastic pellet lost steam, bounced three more times on the wheel and came to rest on fourteen.

"*Fourteen, red*," the dealer called out, bored but still authoritative, setting a glass paperweight shaped like a bowling pin onto the table on the winning number. The college kid with chips on the high numbers shook his head, but the older man was all smiles, happily rubbing his hands together as the dealer pushed a big stack of chips his way, paying off his winning bet. Zeke studied the board numbers, one through thirty-six, lined up. His training as a preacher couldn't help him. Only the gravity of the bouncing ball mattered. He was sure God played no part in this fate, but maybe the Devil was at work, pushing the roulette ball around with his pitchfork, the little sharp tins poking it this way and that.

He spun $100 three more times on thirty-three, losers, before pulling back to $50 for three more rolls, more losers, and then down to $30 per spin. The first spin with $30 came in, the ball ricocheting, bouncing and tricking around until it settled, nestling in the thirty-three slot. The payoff was $1,050, "thirty-five to one on number thirty-three," the dealer said, sliding the chips his way.

The blonde cocktail waitress appeared with a drink for him about the time the dealer slid two black $500 chips toward him, the glossy discs emblazoned with the image of the sphinx. She had a strong liquor drink this time in a heavy highball glass with ancient Egyptian designs etched into it.

"Would you like a coke or a beer chaser, baby?" she said, resting the drink on a coaster then bending to him, her free hand on his shoulder, her nails caressing the skin of his neck above the collar. He took a beer from her and sipped it before setting it down by his liquor drink and his growing stack of chips.

He reached into his breast pocked and peeled off another $100, folded it crossways and set it on her tray. Her shoulders trembled a little. Her full lips spread into a smile. She surveyed the table.

"You are good at this, aren't you?"

He slid one of the $500 chips onto the table and the dealer working the wheel called out to the pit boss, standing behind him with a clipboard, "black in play." Zeke placed the chip on the edge line, betting six numbers, thirty-one through thirty-six. He watched the dealer spin the wheel, releasing the little determiner of fate, about the size of a bullet, to spin around as though it had somewhere to go, somewhere to be, until it clicked, bouncing high this time, trying to see over fate's horizon, trying to break free, trying to determine its own destiny and become more than a bouncing ball. The wheel mesmerized him. As if in slow motion, the ball hopped and scratched in the numbers, jumping from red to black to red again before finally finding its way over to the black thirty-three space yet again.

"Yeah-heah! That's awesome," the cocktail waitress said. Her nametag said she was Brandi and that she was from Los Angeles. She put her arm around him and gave him a sideways hug, running her hand along his arm. The payoff was $2,900. He gave Brandi one of the $100 chips, just for being there.

She leaned close to his ear and whispered. "Did you tip the dealer yet?" Zeke noticed the dealer was not as friendly as he had been, practically scowling at

Zeke's good fortune as he pushed the chips his way. Zeke shook his head no, barely moving as not to draw attention to himself. He took a sip of his bourbon and then chased it with beer, but he was still nervous, the fear of the unfamiliar.

She leaned closer still, brushing against him, speaking in a low voice. "On a win that big, you should give him at least $50—most people tip between five and ten percent." Zeke nodded in agreement and slid a $100 chip onto the table. The dealer looked at him like he was crazy—it wasn't time for new bets yet—but Brandi pushed it on across the green felt.

"He's tipping you," she said. The dealer's face warmed, and he picked up the chip, tapped it on the board as if to make sure it existed, and dropped it into a slot to his left. It clinked in a small metal case attached to the table. "Thank you, sir," he said, and winked at Brandi.

"You haven't played much in a casino, have you?" she said again, still closer, her breath sexy and warm on his ear, but all he could think about was her scent, fantastic, the smell of gardenias.

◆ ◆ ◆

"I'm telling you, that smell shook me up, boy, it shook me up good. *Jolene*—it was like Jolene was right there beside me again—I took a strong drink, almost finishing off that big glass, and I wasn't no drinker then—and I turned right to that sexy blonde thing and asked her what she was doing when she got off. I dropped another hunnerd-dollar bill on her tray.

"She gave me a hot eye but slinked off 'cause of the fact that she was afraid the pit boss was watching her. I sat there and played a few more spins, not winning a thing—I think tipping the dealer is bad luck—until she came back around with another drink and a note on a napkin. It said she and some friends would come by my room at midnight. How she knew my room, I didn't know. That casino seemed to keep good tabs on everyone. I sat there for four hours, watching that wheel spin, losing money but winning a roll here or there, enough to keep me in the game with the first thousand I threw down.

"She kept bringing me big strong liquor drinks. I must've tipped her $800 that night alone. I got knee-crawlin' drunk, warm and happy, knowing I had something good coming.

"Well, by almost midnight, I was damn near falling off my stool. All of my winnings and most of my $1,000 in chips I had started with were gone. I went upstairs and cracked open the mini-bar—that's the first time I'd ever seen a mini-bar—and had me one of those little-sized bottles of Chivas Regal—now that's some smooth stuff, I'm telling you. I was damn near blind, waiting on my harem to come by, like I was King Tut.

"They knocked on the door at twelve-thirty. What a sight that was…Brandi, and two lookers, big tits out to here," he cupped his hands and gestured, "and tight dresses squeezing their asses. I'll be damn if one wasn't a redhead, a lot like Jolene. That's about all I remember."

He smiled, his eyes alive. The sky was getting dark, cloudy, outside the Greyhound bus. A few silent beats passed.

"Now, come on," Timber said, "surely you remember the rest of it."

"Yeah…okay. I was just testing to see if you was paying attention." He paused, grinning. He looked down the aisle. His eyes with the big pupils had a faraway look as though he was recalling the past. "I knew you'd want to hear this part.

"My memory of it is hazy, but seems like they said it would cost $2,000 for all three of them, although the waitress, Brandi, said she wouldn't screw. I said, 'How about $8,000?' I threw the stack of hundreds from my coat pocket onto the bed. 'Bout all I remember then is them pulling my clothes off…rolling on the cash on the soft cotton sheets…I kept calling out the name Jolene…I remember the smell of wet gardenias.

"I learned something, my brother, that night, about fate, about our decisions. We ain't in control of *nothin'*. Some men don't like the roulette wheel, but me…to me that's the only true form of gambling.

"You just gotta put your money down and see where the ball bounces."

ANGEL OF THE WESTERN STARS

Timber knew moving vans well: the various sizes, paperwork required, security deposits needed, the way the trucks handled on the highway. He had packed and unpacked U-Hauls many times, fitting his life comfortably into the fourteen-foot truck. He used a trailer to tow his car behind, the bright orange and silver design of the U-Haul a warning to other drivers that an inexperienced pilot of a large vehicle almost as big as a transfer truck is on the road. It sometimes worried him, coasting down the highway, everything he owned in the world on wheels.

He reassured himself—it wasn't that much to lose. He'd packed up all these times from Houston to San Antonio to Fort Worth to Lubbock to Biloxi to Chicago to Lacrosse, Wisconsin to Fargo to Flint, Michigan. Those jobs were about a year each, except for Chicago where he quit in less than a month, Lacrosse, where he lasted only three months before he was fired, and Flint where he survived for three years. There were ten thousand radio stations in the country; there was always an opening somewhere, especially for a one-time star from a major market like Houston.

It was 1988 and he was leaving Flint behind. It was as gritty a city as they come. He had enjoyed the station, a true country format serving the blue-collar town. Flint had a large community of Southerners, autoworkers with their pasts in little towns in Mississippi and Kentucky and Alabama. People in Flint were impressed with his Houston country music credentials. But again, like Houston, slightly drunk on the air, he had badmouthed a sacred cow, this time General Motors, the holy church of automobiles and employer of practically everyone in Flint. "Those new GM cars move along like old Russian tanks!" *Jesus*, what had he been thinking? His show's ratings had been soaring. He shot them down with one unforgivable slip of the tongue that put him on the road to Reno.

He had a few cardboard boxes he had not unpacked for years, including two full of photos, signed records and mementos from Houston: a plaque that said, "KIX 97 FM—No. 1 in Texas—No. 1 in the World"; a signed record by Waylon Jennings and Willie Nelson; a framed photograph of him with the Derrick Dolls, bulging in all the right places in their baby-blue halter tops. Occasionally, he would putter through the boxes, remembering the good old days. He wasn't quite forty yet but he longed for his past.

Houston was a long way back in his rear-view mirror. He was looking west toward Reno. It was always exciting to him and a little frightening at the same time to up and move someplace where he knew absolutely no one. It was lonely, too, a heavy weight to bid farewell to co-workers. Radio station staffs were small and bred closeness, if not always camaraderie.

There usually was an informal farewell party, even in the case of his firings. Fellow deejays gathered at a bar and got drunk, remembering his funny or trying moments on the air, Timber's first day at the station. They retold stories of getting drunk together, tying on one last buzz for old time's sake. Any excuse to drink was a good one for most radio crews. The sloppy goodbyes at the end of the night always included promises to write, to call and to get back together again when he was in town. These sentiments were always expressed but everyone knew a reunion would never happen. It was a cold truth that nobody wanted to admit—this was the last time he would ever see them. Forever was a long time. The desire to hide this burning fact deep inside made the farewells even more emotional. Sometimes the women, near tears, insisted they would keep in touch when they knew they never would. More than one floozy receptionist had cried her eyes out on his shoulder, including several he hadn't screwed.

The following morning he would sleep later than he had planned and get a delayed start on packing, hungover and dragging. But it didn't matter what time he left as long as he was at his newest destination in plenty of time for his next show. It was important to be early that first day, to put his best foot forward.

The job in Reno was the morning drive-time slot for a pop music station, number three in the market. It had been losing listeners for years. It had taken him about a week to find the new gig after he got fired in Flint. Radio stations frequently dumped their prime-time deejays for one reason or another, often in search of a new voice, a fresh sound when the ratings began to slump and ad dollars declined. That new opportunities ever presented themselves was one reason why he had moved so many times, eight cities in the years from 1979 to

1988. That and the fact that he was drinking heavily and sometimes was late for shifts, every now and then missing one altogether. Stations had little patience for no-show deejays. He'd been demoted in Fort Worth and Biloxi for tardiness, and fired in Lubbock when he didn't show up.

The story in each town often played out the same. He'd come in at the outset, excited and enthusiastic about the job, cutting way back on his drinking, thrilled at the town, happy with his apartment although he hoped to make enough money and get financially stable enough to buy a house. He would make paying off his credit cards a priority. It usually took three or four months for the novelty of the new town to wear off and his resolutions to lose steam. By six months he was bored and the drinking would begin in earnest. By nine months he hated the town, the station, the same *goddamn* songs, the same damn newscasts every single day. He'd find a regular bar, meet some drinking buddies, start showing up late, call in sick here and there. Station management would grow cold on him, or him on them. He'd begin to put letters and demo tapes in the mail. A new offer would come along, or he'd get fired. It was a repeating pattern.

He vowed to change this time. He was getting older, regretting the time he'd let slip away. A neon sign proclaimed Reno the "world's biggest small town." It sat high and dry in the Sierra Nevadas, the few towers of downtown and glittering casinos dwarfed in the vast mountains and big sky. He'd never lived out West before, and, other than the annual broadcasting convention in Vegas, he'd not traveled there except for one visit to L.A. That, like much of the H-town years, had been a blur.

Driving the U-Haul with a trailer pulling his car clear across the western half of the U.S. took much longer than he anticipated. He arrived in Reno at midnight on a Friday after four days on the road, bone weary, his eyes blurry from staring at that yellow center line. It had been slow going towing his Pontiac, the U-Haul never getting much above fifty. Tired as he was, he still got a boost from seeing the flashing lights of the casinos—GET LUCKY TONIGHT!!! a billboard screamed. The mountains towered quietly in the black distance and he imagined cowpokes out there in sleeping bags around campfires. He'd always dreamed of being a cowboy, riding a horse into the canyons, under the western sky. He saw a shooting star, gliding through the darkness over his head, fading in the black horizon, behind a mountain.

The first night he took only his suitcase into his new apartment—a functional one-bedroom in a newish complex, complete with a small swimming pool, tiny exercise room and a laundry with quarter-powered washers and dryers. He piled his clothes onto the bedroom floor and spread them out into the shape of a single mattress. He fashioned a pillow out of a sweatshirt and slept on top of this makeshift bed, his arm stretching onto the white carpet. He was so tired he could have slept anywhere.

The next morning two deejays came by to help him move his furniture. It was a code among the peripatetic radio men that the new guy always got moving help. All deejays, if they were serious about the business, would need help moving sometime sooner or later. Timber needed more help than the average man, unable to manage a heavy load on his bad foot.

He didn't have much to move. A bed, a couch, TV, stereo, coffee table, a nightstand, shelves, a small kitchen table and chairs, three boxes of dishes, books, records and mementos, a shotgun that had been his daddy's, and his recliner. He loved this particular chair, having bought it in Houston, brown leather and soft. It was perfect in front of the television. All his furniture he had bought back when he was making real money. The recliner and couch were top of the line, costing him $2,000 for the set, serious cash back in 1979.

The white couch, a long cushy piece, was dingy after eight moves and steady use. Under it he kept the shotgun he had never fired. The recliner was soft and worn and molded to fit his body but it also was broken, the handle on the side that unwinds into the reclining position immobile. The chair would still recline and pull forward, but it required a great effort to take it with both hands and push it back or pull it upright.

The deejays who helped him move were about his age, late thirties, radio journeymen as well. He had heard of Jack Simpson, the afternoon drive-time guy. Simpson had been on the air in L.A. about the same time Timber was in Houston. Ernie Williams was a deejay who'd spent all of his time in smaller, secondary West Coast markets like Reno. Both wore sneakers, gray sweatshirts and baggy jeans, dark beards and seventies hairstyles, shaggy and unkempt, like Timber.

They unloaded the U-Haul quick, an easy move into a first-floor unit. In one move past Timber had to go up to the third floor, traversing winding narrow stairs, wedging the long couch through the doorway, turning the recliner at all angles to get it inside. Climbing the stairs had caused his weak ankle to throb. Nowadays he chose first-floor apartments whenever he could find them.

They finished up about noon, getting it all inside in less than two hours.

"You want to go for a drink?" Jack asked. "There are some good ball games on…We can go to Harrah's. It's right near here."

It occurred to Timber that he lived in a town where he could gamble and drink anytime he wanted. His apartment complex on a side street near downtown was less than a mile from the cluster of casinos, glittered up all neon red and purple and pink, bright even in the midday sun.

They went to Harrah's and plopped down in the plush chairs in the sports book room, filled with six big-screen televisions, each featuring a different sporting event: three baseball games, bowling, stock car racing and a lumberjack competition of some sort, men spinning on a log in the river or chopping at a tree with an axe.

A cocktail waitress brought cold beers. The first few sips were crisp and refreshing after the hard work of moving. Timber was pleased to have some companionship after four days alone inside the U-Haul cab.

"You ever bet on baseball?" Jack asked.

"No, I haven't," Timber said. "Never really had the chance much. I'd like to give it a shot. I know the game pretty well. Watched it all my life."

"Yeah? Well, there's a good game this afternoon, starting soon…the Cardinals and Dodgers. I'm putting $200 down on the Cards. They are underdogs but they shouldn't be—they got a rookie pitcher going who's red hot."

Jack's voice was strong, smooth, a professional radio man. He glanced at the digital tote board, eyes scanning the odds and statistics.

"The Dodgers are throwing their ace, Hershiser, but he has been injured. Besides, the game is in St. Lou-ee. It's not often I won't bet on a home team underdog. That's almost always a sure thing. A *sure* thing."

Ernie chimed in. "It says on page seven of the Gamblers Anonymous book that there is no such thing as a sure thing."

"That's true, Ernie." Jack laughed. "How much you in for?"

"Probably just a hundred," he said, never pulling his eyes from the bank of TVs. "I don't think the line is high enough. It should pay more than $120 betting against Hershiser."

"I guess the oddsmakers know what a pitcher our young Cardinal boy is," Jack said. "The house don't miss much."

The baseball chatter continued. Timber, still a Cards fan, had much to contribute to the discussion. It was early April and there was nothing like a fresh new baseball season when every team had a chance at the World Series, seemingly so far off in October.

Timber thought about the matchups, agreeing that the Cards were a good bet. He visited the ATM machine at the casino's entrance, withdrew a $100 bill and bet it on the red birds. He didn't let himself think about the fact that his balance was down to $80. At least he would get paid in a week. His rent was covered. And he could always win.

The chairs in the sports book room were big and comfortable, reclining a few degrees. The scores of every game going on in the world were visible at all times. The beers were going down good, loosening Timber up, a warm rush, the patter of Ernie and Jack, the fleeting glimpses of long-legged cocktail waitresses as they strutted by, heading for the big casino floor with trays of drinks.

Women. He had not had the intimate company of one in quite some time, six months at least. He'd had a liaison with the wife of the news director back in Flint, a schoolteacher he'd hooked up with at one of the radio parties. It was always on the sly and infrequent and hurried, always at her convenience. Nor was it that great to begin with. She moved away when her husband got a better job in Detroit, taking off to another promise of radio glory, believing, like Timber did, like they all did, that something better was just around the corner. He didn't think much about her at all after she left. However, watching the cocktail waitresses come and go, he missed her. It was only logical being she was the last he'd had. He wanted to hold a woman tonight. He was on the downside of his thirties but he'd never been with the same one very regular. Maybe there was a woman for him here, somewhere in Nevada.

"Hell yeah, baby! Here we go!" Jack startled Timber from his lecherous fantasies as the Cards got a three-run homer, putting them six runs ahead in the seventh inning. He slapped Ernie on the shoulder and they exchanged high fives.

"I told you doubters to put more than a hundred spot on them," Jack said.

More beer flowed. The Cards closed the game out. They cashed their tickets and bet on a night game, taking the Giants against the Mets.

The cocktail waitresses changed shifts and a perky blonde Timber had been eyeing went home for the night. He tipped her $10 on her last go around. She smiled, squeezing his forearm.

"Hope to see you around again soon," she said.

The casino began to fill up, people in their Saturday night best, young gamblers replacing the gray-haired patrons who packed the slot machines in the daytime, punching buttons to beat the band.

The Giants got off to a big lead in the next game and never lost it. More beers and more money, even bigger winnings this time as Timber had invested $200 in the Giants. He would walk out of the casino $350 richer than he had come in. That was cause for yet another beer. Seven hours of drinking in the same seat yet it seemed like he had just gotten there.

It got late and the last games of the day ended. The three men were the only ones still sitting in the sports book. Reruns of ESPN's SportsCenter played on all six screens.

Jack, counting his money, looked over at Ernie.

"You think our friend Timber would like to meet Cecelia and some of her girls tonight?"

Ernie looked Timber up and down, as though he were looking at him for the first time, and grinned.

"Yes...yes, indeed...I believe he would."

"I'll be right back, then," Jack said.

He crossed the sports book and headed toward a sign for phones and restrooms. He was back in a few minutes.

"The only one she's got available is Jenna Rae. But she can see us in an hour. She'll do all three for $300, a two-hour block."

Timber had shied away from prostitutes since a bad spell a few years back in Fargo where the Indian streetwalkers were only $25 for blowjobs and $50 for sex. Over a course of about three months he spent about all of his expendable cash on a cute little Sioux named Cotton. Why she was called Cotton he never knew because she had raven black hair and eyes as dark as fresh paved asphalt. She was short and a little pudgy but she would wrap herself around him, squeezing him like he was her first crush. But then one day she up and disappeared from Fargo, never to answer her pager again.

Timber had cruised the streets looking for her with no luck. He went for months without getting laid. On a bitterly cold night when he couldn't take the loneliness anymore, he cruised down the boulevard where he first met Cotton and picked up a tall Indian woman with short dark hair who had a face like a possum. She had on a parka and a wool hat and boots but no gloves; her knees, in dark stockings, were exposed. She ran to his van like a refugee dashing to the last boat off the island and touched his hand with her freezing-cold fingers.

He asked her what she wanted to drink. "Vodka," she said. He pulled into a liquor store and left the engine running, the heat on full blast. He touched her knee, the stockings chilly to the touch, and said he would be right back. A tentative smile crept onto her pointed face.

It couldn't have been more than ten degrees outside. He stamped his feet to warm himself as he surveyed the brightly lit liquor bottles. He found the vodka on the back wall and searched for the cheapest bottle. He was about to settle on a liter of Smirnoff when he turned to glance out the front window and saw the tail lights of his van going down the street. He ran into the parking lot, cursing her—he didn't know her name—and watched the red lights fade as she picked up speed on the open stretch of road beyond the intersection. He ran to a pay phone to call the police but paused when he picked up the receiver. What would his story be? "I picked up an Indian prostitute who stole my van"? They probably would never find his van but they might just arrest him. He was on the radio, a mini-mall celebrity. He decided on calling to say he was in the liquor store when someone stole it. The cops wrote down the license plate and a description and said they would do what they could. He knew he'd never see his van again. Fifteen hundred dollars down the goddamn drain. He vowed to himself to give up prostitutes, once and for all. It was a cold walk back the half mile to his apartment, only a few days before Christmas. He wasn't going home to see his mama, but instead was working twelve-hour shifts on Christmas Eve and Christmas Day. He had needed the overtime since he had to buy a new set of wheels.

That had been almost five years. He was proud of himself, not in a way that he would ever tell anyone, but proud nonetheless of kicking the prostitute habit, once and for all. It was one of those secrets he kept to himself, one of the many he figured most lonesome people had.

But here he was in Nevada with the opportunity for some time with a professional woman. She could be paid for with his casino winnings and he would still go home with more cash in his pocket than he had when he started the day. What a great country—all the beer he could drink, sex and then home, still turning a profit. He could break the streak of lonely nights. He thought about a Willie song, *one night of love can make up for six nights alone…I'd rather have one than none, Lord, cause I'm flesh and bone.* He was flesh and bone, no doubt about it. Hadn't he heard that it was better to regret something you *have* done, than something you *haven't* done?

The whore was in walking distance. Jack led the way. The night was clear and cold, a brisk dry wind blowing down the streets of downtown, swirling around the casinos, the big signs glowing in the night, stars on the horizon visible over the Sierra Nevada Mountains. She did her business in the same neighborhood where Timber lived, almost across the street, catty corner, in a two-story complex called the Reno Resort.

Jack mounted the stairs, Ernie and Timber behind him, and knocked on the door. A short blonde girl with long hair in a tight black dress answered. Her body was firm and curvy in the tiny dress, but her eyes were crossed and she had a mild speech impediment, some type of muckle-mouthed lisp that made her voice deep and strange. Maybe it was just an inebriated slur. She ushered them into the room and shut the door behind them, dead-bolting it and fastening the chain.

"Hey dere, Jack," she said, giving him a peck on the cheek. "Tha'll be three hunnerd. Who first?"

Timber handed a $100 bill to Jack, who also took one from Ernie. He added a bill of his own and set it on the dresser. The girl counted it, and stuck it away in a big black purse. Then she smiled, turned to them and pulled her dress down to reveal her breasts, large and round, the left one pierced with a gold loop hanging from her nipple. Something about the way she moved and the way she wore her hair reminded Timber of his sister, still long gone. He rarely thought about Bev anymore.

But suddenly she was on his mind. The images of those photos he'd found in his room would be with him forever, somewhere deep inside his consciousness. He couldn't shake them.

"Jack, I'm gonna take off…I'm not feeling too well."

Jack, already on the edge of the bed with the topless girl in his arms, waved him away. Timber left without trying to get his money back.

The walk home took only a minute. He wondered what went on in all these apartments around him. How many prostitutes, drug dealers and other vices were there, liaisons best kept quiet? He opened the door to his apartment, feeling like a stranger in someone else's home.

He needed a liquor drink. He searched for a bottle of bourbon in a box in the kitchen. He dug around until he found the liter of Jim Beam, a farewell gift from a fellow deejay in Flint. He wished he could listen to Willie, one of those mournful, sad lost-love songs, but his stereo was still packed up. He didn't bother hunting for a glass but sipped straight from the bottle. He stood before his recliner, angrily forcing it back with his hands, tipping over the liquor but catching it before more than a shot spilled out. He sat in the silence and stewed, slugging down several stiff gulps.

The bourbon eased his anger. Soon he was drunk and warm again. He passed out there, amongst the boxes and furniture, arranged in no particular order other than where it all came to lie after being moved in from the truck.

His first thought when he woke up the next morning was that he had all the time in the world to unpack. He didn't feel like doing it with a solid hangover weighing on his head, clouding the oncoming day. He didn't move from the chair, but lay there studying the spackled ceiling overhead.

He realized as he woke up that he had forgotten to call Mama on Saturday, his weekly call. He knew she was waiting to hear from him, how the move went, and to get his new phone number. She was all he had and yet he had forgotten her. He could have driven his U-Haul over a cliff for all she knew.

He dug around in the boxes until he found his phone in a box. He plugged it in, the loud dial tone irritating his headache. He dialed her number. No answer, even after ten rings. It was, he realized, noon Sunday in Whitcomb, and she was without a doubt in church, praying for his poor lost soul. He sat up, the movement causing a sharp pain behind his eyes, a numbness going to the back of his head. He surveyed his shabby possessions in the clutter of boxes, random furniture and odds and ends he had accumulated over the years. The couch had a new rip, a tear on the back, and the worn recliner sat at an angle. He thought back to the day it was delivered in Houston, the party he'd had that night in his new condo, the woman he had slept with, a tall blonde of glamorous proportions.

He spent the day doing nothing except napping and waiting for his hangover to pass.

He woke long before dawn on Monday. He was eager to go on the air, to get in front of a microphone, to broadcast his booming voice into the Sierra Nevadas. He was most at home in headphones.

The station's program director welcomed him at five-fifteen to prep him for the show and introduce him to his sidekick, a small, fiftyish man whom everybody called Igor. Chuck, the program director, was a clean-cut, young-looking guy whom Timber guessed to be in his early thirties, a few years younger than he was. Timber with his gut and longish hair, graying a little here and there, looked twenty years older than Chuck—he felt it, too, as though he were old enough to be this organized young man's father. Chuck, cut from the cloth of radio management, seemed genuinely sincere in his praise. It was rare that a program director would ever darken the doors of the station before nine in the morning. Timber liked him right off.

"I remember hearing you in Houston when I was there, great stuff. I could hardly believe my eyes when I saw your letter and demo tape. We are lucky to have you here."

"You were in H-town?"

"Yeah. For a short time, my first job. Promotions, at KRTS, the top forty station. I think I started only a few weeks before you left."

"Ah, okay," Timber said. So he knew Timber's history. He guessed everybody in radio did. "Did we ever meet?"

"No, I was just married back then. Didn't get out much."

"Well, you missed a hell of a time. Those were the days. Those Texas women. Gilley's. Oilers games at the Astrodome. The rodeo. It was *something* else."

"Oh, I heard. And I did marry a Texas girl. Lost her along the way, of course, when I moved her out of Texas."

Chuck's eyes looked sad. Timber didn't know what to say to that.

"Let me show you around," Chuck said, pointing out the recording rooms, and more importantly, the coffee machine and the bathroom. There wasn't a radio station Timber had seen yet that could take more than five minutes to tour.

Chuck noticed his limp and Timber explained the football injury, "the bad break that never healed right, tendon damage too."

They sat in the news booth waiting for his time on the air to begin.

"Now, you can talk about anything you want on the air here," Chuck said. "The previous morning guy told some pretty raunchy jokes. His ratings weren't bad, although we think they could be a lot better. I don't need to tell you how to do a show. There's just one thing you can't do around here."

"What's that?"

"Just don't piss off *any* of the casinos. They are big spenders—the biggest game in town here, obviously. They stick together, too. There was a classic rock station that had this ambitious news director who did a story about repeated armed-robberies in the parking lot of the Lucky Horseshoe, claimed it wasn't a safe place for people to go. Cut the casino's business in half. Every single casino in town pulled their ads. That station went under. It's a religious station now."

Timber laughed. "I guess that's a station that doesn't care much for the casino business." He thought of his sanctimonious mama, whom he had finally talked to Sunday night. He had told her about his visit to the casino with his fellow deejays. There had been a long pause on the line.

"I hope you didn't bet," she said. "Did you?"

He'd responded, "just a little one. I won, too, a bet on the Cardinals."

"That's the Devil's money, Timber. You should stay out of those places, go to church."

"Yes, ma'am," he said, changing the subject.

Chuck continued talking.

"It's a station that doesn't care about selling ads, either. You'd be surprised at their ratings, though. They do pretty well. Just behind us, as a matter of fact. They got this one shouting Southern Baptist preacher who goes on the air every single day. His shows do really well, lots of listeners. He's got quite a following in Nevada, in all of the West, really."

"No kidding. A Southern Baptist in Nevada?"

"That's right. I'm betting that a Southern deejay will do well here too. Our last morning guy was from L.A. Had the nickname of Hollywood. Thought he was too cool to be here."

"What happened to him?"

"We…I fired him. He pulled a no-show…and his ratings were poor anyway…but I see big things for you here, Timber. Go with the Southern thing. And don't hesitate to go after politicians at any level. Everybody out here hates 'em. You're going to go over well out West. Just don't—"

"—Piss off the casinos," Timber said. "Don't worry. Oil companies and carmakers I've got no respect for. But casinos, now, I would never say anything bad about such venerable institutions. Where do you think I plan to spend my Saturday nights?"

Chuck laughed.

"And Timber, if you ever need a wake-up call, let Igor know and he can give you a ring. I want you to be happy here. You work with me, I'll work with you."

They shook hands, Chuck vigorously, giving him a firm look in the eye.

Fifteen minutes later he was live.

"Good morning, Reno. It's six o'clock *Timber* time. A good Monday morning to you and yours. This is Timber Goodeneaux, fresh in town from the swamps of the bayou. Hope y'all won some money this weekend in one of these fine casinos in town. I sure did, let me tell you. But no, don't you worry, Old Timber's not going to retire just yet on my newfound riches. I just got here. I'm happy to be here. We are going to *enjoy* our mornings together."

Timber leaned back in his chair and the red light flicked off when he cut his mike. Igor nodded his approval. Chuck opened the door and told him he sounded great.

Radio was no big deal if you had the *voice*. He could recycle the same line a hundred different ways, applying it to celebrities, politicians, athletes, whomever. The jokes didn't matter. The *voice* was the thing.

His shift went very well. He was glad to be back on the air again, the place where he could open up. He could do this job in his sleep. In times past, he almost had.

He got off at ten and hung around the station till noon, visiting with Chuck, meeting the staff. After Chuck took him to lunch—a Mexican place where they toasted to future success with margaritas—he went home and took a nap. He awoke and spent a little time rearranging his furniture into an acceptable pattern, putting away some of the boxes, clearing out the living room.

He flipped on his television but he could pick up only one local station carrying a talk show, women blabbering on about some sort of health problem. His cable wouldn't be hooked up for a few more weeks. He checked the newspaper to see what baseball games might be on tonight. The Cardinals and the Astros were starting in an hour. If he hurried, he could put down a bet and watch the game. There was a game between the Braves and the Dodgers later that he had a good feeling about. Soon he was in the casino, placing his bets. He won both games, bringing home another $225, pushing his two-day winnings to more than $500.

After that, betting on baseball became his regular thing, his daily routine. He was so much more confident in his knowledge of baseball than in any of the card and dice games or the insanity of betting on a white ball bouncing around the roulette wheel. Even more pathetic were the keno players, most of them older than the black mountains, sitting, waiting, watching the ping pong balls bounce, hoping, praying for their combination of numbers to come up as though summoned by God.

He'd been to Vegas enough times back in his good days to know those games were like throwing money down a hole. But he knew baseball, had followed it all of his life. He understood all the stats and what they meant or didn't mean and what stats would affect the game and what stats wouldn't. Soon every morning after his shift ended, he snatched up the USA Today sports sections to study the pitching matchups. With a copy of the weekly baseball statistical tabloid, he analyzed the earned run averages of pitchers in agonizing detail, examining the result of their five most recent starts. He tried to picture who the house oddsmakers he was competing against were, what they were like. He figured they were old baseball fanatics as well, men who at seven years old had kept scorebooks of games like he had. He would put his knowledge of baseball up against anyone.

He was red hot for the first three weeks, winning almost two-thirds of his bets, going more than $3,000 into the black. He developed a system of betting two games a day: one big favorite with a strong pitcher, and one big underdog that had a pitcher with a decent ERA, the best he could find. The system was working like a charm. The real success of it depended on picking the underdog.

When the underdog won, he always made money, even if his favorite lost, although that usually didn't happen. Win both bets, he could bring in $350 on a $200 bet. When the underdog was the only winner, he would still bank as much as $150. When the favorite won and the underdog lost, he might lose as much as $25, but sometimes he would break even, depending on the favorite's line. Only when both teams lost did he lose it all. But that only happened one out of four times. He was happy with only a 25 percent shot at total failure.

And he enjoyed the free drinks brought to him by the parade of cocktail waitresses strapped into tight costumes, their hair coiffed and eye makeup heavy, sauntering back and forth. It beat the hell out of watching TV and sipping bourbon at home alone.

Jack and Ernie were back on a Saturday night several weeks later. They only went on weekends, but Timber had been there almost every night since moving to town.

There was a new cocktail waitress that night, a tall brunette who cruised by every inning or so to bring them more beer. Her name tag said she was Tammy from Bay St. Louis, Mississippi. He watched her come and go for the better part of the evening. She had big boobs and slim legs and he would have guessed she was twenty-five were it not for the subtle lines on her face, crinkles around her eyes. He couldn't tell if the lines were from worry or too much sun and wind, maybe both. He guessed her to be about thirty-three. But she had the steps of a girl and the smile of a teenage beauty queen. She was flirty with him, but he suspected that it was for the $2 tip he gave her for each beer. He had the urge to introduce himself as a fellow Southerner, imagining what he'd say, practicing it in his head, but then Jack started to flirt with her, calling her Mississippi Long Legs to her face and Big Rebel Titties behind her back. Timber just sat and smiled at her. She had big brown eyes that made direct contact with him a time or two. It made him weak.

He was tempted to ask Jack for the number of the escort service he used, to hook him up with a woman for the night. But he held off. He had been down that road before and didn't want to try it again. It was one of those things if he started, he couldn't stop. He watched Tammy the cocktail waitress come and go, her long brown hair drifting down her back, and drank himself numb.

The radio station had taken to him well. Ratings were up. Advertisers were happy. Timber talked about gambling on the air often, prompting more casino purchases of ad time than the station had ever seen.

And the Southern thing was working. He got a little more down home every day.

"I've been here about a month now," he said one Monday morning. "And I need your help, folks. I need to find me a restaurant with good Cajun food. You can take the boy out of Louisiana, but you can't take the Louisiana out of the boy. If you know a good Cajun place, give me a ring here at 102.7 FM—KTOP, the Big Top—all the hits that are fit to play, and some that aren't. Time for the news, so I'm going to turn it over to my good buddy Igor, and then a song."

The phones lit up, six lines flashing red.

Timber grabbed the first line. It sounded like an old black man from Mississippi, telling him, "There ain't no good Cajun food around here, boy. You got to go to Vegas for that. *But* there is some mighty fine Southern cooking out here on the airline highway—*Angelique's*. They got the best fried chicken, chicken-fried steak, collard greens and mashed potatoes you ever put in yore mouth."

Timber wrote down the address and thanked him, said he'd mention it over the air.

Igor wrapped up the news and began to help Timber field phone calls while a song began. He tapped on the window to get Timber's attention, holding up his hand and telling him to take line four. Timber picked up the flashing line.

"Good morning."

"Well, good morning to you too," a woman said. She had a lilting Southern accent. "You sound *so good* on the radio. I *love* your voice."

"You've got a nice voice yourself." He hadn't heard a girl's voice like this one in awhile. She reminded him of the women in Biloxi.

"*Aren't* you sweet?…To answer your question, *I* know where you can get the best Cajun food—gumbo, jambalaya, and even a good strong hurricane to drink. It'll blow you away."

"Where's that?"

"My house."

"Your house?"

"That's right. I'm from New Orleans. My mama was a Cajun girl. I know how to cook up beans and rice like nobody's business. There are no restaurants that could ever compare."

"Yes, but I haven't even met you."

"Of course you haven't, *silly*," she said. "You are new to town. How could you know me? But I'm a Southern girl. My mama taught me good manners. Probably yours did the same with you. So I know you wouldn't decline an invitation for a good dinner. I want to welcome you to Reno."

Timber checked the time on the song. He still had a few minutes. He thought back to the many radio women he'd known with sexy voices, voices that didn't match their appearance. He figured this poor girl was quite ugly, probably as big as a house the way she seductively talked about food, the kind of woman who would call up the deejay and hit on him at seven in the morning.

"Well, what do you say?" she asked.

Good sense told him to blow her off, to say he was married, to avoid her. There was a world full of lunatics, and a town built on gambling and drinking had more than its share. But, *damn*, he was lonesome. And he didn't want to start paying for it again. He had been strong, even with all this gambling money in his pocket. He would take whatever kind of free female company he could get.

"Why don't we meet someplace first?"

"I could come down there to the radio station when you get off."

"No, not here. How about a bar? Later this afternoon?"

"Well, okay. There's a place just south of downtown, near where I live, called Lucky Seven. Can you meet me there at four? I'm off today."

Timber wrote down the name of the bar.

"OK. What do you look like—so I'll recognize you?"

"I'm about five-eight, with long brown hair. I'll wear—let's see—my silver dress. You can't miss me. My name's Tammy."

"OK, Tammy." He had a good feeling about her. "See you soon."

Timber trimmed his shaggy beard that afternoon and sprayed on some cologne he bought in a drug store in the strip mall next to his apartment complex. He had not been on a date with a woman in more than two years, back before his affair in Flint had begun. And the Flint liaisons were never dates, but usually just drinks and sex in his apartment, or an occasional session in his car on the playground behind the elementary school where she taught, exciting rendezvous early in the relationship when it was new and different, before fatigue and boredom took hold.

He walked into the Lucky Seven, his eyes adjusting to the dark bar from the bright sunlight. He couldn't believe his eyes. *This* Tammy was the *same* Tammy from the casino, the tall cocktail waitress he had been watching Saturday night, bringing him beer after beer, the one he'd been preparing to chat up until Jack pre-empted him.

She looked magnificent, out of place in the afternoon alcoholics' dive, a long narrow room with the bar running the length of it. Her long dark hair was brushed forward and down past her shoulders. The low-cut tight dress accentuated her chest—too round to be human, implants, certainly—that he could hardly take his eyes off. His mouth went dry. He could hardly speak. He was very self-conscious of his limp.

"Tammy?" He was weak-voiced for a change.

"So *you* are Timber? It's so nice to be properly introduced. I remember you from the other night. I thought you were cute. Too bad I didn't get to hear you talk. I didn't know I was serving a celebrity."

He held out his hand, but she hugged him, pressing herself against him. She smelled good, like a magnolia. It had been a long time since he'd been in the South. Houston girls had smelled like that.

She clung to him, almost nuzzling, before letting him go and sitting back down on the barstool. He sat next to her. Her glass was almost empty.

"What are you drinking?"

"Gin and tonic," she said. The words rolled up and down in her mouth, from high to low to high again.

He ordered two gin and tonics.

"So you said on the phone that you are from New Orleans but your name tag said Bay St. Louis."

She tilted her head slightly and cut her eyes, opening them, almost as if she could make them brighter.

"My mama was from New Orleans, and we went there a lot, but I lived most of my time in Mississippi. I tell most folks around here New Orleans cause they know where that is."

"Yeah." He laughed. "Me, too. I'm from Whitcomb, Louisiana, but most of the time I'll say Baton Rouge, but every now and then I can pass for a native of the Big Easy. We are both a long way from the bayou up here in these dusty mountains."

"Tell me about it, sugar." She put her hand on his forearm.

The drinks came and they clinked the glasses together and took a sip. The door to the bar was propped open. It was a warm day, in the seventies. To Timber it seemed like a spring day back down South.

"A Mississippi girl. How'd you end up way out here?"

"*Lord*, it's a long story. I married the wrong man…I'm telling you, I loved him something fierce. He brought me out to Las Vegas six years ago, when I was only twenty-three."

"You're twenty-nine now?"

"That's right. My last year of my twenties. I plan to go out with a bang, too. I wasted a lot of this decade. I want to send it out right, too. You want a cigarette?"

She pulled a pack and a lighter from her small silver purse that matched her dress. He watched her. She had the body of a twenty-nine-year-old or younger, although her face looked older. Perhaps the desert sun—she was tanned dark—had aged her. Maybe she frequented tanning beds. From the glimpses he could get down her dress when she leaned over, she had no tan lines at all.

She got her cigarette burning and started talking again, gesturing this way and that with the smoldering flame. She looked him up and down.

"I'm guessing you are…. forty-three, forty-four? And a Capricorn."

He started to shake his head, tell her that no, she was wrong, he was only thirty-six, and a Gemini, but why confess to looking older than he was? He would be whatever she wanted him to be.

"That's right—forty three. And yes, I'm a Capricorn."

"I can always tell." She leaned close to him. "You know, I *love* your voice. You talk like you are on the radio even when you are not. Talking on the radio, I mean. I wish it wasn't so hard to hear you in here."

The jukebox was thumping with another Madonna song, popular music he despised and heard too much of already working for a top forty station.

"You want to go someplace else?" he said.

He could feel himself falling, drifting down, going wherever this woman wanted to take him. He was a rudderless boat on the water, following the current, defenseless to the undertow, easy to be pulled along like an empty beer can in a rip tide.

"Yeah, of course," she said. "Let's go to my place. I've got some gumbo to fix and some jambalaya. I also make crawfish étouffée but it's hard to get good crawfish out here. They get these scrawny little ones from Asia at the seafood place I go to. They ain't worth eating."

She kept speaking and didn't seem to know the power she had over him, or maybe she did. (Timber had overheard his daddy say to Hyatt Delacroix once, "Women's got half the money in the world and all the pussy—what more could they want?") Her eyes almost danced when she talked.

"I live right near here. You can just follow me home. Now don't laugh at my old car. It's all I can afford since my ex won't pay his alimony. He's got money, too. Oh hell, I'll get back at him, sooner or later. I got a lawyer working on it."

"Where does he live now?"

"Oh, don't worry," she said. "He's not around here. Let's go."

Timber ushered her out the door, a hand on the small of her back, down where the dress narrowed before fanning out snug over her hips. The smattering of men at the bar, most of whom had been sitting with their heads hanging down over their drinks, watched them go.

They stepped outside. The sun was beginning to descend toward the mountains in the west, glorious red and orange and brown in the dusty rocks that had been there for eons, and would weather the sun and heat and darkness and cold long after the casinos were gone, maybe until the earth perished. He was in the car, thinking about these things, when he realized his radio was tuned to a Southern Baptist preacher, the one Chuck had told him about. The preacher was damning the modern world to hell and good.

Tammy drove a Ford Escort, red, an eight-year-old model with a crease in the front bumper and a big dent in the passenger's side door. Timber followed her. These days he was driving a fairly nondescript Pontiac Grand Am, blue, a two-year-old model he had bought before leaving Flint. It wasn't a car that screamed money and drove the ladies wild—like his Karmann Ghia in Houston had—but it was nothing to be ashamed of, either.

He followed her to her apartment complex, a cluster of two-story stucco buildings. She led him up a flight of stairs. He watched her ass move around in the shiny silver dress, her calf muscles tanned and firm and smooth, the legs of a nineteen-year-old. He was glad she couldn't see his limp, exaggerated when climbing.

She had not lived in the furnished apartment very long. There was nothing on the walls, no photos or knick-knacks or souvenirs. A big bottle of gin was on the counter.

"You want a drink? I've got gin—Tanqueray—the good stuff." She was in the kitchen, behind the counter. It opened up into the den, decorated only with one couch and a pinewood coffee table, a blonde-colored wood.

"Sure. That sounds good."

"Have a seat. I'll bring it out to you." He settled down onto the couch, a cheap beige sleeper sofa. She brought the drinks out and handed him his glass. They clicked them together and each took a sip. It was heavy on the gin, much stronger than in the bar.

"So I listened to your entire show this morning. You are so funny. You crack me up. And I *love* the way you introduce songs. You sound *so* smooth. I feel like I know you."

She kicked off her shoes and shifted on the couch, bending her legs up under her, her knees flexed, her short dress riding up high on her thighs. "I don't know what it is about your voice."

"I've been on the radio a long time—since I was thirteen."

"I don't even guess I was born yet," she said, laughing and cutting her eyes at him. She reached out and touched his shoulder. She smelled terrific. He wanted to kiss her right then and there. He took another sip of his drink instead. It was extra strong, the gin taste permeating his mouth like a chemical.

"So, tell me about you—you didn't finish telling me your story. How'd you end up a cocktail waitress in Reno, listening to the radio at six in the morning?"

"Honey," she flipped her hand in a wavelike motion, "that's a long one. It would take all night to tell the half of it. Me and my ex did good for a while, living high on the hog and all that, but then it all went to shit."

"How long have y'all been split up?"

"About a year."

"What does he do?"

"*Now?* He's in jail. He's got another year or two."

Timber didn't know what to say.

"It's okay, honey. I'm sure you've been married at some point too."

"Nope, never have…moved around too much. I never did let myself get tied down."

"You just haven't met the right one yet." She leaned forward and kissed him, her lips soft against his, partly open, inviting. But she pulled back.

"You need another drink," she said, taking his empty glass from the coffee table. He watched her shimmy into the kitchen and back with the drinks.

She handed him his refill, and proceeded to tell him the story of her life, of growing up Catholic in a Mississippi town full of Baptists, of going to college at Ole Miss, of meeting a gambling man on a visit to New York with college friends. She thought he was a legitimate businessman for a few years, until they moved to Las Vegas.

After he got locked up, she worked as a cocktail waitress at Harrah's in Vegas for six months. The money was good and the people in the casino treated her well. She rarely had to work the overnight shift there. But she had wanted to get out of Vegas, the bad memories of her ex, and start over. That's when the job in Reno opened up.

She talked and talked like Southern girls tended to do, a slew of hand gestures and smiles and blinks, more expressions than he could count, her voice rising and falling like a barometric pressure needle during a hurricane.

After their fourth drink, she began to kiss him again, this time straddling him, her fingers grasping at his shirt collar, unbuttoning it, and kissing him, moving slowly down.

He had never been so lucky, not in a long time, anyway, since Houston. She called his name over and over, holding him like he'd not been held before. Timber fell asleep in her arms, her stroking his hair, calling him a "sweet baby." He forgot all about her plans to fix him dinner.

She woke him at five. "Honey, don't you have to go on the air soon?" He never would have woken himself that day. It was hard to leave her warm bed. He made love to her one more time. He smiled all the way down to the station.

His show that morning was one of the best he'd ever done. He felt like a new man. Every song sounded good, his jokes went off just right. For the first time in a long time, he was happy to be alive.

That afternoon he collapsed into her arms, her long nails caressing his back, scratching his neck, running through his bristly hair. He began to call her an "angel" with multiple variations: "my Mississippi angel," "my angelic gin-drinking darling," and most often, "my sweet *sweet* angel girl."

On the fourth consecutive night in bed with her he opened up and told her everything, things he'd never told anyone about: the truth about his limp, the childhood fishing accident; that he'd never played football; about his boyhood with Mama; his daddy's killing; his sister's disappearance; his high times in Houston (some of these stories he'd told before, but she enjoyed them, particularly the references to famous people); his fall from Houston and drifting down: the loss of his van to a prostitute, the dismal affair and firing in Flint. He told her how lonely he'd been before he met her. How he loved her.

"I think," she said, "that God sent you out here to find me."

"Oh my angel. I do too. I do too."

He talked all night long, like he'd never talked before. He hadn't opened up to anyone like that ever, to let the gates down and spill everything inside of him. He hadn't even entertained the thought that maybe there was a God or such a thing as fate in many years, almost since the time he left Whitcomb and his mama behind. But he felt that spark again. He would take Tammy to see his mama soon. He would take her to Louisiana as soon as they were married, hopefully by the end of the month.

The wedding was held six weeks later, a mid-June Thursday night, in the small Harrah's casino chapel, officiated by the casino preacher, a retired Baptist minister from Mississippi whom Tammy had befriended.

Reno was an easy place to get hitched. All it required was to fill out a form and pay $75, although one could run up a much bigger bill depending on how many frills were desired, such as the purple and gold bells, the rock 'n' roll wedding band, an Elvis impersonator to conduct the service.

Timber and Tammy had guests enough to fill the eight-pew chapel, almost to the fire marshal's capacity of thirty-eight persons. Timber chose Chuck as his best man. Jack and Ernie and Igor and ten other men from the radio station showed up, including all the deejays, engineers and the board ops except for the ones on the air. Wendy, the saucy receptionist, and Jean, an overnight board op who Timber didn't know, were the only two women employees of the radio station who attended.

Tammy had a new family of her own. Ten of her fellow cocktail waitresses attended, including the three best-looking ones she chose as bridesmaids, adorned in gold dresses with plunging necklines and high side cuts that showed their legs when they walked. A few brought their children—six kids from the ages of one to nine played in the back of the chapel.

He hadn't told his mama about the wedding. He knew she would never approve, would never set foot in a casino, and most likely would never even recognize the validity of such a wedding, preferring to believe he was living in sin to actually being betrothed in the eyes of God. Even worse, he was marrying a Catholic girl, although Tammy said she hadn't been to Mass in years, since she left Mississippi. His mama might say one of the only things worse than a Catholic was a disgraced Catholic, and that was only slightly better than the hordes of non-believers that populated the ragged earth. She might not ever say it, but Timber knew what she would think. He had not been home since Christmas more than two years ago. He was ashamed of himself for that. But he would be home for her birthday in only a few weeks, his new bride by his side. He was even entertaining the idea of going through with a church wedding in Whitcomb to satisfy Mama. He'd bring that up with Tammy soon enough.

But for now he was standing up in the small chapel at Harrah's, marrying one of the sexiest cocktail waitresses, an audience of hair-dyed, booth-tanned women on one side and a slumping assembly of shaggy, leering men on the other, their physiques soft and beaten down from years of radio, bodies strong of voice only. Timber beamed with pride when he saw Tammy come down that aisle, a smile blinding like white lights, brown eyes dancing like marbles in a candle flame, her white dress cut low on her cleavage and her hemline halfway up her thigh, her shoulders tanned and smooth and smelling of magnolias, the Mississippi state flower. His mama at least should be happy that he was marrying a girl from her home state. Tammy had that going for her with his mama. The service lasted all of ten minutes before they were declared man and wife.

The wedding reception was held in the bar of the casino's steak house. It was a hard-drinking affair, the radio men at the end of the bar doing shots, standing together, while the women stood out away from the bar in a tight circle, drinking vodka and water and talking nonstop to one another, the mothers in the group eyeing their children who played around the house piano, unused that night. Occasionally one of the radio men, bolstered by a shot, would amble over to the bridesmaids' party and try to flirt, but it was to no avail. The cocktail waitresses made it clear that they were off duty, and the haggard men got nothing but cool brush-offs, not the smiles they were used to when the girls had on their standard-issue purple and gold tights and were working for tips. These men had no chances of hooking up tonight. Timber could see the jealousy in his peers' eyes as they returned to the end of the bar, defeated, shot down by the stable of statuesque ladies. None of them spoke of defeat, however; instead they raised their glasses to Timber, toasting him, as Jack said, "to one lucky dog."

The drinks were all on the house as long as they stuck to the bottom-shelf liquors. And the presidential suite on top of the casino, twenty floors up, was comped for their first night as man and wife. It was a giant room with a king-sized waterbed, a hot tub and a fully-stocked liquor bar. The room had huge windows spanning the east and north walls, twelve-foot-tall arches reaching up to the high ceiling, giving a vast view of the blackness of the desert, the mountains dim against the starry night sky.

The party was still going at midnight when they went upstairs, drunk, and took a bottle of gin into the hot tub. He poured it on her, licking it off her stiff nipples, and calling out to her, "my angel bride, my angel bride."

He awoke the next morning and rolled over, the waterbed sloshing along with the pounding in his head. Tammy was not next to him. He raised up, disappointed, a slight panic that she was not there. He was fond of opening his eyes to see her long brown hair fanning out over the pillow, her lips pursed in her sleep. He sat up and saw her at the huge window, completely naked, her hair falling down her back, ending just above her ass. She was looking at the sky turning blue and pink, clouds lit up like they were plugged-in signs, burnt orange around the edges. He could see her reflection in the glass but she did not see him. She was lost in the landscape, her brown eyes troubled in the morning view. Her lips were tight, mournful, the lines in her face exaggerated as she surveyed the world from twenty stories above the desert. It was an expression he had not yet seen.

She wanted to honeymoon in Vegas. They could get another free room, this time at the Mirage, courtesy of an old friend of hers, for as long as they wanted. Timber had wanted to go further west, to the California coast, L.A. or San Francisco, or maybe even Hawaii. He had more than $3,000 from his baseball winnings stocked away. It was their only disagreement. She won the mild argument rather easily, batting her eyes, pursing her lips in a pout.

The suite on the Mirage's fortieth floor—the top—was spectacular, a grand space larger than most homes, a Louis XIV-style opulence complete with two big-screen TVs, a waterbed, a hot tub and a liquor cabinet stocked with top-shelf spirits. The windows were even larger than in the room in Reno, twenty feet high, allowing views looking straight down into the Mirage's volcano, a mechanical fire spout that went off every fifteen minutes. Beyond that were the bright lights of the Vegas strip, and then the vast Mojave Desert that melted away into distant mountains, snowcaps visible in the daytime even on summer days above a hundred degrees.

The first two days in Vegas they drank, ordered room service and frolicked in the hot tub and the bed, going out only for dinner and to the spa for full-body massages, also compliments of the house. Timber was in heaven, a wet dishrag of a man, drained of every ounce of stress.

He awoke Sunday to find she was not in the bed, not anywhere in the suite. She'd left a note on her nightstand that said she had to go visit her lawyer, and also was going to have lunch with some old friends in Vegas. Seeing a lawyer on a Sunday? He frowned. He wished she had told him the night before instead of just leaving a note. He could have taken her to the lawyer's office. He would have liked to have met some of her old Vegas friends.

He checked the clock: nine-thirty Vegas time. It was Sunday, time for afternoon baseball. He'd have to hurry to bet the early East Coast games starting in half an hour. He had his eye on a few of today's matchups.

He was aggressive that morning, dropping $500 on the Yankees at home against the Red Sox, and $500 on the Padres at the Braves, his underdog pick. He sat in the sports book and drank a Bloody Mary to ease the lingering headache from the gin the night before. Both games started out brilliantly for his teams, staking leads of three and four runs early. His pitchers looked strong, taking care of business. This would be the easiest $1,300 he ever made. He would take Tammy out to the most expensive restaurant he could find that night, or maybe even surprise her with plane tickets to L.A. for a day trip on Monday, before they went back to Reno.

He ordered another Bloody Mary from the cocktail waitress, took a sip, and watched his games go south. His pitchers lost their leads and were pulled. His teams went into the bottom innings tied, calling on their respective bullpens to hold. The Padres collapsed first, the Braves lighting them up for six runs in the bottom of the eighth. He was sure the mighty Yankees playing in the House That Ruth Built would hold out against the hated Red Sox. But the Yankees bullpen fell apart like a dam of sandbags giving way to a tidal flood, collapsing in the top of the ninth inning and falling into a hole from which they could never get out.

He was almost sick to his stomach, unable to believe he had lost $1,000 and it was not even one o'clock yet. He'd had his eye on another pair of later games, starting soon. There was little chance that he could lose four in a row. He was still up $2,000 for the month, since his baseball betting binge began. Why not go for a big win? He was in Vegas, on his honeymoon. Time to lay it on the line. He could afford to do it. He had a *feeling* about these next two games. He finished off his third Bloody Mary—the hangover long gone—placed his bets, $500 apiece, and went up to watch the scores in his room and wait for Tammy to get back. Surely she would be back soon.

He stretched out on the bed that had been made while he was downstairs and ate the piece of chocolate the maids left on his pillow. He was tempted to eat Tammy's but instead set it aside on the nightstand. The games started out poorly and quickly got worse. He flipped back and forth with the remote between the two games until he could take it no more. The realization of losing $2,000 began to settle on him like a cold chill.

It was getting close to four and she still wasn't home. The sun outside the giant windows was blazing, searing the red-brown desert below, the big blue sky unmarred by clouds. He wished he could sleep. There would be nothing better than to drift off and wake to her kissing him on the forehead, her joining him in the bed. But he could not sleep. He lay there staring at the high ceiling, the sky and the slow progression of the digital clock.

She got back several hours later, as the sun began to set, an orange ball knocked over the distant mountains. She was in her silver dress again, that one from the first time he met her.

She barely smiled at him, a forced expression, far from her sweet grin.

"Did you get things worked out with your lawyer? How'd that go?"

"Oh." She sighed, deeply, a long slow breath. "It's going to take some time, a long time. I don't know what'll happen. I don't really want to get into it now. I was there most of the day. I *hate* goddamn lawyers."

"His office is open on Sunday?"

She glared at him sharply. "*Yes.*"

"Is there anything I can do? You want me to talk to them?"

"No, Timber. I can handle it *myself*. I'm a big girl."

Her tone was icy. He paused. She walked to the mirror and took off her necklace, gold with a single pearl.

"How were your friends? Did you get to see them?"

"Yeah, I had a drink with them. But I wasn't in the mood for it."

She was standing before the mirror at the dresser, facing it, but not looking into it. He walked over behind her and put his arms around her, hugging around her stomach, pressing his body to hers. She didn't respond, but began to cry, slow quick gasps that grew into a deep whine until finally a loud wail. He squeezed her tight and turned her, still unresponsive, until she faced him, dropping her head onto his shoulder, tears trickling down. He picked her up and laid her supine on the bed, covering her with a blanket. She cried herself to sleep, napping for an hour, her mascara smeared down her face in tracks like spidery veins. She awoke, her only movement opening her eyes, and looked at him like she had never seen him before in her life. He asked her what was wrong, if he could get her anything…water, a drink, something to eat. She said nothing, only shook her head no. He reached to hold her hand under the blanket but she pulled it away. She lay like that for an hour.

When she finally rose, she was still in the silver dress, too tight to wrinkle. She went straight into the bathroom and locked the door, running the water. He couldn't understand why she would use the tub in the bathroom when there was a huge hot tub with a view in the corner of the suite, elevated to see out the big windows and into the desert.

He tapped on the bathroom door when the water shut off.

"Can I get you anything?"

"No."

After fifteen minutes, he tapped again.

"You okay?"

"Yes. I'm fine," she said, icily. "I just need to be alone for a while."

He looked at the clock. There were two late games that he could bet and recover the day's losses. He wanted to get out of the room, away from the chill she'd brought. Maybe watching a game, a drink, would relax him and give her some time alone. He could hear her sloshing softly in the tub.

He went back downstairs to the sports book and put $500 on the Mariners at home and another $500 on the Mets at the Dodgers, his underdog pick. He looked at his watch and could hardly believe it was only seven.

Both games started terribly again, his money riding on pitchers that fell into deep holes, the Mets and Mariners looking like they were in slow motion, lethargic, unable to get a hit, unable to throw good pitches, unable to get anybody out. It was like the players were underwater, standing around like mannequins, pissing away his last $1,000 and not giving a damn.

That was not even the worst of it. He had no idea what was going on with his wife. His *wife*. He sat there in a daze, sipping on bourbon, numb. He stayed through the end of the games—two of the sorriest contests he had ever seen. He got up slowly and wandered around the casino, randomly stopping at a roulette wheel where an old bald-headed man was trying his luck.

He reached into his wallet, pulling out the last bill there, a wrinkled twenty. He smoothed it and laid it flat on black. "Cash in play," the dealer shouted out to no one in particular. He spun the wheel. The white ball raced around madly, slowing down to bounce in a series of clicks before coming to rest on the green double zero.

He took the elevator forty stories up to the room. Tammy was in bed, sleeping, the lights off, the huge curtains drawn over all the windows, Vegas-thick drapes that kept the bright neon light and the ferocious sunshine out. He stumbled to one of two big chairs in the spacious room, large recliners reminiscent of when his battered chair was new, and stared into darkness.

Tammy awoke the next morning and she was fine, a new person, apologizing for her mood. She blamed it on the beginning of her period.

"I'm sorry, but sometimes it just makes me absolutely crazy. I need to see a doctor about it."

He kissed her, rubbed his hands across her back. "Oh, baby, not today. I just started. I'm a mess. Give me a few days."

They checked out of the room and went to a nice lunch. Timber paid by credit card. Afterward, they drove around Las Vegas, out to Hoover Dam, sightseeing in the desert, killing time until their flight back to Reno. They were home and in bed by midnight.

Things were fine between them for three weeks, although he'd had a *bad* betting streak since that fateful day on the honeymoon when he lost all six games. He'd dropped his average bets from $100 to $50 per game, and still continued to lose most of them, sometimes splitting his two daily games, but always losing the profitable underdog, and on several occasions losing both games. He was down about $2,000, running up his credit cards again.

He had been ready for a night off from the casino when Friday rolled around. Chuck had scheduled him with a remote broadcast from a local Ford dealership that was going to give away a new model Thunderbird to anyone who could hit a golf ball from the parking lot through the "O" in the Ford sign. The station's promotions director, T.J., an excellent golfer, had come up with the idea, assuring the Ford dealer that no one could make the shot of more than two hundred yards because the "O" was much too high in the air. A large crowd of would-be Thunderbird owners took their shots to no avail.

Timber got an extra $300 for his time. He needed it. In addition to the losing bets, his new bride was expensive, running up bills for clothes and a few new pieces of furniture for the apartment, as well as other household odds and ends like the $125 shower curtain and $90 placemats. She'd opened up numerous charge accounts, and got them both joint VISA and American Express cards.

But she took care of him in bed each night. He was a simple man. He worried about the expenses but then he would think about all the money he'd given to North Dakota prostitutes and figured a few thousand dollars in credit card bills wasn't so bad.

Timber went out for drinks with the radio crew at a bar near the station after the Ford remote. Jack, Ernie and a few of the engineers who had been at his wedding were there. They kidded him, wanting tips on how to marry a cocktail waitress, wanting to know what she was like. He laughed, said he was lucky, that was all.

He got home at midnight, but Tammy wasn't there. She got off at nine. She had mentioned something about going out with the girls one night after work, so he figured maybe she went tonight. He went to bed tired and slightly drunk.

He woke up Saturday morning and she was still not home. He went into the bathroom and realized that her toothbrush was missing, along with most of her cosmetics. He checked the closet—her silver dress and a suitcase and some other clothes were gone. He called the casino and her boss told him that she had called in sick Friday, but still came in to get her check. She also had asked for all of the weekend off.

Timber hung his head. He had bought plane tickets to Louisiana for the first weekend in July, Mama's birthday. He had planned to surprise her with his new bride.

He waited all day Saturday for Tammy to call. Maybe there was an explanation. Maybe she had been kidnapped. If only her toothbrush and suitcase weren't gone. Maybe she had a surprise in store for him. She was like that, full of unpredictable acts, whims, like the morning she had called him on the radio. He scoured the apartment three times, looking for a note, some type of clue as to where she had gone.

The darkness came Saturday and he decided to call the police. They sent out an officer to take a report, an old man with a smoker's voice, glasses and loose wrinkled skin that hung on his bony frame like a black banana peel.

Timber described Tammy, the details of when he'd seen her last. The old man raised an eyebrow when he told him she had taken her toothbrush and packed a suitcase.

"Had you been fighting?"

"No. We'd been fine."

"And you said you were married only three weeks ago?"

"Yes, that's right."

"Humph." The old man scratched his head. "Well…we can see if we spot her. But it don't sound like foul play. If we do find her, we can't make her come back. You got a picture of her?"

They had gotten the wedding pictures in the mail that week. He retrieved one from the bedroom, a close-up of Tammy in the tight wedding dress, her cleavage boosted up.

"Wow. She is a looker all right. How old did you say she is?"

"Twenty-nine."

"I'm not saying she doesn't look great, because she does, but she looks a little older than that, but I'll go with what you tell me. Maybe she got too much sun. I'm sure all the guys down at the station house will want to see this…Any where you think she might have run off to?"

"Vegas, maybe. She had lived there for a while. Her ex is there."

"You know his name? Where he lives?"

"No. She said he is in jail. But I don't know a thing about him."

"Well…we can run records on her."

"Okay," he said. "When do you think you'll have something to tell me?"

"There's no telling, son. It might be an hour, it might be never. It's a big old world out there for people to disappear into. They do it all the damn time."

Timber thought about calling Chuck, to have someone to talk to, to see if he had any ideas. He also thought about calling some of the girls Tammy had worked with and see if she said anything to them. But he didn't know their last names, their numbers. He could talk to them later if she didn't come back. And Tammy had only been in town a little more than a month. She wasn't that close to any of the girls anyway. Maybe she would come home. He didn't want to run out blabbing his troubles all over town. He so badly wanted to talk to someone, but there was no one to whom he was close. She was the only person he'd had. He could never tell Mama. He sat awake all night in his chair, flipping through the TV channels, the sound down low, the phone at his side not ringing.

The next morning about ten his phone startled him from a light sleep. He was still in the recliner, all the way back. He struggled to get out of it and answer.

"Mr. Goodman, I'm Detective Robinson," a deep voice said. "I've got some information about your wife."

"Did you find her?" Timber's heart palpitated, imagining her dead.

"No, but we are looking. She's got a number of warrants out for her. Why don't you come down here and see the file. I don't think she *is* who you think she is."

Twenty minutes later Timber was alone in an interrogation room with a file an inch thick. The detective had given it to him, saying, "this will explain everything."

Her real name was Stacey Runyon. She was forty-one, born in Mobile, Alabama. She had been married eleven times. In the seventies she'd had a lucrative career as a stripper in Vegas. She'd been arrested fourteen times, including a number of theft charges, twice on prostitution and most recently an assault, burglary and theft charge in Vegas. The police report said she had sex with a wealthy man in his sixties. After he went to sleep, she hit him in the head with a fireplace poker and stole his wallet and several pieces of artwork, including a Salvador Dali drawing worth $25,000. She'd been released on $500,000 bail. She missed a court appearance on Friday and a nationwide alert was out for her arrest.

Timber would have never believed it had he not seen the photocopies of her many mug shots, ranging from 1974 to the most recent one. In all of them, she looked beautiful. He longed for her still. He knew it was stupid, completely illogical and ridiculous, but deep inside himself he loved her, a fiery passion he couldn't extinguish, an overwhelming feeling in his subconscious. He wished he had a switch and could turn it off. But instead he held out the hope that maybe she really did love him, that those nights since they met six weeks ago where she held him and called him her "sweet, sweet baby," stroking his hair, rubbing his back, the mornings she woke up and was eager to take him inside her, wherever he pleased, *surely* that, some of it at least, had been real.

He sat in his recliner that afternoon with a big glass of bourbon, large chunks of ice melting fast, his mind racing through her police file, her fourteen mug shots etched sharply in his brain. Their framed wedding portrait sat on the chest of drawers. When his clear mind was thinking he told himself he was better off without her, she was high maintenance, difficult. She was old, after all. There were many younger women who would be interested in him, who would love him, dote on him, call him "baby." But when he relaxed and let his thoughts wander, he missed her, longed for her, would do anything if she would come back. He could forgive her. He would help her. He loved her. If only he could tell her. If only he knew where she was, how he could find her. He slumped back in his seat and took another drink.

He awoke the next morning at six to the phone ringing. It was Igor. Where was he? His mouth was dry as the desert, crusty. He could hardly speak a word. His head pounded, his neck and shoulders aching, sore. He was still in his recliner.

"I'm sick," he said, sounding it. "I'm getting the flu, I think."

There was a long pause. Igor was a slow thinker, the type who scripted out most of his on-air lines.

"What do you want me to do?" Igor finally asked.

"Can you cover for me? Just today?"

"I'm not a deejay. I can't do the whole show. I've got to run the board and put together the newscast."

"Okay, okay," Timber said. "I'll be down there as soon as I can. Can you cover for me, till seven?"

"I don't guess I have much of a choice, do I?" Igor hung up.

Timber splashed water on his face and pulled on a baseball cap with a Ford logo. He was about ready to go when a wrenching in his stomach sent him reeling to the toilet. He hunched forward and leaned over it, spewing up a yellow stream of vomit, a mixture of stomach acid and bourbon. The volume was tremendous. It roared into the toilet bowl like a hose, the putrid liquid pouring out of him until he began to wretch with dry heaves.

Eventually, the vomiting subsided. He sat for a minute, crouched over the toilet, trying to catch his breath, his chest and throat in pain—the liquor had burned on the way back up. He noticed in the corner beneath the sink one of her lipstick tubes, a silver one. She must have dropped it as she gathered up her things to go. He opened it, swirling the deep red stick up. In the shape of it he could see the curve of her lips, the round smooth lips he had kissed, that had kissed him all over. He hung his head, and for the first time in his adult life, he cried, salty big drops splashing into the toilet, running down his face, washing away some of the vomit from his lips. His sobs slowed down to low whines. After awhile, he got to his feet, his bad ankle killing him from squatting. He washed his face, brushed his teeth and looked in the mirror. He felt better but he looked like shit.

He got an idea. He put into his duffel bag a copy of Willie Nelson's "Red Headed Stranger" and "Willie and Family Live," recorded down the road at the Lake Tahoe Harrah's in 1979, both albums the top forty station didn't own. He took a bottle of bourbon, a fresh one, from the liquor cabinet. Four of his radio buddies had each given him a bottle of liquor as a wedding gift. He was down to the last one, but suspected maybe Tammy had taken one with her when she left. He noticed a bottle of gin was gone too.

He was in front of the microphone by fifteen after seven. Igor glared at him and walked out. A Madonna song was playing, something preposterous about her being "like a virgin." He locked himself in the deejay booth and wedged a chair under the doorknob. He let down the thick red velvet curtain that covered the window between his seat and the news booth where Igor sat. He cued up both Willie albums. He cracked open the bottle of Jim Beam and took a drink. He pulled on his headphones and hit a switch that put his sound board in control of what went out over the air, stopping the song mid-lyric.

"Good morning, y'all," he said, his voice lower, less his radio voice and more his real voice, still deep but not as charged. "This here is Timber. And I've got a story to tell y'all this morning, so sit back and listen, sympathize with me a little. I was just a simple man from Louisiana when I moved out here to spin some records and tell you a few jokes. Every now then and some of the jokes might even have been funny.

"But Lord, I was a lonely man when I got here. I'd never been married even though I was thirty-six years old. I'd never even told a woman I loved her, except for my mama, of course, and this one good-looking gal in Houston who was already married and not interested in me one bit. I did that on the radio. Made a pure ass of myself. Got me fired. And I imagine what I'm doing here today will too.

"But I don't give a good god*damn* about that. In Reno I met the most beautiful brown-eyed, long-haired woman you've ever seen. Curvaceous, with eyes that lit up like ten thousand jewels in the night. *She* sought me out. Called me up right here one morning and invited me over for some Cajun food. Now I should have suspected that maybe she wasn't who she said she was when her gumbo and jambalaya came out bland, but I was lovestruck, helpless as a child. Her kisses weren't bland, I tell you that. And she smelled like a big magnolia bud. She could do about anything she wanted to with me. I guess she just about did.

"After six weeks—and I know some of you mamas in the crowd with sons out there are shaking your heads, my mama will shake her head too if I ever tell her this story—after *six weeks* we got married. She was the best-looking bride you ever did see. We went to Vegas for our honeymoon, had a great time except for the day she disappeared and came back with a raging headache. I lost $3,000 on baseball games, like a dumbass.

"Now a quick little message for all you gamblers out there: You know the house has everything in its favor. You know you *can't* beat the house. If you've ever gambled more than a few times, you know what I'm talking about. You just don't want to admit it. I'm telling you, it's all rigged against you. The casino ain't nobody's friend. Get help if you got a problem. Get the hell out of this town, this state, if you have to.

"But that's not what I'm here to talk to you about this morning. I want to talk to you about love. The kind of love I had for Tammy, a blind love that ate at me from the inside, and always will, a totally unreasonable emotion, tearing me all up. If I was a violent man with a gun, I might just go down to Vegas and hunt her up myself and kill her, shoot her ex-husband right between the eyes and turn the gun on myself."

Behind him he could hear pounding and shouts, muffled by the thick soundproof door.

"But I ain't going to do that. I understand why people sometimes do. Love makes you do crazy things. I can see good and well how people go plumb crazy. I'm there in my own mind right now.

"And I got a feeling I ain't going to be on the air much longer. Old Timber is going to be shut down. So, Tammy, my angel, wherever you are, I hope you are out there listening. I love you. I always will. And I don't believe all these things between us was fake. I'll help you baby, if you get in touch with me. I'll forgive you. I'll be here all this week…you know the number.

"And Mama, I know you can't hear me down there in Louisiana, but I'm sorry, Mama, for being a sorry son. I'm sorry for running off on you and chasing this radio business and women all over the country. Lord, Mama, I'm a mess…I'm coming home, Mama. I know you've been praying for me. I know you always will do so. I appreciate it, Mama, and I love you…I'm sorry for being *so sorry*…But I'll be home soon, Mama…I'll be home soon."

THE GOSPEL ACCORDING TO LITTLE JOHN

Zeke's second day in a Vegas flophouse he met Little John. He was from Galveston, Texas, and came by his name honestly, standing only five feet four and weighing about 130 pounds with droopy ears and a big nose and a thick pair of glasses, plastic brown frames. He had faded tattoos, picked up in Vietnam, of a rifle and a heart on his wiry arms. His short hair was thin and brown and greasy, parted in the middle.

Little John was a feisty man, edgy, always fidgeting. Zeke liked him despite his obvious boasting. He talked loud, much louder than was necessary in the cheap motel room that Zeke called home. He smoked one Marlboro after another, burning them right down to the stub before flicking the filters with a violent motion of his thumb and forefinger, vaulting the smoldering butts out the open door and into the parking lot. Little John was always wound up about something. He loved the sound of his own voice.

He apparently had no one to talk to until Zeke moved into the Old West Motel, a twenty-four-room dive offering lodging for $149 a week, not too far from the famous neon cowboy sign on Fremont Street. This was the *old* Vegas, downtown, a neighborhood where some of the casinos had penny slots, the prostitutes offered services starting as low as $20 and the strip clubs had size-twelve women dancing there, scars on their bellies, big asses jiggling.

Little John introduced himself to Zeke on January 4, 1998, by offering him a can of Busch beer. Zeke accepted and Little John just started talking to beat the band. He talked and talked and talked without a break for six hours. He said he left his job on a fishing boat in his grubby little Texas-island home four years ago when he won $63,000 on a scratch-off lottery ticket. He came west, certain of his expertise in blackjack, with the intent to multiply his money. It hadn't quite worked out like he planned. But it was not Little John's fault. *The man* was keeping him down—one damn conspiracy after another. Little John lived under the boot heel of politicians, corporations, tourists and card dealers.

He drove a taxi, a 1988 Chevrolet Caprice, dark blue. The heavy rectangular car burned a gallon of gas every eight miles, but it was *smooth riding*. His cab had a cassette player and a collection of every Muddy Waters song ever put on record. He was a chauffeur to the tourists, a class of people he despised.

"These sons of bitches don't tip worth a damn. Not for taxi drivers anyway. They'll give some big-tittied cocktail waitress a twenty-dollar bill for a watered down liquor drink. But drive 'em across town, sit with their sorry ass while they blabber on the cell phone, talking the whole time like they are important—talking nonstop but saying *absolutely* nothing—sit waiting on asphalt that's two hundred damn degrees, and I *might* get a dollar tip out of a thirty-minute ride. Sons of bitches. I gouge those fuckers every chance I can."

Every minute of the day Little John had a cigarette and either a cup of black coffee or a Busch. He drank his beer from the can, popping the first one at nine in the morning, when the desert sun was just beginning to get started good, bearing down on the parking lot.

He had an opinion on everything. Zeke, being a man with no money and nothing to do, was glad to sit and hear Little John's version of the world. Zeke enjoyed the camaraderie, something he had not had when he was a preacher. Little John had taken a philosophy course at a Texas junior college and swore up and down that he knew the meaning of life. He was certain the meaning was that there was *no* meaning.

"This old French dude, with a name something like *Dare-ya-doo*. Something like that. Anyway, he figured that out—that there ain't no meaning to life— sometime in the sixties. *Duh! Hello!* People knew that shit all along. Just nobody wanted to admit it."

Little John also encouraged the use of acid, claiming that LSD had straightened out his thinking on the world.

"Now, I'm telling you what, if you want to really explore your mind, to dig deep down into what's really going on back there in your subconscious—I do believe in Dr. *Frood's* theories—you need to drop acid with me sometime. That'll wake you up. You can figure out who you really are. It cleared up my mind for me good."

Little John talked all day, for three days straight, covering subjects such as the Vietnam War, blackjack strategies, a college football playoff system, the history of General Motors, oil drilling in the Gulf of Mexico and the sorry state of country music. Zeke nodded along, sipping beer until late in the afternoon of the third day of their budding friendship when Little John finally asked a question.

"So what's your story, anyway? How did you end up in this lonely place? You a Southerner, ain't you?"

"That's right," Zeke said. "I used to be a preacher. Had a Baptist church in Georgia. Was there twenty-three years."

"Well I'll be damn. Not many preachers end up in this place, that's for damn sure. I guess you done lost your faith. Or maybe you didn't lose it. Maybe you just put it away. That's the logical thing to do, 'cause like I said, the *only* meaning is that there *ain't* no meaning. I grew up in a little Methodist Church in Texas. When I was about nine years old I figured out they was all crazy, that this whole Jesus coming to save your soul story was a fantasy. I quit wasting my time down there as soon as they let me quit going."

Little John took a sip of Busch and a long drag on a freshly lit cigarette.

"So how did you fall?" he asked, exhaling a stream of smoke toward the open door. He gestured around the sparse room, walls of wood paneling. "How did a preacher like you end up here at the *lovely* Old West Motel?"

So Zeke told him, a long story, starting at the beginning with his childhood in Armstrong and continuing to recent history…

The bankroll he brought to Vegas had run out only a few days prior, New Year's Eve 1997, about the time the clock struck twelve. It had taken only seventy-five days for Zeke to burn through $100,000 on drinking and gambling and strippers and sex with prostitutes, not to mention the room in the Luxor.

Zeke (known in Vegas and to Little John as Johnny Sands) lost more than that taking into account the few hot weeks he had at the blackjack table, doubling his take at one point to about $200,000. "That's twenty percent of one million, by the way." He had learned how to play cards, mastering the game as much as it could be. He had studied the odds and knew when to hold, when to hit, when to double down, and when to split. At one time he was strutting around with the fat $1,000 chips in his pockets, regal-looking discs of purple and gold. Hotel security always had an eye on him, both for his safety and their own.

But it didn't last. "It's amazing how quick $500 a hand of blackjack can push a man up into the riches or how fast it can bring him back down." The cards turned against him in December. He lost money from then on out. Some days he'd sleep to almost six in the evening and gamble for only a few hours, dropping out after losing only $3,000 or so. Other days, when he woke up earlier, about noon, he'd spend six or eight hours at the table, including one day he left after dropping $20,000 in one sitting. At least the liquor drinks were free.

The free spending kept right on after leaving the card table. He discovered a strip club not far from the Luxor, the Pink Palomino. It had more than a hundred women, at least twelve dancing on stage at all times, gyrating and twisting and spinning around metal poles. The rest of the women scoured the club like coyotes looking for fat chickens. He would watch the dancers until one would lure him back into a private room and pour champagne down his throat from a bottle that he bought for her.

And there were the prostitutes, the two from the first night and Brandi the cocktail waitress, all who converged on him like jackals after midnight. If he wasn't at the Luxor, they left notes, sometimes waiting at his door for an hour, or watching for him at the casino bar. Brandi and her friends didn't like it when he started going to the strip club, jealous minxes. He took pleasure in their envy, working it up as much as he could. Every now and then he would call in some *strange* from one of the many catalogues of women handed out by Mexicans along the boulevard. He loved Vegas. "Just think about it. Ordering women from *catalogues* handed to you in the street!" He had reveled in nine glorious weeks of liquor and gambling and sex, tossing money around like confetti. "I was the *king* of the strip, at least for a while."

It was a shock when the big bills began to run out, when the safe in his room and the big blue hard-shell suitcase was empty. He'd been drinking so much that he had no idea the bottom of the cash was near. He had given up on keeping track of it in the height of his winning streak. "I got to the point where I was counting it by thickness—one inch of hundreds was about $3,000." At the end of November it had been so much money he couldn't fit it all in the safe. He had stored some of it in the suitcase and jammed it under the bed when he left the room. But since then the stacks of money had dropped like lake levels in a dry spell.

On New Year's Eve he was surprised to find he was down to only two short stacks of bills in the safe. It was $15,000, all hundreds. He thought for a moment of not gambling, of not even going out, saving the money and living a little more frugally. He could get by for a good long time on that much cash. But it was only a momentary thought. He could double or even triple that at a good night at the tables.

And every New Year's Eve of his life before this one had been boring. Sometimes he and Mary had gone to bed early, before the clock struck midnight. This time, however, he would ring in the new year with a bang, either shooting up the charts winning money or going down in flames. He sang "Whiskey River" while dressing, putting on his shiny Italian suit, a dark glittering silver with a thin matching tie over a white silky shirt, an outfit that had set him back about $2,000. Brandi had recommended it to him from the men's store in the casino. He stuffed the breast pockets with cash. He looked in the mirror to slick his hair back with gel and admire the thin mustache he had grown. He was sure he would win tonight, multiplying his dwindling money, just like Jesus had done with the loaves and the fishes, begetting a lot from a little.

The cards, however, were determined to clean him out that night. In two hours, he lost $10,000, a wave of bad cards, more sixes than he would have ever thought possible. Every time the dealer threw him a six card, he slammed his fist down on the table and proclaimed, "the sign of the *beast!*" The beast was in from the Mideast all that night, the Big Pharaoh, working through the dealer, dropping him a face card but then a six on most every hand. The dealer was always sitting on face cards, or eighteens, rarely having to take a hit at all, or more than anyone else at the table, hitting straight to twenty-one. "Black-*ass*-jack," Zeke said each time the dealer hit it. The Pharaoh was sitting right up there in his pyramid, scowling down at the fallen preacher man, dictating the bad cards to him. Zeke was no Moses to face down the Pharaoh inside the great pyramid. The shoe of the Egyptian king came down on his throat again and again, *numero six, numero six.* "But old Pharaoh couldn't keep me from getting a little tail. I still had some money left."

He walked away from the table with two hours until the new year. He had $5,000 he was determined to spend before midnight. He took a taxi to the Pink Palomino. Several girls recognized him, charging him the minute he was in the door, escorting him back to a private room, recruiting their friends along the way, six dancers in all. A waitress soon appeared with eight bottles of champagne, and they each took a bottle of their own, leaving one in the ice bucket as a spare.

They toasted New Year's Day to Johnny Sands, and the girls starting dancing—on the couches, on the table, on his lap, pouring the bubbly down their slick bodies, letting him lick it from them, their nipples, crevices, wherever the sticky gold drops settled. They were buck-ass wild that night, wilder than usual, their bodies throbbing in the black light. One of them, a tall brunette, maneuvered an armchair in front of the black heavy door and draped her bra over the small security camera in the corner. They stripped him out of his silky suit, tossing it on the chair, and then were on him like a pack of hungry puppies on the mother dog, lips and asses and orifices, hot saliva on his ears, fingers, feet and all places in between, smooth and slick and warm. Two girls with nothing left of him to kiss began to kiss each other, pointed tongues flicking pierced pink places he never could imagine would be pierced.

Zeke had held on tight to the stack of $100 bills in his left hand as they nibbled him, his right hand partially inside a perky blonde, a thumb and three fingers exploring her. With his left thumb, he tore the wrapper off the bills and tossed the money straight up to the ceiling. The money fell, some bills fluttering, spinning in circles, the room's black light illuminating Ben Franklin's big bald forehead and highlighting the lettering that said IN GOD WE TRUST.

Whenever it was that he got back to his room, he was too drunk to tell time, Brandi and the big-breasted prostitutes converged on him. They had been waiting pensively in the hotel bar. He'd forgotten that he'd invited Brandi and the girls to his room at midnight. Brandi right off saw that the room's safe was open and empty. He shouted, "I ain't got no money to throw at your asses. But come on girls, don't you love me?" He unzipped his pants and pulled it out, tired and chafed and red as it was, and waved it at them. They left without even saying a word.

Zeke woke up at three in the afternoon on New Year's Day, alone, in his suit, wrinkled and stained with champagne. The money he had on deposit for his hotel bill the only currency of any sort he had in the world.

He inquired of the front desk of how much he owed— $9,500 if he checked out tomorrow. He would check out with only $500 to his name. He flipped on the television, a big flat screen, and watched the college football bowl games, wishing he had some money to bet, but in a way, relieved that he didn't.

The next day he checked into the Old West Motel, the room adjacent to Little John's.

"I knew living high on the hog like that wouldn't last forever," he told him, wrapping up his story. "But I had me a good time. I hadn't done nothing wild in my life until then. I figure I made up for it—and good."

"Damn, boy, that's some story." Little John paced and smoked. "The way you tell it, I almost believe it's true. But you all right, boy, you all right. You my kinda people."

Little John then launched into a diatribe about how organized religion brainwashes people's minds, jabbing the air again and again with his cigarette.

Zeke admired Little John's grit, his determination, his passion in a world where there was no meaning. He got Zeke to thinking. Zeke—now that he had a little time to sit back and not spend every minute of every day doing something totally self-gratifying—contemplated his soul, wondered if he really had one or not. All these years he had preached and believed, passionately, had *felt* the Holy Spirit inside him. But now he wondered if it hadn't been a waste of time, if he wasn't just like a wild dog following the pack.

Zeke had heard of "Dr. Frood's" theories that Little John spoke of, way back in college and on a special on educational TV. He remembered that Freud believed that sex and death were the only two motivating factors in a man's life: getting laid and staying alive, the burning desire to procreate and continue the forward march of his genes. He couldn't disagree.

On Zeke's sixth day in the Old West Motel, Little John woke him up early, about seven.

"There's money to be made down at the convention center today. They got this big convention in town, C-E-S, they call it. Where they display new TVs, computers, all kinds of shit like that. And they need workers, anybody they can get to unpack boxes and set up. They called me in this morning and told me to bring anybody I could. They're giving $150 a day. Cash. Come on down there with me."

Zeke had never seen anything like the Consumer Electronics Show when it was in full blast. The newspaper said there were a hundred thousand people in town for it. He didn't see how that many people could come for one event until he saw the vast room of the Las Vegas Convention Center, the size of twenty-five football fields, booths and signs and buzzers and neon and noise and people, including girls in bikini tops with silvery mermaid bottoms handing out buttons and brochures. Little men in tights spun on a trapeze above a net over the convention floor.

His job was to deliver boxes to the company booths and retrieve the wooden pallets. It was an ocean of signs and company names and products and services. The only companies he had ever heard of were Microsoft, Sony and Panasonic. The others were mysterious to him, companies with huge exhibits, bright lights and highly organized staffs. The only events he had ever seen that were similar at all were the county fairs in Armstrong and Piney. It was that kind of noisy, busy atmosphere, only corporate instead of carny. He delivered giant black plastic cases containing God only knows what to the booths.

Each company had its own little organized army. Many of the men were slick, glossy almost, in neat suits or, more commonly, matching uniforms of golf shirts with logos and lettering and khaki pants, men who had not a single hair out of place, men who looked like they wore eyeliner, their faces covered in cake makeup to fill in their tans. Some of the other men, mostly the older ones, were pot-bellied with bad toupees and spackled complexions. All of the men had vigorous hand-shakes and supersonic smiles, grins perpetually implanted, their natural resting position of the face in the turned-up mode—not unlike preacher smiles.

There were two kinds of women: the kind he was familiar with, the sexy made-up kind in high heels and slinky skirts, halter tops snug below their cleav-ages, implants plump like Florida grapefruit, ripe and ready to be picked. They had long hair washed and blow-dried and coifed until it was perfect and smelled like, well, *hell yes*, gardenias. These girls were trotted out in front of the booths like decoration or landscaping.

The other type of woman he saw confused him, a breed of woman with whom he was not familiar. Some of them were tall and thin and attractive, some of them not, but all were in slacks and golf shirts just like the men, wearing cell phones on their belts like a sheriff wears his gun, their hair neat and straight and short, some collar length, others just like the men, over the ears. Quite a few of them stood in front of the booths shaking hands and smiling just like the men, many of them wearing headsets like he had seen the staff at McDonald's wear, filling the orders at the drive-through. The women had the same demeanor as the men, smiles and handshakes, feigned enthusiasm for whatever stepped in front of them as long as it was somebody in a position to buy something.

Everyone ignored Zeke in his blue work shirt. Little John, when he walked out onto the floor with Zeke to move a stack of pallets, said, "Welcome to the corporate carnival of whores who'll do anything for the almighty dollar. Disgusting, ain't it?"

After work, Little John invited him to an impromptu gathering of a handful of the floor crew in the parking lot outside the convention center. The men stood around drinking beer from a cooler in the back of a pickup truck. Little John said a friend of his had some acid, "some strong stuff, in from Mexico."

He gave Zeke a speck of paper, a tiny perforated square. He held it in his palm, studying it. It was like a very small stamp with a tiny picture of a pyramid on it, similar to the image on a dollar bill except it had no eye on top.

"Don't eat it too fast," Little John said. "Hold it on your tongue as long as you can. Five minutes or so. Then swallow it."

He didn't feel anything for the first half hour. He stood in the parking lot, the sun beginning to drop to the horizon, with Little John and six men from the convention floor crew. Little John was holding court with stories of how the city council held down the rates paid to workers at the convention center and taxi drivers.

Zeke was wondering if anything was going to happen, skeptical that such a tiny slip of paper could affect his brain, when his beer started to feel heavy in his hand. He focused on gripping it, not letting it slip from his fingers. Taking sips from it was a struggle, a concentrated effort as he lifted the can to his mouth. It seemed like he had taken a hundred sips from the can but it was still more than half full, like it was a never-ending beer. All of a sudden it seemed to weigh twenty-five pounds.

The first wave rushed over him. It was a warm feeling, like the warmth built up in a blanket during a long nap, when the cover shifts and some of the body heat slips away, dissipating in the colder air, except this time it was in reverse, the warm air was coming to him, encircling him, like his own special friendly cloud. Soon the colors of the sky were more vivid, the glittering glass of the hotels on the horizon, the sunlight dancing on the Mirage's golden towers, the MGM Grand glowing green and eerily like a giant emerald in the distant dark sky.

Little John was talking still, his voice loud and constant, a whoosh of words. The men were standing in a circle listening to Little John, nodding their heads and laughing, often looking at Zeke as Little John pointed and gestured at him.

Little John was talking about him but Zeke couldn't follow the barrage of stories about his own life. He tried to concentrate on Little John's monologue, but all he could make out were random words, words that triggered images in his head: "banks…Georgia…pussy…church…strippers and whores…sheriff…and gun." He would follow Little John for a while, but would be distracted, watching instead the tip of Little John's cigarette being waved around, back and forth, the smoldering fire being poked into the air as an exclamation point, or swung back and forth like a bouncing ball to follow in the oncoming darkness of the parking lot. When he flicked the butt away and lit a new one, it was the most amazing thing Zeke had ever seen.

"Johnny," Little John said, calling Zeke by the name he knew. "You okay? You feeling all right, preacher?"

Little John shifted his cigarette to his left hand—Zeke watched the burning tip leave a fading red trail in the air—and playfully punched him in the arm. Zeke saw the fist coming like it was in slow motion, as though it were someone else's arm that was getting punched. He tried to speak but no words came out. His tongue was like a dead fish in his mouth.

Little John spoke again, his voice sounding like it was coming from inside a large barrel.

"Hey man, you all right? Sometimes people freak out their first time on this shit. Tell me something—tell me you are okay."

Something about the way Little John cared about him, the concern in his voice, touched Zeke in a place he didn't know that he had. Little John *loved* him. Little John *cared*.

Zeke nodded his head, mustering up the loudest voice he could manage although he was barely audible, "I'm fine, great. Thank you." Then he started to cry, tears of joy flowing down his face. Wet, salty tears ran through his thin mustache and dropped off his chin onto his shoes, forming a tiny puddle at his feet in the black parking lot.

He couldn't recall someone caring about him, his well-being, sincerely, for so long, since Reverend Thomas set him up in house and church. In most everything in life he had played an official role: son, student, husband, preacher, gambler, client. All of these roles required nothing more than to fulfill a job or duty, to do what was expected. But he had no official category with Little John. Little John cared for him out of the goodwill of his heart. There was no sex or money or power or fame at stake, just love of his fellow man. Zeke wept.

The tears felt good coming out of his eyes, plopping down like little raindrops, the only precipitation the parking lot would see all month. It was like a clogged-up hose had been cleared out. His eyes finally ran dry and he rubbed them, bloodshot and scratchy but relieved.

Then acid wave number three poured over him, the color of the skyline turned up another notch, the shining buildings like when Dorothy and Toto and the Scarecrow and the Tin Man and the Cowardly Lion happened upon Oz. He imagined himself eight years old again.

"Hey man, you all right?" Little John asked again. Zeke had his voice back and he felt good, strong, like he was standing in a pulpit preaching.

"Yes, Brother John. I've never been better, never better, my friend. My yoke is easy, my burden is light."

Little John threw back his head and laughed, loud and scratchy.

"Well, I'll be *damn*, preacher. I'm glad you are enjoying yourself. This *is* some good shit, ain't it?...let's go walk down the strip and take it all in. You ain't never seen anything till you've seen Vegas on acid."

"Amen, Brother John, *amen*," Zeke said. "Shall we walk through the valley of the Lord?"

Little John laughed again, a deep sandpapery chuckle, and slapped him on the back.

Soon they were on Las Vegas Boulevard, the sky dark and the neon miracle all lit up as far as the eye could see. Cars whooshed by, tail lights and headlights in intricate patterns, a living kaleidoscope. The sidewalks glowed, little sparkles of light embedded deep in the beige concrete, dancing and zigging and zagging. Light posts stretched like sinewy giraffe necks into the sky. Coming out of every door they passed were sounds of slot machine bells chiming, a chorus of bells, an advancing army of ringing and clanging, endless tintinnabulation.

Looking up, beyond the miracles at his feet and eye level, were the great glittering towers, shining in the night sky, screaming of light, spheres of happiness standing in the desert, defying gravity, logic and all that the Devil and the government and the preachers said shouldn't be possible. It was a great big world of wonder and joy.

That's what the *voices* said.

The voices had begun speaking to Zeke, voices he'd heard all his life but didn't understand, voices familiar but that he'd never heard before so clearly. The voices pulled him on down the street toward the crouching sphinx and the great black glass pyramid, a towering light shooting from the top, beaming up farther than the human eye could see. The voices and bells swirled together, beckoning him down Las Vegas Boulevard toward the infinite white light—a light that shone all the way to heaven's gate, the voices said.

PRAYER LIST

Timber had been home in Whitcomb a week when, one night after Mama had gotten in bed to read herself to sleep with the Bible, he drove down to the old radio station on the south side of town. The flashing antenna lights were visible for miles away, blinking in the haze of the overcast summer evening.

The industrial neighborhood was quiet with none of the rumbling of trucks like during the day. Fat raindrops fell sporadically on his windshield, the threat of an oncoming storm. The sky was gray and he could hear thunder rolling in the distance. The roadside Chicken Fried Chicken sign was still there, although it had changed from white to a deep shade of rust, the once black painted letters barely readable on the weather-beaten metal. The lumberyard and the trucking company that sandwiched the station were still in business, their gates locked for the night, big black guard dogs roaming inside chain-link fences.

He pulled into the empty driveway of the abandoned station and his heart sank. The WKAL sign on top of the hutlike building was a ghost of itself, the once bright red call letters a faded dingy pink, the K missing and the L listing hard to one side, only a strong wind away from toppling over. A ten-foot-high security fence had been put up around the base of the towering antenna that sat in the back left corner of the lot. Pieces of plywood were nailed over all the station's windows. He cut the engine and the lights. The rain had gotten a little steadier as darkness began to settle. A huge deadbolt had been placed with a padlock on the front door, a DO NOT ENTER sign warning away trespassers, claiming that the Radio Signal Corp., owner of the station, would prosecute. He wondered what, if anything, was left inside the tiny four-room structure. They had probably scavenged the equipment and furniture. He stared at the building and pictured his daddy behind the microphone in his coat and tie like it was yesterday, could see him hunched over Delores Arceneaux on the desk. Timber had not been back to the station since before Daddy's killing, eighteen years ago. He regretted coming tonight.

He stayed in the car, watching the rain and the darkness take hold. He turned on the car radio and spun the dial to the right, to the old 1450 AM channel. The New Orleans station that used that frequency was running a talk show out of Chicago. He tuned it out, and thought about his plans. He had left Reno intending never to do radio again. He had wanted to settle down in Whitcomb or somewhere nearby, to find a stable job with decent pay and adequate vacation. He had an application to go to college and get a teaching degree. The promise of reasonable hours, summers off and a pension had appealed to him. He could substitute teach in the meantime. But after a few days at home he realized he could never be an aging college student, living with his mama. The only other jobs in the area were as prison guards. He even considered that, briefly, but then figured they would never take him with his bad foot.

And Mama wasn't well. Her mind was going, if not gone already. In the week he had been home, she cooked meals large enough for eight people when it was only the two of them. She often called him Phil, the name of the church's pastor, or Wilbur, her long-gone older brother from Mississippi. And she got crazy notions in her head, believing that former Governor Earl Long, dead since 1960, was coming to the house to pay a campaign visit.

The talk show rambled on but Timber didn't listen. Over dinner that night, enough fried chicken for six people, he had suggested that he would make a doctor's appointment for her. She scowled, insisting that God would cure her, that all she needed to do was pray, she would be fine. It was God's plan, she said. But Timber knew otherwise. He had to get her to a doctor.

He cut off the car radio and cranked up the engine. He took one last long look at the old station, hearing his daddy's voice, all those years ago. He turned around in the small driveway and headed home, the lumberyard's guard dog barking ferociously in the rain.

A few days later, he told her he was taking her to a new Christian bookstore in Baton Rouge, that he wanted to buy her a birthday present. She would be sixty-eight in a few days. Her eyes lit up. She was like an excited child.

He told her the store was by appointment only and sat with her in the waiting room, thumbing through old magazines. She didn't realize she was in a doctor's office until a nurse in scrubs called her back to an examination room. She glared at him, her eyes angry, her brow wrinkled. But she didn't say a word, succumbing to the beckoning nurse.

The exam revealed that she had suffered a series of strokes over the past year. The strokes caused problems of memory and reasoning. She shouldn't be living alone, the doctor said, and recommended either around-the-clock care or a specialized nursing home in Baton Rouge. She would never get better, but with proper care and an improved diet, she wouldn't get worse. The doctor gave her a shot to calm her down and prescribed four different medicines.

She was very subdued after the doctor's appointment, riding in the car without speaking, her eyes glassy and fogged over.

Two days later they visited the Baton Rouge nursing home recommended by the doctor. It had a white-columned entrance, a big lawn with magnolias and azaleas, a two-story building with private rooms. It sat in a fenced ten-acre lot set off from the interstate far enough that the traffic noise was barely audible, only the rumbling of pulpwood trucks and gasoline tankers within muffled earshot. But it was expensive and Medicare covered only sixty percent of the cost.

He went over her bank statements that night. She had given most of her monthly Social Security income to the church and had very little savings. She had refinanced the house a few years back. It was worth only slightly more than what was owed on it. Timber was in no position to help her financially. He was out of work and more than $11,000 in the red, saddled with Tammy's credit card debt. Another month without a job and he might have to file bankruptcy.

The next morning he was looking through the yellow pages for cheaper nursing homes when an old radio friend from Flint called. The fellow deejay was moving to a New Mexico station that was adopting a country format. He said the Albuquerque station was hiring several deejays and wanted ones with country music experience. He said he would vouch for him and hoped Timber would take a job there. Timber called the station manager and got a job offer that morning, right on the spot. It was a night shift, much less than he'd been making, but he took it. He was eager to get back on the air and get out of Whitcomb. He was scheduled to start his new job in August. That allowed three weeks for him to get Mama settled and to move out of his apartment in Reno and into a new place in Albuquerque.

He found a cheaper nursing home east of Whitcomb that was populated mostly by retired refinery workers and their wives. He drove over to see it that afternoon while Mama napped. It was a large one-story prefabricated structure behind a strip mall anchored by a K-Mart on U.S. 61. She would have to share a room, but at least Medicare would cover most of the costs and she could afford to keep the house. He was tempted to sign the admittance papers then and there, but he decided to wait until he could talk to her, the next morning, to break the news of his leaving.

She was at the kitchen table reading the Bible when he woke up and went in for coffee. He sat across from her and slowly stirred a spoonful of sugar into a chipped porcelain cup. He didn't have any appetite for the dozen warmed-over sausage biscuits she had put out.

"Good morning, Mama."

She smiled wearily at him, her eyes glassy. He'd hoped she would be more alert. She was the most lucid in the morning, but then she went downhill each day, sleeping more and communicating less. By late afternoon she didn't seem to even recognize who he was, calling him Wilbur. At least the medicine kept her calm.

"Mama, I want to talk to you about what we are going to do."

She didn't look up from her Bible. She was reading with her finger on the page, moving it along shakily. He leaned closer to her and put his hand on her forearm.

"*Mama.*"

She looked at him like he was a stranger.

"Mama, I want to talk to you. I think you'll like this nursing home I told you about, east of here. I saw it yesterday. It's got a lot of nice folks and it's close to Whitcomb. People from the church won't have to drive too far to visit you. It's a lot closer than that one in Baton Rouge."

She looked at him, her head starting to nod in short motions, the beginning of a shake.

"You can move in over there week after next. There are lots of nice folks there. You can make some new friends."

She looked as though she was going to speak but stopped. She nodded again. He wondered if she was taking her medicines properly.

"And Mama, I got some good news. I got a new job. Another radio job—I know I said I was going to try something different, but this is a big station. I'm too old to go back to college."

He still had his hand on her forearm. Her hands began to tremble, slightly. She looked to him like she recognized him now.

"Where?" Her voice was weak, a whisper.

"It's in New Mexico, Mama. Albuquerque. But not until August. I've got three weeks here with you. And I'll visit you often."

Her head began to nod again and the trembling increased. He could see her eyes began to moisten as her head shook in small quivers. He put his arm around her shoulders.

"It's all right, Mama. It'll be all right."

"I thought…" She paused, unable to get the words out. "Here."

"Mama, there's no radio jobs for me here. I've got to take what I can get. I promise I'll come see you often."

Her trembling got worse. She looked away from him and down at her Bible, her hand almost thumping on the table. She flipped the pages randomly, as though she were looking for something. It seemed to calm her.

She looked up at him again, her eyes wild.

"Wilbur, can we go to church tomorrow? I'm supposed to sing in the choir."

"Mama, it's me, Tommy. Not Wilbur. Church is not for a few days, but I don't know if you'll be well enough to go."

"Wilbur, don't say that or I'll tell Daddy." Her voice picked up strength, anger. "*Wilbur… Wilbur… Wilbur.*"

He put his arms around her and held her. The trembling stopped, but tears trickled down her cheeks.

The preacher, known to everyone as Pastor Phil, paid a visit the following Monday. He was another East Texas gasper, screaming his sentences in a rhythmic cadence so strong that he had to gasp for breath at the end of each statement. But he seemed to be more reasonable than the Reverend Shaver, the preacher Timber had gotten to know when Bev disappeared ten years ago.

Timber watched through the front window as the preacher parked his car at the curb and got out. He carried his Bible in his left hand, walking slowly up to the house, as though he was surveying the overflowing gutters, one of which had fallen on the side, or the frayed roof tiles, curling up like Fritos after years of baking in the sun.

The new preacher was only about thirty. He seemed like a child to Timber, too young to be in charge of the church. He dressed casually, in a light blue button-down shirt, jeans with a big silver belt buckle with a cross on it, and cowboy boots. He had slightly long hair, a seventies style even though it was 1988, with a bushy mustache that curled down around the corners of his mouth. He had been in Whitcomb less than a year. Timber heard him preach twice, both the morning and evening service, the first Sunday he had been home. Pastor Phil was a vast improvement over Reverend Shaver—there was no more speaking in tongues—but Timber still did not trust him as far as he could see him. He suspected the preacher was coming around because Mama hadn't sent her monthly check. Timber figured her to be one of the bigger donors to the church, if not the biggest.

Timber greeted him at the door before he had a chance to knock.

"Hello. Thomas, is it?"

"Yep, that's me." Timber returned the preacher's vigorous handshake. He stood in the doorway, not inviting the preacher inside.

"How's your mother? She wasn't in church this past Sunday. I've never known her to miss a day. She's the best member I've got."

"I bet she is." Timber made direct eye contact with him. The preacher glanced away.

"Is she okay?" the preacher said, raising his head.

Timber paused, shook his head slowly.

"Not really. The doctor said she has had at least three or four small strokes."

"Oh, I'm so sorry to hear that." The preacher was much more soft spoken out of the pulpit, meek almost. Timber was surprised to see, standing next to him, that he was a little man, only about five feet six. He had seemed much bigger on Sunday.

"I wish I'd known yesterday. I'd have put her on the prayer list—"

"That wouldn't help her none."

The preacher kept on as though he had not heard Timber's statement. "I'll be sure to let everybody know. A lot of folks in the church are worried about her. You are so kind, such a good son to stay here and take care of her."

"I'm *not* staying here. I've got a new job, out West again, in New Mexico."

"Oh…who's going to take care of your mama? Can she live alone?"

"No. The nursing home. That's what the doctor recommended. I'm taking her next week."

"Oh…I'm sorry," the preacher said. He looked down at his feet, as though he was speaking only to himself. "Bless her heart." He looked back up to Timber, still in the doorway. Sweat was beading up on the preacher's brow. He had a large forehead and his light brown hair had begun to recede.

"Can I see her?"

Timber frowned. He wanted to keep the preacher away from his mama. She might just sign the house away. But he knew his mama would want to see the pastor. She had talked very little since starting the prescriptions. The only thing she had asked about was the church.

"Hold on," Timber said. "Let me see if she's awake…how she's feeling."

He shut the door and walked down the short hallway into the den where Mama was sitting in a recliner. She was spending most of her days in the chair, napping.

"Who's there?" She was more alert than he'd seen her in several days. "Is that Pastor Phil?"

"Yes, ma'am."

"Well, let him in."

"Mama. Are you sure you feel like seeing him? I don't know if you are well enough for company."

"Yes, *please* let me see him." Her voice wavered, crackling. She pulled the recliner to its upright position, exhausting herself. She reminded Timber of someone on a bad drunk trying to get herself together.

"Okay, Mama. Just a minute."

Timber opened the front door and shut it behind him. The preacher was sweating fiercely in the midday sun, stains in his underarms, drops on his face. Timber held the screen door open, standing close to him on the stoop.

"Okay, Pastor Phil, she can see you. But only for a little while. She gets exhausted easy…And you might want to know, I've got the power of attorney for all her finances, the house, everything, so any more donations would have to come through me. And to be honest," Timber let the screen door slam shut and stepped forward, bowing up to the small man, "I think she's given more than her fair share already. A lot more than she could afford. So I'm afraid your gravy train has come to an end."

"Brother Timber, I understand. Your mother has been a saint in the eyes of the Lord. I appreciate you letting me see her."

Timber, having expected resistance from the preacher, was embarrassed at his tone, guilty for staring down the little man of God.

"Hey…uh…thanks," he said. "Come on in."

The look on Mama's face when she saw the preacher beat anything Timber had seen. She produced a smile he had not seen in years, not since he was a little boy and she doted on him.

She stood and hugged the preacher, tears down her cheeks dripping into her wide smile.

"Oh Pastor Phil, *thank you* Jesus. Oh *Jesus*, thank you pastor."

Timber stood outside the doorway in the hall while the preacher sat with her and said how sorry he was to hear she was ill. He said the folks at church missed her and would pray for her. He promised to visit every week at the nursing home.

"Mrs. Goodman, you are lucky that the Lord gave you such a wonderful young son in Thomas. I hear he's a talented man in radio. Has a *great* voice. He has a big job offer out there in New Mexico. I know it hurts him to leave you here—I can see it in his eyes—but I believe the Lord has given him that voice and called him to do a job, just like He called me to the church."

He began to read to her from the Bible in a preacherly tone: "'Is *anyone* among you sick? Let him call for the elders of the church, and let them *pray* over him, anointing him with oil in the name of the Lord. And the prayer of faith will *save* the sick, and the Lord will raise him up.'"

And then he prayed, asking for the Lord's help with her illness, Timber's new job, a good move into the nursing home, and many other things.

Timber listened, staring at his shoes. It was hot inside, the air conditioning too weak for the summer heat. The old house needed a new heating and air unit, a new roof, painting. He didn't know what he would do about the house. He couldn't bring himself to sell it—not while his mother was alive.

On the way out, the preacher shook his hand. Timber walked him to the car, his head hanging. He wished he and Tammy had been married in Whitcomb Baptist Church by this preacher for his mama to see.

Pastor Phil said, "You know, your mama loves you very much, Timber. She always talks about how proud she was of you, you and your radio success. She said you were the sweetest little boy ever."

"Thanks," Timber said, meekly. He shook hands again with the little preacher and watched him drive away.

A week later he drove Mama to the nursing home. She was quiet, sitting low on the passenger's side and looking straight ahead. She had talked to him very little since the doctor's appointment. The medication, he figured.

"Mama, Pastor Phil is going to come visit you tomorrow. He's planning to bring folks from the church to see you."

A thin smile formed briefly on her face before slipping away.

"This place is going to be good for you, Mama. You can make friends. The food looks good. I saw the menu. They have some of your favorites: fried chicken, pork chops, meat loaf. Lots of things you like. But remember what the doctor said about eating healthy. Make sure to eat some salads, fruits. And drink lots of water. Okay, Mama?"

He continued with nervous conversation, trying to break the icy silence in the car. Mama didn't respond other than to nod or give him an occasional confused stare.

He pulled into the parking lot and led Mama slowly to the front desk. The home had a strong sterile smell of ammonia. A tired, heavyset black woman gave them a cursory tour of the campus, speaking in monotones. She showed them to Mama's room. Timber followed along, carrying her large fifties vintage hard-shell suitcase. It was very light, half full with only her simple clothes and Bible. "You'll be in this room here with Mrs. Mouton," the woman said, pronouncing it in the Cajun style, *Moo-ton*.

Mama's eyes glared at him.

"Is Mrs. Mouton a Baptist?" Timber asked, knowing the answer from her French last name and picture of the pope on the mirror.

"Uh...I don't know," the woman said, perturbed. She seemed to want to hurry back to the magazine she had been reading. "I guess you or your mother can ask her when she gets back from lunch."

"Okay," Timber said. He stood up straight. "But if she's not, my mother would like to have a Baptist roommate. When I signed the paperwork and wrote out a check, I was told she could have a Baptist."

"Well, I'll see what I can do. But that's the only opening we have. Rooms do open up. People are—uh—*leaving* all the time."

"Thank you. Can you please check on that? My mama would appreciate it. I'll get her set up in here."

"Okay," the woman said. She pointed lazily to a piece of paper on the dresser. "There's a schedule of meals, activities and a list of contact names—you know, people who run the place, doctors and stuff." The woman then slipped off.

Timber told Mama to sit down in the armchair near the end of her bed. He opened her suitcase and took out her clothes, putting her undergarments and nightgowns in the top drawer, her two dresses and sweaters in the second drawer. He unpacked a little cosmetics kit and organized her toothbrush, toothpaste, a hairbrush and powders in the bathroom, the smell of cornstarch permeating the air. He put her walking shoes and slippers in the closet, lining them up neatly. He looked around the bare room and wished he'd brought some photographs, a cross or something from home to put in the room.

He was anxious to get out of the nursing home, away from the sterile stench of madness, the scent of oncoming death, the loneliness that was palpable in the air.

"Well, Mama, you are all set," he said, pausing, trying to be strong. "I...I love you, Mama."

This got her attention for the first time all day. He had told her he loved her only once in the two weeks he had been home. She looked right up at him.

"I love you too, little Tom-Tom."

They hugged, him leaning over her in the chair. Her eyes moistened. Timber fought to keep from crying. They broke the embrace after a few seconds.

"Okay, Mama, I'm going to leave for Reno later tonight or early in the morning. Then moving my stuff to Albuquerque. I'll call you from the road to let you know how I'm doing. Don't forget the church folks are coming to see you tomorrow. That'll be a good time."

He looked around the room to see if he was forgetting anything.

"Now, Mama, you are all set. Is there anything I can do for you before I go?"

She gulped, her throat trembling.

"Yes, Tom-Tom," she said, her voice cracking.

She reached her hand up to his shoulder. She seemed to want to say something but the words never came. He leaned over, kissed her on the cheek, and left.

+   +   +

Six years later Timber was alone, as usual, in Sandusky, Ohio, the shores of Lake Eerie, a late April day, 1994. It was still as cold as hell, low thirties for a high, a wind out of Canada, bitter. It cut through coats and scarves and hats and made everyone who ventured outside shiver. He'd been through three more jobs since his move to Albuquerque, his usual pattern.

He finished his Saturday deejay shift that evening and went straight to the Lighthouse Bar, a little dive on the edge of downtown that sat on the coastline. It had cheap drinks and a selection of bourbon, the only bar in the area that did. All the other local bars had only Jim Beam. Not that there was anything wrong with that, but a man liked a choice every now and then. The bourbon drinkers of the world were dying out, replaced by young people who drank beers that looked like Sprite or liquors with fruity flavored vodka or minty rums in all kinds of colors.

The bar was a good place to sit. He had sat there many hours, listening to the jukebox, an eclectic mix of the usual popular trash and Irish drinking songs, but it also had a healthy representation of old country music, including classic Willie, Johnny Cash, Waylon and Merle. It even had an old Ray Price record, Buck Owens' greatest hits, three Hank Williams Sr. albums, two by Hank Jr., and two Patsy Cline records. He would put in a five spot, choose eighteen songs, and sit there for hours, sipping his bourbon. His foot bothered him more on cold nights like this. The liquor helped ease the pain.

The bar was devoid of single women, any women for that matter. The only semi-attractive women he encountered in Ohio had diamond rings on their left hand, two or three children each, and drove silver minivans. The ad sales team at the radio station was typical of the average suburban Ohio woman: all were married, thirtyish, regular churchgoing Catholics, Methodists and Presbyterians all with short bobbed hair and practical, color-coordinated outfits that didn't give him much of an idea of what was up under the loose-fitting sweaters and long skirts. The ad women regarded Timber as an oddity, like a character from a television show. He figured they'd worked in radio long enough to see many scruffy deejays come and go.

Tammy, *goddamn* her hide, was still on his mind, always. She was, as far as he knew, somewhere with a new identity, blonde or black hair, a new man to suck off every night until she found a way to scam him or the law tracked her down. Maybe she'd had more plastic surgery, got some new parts, to keep her aging body young. She was the one great love of his life, the only woman he'd ever held in his arms and could find nothing wrong with, the only one he'd worshipped, adored. Of course she turned out to be the most troubled, manipulative person he'd ever known. That obvious fact still didn't put her brown eyes and soft red lips out of his mind.

The first few years after she left, he suffered greatly, drinking himself to sleep, every waking moment torture, a painful existence, days upon days without smiling, until he got drunk and began telling anyone within earshot about her. Then he would smile, a smile that frightened people away, giving them an excuse to gather their car keys and coats, finish their drinks and go home, anywhere but near him and his rambling, pathetic story.

He took another drink of his Southern Comfort on the rocks, the half-melted ice cubes clinking in the glass when he set it down on the bar during a break between songs. A song Willie Nelson wrote for Patsy Cline started up, her singing mournful, his last selection on the jukebox, about how she was "crazy, crazy for feeling so lonely…I'm crazy, *crazy* for feeling so blue." He had always, for the first few years after it ended, figured that he would get over Tammy. Sooner or later it was bound to happen. But after three years of not getting over her, he gave up hope, resigned himself to the pain. At that point of defeat it faded from a sharp ache to a dead numbness inside him, eased only with alcohol and an occasional Cleveland prostitute.

But at least worrying about Tammy kept his mind off his poor mama. Bless her heart, her mind was long gone. He had seen her only once a year, at Christmas. Each time she was worse, more incoherent. She didn't even recognize him anymore.

He had not sold the house. A realtor had rented it out for him. The income was barely enough to pay the mortgage and taxes, but at least they still had it. Not that he ever planned to live in Whitcomb again. But then again, he didn't know if he'd be any more miserable there than he was in Sandusky, Ohio.

He finished his drink and ordered another one. It was getting late, ten o'clock. He thought about heading on home, getting some sleep. He had to work again on Sunday, another twelve-hour shift. But he wasn't ready to go. At least in the bar there were other people around, an occasional person to talk to about baseball, music, radio—something. It was better than sitting alone in his one-bedroom apartment with his aging, dinged-up furniture. He put another five dollars in the jukebox and ordered a fresh glass of Southern Comfort. Willie Nelson's twangy guitar pierced the smoky air.

Soon it was midnight, closing time. He had to be on the air again in six hours. He pulled himself off the bar stool and walked out to his car. A stiff wind blew in off the lake. It seemed much too cold to believe that baseball season had just started, that the Indians had played a game in Cleveland tonight. He shivered, doubting that summer would ever come. The weather was so cold that he couldn't get drunk enough not to feel it.

He had made the drive through the empty Sandusky streets at midnight many times before. It was a straight shot through several red lights on the quaint Americana main street, a gauntlet of flags hanging from faux antique lampposts. He made it onto the four-lane highway that took him away from the coastline and to his apartment complex south of town, a long-dilapidated area undergoing revitalization with strip malls and new subdivisions. He drove slowly, cracked the window to get fresh air, chewed gum, kept the radio off. A deejay friend of his who had two drunk-driving charges had advised him of these tips, learned at safe driving school, on how to avoid arrest.

At home he decided to have one more drink. He had just enough Jim Beam for a stiff one, the nearly empty bottle sitting on the counter. The sink was full of dishes and the garbage can overflowing. He picked a dirty highball glass out of the sink and wiped it clean with a paper towel. He emptied the bottle and dropped two ice cubes into the glass. The red light on his answering machine blinked, indicating one message was there, most likely an automated recording trying to sell him something. Marketing calls were about the only messages he ever got. He hit the play button. The machine started up with a loud beep.

"Mr. Goodman. This is Cheryl Richmond from Bayou Lakes Nursing Home.

We have been trying to track you down all day…Please give us a call regarding your mother. It's urgent…She—she passed away Friday night at dinner. Deveneaux Funeral Home is handling the arrangements. They hope to have the funeral Monday if they can get in touch with you."

Timber stood for a few moments, replaying the message in his head. The white kitchen opened up into the beige den, separated by a counter with stools, the spot where he sometimes ate his meals since he had no dining room table or chairs, but usually he just sat in his recliner and ate off the coffee table. He walked over to his old chair and sat down, the drink still in his hand. He stared across the sparsely furnished room with nothing on the walls for decoration. The only light burning in his apartment was the overhead fixture in the kitchen, throwing a shaft of light over the counter and into the den. The coffee table was littered with stacks of newspapers and junk mail. He didn't bother trying to lean back in the broken chair, but sat there, still, waiting for what he was not sure.

He didn't have a photo of his mama up anywhere in the apartment. There were a few old snapshots of her, taken when he was a kid, stuffed away in boxes back in the closet, unopened for years now, taped up tight many moves ago. He couldn't remember the last time he and his mama had their picture taken together, probably fifteen years at least. He thought awhile and remembered. It was a church picnic, one of his rare visits home from Houston before Bev had disappeared, although Bev was not in the photo. One of Mama's fellow Sunday school teachers had snapped the shot of them eating ham, green bean casserole and potato salad at the end of a long picnic table under the shade of an oak tree. The church lawn was green with freshly cut grass and the oak tree was thick with leaves. Mama looked happy, her eyes bright, surrounded by her church friends, eating a good meal on a nice spring day with her son. Timber was looking at the camera with a forced smile.

He hung his head forward, his weight like lead in the chair, the room half dark. He closed his eyes and inhaled. He expected to cry but the tears wouldn't come. He took another deep breath, his arms and shoulders trembling for a few moments. He sat that way for a long time, his breathing the only sound, the quiet stillness of the blank room almost enough to kill him.

He opened his eyes without lifting his head and took a long slug on the bourbon. This one glass would never be enough to get him through to the morning, but then nothing he knew would be good enough to get him through the desperate, lonely night ahead of him. Mama would have wanted him to pray for her. But he didn't think that would do any good either. He flipped on the TV, hoping the sound of other voices would comfort him until it was time for him to go back on the air at six.

♦ ♦ ♦

The sky seen through the Greyhound's tinted windows looked like faded silver, displacing the wide open blue with a coin-colored dome; the clouds hung like gray dirty sheets on an invisible clothesline.

Timber paused, thinking about his mama, the stories he'd told the preacher fresh on his mind again. He didn't know why he had opened up and told this hick preacher everything, these memories that hurt the most, emotions he'd held inside all of his life. These had come pouring out on a bus this Sunday morning. Once he got started on a particular episode in his life, he couldn't stop himself. And crazy as Zeke was, there was a kinship, a shared understanding of their lonesome existences, their poor mamas and their jackass daddies, their Southern roots that ran deep and were inescapable. They had taken different paths but ended up in the same place, a rumbling silver, red and blue bus two hours south of Salt Lake City.

"So, I went home and buried Mama," Timber said. "Put her in the ground right next to Daddy.

"I thought about selling the house. The realtor renting it for me said the tenants were good payers and took care of it. I had refinanced it again, so it still wasn't worth much more than was owed on it, so I kept it. I still have it. But I haven't been down there since Mama died, eight years ago.

"The radio business continued to go to shit. *Some* career. I stayed at the Sandusky station almost five years in the same position. But about three years ago it was sold to one of the big corporate owners. They fired most of the staff, including yours truly. They automated all the after-hours programming. Only two real people work there now: a daytime news director-deejay and a woman to sell ads. Most of the programmers these days, they just flip a switch.

"I landed in Youngstown, an overnight shift. I'll be damned if the same thing didn't happen there six months later. This giant corporation, Clear Channel, has been buying stations all over the country, milking them for every dollar they can get.

"After that, I got on in Akron with an AM station. It was another bad shift, starting at seven at night and ending at seven in the morning. Five days a week. I did everything on that shift...ran the board, did the news, played all the songs.

I was all alone there the whole time. Not even a janitor in the building. That sorry station didn't have but ten employees in all, only seven on-air staff. The pay was the lowest I had made since I left Baton Rouge more than twenty-five years earlier—*fifteen* thousand dollars a year at the turn of the millennium. I think that's right below the poverty line.

"I started thinking again about doing something else, trying a different line of work. But radio is all I've ever known. I couldn't see myself selling life insurance, used cars, working in a grocery store. Nothing else I could do would pay worth a shit either. At least I was doing something I enjoyed. Most of the time, anyway.

"Then I got a DUI one night coming home from a bar in Akron. I wasn't nearly as drunk as I usually got. Some eager cop just wanted to check my insurance card. He *checked* it all right. My insurance was cancelled after that. The fines were high, almost two thousand dollars. So I gave up my car. Couldn't afford the payments and the high-priced insurance they offer drunks.

"I needed money bad, so I begged station management for a raise. They blew me off. Said after one year of service—I'd been there six months—they would evaluate me and give me a raise between *one* and *three-and-a-half percent*. That's *only* five hundred and twenty-five dollars, max. I'd asked—*practically* demanded—a raise of five thousand. I had good ratings, but they didn't give a damn. Said if they wanted they could replace me with someone cheaper, or maybe even automate the off hours.

"So I sent around more demo tapes and resumés. I landed the job I have now in Pierre. Never dreamed I would end up living somewhere like South Dakota again. It's not a bad station…number four in the market and can be heard from a hundred miles away. They started me at the grand total of sixteen-five but promised to bump me up next year to eighteen, or maybe even nineteen, if the ratings keep going up. But *damn*, I'm on AM again. Back where I started with my daddy. Most young people don't even know what AM is. Nobody but farmers and old people listen to AM stations.

"Anyway, I've decided that I want to shoot for another big job. I haven't been fired for pissing off an advertiser in fourteen years. A lot of people have forgotten about that time in Reno, I hope. I did miss a few shifts down in New Mexico, but that's been a long time, too. My job search brought me out to Vegas this past weekend. There was a big broadcasting conference in town, lots of station managers there. Maybe one day I'll climb back into a big job like I had in Houston."

Timber stopped, sad that was where his story ended. He knew he would never get back the glory he had in 1979, the big time slot he'd thrown away. He didn't want to admit to Zeke that the job hunt part of the trip had been a failure, pre-empted by his gambling and drinking binge. Nor did he tell the preacher that on Friday night, when he was in the money after winning both his baseball bets, he'd had a call girl up to his room, a perky little brunette named Shasta who set him back $500.

"So how's it look for a new job?" Zeke said. "D'you find one?"

"Ah…yeah…well, no. I didn't get an offer. I talked to a few station managers. Handed out some demo tapes, resumés. Radio isn't what it used to be. There aren't nearly as many jobs out there. Pretty soon won't be but one or two companies that own every radio station in the U.S. They are automating a lot of stations, putting people out of work."

He didn't say that walking the huge trade show floor caused his bad foot to ache, that he only spent about thirty minutes there before heading to the casino, but Zeke sensed the truth anyway.

"Aw, come on, boy," Zeke said. "You didn't look that hard for a job. You just drank and gambled the weekend away. You ain't gotta lie to me. I can't hold it against you, seeing all that I done."

Timber shrugged. He didn't care what Zeke knew. He hoped pretty soon he would get away from this preacher. Seven hours next to him on a bus was a long time. He hung his head and sighed.

He reached for the bottle, under his seat, and took another drink. It felt good going down, warming his insides. There was nothing like bourbon for warmth from the inside out. The liquor was close to gone.

After a moment, he turned to Zeke and grinned.

"Hell, I ought to go back to Louisiana and become a preacher. Sounds like a good job to me. Maybe I'll get *my* calling too."

Zeke laughed, a rough cackle.

"I wish you would get your callin', boy. There's men that have made a killing at it, that's for sure. But the ones who did sure will have hell to pay if they don't come clean before judgment day. I'm so thankful to the Lord for showing me the way, for bringing me out of the path I was headed down, the road to ruination. The Lord spoke to me, Jesus *Hisself*, and I followed. I done what was right."

"I guess there's a part of your story I'm missing," Timber said, "this big ending you've been telling me about."

"You are right there, my brother Timber. It's time for you to hear it. And if you got ears, you will hear it…you will hear my story. And you won't never be the same."

AND JESUS SAID

Zeke reached over and took the bottle of liquor from Timber's hand. "Let's finish this off once and for all," Zeke said.

He uncapped the almost empty liter and took a pull on it, leaving barely a splash. He handed it to Timber, who finished it, not even enough to fill half a shot glass. Timber held the empty bottle in his hand, reading the label, wondering what to do with it. Zeke took it from him and jammed it under an empty seat across the aisle.

"Ain't no need to keep it around anymore. It's like the human body—just a vessel for the spirit."

They had finished the Jim Beam in about six hours, stretching it out in sips over the long haul up I-15, the bus climbing steadily through the corner of southeastern Nevada, cutting across the rocky corner of Arizona—not far from the Grand Canyon—and then the big ride in Utah, through the dramatic vistas of the Black Mountains, on through the Black Rock Desert and into the Juab Valley, flat and snow covered. The interstate through Utah stayed in valleys but the scenery on both sides of the bus was mountainous, majestic.

Timber had a good buzz. It wasn't what he'd describe as drunk, but a buzz about like he had when he was arrested for drunken driving—legally drunk but sober enough to do most anything. He was far from incoherent, from blacking out, like he had been in Vegas the night before, like he'd been on many nights. He'd been drunker on the radio many times and no one had noticed. He could hold his liquor. It was obvious the Reverend Blizzard could as well.

"Brother Timber, my friend, the bottle has come to an end—so must my story."

Zeke spoke as though he were beginning a prayer in preparation of the call to the congregation to come on down and be saved. "I'll get you to the end. I'll answer your question, your skepticism of *'what's* a preacher man doing, roaming around out here in the desert with a bottle of liquor?' and other such doubts about me and the word of the Lord that you've expressed…*Such* doubting—*doubting Thomas*, that's your name after all, ain't it? Thomas? Your real name?"

Timber nodded.

"Well, son, let me dispel the doubts in your heart and bring you around to Jesus. I'll tell you how my story ends:

"I spent four years running with Little John. The man had the energy of a go-cart, always running. I started driving his taxi for him overnight, from midnight until sun-up." Zeke's voice was passionate, excited, a cross between a drunk man and an enthusiastic preacher giving his Sunday message. "I'm telling you what. You ain't seen nothing—even with what I'd been through before that—you ain't seen nothing till you've driven a taxi overnight in Las Vegas. Lord help us all…the freaks and the pimps and the prostitutes that roam those streets, the sluts and sleazeballs that slither out of those seedy clubs…*three, four, five* in the morning, sometimes even after the sun comes up. Sodom and Gomorrah ain't got nothin' on Vegas, not a single, solitary thing. It's *unreal*. Absolutely *unreal*. Women with penises. Men with vaginas, breasts, in *dresses* no less, letting it all hang, letting it hang out like they are proud of it. Some people you couldn't never tell if they were a woman or a man. Some of them you'd ask and they wouldn't even tell you.

"The whores. I'd already seen them before, but this was a different perspective. Every night I watched these evil harlots, these reptilian women. I watched them working it, using what God gave 'em—of course, they'd all monkeyed with it, getting bigger and rounder parts, injecting themselves with chemicals, lying under lamps built to mimic the sun. *Imagine* that! These women think they can get *the sun* from a box! In the long run they'll find out that they've ruined what God gave 'em. These women, derived from Eve. They would swallow a snake if there was a little gold and silver in it for 'em.

"And the whore*mongers*. These men—beady-eyed with leathery skin—in suits and ties. Lots of Oriental and Egyptian-looking men. Leering, sweaty…slaves to their loins."

He paused, slowing down the rhythm of his speech.

"I didn't have any more sexual desire. I had burned it all out of me and seen it for what it was: the urges put in me by the Devil.

"Read Genesis. A man shouldn't spill his seed on the ground. A man shouldn't waste his seed. I done bred my seed back in Georgia, done put three young'uns on the earth, so I had no more to do.

"I had tested God's patience, running with the women like I did, flaunting the money I'd stolen. When I first got to Vegas and had all that cash, I was thinking with the *little* head—he don't care 'bout nothing but pussy," he gestured to his crotch, "and wasn't thinking with the *big* head," he said, tapping his temple with his pointer and middle finger.

"Only when I took to driving that taxi, seeing all these folks lost from the word of the Lord, little pawns of Satan that they were, did I realize how far I had fallen…

"But *Jesus* loved me enough to see me through it, to give me that taxi to drive. Driving that car around helped me to get my thoughts together about who I am and what I wanted to be. I am a preacher. I had been called by the Lord at a young age. I answered that calling pretty good for a long while, until I ran into Jolene and neglected the Lord's word when I came out West."

Timber shifted in his seat, turning his head to look out the window. The bus had entered a long flat valley, snow covered as far as the eye could see, with huge mountains, mostly whitecaps with patches of black rock showing through in the distance. The clouds had parted and they were heading into a break in the clouds with strong rays of sunlight. The sky ahead was fantastic blue, shining on the snowy plain, a brilliant gleam. He zoned out for a moment. The Reverend Blizzard was beginning to repeat himself, something all preachers tended to do. They were out of liquor and Timber was running out of patience.

"So," Timber asked, cutting him off. "Were you still doing acid, and smoking weed at the time? When did you find this peace of mind you were telling me about?"

Zeke gave Timber a sharp look, his big pupils black and angry in the silver-blue rings.

"I'm *going* to get to that, my brother. Be patient. Patience is a virtue… Yes, I continued doing acid, once or twice a week, while I was driving the taxi. Little John and I would do a hit, usually on Wednesday night when the taxi business was slow. We'd wander all over that city. Sometimes we'd drive out into the desert listening to music. Blues. Muddy Waters. That's all Little John ever listened to. It is something else to see the sun go down in the desert, all fiery red and orange, when you on acid.

"All this time I could feel my religion coming back up in me. I could feel Jesus in my heart, working on me to bring me back to Him. Those beautiful sunrises in the desert helped me to believe in God again.

"I started talking to Little John about Jesus, about the Bible. He was skeptical at first—I told you about his belief in meaning is that there ain't no meaning, and all that—but he listened, asked questions. As a child in Texas he had learned more about Jesus than he wanted to let on.

"Then one night, it hit him. He was saved. He—"

"Oh, enough about Little John already," Timber said. His head was starting to hurt as his buzz faded. "We don't have that much time before we change buses in Salt Lake. Tell me your secret about whatever it was you did out in the desert. Tell me what gave you this peace of mind you are so proud of. Did anything at all happen out there?"

Zeke glared at him.

"All right, boy, you'll get the story...I went on driving the taxi for several years, doing acid with Little John...I'd also started working construction. Turned out I was a pretty good carpenter. There's so much new building going on around Vegas that anybody who can drive a nail can get a job. There was something I liked about building these houses. I ended up working for a Christian business-man who I told I was a preacher. He asked me to give the prayers in the morning, before the workers got started.

"About a year ago he set me up in a tiny little church in a strip mall he owned south of Vegas. I had a small congregation, eight or ten people at the most. Little John was always there. He'd usually drag someone from the motel along. Two fellow construction workers and their families came sometimes. It was good to get up and espouse the word of the Lord, to spread the news about Jesus. I also took the opportunity to talk to people in the taxi about how Jesus loved them, how He wanted 'em to do right.

"Things was going pretty good. Little John and I began handing out flyers for my church all up and down the strip on Sunday afternoons and evenings when we weren't driving the taxi. We still did acid once a week, each Wednesday. I know most preachers and everyone else will argue with me, but that helped me to hear the word of the Lord more clearly. It was like His voice was speaking directly to me.

"We dropped a hit last Wednesday night. We were downtown, right outside our room, when we began tripping." Zeke's tone softened to almost a whisper. "The voices came back to me.

"But this time, *it was* Jesus...speaking right to me. He had a soft voice, very kind and warm, but strong too. Smooth and measured. His words came straight down from the sky. I was the only one who could hear it.

"He told me, 'Son of man, go to the light. To the brightest light in the desert—the Pharaoh's light. You must follow the light. Follow it to the end,' he said.

"I set out for the Luxor. Little John walked along with me. We was downtown, a long way to the pyramid. Jesus spoke again, 'Go alone, son of man. But before you do, eat another scroll.' I did not know what He meant by that. Then He said, 'Look inside your front shirt pocket.'

"I looked. There was another hit of acid in there, where there had been nothing. It was wrapped in white paper...thin paper like the pages of a Bible, but blank. I looked at the hit closely. It had a purple cross on it, a cross on a mountaintop. I'd done a lot of hits of acid by then, but I'd never seen a hit like that. I ate it. Held it on my tongue a long time before swallowing. It had a sweet, sugary taste to it.

"Then He told me, 'That's good, son, that's good. You must go to the pyramid. And go prepared to spend three days in the desert.'

"I told Little John what I had to do. He said I was trippin', that I had been trippin' too much. He said to drink some beers and smoke some dope and calm down. He said I could not use the car. He also did not want me to leave him alone. He said we could get through it together. But I insisted. He cursed at me, called me a Jesus freak.

"I walked back to the hotel and went into my room. I locked the door and gathered my things together, packing my old suitcase and this briefcase a man left in the taxi a few weeks back. I got my Bowie knife, a flashlight, blankets, extra clothes, a hammer, a pack of six-inch nails, some rope. And my Bible.

"Little John banged on my door, yelled at me to come out. After a while, I heard him go into his room. When he did, I ran into the parking lot with my luggage and took off in the cab. I had my own keys since I was driving nights. I knew he wouldn't call the cops on me in the condition he was in, not right away. Even if he did, who was I to ignore Jesus? I trusted His plan for me.

"I drove up the strip, busy with traffic, prime time. The radio was on a religious station. It was playing 'Amazing Grace,' sung by some big choir. I turned it up loud. Everything was all lit up. Crowds of people thronged the strip, watching and *ooh*-ing and *ahh*-ing the dancing fountains, the volcano, the fightin' pirates.

"After Amazing Grace, Jesus spoke to me over the radio, His voice coming through the speakers, 'Go to the pyramid and wait for my instructions.'

"I parked at the Luxor, up there on the top level of the giant deck, the area marked for employee parking. I could see the hotels down the strip shining. I could see around the pyramid, black and shiny glass at night, to the back of the sphinx's head and the ivory obelisk. It glowed. The sphinx was alive, like a big cat ready to pounce.

"And here Jesus began to preach to me. He said, 'Son of man, see how far the world has gotten from my word? Look at these lights, this glitter, these women—harlots all—strutting all over my Father's creation. They do not worship the Lord. They worship the almighty dollar. They do not worship me. They worship instant gratification. They do not worship the Holy Spirit, but they worship their own carnal desires. They are prisoners to their own sexual pleasure, prisoners to the prince of darkness.'

"He said, 'My own son, Ezekiel, I know you have been down the path of the unrighteous. I know you have tasted the evil fruits of sin. You have worshipped at the tables of money. You have put yourself before the Lord.

"'But Ezekiel, even though thou art a son of man, thou art a man of God. I chose you because I know you have fallen far but are recovering, seeing my way again, witnessing to the unclean in spirit.'

"I began to try to talk to Him. I began to tell Him…to tell Him I was sorry for my sins, my many sins, but that I loved Him and would dedicate all my days to His work. But He stopped me. He said, 'Son, I *know*. I know *all* you think. I know your past, your present and your future. I see all. I know all. I know what is in your heart, my dear Ezekiel. That is why I chose you.'

"He said, 'I have a very important job for you, a job that will earn you a seat in the Kingdom of Heaven. It is a job that people will not understand. You will be scorned and maybe even crucified, but it is the right thing to do, my son, to try and take back the world that we have lost, the world of men who worship idolatry, who worship raw lust. Sex, money and *earthly* power have become the gods of men today. I fear these men will create a false second coming…that they will choose the wrong Messiah. You must counter this sex-crazed generation, this lust, this money, this imagined power that all men chase like vermin in the gutters. Show them they are following the wrong path, show them that only *I* was on the cross, that *I* am the only one whose arms were outstretched and nailed to those rugged beams.

"'I want you to send a signal to Satan to let him know we are not giving up the battle. That we will not be defeated.' His voice was the only sound I could hear.

"He said, 'There is a woman here, whom you know, with whom you have been *carnally* intimate. Take her to the Valley of Fire, near the Virgin River that flows down from the mountains. Stay with her for three days. Preach to her of the ways of the Lord, of my ways, of the ways of the Holy Spirit. She will accept me as her savior and ask for forgiveness. Grant her this.

"'And then you must show her—show the world—that my arms were the only ones that were stretched betwixt the beams of the cross. Remind the world that if your arms sin against you, it is better to cut them off than for all of your body and soul to perish in hellfire. Her conversion should be a symbol of God to all mankind.

"'After your mission in the desert is complete, you shall travel north, to the lake of salt, converting others as you go. Remember, Ezekiel, my son, I am always with you. You will not be alone.'"

Zeke's eyes were intense, the pupils seemingly even larger than they had been. Instead of looking at Timber, as he had done when telling earlier episodes in his life, he looked straight into the seat back in front of him. Timber hung on his every word as he continued.

"Jesus was speaking in parables, but I understood. I was born to understand. I knew He meant Brandi, the loose cocktail waitress I had known. I knew she would have to die so she could live. He knew that she was still there, at the Luxor, four years since I'd seen her last. He knew she would come out at midnight, where I was waiting on top of the parking deck."

Zeke turned his head to look straight into Timber's eyes. His eyes were blue and bloodshot but overwhelmed by the giant deep pupils. Timber was leaning forward, close to his face.

"He knows everything, my brother. *Everything*," Zeke said, pausing three beats before continuing.

"So I waited. At midnight I got out and unlocked the trunk of the car, leaving it cracked open. I put my knife on my belt, looping it through the sheath. She came out about ten minutes after midnight, by herself. She had changed out of her Egyptian cocktail waitress getup into a silky red dress. That thing was tiny and stretched tight. She didn't look very different, only her breasts were bigger, like she'd had them enlarged once again. She had on big high-heel boots—black leather—like strippers and whores wear.

"I watched her walk to her car in the far corner of the parking lot. I drove over and parked behind it as she got in. I blocked her in her spot. She looked back at me, all mad looking. I got out and walked to her door. She was still in the car. She did not recognize me at first.

"'Brandi,' I said, 'don't you remember me? It's your old party buddy, Johnny Sands.' She smiled a big phony smile like she was glad to see me.

"'Hey, it's been a long time,' she said.

"'Yeah,' I said. 'You want to go for a ride? I'm in the money again.' She smiled, crinkling her eyes.

"'I'd love to,' she said. 'But I've got plans tonight. Maybe tomorrow? Are you staying here again?' She gestured at the giant pyramid behind us.

"I guess I could have waited an eternity if Jesus had wanted me to, but He wanted the job done that night. I'm not a man would keep Jesus waiting. So I leaned down to her window like I was going to whisper something soft and low in her ear. She turned her head to me, giving me the eye, smiling that money-grubbing whore smile. I reached in fast and turned off the engine. I snatched the car keys out of the ignition and put them in my pocket. She tried to roll up the window but couldn't without the keys.

"Then she started scrambling for her bag. Mace, I figured, and I yanked the bag out of her hand. She couldn't grip anything too tight with these big fingernails she had. I threw it on the ground near my car.

"She tried to crawl out of the driver's seat to the passenger's side. I grabbed her by that long blonde mane and pulled her right out the window. She screamed and hollered like a stuck pig. She scratched my face good with those nails," Zeke gestured to the healing wounds on his face, "and tried to knee me in the balls. I smacked her good. She fell to the ground, still a-hollerin'. I took my knife and held it hard to her throat. I told her if she didn't quit squealing and tried to hurt me again, I'd slice her open like a hog.

"I put her face down in the trunk—there's a lot of room in those old Caprices. I coulda fit her two whore friends in there too. I tied her hands behind her back with the rope. She was moaning, sobbing the whole time now. I told her that if she didn't hush the hell up, I'd gag her, maybe even cut her to pieces right then and there and she'd go to hell unsaved. I told her that if she would be good, she'd get saved and go to heaven before she died. That was more than fair…I told her, letting her get saved…forgiveness…even after a life of sin, all the whoring and money grubbing she'd done right up to the last few days of her life. A life of sin and only a weekend of repentance sounded like a good deal to me."

He turned to Timber again. "To think that our God, and His son, are so gracious as to forgive our sins, *whatever* they may be. All you got to do is ask Him for it." Zeke then fell back into the trancelike state as he continued the story.

"So I shut her in the trunk and drove off. Not a soul came into that parking deck that whole time I was struggling with her. I figure He took care of that for me. I could feel His hand guiding me, His eyes watching me. I'd never felt the Lord's presence so strong, not in all my years of preaching.

"I got on I-15 and headed north, driving about thirty miles. I stopped at a truck stop and sat in the car. I could hear her screaming and crying in the back. I opened the trunk and took an old T-shirt and gagged her with it. I threw my coat on her, propped her head up on her bag for a pillow. It wasn't cold that night, about fifty degrees, but she might as well have been naked in that little red dress. Her crotch was wet where she had peed on herself.

"I spent the rest of the night sitting, listening to the radio. You'd be amazed at how much good religion you can get on the radio out there in the desert. It came in so clearly, stations from far away. Jesus was not talking to me anymore, but I know there was divine intervention because every station I tuned into had one of the great preachers. I listened to the Reverend Jerry Rodgers, the man Jesus had sent to get me through the bank robbery that first time. He was there for me again, urging me on with my fight against the Devil. He said when we fight evil—when we take on sin—we are locked in combat with Satan *hisself*. He said because the Devil didn't fight fair, we can't fight fair. He said we have got to do everything in our power to keep the Devil down in his hole. And he's hard to keep down in that hole. He's out amongst us most of the time, picking at our souls, tempting us every minute of every day, *twenty-four* seven.

"I heard a sermon by Swaggart, too. Who would've thought you could get the great country preachers out in the desert? He talked about his fall from grace, how sexual desire had tainted his mind, his religion, had caused him to go to prostitutes. He said we can't let the lust and evil injected into our blood by the Devil overtake us. He said we got to resist those temptations, as strong as they may be. We gotta try hard to follow what Jesus would have us to do. And he said if we have fallen, if we have been weak—and many among us have been weak, including me, Swaggart said, as you well know—Jesus will forgive us of our sins. He's a forgiving God, a *loving* God. I sat there all night, just taking it in…

"The sunrise that morning was brilliant, the rays dancing on the red rocks of the Valley of Fire. The sky changed from black to a light greenish blue before pink and orange and red and then fading into light blue. I watched with wonder in the truckstop parking lot. On the radio came a big choir from somewhere up in Utah singing beautiful songs. *Glory Glory Hallelujah.* There was so much good Christian music you couldn't believe it.

"Once the sun was up and good, I went into the truckstop store and bought two bottles of liquor—the second one you and I just finished—a bag of ham sandwiches, several bottles of water, and a handful of beef jerky sticks. We were going to be out in the desert for a while…three days. I got a cup of black coffee for myself.

"The drive to the Valley of Fire once you get off of I-15 does not look that far on the map. It's about thirty miles or so through the desert. About the first fifteen miles of that road is the same, every inch identical, flat and seemingly never-ending, the shoulder rocky and dry, all shades of red and brown and black. The landscape is so big and wide open it swallows you up like a crumb. You feel like a tiny speck of dust on a huge canvas.

"And the acid was still going strong in my brain that next morning. That second hit was powerful. The red desert floor looked like it was bubbling up in spots, a boiling liquid on the face of the earth. The road looked like it was made of rubber, stretching out before me. It stretched further and further away the faster I drove the car. I had it up to almost ninety miles an hour but it seemed like I wasn't moving at all. Instead it felt like I was in a boat on a flat smooth lake, sort of like I was back in Piney on my old preacher's pond, waiting for the fish to bite.

"After what seemed like a very long time, the road started to wind and curve around rock formations that began to rise from the desert. We started climbing higher, a gradual incline. The rock piles were brown at first, dust-colored rocks. The closer to the park we got, the redder and redder they turned. They call it the Valley of Fire because the rocks turn the color of flames when the sun hits 'em. And those things was blazing with sunlight that morning. It beat anything I'd ever seen…Little John and I had driven out in the desert before quite a bit. He never would go into a park, however. He said it was against his official code of ethics to support a government facility.

"But I was happier than a pig in shit to be there. The sun and the earth put on a show, I'm tellin' you. Red rocks burning in the morning sunlight, deep red and orange, a color like no man can make. It was like all those rocks were talking to me. There were faces in all those forms, little heads and big heads. I could just see people I knew in those rocks, everybody from Jesus on down. Moses…Paul…my daddy…the Reverend Daniels…Dean Green…Reverend Davis. It was like they were there talking, moving around the whole time, watching me from the rock cliffs.

"I drove all around that big ole park that morning, drinking in the scenery. I was looking for a place to hide out, to leave the car where it wouldn't be suspicious. That park is huge. I needed somewhere to set up for a few days where I could do my preaching to this lost girl, somewhere I could save her soul, somewhere I could do what I was called to do. I figured I'd just drive around till He showed me a spot.

"And sure enough, after awhile, He did. It was down a narrow path between two hills, big boulders shaped like giant skulls about three stories tall, a good ways off the road. On the far side of the giant rocks there was a split into the bottom, a small cave. It was about the size of a one-car garage 'cept it was shaped like an A-frame. It was just a crack in the rock, with only a narrow opening. It faced east…toward Jerusalem, toward Bethlehem, toward the sun. There was a good rock for sitting, right outside the entrance. In the distance we could see the gorge that led down into the Virgin River, the mountains sprinkled with snow far away. Down in a sandy gully below the cave was a lone Joshua tree, a cottonwood I think they call it—about thirty feet high. The only tree around for miles. The spot was off the beaten track, too, although that park is so big and wide open it seems like there's nobody anywhere in there. I never coulda found it on my own."

He made eye contact with Timber, and nodded his head down to make a point, jabbing his finger in the air.

"Let that be a lesson to you, boy. When you don't know where you want to go with your life, ask Jesus. Ask God. Open your heart and they will show you the way."

Zeke's eyes lost direct contact with Timber and got that distant look again.

"Later that afternoon, as the few hikers and tourists who were there cleared out, I parked near the little path. I got Brandi out of the trunk. She was sweaty. Smelled like piss. I told her I'd take the gag out of her mouth and give her water if she wouldn't scream. She resisted me at first so I left the gag on. I told her if she wanted to be saved, she'd cooperate. Her eyes were wild, like a cat in the headlights.

"I walked her down the path to the cave I found. It was the perfect spot to tie somebody up. The walls were full of crevices. I looped the rope in one big hole that had a narrow but solid strip of the rock cutting through it, almost like a concrete pole, and tied her to it. Her hands were still tied tight behind her back. I knew she wasn't gettin' away. I'd done enough fishing to know how to tie a good tight knot. I decided to keep the gag on in case anybody happened to walk nearby and hear her scream. With her quiet, there was no way anybody would find us. The little cave in the rock was shaded so nobody would even think anything was there unless they happened to come right up on it.

"Think about how many little hiding spaces there are out in the desert like that. Must be a million little caves that nobody ever sees or thinks about. I'd heard the story of this Indian who killed some men about a hunnerd years ago. He hid out there for years before anybody tracked him down.

"I went back to the car and hauled my stuff and her bag to the cave. The car empty, I drove it to the large campground area. People were there setting up RVs for the night or they were in trucks and SUVs, pitching tents on the ground. I parked Little John's cab near the far edge of the campground. A few of the campers looked at me strange. I guess it looked a little odd to be parking a taxi in the desert. But after a glance or two, nobody paid me any mind.

"I walked back the way I came, taking a shortcut across a flat dusty spot between the hilly campground and the rock formations. It was about two miles back from the campers. I figured Little John might have gotten 'round to reporting the car stolen. The park rangers would tow it off sooner or later.

"When I got back to where we was hiding, the sun had fallen below the horizon and our side of the hill was getting dark. Only gray fading into twilight remained. I'm telling you that you need to see the desert at dusk to know what it's really like. Ain't nothin' like it.

"It was getting very dark in the cave, although I could still see. Brandi was sitting down with her arms stretched behind her toward the rock she was tied to. She had hate in her eyes. I took the gag off her. Wasn't anybody anywhere near to hear us. She breathed hard, deep, almost like she was hyperventilating. I told her I would untie her, for a while, if she wouldn't cause any trouble. I showed her my knife. I sharpened it right in front of her to get my point across.

"I got out my flashlight and shined it on her when the sun went all the way down and the desert turned to black. I took a good long look at her. She looked like hell to be such a good-looking woman. Her mascara was running down her face and her hair was stringy. Her little red dress was ripped in a few places, showing her black bra. The dress had wrinkles and grease stains, tire marks from the trunk of the car. A few black streaks marked her long legs and shoulders. She still had on the big boots that came up just below her knees.

"She caught her breath. She didn't say anything right off. I didn't want to make her talk. I didn't ask her no questions."

Zeke shifted his head, looking straight at Timber.

"I know you find it hard to believe, but I am a quiet man, not prone to talking a lot, running my mouth like some people do. I'm only telling you this now 'cause I have to."

He studied on Timber for a while, his eyes with the big pupils scanning his face, looking him up and down in the bus seat.

"And son, I want you to know that I'm counting on you to help me out, and to help Him. Don't think my sitting down here was accident, some sort of coincidence. I've only been talking to you because Jesus wants you to hear my story. I've been preaching to you this whole time."

Timber shook his head in short, rapid side-to-side turns, crinkling his eyes, disbelief. He was scared, hardly able to get out words.

"How in the world could I possibly help you?"

"You have the gift of voice and the power of the airwaves at your command."

"No. It's only an AM radio station, in Pierre, South Dakota, of all places."

"That's a start, my son, that's a start. I think you can—*and will*—take my story and much more importantly, the story of Jesus, nationwide…*world*wide."

Timber didn't say anything; the hum of the bus engine and the tires on the pavement filled in the pauses. He was becoming fearful of Zeke. He wished he'd never met this lunatic. Zeke resumed his storytelling posture, looking at the back of the seat in front of him.

"So I untied her. She didn't try to run, just rubbed her wrists. She also rubbed the side of her neck and kept twisting it. I offered her a sandwich and water. She gulped the water like she'd never seen it before. Then she gobbled down the sandwich. She was refusing to look at me. She kept her head down.

"I decided I would wait to let her speak first. Way back at the seminary there was a young preacher who taught a psychology class. He was sort of a liberal guy and I think they ran him off a year or two after I left. But he was good at teaching classes on counseling. I remember he said when counseling somebody, you should let them do most of the talking, let them get things started. I think he said that the person getting counseling should do eighty percent of the talking. I think he called it the eighty-twenty rule, if I remember right.

"After she ate, she splashed some of the water on her face, washing off the mascara and the dark lipstick. She used the old T-shirt that had been her gag for a towel. I set her bag down next to her and she pulled her cosmetics case out of it. She got a mirror out and looked at herself. Then she took a brush and brushed out her hair.

"Now, I'll never understand why a woman kidnapped in the desert would want to look in the mirror to see how her appearance was faring, but then I don't guess I've ever understood women, why they do what they do. The only thing it can be is the vanity of the Devil inside her. It had to be the Devil, his worship of *physical* beauty, instead of spiritual beauty.

"I had three days to cast the Devil out of the poor girl. I decided to get started with her on Friday morning. I'd let her rest a night. She could ignore me if she wanted to.

"Besides, the acid in my brain was beginning to fade, bringing me down slowly. I was serene, happy, relieved to have things figured out, lucky to have the savior *Hisself* guiding me." He looked back at Timber again. "He's guided all of us, just not everybody knows it. If you don't know it, that's when you'll fall prey to the tricks of the Devil.

Zeke paused, looking down the aisle toward the bus driver. Signs indicated they were near Provo, getting close to Salt Lake. Traffic picked up along the roadway and more billboards and exit signs appeared along the shoulders of the highway. He went on:

"I was hungry, so I ate one of the sandwiches. Then I started to get sleepy. I hadn't slept in thirty-six hours. I tied her up again, tying her wrists in front of her this time. Then I knotted the rope loosely around my right palm and pulled it snug between us. That way if she tried to untie it and run off, I'd feel it and wake up. I gave her a blanket and I covered myself with one. It was pitch black now, gettin' chilly. I lay there thinking that tomorrow I wanted her to dress up in that Egyptian getup she wore at the Luxor. It would help me make my point when I preached to her. And it would be a symbol to the world.

"I fell asleep. I slept lightly most of the night, turning and waking up often to check on her. Later into the night, however, maybe only an hour or two before dawn, I fell into a deep sleep. Jesus came to me, this time in a dream. He was just like I'd always pictured Him, in long flowing robes, with a white shroud over His shoulders, a crimson red robe underneath. He was walking down the road to the Valley of Fire, the long flat section I told you about, leading a huge flock of sheep—lambs as far as the eye could see. I was standing in the middle of the road as He approached me.

"I bowed down to him and he touched me on the top of the head. 'You've done well, my son, Ezekiel. I am going to leave you to finish our business. You know what you must do. I am with you in spirit always. I shall see you twenty-four years from now, on the other side.' He touched my head again and I felt warm.

"He turned to go, but then He stopped. He said, 'Just remember that as I healed the sick, you are healing a sick spirit, curing a soul plagued by the illness of the Devil. I was a young man when I cured people on earth. Healing their physical ailments was only a way of making men see my powers, who I was. Curing the soul is a much more important act, an act my father cherishes and rewards. Physical life is only a speck of sand in the ocean of eternity. The afterlife, for the saved, is the water: cool and cleansing and never-ending. You must give your all to make people understand that.'

"Then He walked on past me, down the road, toward the eastern mountains. All of a sudden the mountains disappeared and the ocean appeared. He led the flock of sheep across it and into the horizon, vanishing from sight. The sheep were so many they covered the sea like a huge wool blanket, walking across the smooth waters.

"I woke up to the sun shining in my eyes. I could feel the rope tugging gently at my hand. Rays of light were flickering into the cave, dancing on the walls. The rocks glowed red in the sunlight.

"I opened my eyes but lay still. She was struggling with the rope. She was giving it little tugs. It was almost like I had a line in the water and a catfish was nibbling on my worm. She was still under the blanket, turned away from me, on her side, about eight feet from me, facing the opening in the cave.

"This continued for a while. I could hear her breathing speed up. She was getting frustrated. I knew she couldn't get my knots loose. She sighed…deep breaths…several times.

"She sat still for a minute or two. Then there was a lot of rustling as she turned over to face me. I closed my eyes. I could feel her looking at me. I loosened my grip on the rope, giving it some slack.

"She watched me for a second and then jumped to her feet. She ran toward the opening, yanking as hard as she could. She was quicker than I expected and a few feet of rope slipped through my hands.

"But it was a long rope. I tightened my grip on it and sat up and yanked her, *hard*…This was one fish that was *not* going to get away. The rope was tied to her hands out in front of her. She spun back around and fell against the wall and then collapsed on the floor. I know it hurt her shoulders like hell the way I yanked.

"She really started hollerin', bawling like there was no tomorrow. I guess she figured there was no escaping me. Well, she was right about that.

"She sat there, hunched over, crying up a storm. Her screams echoed in that tiny little cave. It wasn't really even a cave, just a big crevice in the rocks. Her sobs petered out, becoming little whines, and then finally, silence.

"I went over to her. She cowered like I was going to hit her. 'No,' I said, 'I was going to untie you.' She cut those brown eyes up at me and a ray of sunlight through the door illuminated them. I'm telling you for a second I got weak cause there are few things prettier than a brown-eyed girl when the sun hits her face and those big marbles light up. She looked so sweet and young and innocent—*ah*, how deceptive looks can be. Here I was enamored with her physical beauty only minutes after a visit from Jesus. Looking in her eyes I had forgotten the whole purpose of why I was here. I am weak…I know it…I admit it. I resolved myself to be strong, to resist, to not let the Devil in her get the best of me. I undid the rope. I left her on the floor and went outside in front of the opening of the cave.

"The sun was just peeking up over the horizon, the sky red and orange and pink above the mountaintops. It was still deep blue over my head, streaked with thin, wispy clouds. The wispy cottonwood tree was gently swaying in the cool breeze. I never get tired of watching the sun rise and fall. The way the light dances on those rocks, there ain't nothing like it anywhere else I've ever seen. It made me want to pray—and I did. I didn't close my eyes—people only close their eyes when they pray to help themselves concentrate—but I left mine open because I wanted to soak it all in, to bask in God's wonder, all of this beautiful earth. I thanked him for giving us such beauty to revel in, to enjoy.

"I was deep in my prayer and barely heard the quick steps coming up behind me, out of the cave. I turned just in time to see my hammer coming down at my head, the glossy red of her long nails around the handle glittering in the morning sunlight. She just missed me. I ducked to the side as she stumbled past. She had my knife in her other hand.

"She turned and faced me. We squared off like two boxers in a ring. But I knew she was weak. A skinny girl with thin arms. The only thing not skinny about her were those fake tits. And those were plastic. She was a little wobbly in those high-heel boots.

"We shuffled around, sizing each other up. I knew all I had to do was to be patient, to let her make the first move and counterpunch. Her long hair kept falling down over her eyes, shiny in the growing sunlight. She had a hard time brushing it back with my knife in her hand. We stood there for a long time. She was scared to make a move.

"I'm not much of a fighter but I was confident. I had the Lord on my side, after all. She wasn't going to charge me, so I faked like I was coming at her. She swung the hammer down, lost her balance, and fell sideways on her ass. I pounced on her and grabbed her arms. My hands are strong from all the construction work. I squeezed her bony wrists until she dropped the knife and hammer. I dragged her back in the cave and put her down on her blanket.

"She was just about all cried out. She looked up at me again, her voice cracking. 'What do you want with me?' I touched the top of her head in the way Jesus had touched mine in my dream. 'To save, you,' I said.

"We spent the rest of the day without talking. She lay on the blankets in the cave, her bag under her head for a pillow, staring straight up. I sat on the rock by the opening and read my Bible, to myself. I started reading at the very beginning of the New Testament.

"I had been a long time without sitting down and reading the Bible—I mean serious reading of it. Probably ten years or more. I'd done plenty of short readings in church or in prayers, but that was quick passages, just doing my job. And the first three years in Vegas I didn't even touch my Bible. I didn't lay a finger on it. You know I had thought about just leaving it behind in my room at the Luxor, but even as unbelieving as I was at the time, I couldn't bring myself to do that.

"To sit down and really read the word of the Lord again was a thrill, a heart-shaking experience. All of the passion and feeling from my childhood in the church, of those long nights reading and praying at the seminary, reading and rereading and rereading again, that all erupted in me like a volcano. It had never left me, had been deep inside me all this time. *Even* when I was in a room full of strippers, *it* was there. *Even* when I was in bed with three whores, *it* was there. *Even* when I was drinking like a fish and betting thousands a hand on blackjack, *it* was there.

"It was there, inside me. It has always been there, deep inside me from the second I was born until the day I die, it has been and will be there." Zeke locked his eyes with Timber's again. "It's inside you, too, somewhere in there, son." He tapped his chest and turned his head back toward the seat in front of him, continuing his sermonlike story.

"I moved outside and sat down on a rock outside the opening of our cave and read the Bible the rest of the day. I was out there all afternoon. I read all four Gospels, finishing John as the sun began to fall behind the two large boulders that formed the cave. I read until it was too dark to read anymore. I was ready, finally ready, to begin giving witness to her soul, to save her from the fires of hell for which she was bound.

"She'd slept most of the day. I guess she'd been awake all night the night before, trying to get loose. She sat up and rubbed her eyes when I went back in and turned on the flashlight. It was too dark in there to see without it.

"She asked, 'What…what time is it? What day is it?'

"I told her, 'Friday night.'

"She asked, 'Where are we?'

"I said, 'We are in the valley of the lost souls.' I had not planned to say that, it just came to me that way. Words continued to pour out of my mouth, inspired. I said, 'We are in the valley of the Devil's fire. The fires of hell, fires that you can avoid if only you'll repent. The Lord will grant forgiveness for your sins…your many, *many* sins.'

"She looked at me strangely, as though I had two heads. She started to speak, and then paused, thought for a moment, and then started again.

"She asked, 'Who are you?' but did not give me time to answer before she said, 'I remember…you paid us thousands, *cash*, for sex. I remember you playing blackjack and drinking like a madman. The last time I saw you, I remember now, you pulled out your dick and waved it at the three of us. The night you ran out of money.' She said this with a look on her face like she remembered something important she had forgotten, smiling slyly.

"I told her that yes, I had fallen. I had been a pawn of the Devil, for a while. I told her that I had gotten up and was working for Jesus. I told her I had been a man of God. She didn't say anything to that.

"She looked uncomfortable in that dirty dress. It had stains on it. And I wanted to see her in that Egyptian getup. I asked her, 'Why don't you put on your Luxor suit? I'll leave you in here to change.' I wanted the Pharaoh to see this.

"She nodded and asked if she could go outside and use the bathroom first. I followed her with a flashlight and pointed to a spot where she could go behind the Joshua tree to do her business. I kept a close eye on her in case she tried to take off running. She had taken off those boots with the big heels. She wasn't nearly as tall without them. She came back from behind the tree with her panties in her hand—a slinky black little thing, just a piece of thread and a small patch.

"I gave her the flashlight to use while changing and she went in the cave. I kept the knife and hammer outside with me. I had taken to wearing 'em on my belt ever since she damn near split my head open.

"I told her to get a sandwich and a bottle of water if she wanted it. I sat back down on the rock and looked out across the darkness, the desert landscape barely visible. There was no moon that night. It was very dark—the light of the stars was it. I know nothing about astronomy but I always liked to look at the stars. The thin clouds of the morning had disappeared. The sky was crystal clear. I could see the Milky Way, the light fluffy streak floating in the middle of the sky. It was cooling off quick, like it does in the desert at night, but there was no wind.

"I went back into the cave to check on her after almost half an hour. Would you believe that she'd had a big wax candle in her bag with her and had lit that thing? She'd sat it in the far corner of the cave, near where I'd been sleeping. It lit up that little room, not much bigger'n a rich person's walk-in closet…mighty nice. And she had changed into her cocktail waitress outfit. That tiny little black and gold getup was sexy the way it squeezed her chest and showed off her legs, all the way up those long thin thighs to her hip bone. She had brushed her long hair back and pinned it with this big gold piece that matched her tiny little costume. She'd put on fresh makeup, lipstick heavy and dark red. I'm tellin' you, she looked good in that flickering light.

"She smiled at me, sort of raised her eyebrows slightly. You've seen a woman do that—one of those subtle moves? You know what I'm talking about. Where they do something so small that you'd never see it unless you were paying close attention. And they, of course, know when you are watching 'em. That's why they did it in the first place. Good-looking women have got all those damn near hypnotic moves. A woman like that can get you eating out of her hand if she wants to.

"She said to me, 'You know, Johnny,'" Zeke said, doing his best to imitate a sexy-voiced woman. "'I saw those bottles of liquor. Why don't we have a drink? It'll keep us warm here tonight.'

"She had changed her tune, boy, and good. She was like I remembered her when I started throwing that money down…I hadn't been with a woman in a long time." He smiled lasciviously at Timber. "So, yes, I had some strong tingling down in my loins, them old lusts that had caused me so many problems before. As Jesus said, I'm a 'son of man.' I'm telling you those manly longings were urging up inside me. So, *of course*, I told her I would love a liquor drink.

"I didn't have any cups, so we just drank straight from the bottle. Like you and I've been doing. I broke one open and gave her the first sip. She pursed her lips dramatically and softly stuck the opening of that bottle in, her watching me the whole time as she tilted it back. The candle flame reflected in her eyes, dark in the dimly lit cave. Unlike the sun, that little flame couldn't penetrate those eyes enough to light 'em up. Everything in there reflected back at me in those black eyes. I could see myself in her eyes. I could see the Devil that was inside me, wanting to get out and go to her. I could feel him. He was jittery…aroused at having this good-lookin' young thing before him. She was a sight to behold.

"She took a big pull on that bottle and handed it back to me and said, 'Are we going to stand up all night long?' It hadn't even occurred to me that we were standing. I looked around the tiny little cave. I said we should take the bottle out and look at the stars, sit on that rock there where I'd been reading. She said, 'We *could* just lie down over here.' She had spread a blanket out on the ground and straightened my suitcase and briefcase into a neat little pile. I know it sounds weird to say, but it was kind of homey. Reminded me of the bedroom I'd shared with Mary. That seems like a million years ago. Hard to believe it was only five.

"Anyway, that blanket looked mighty fine smoothed out. I could see myself screwing her right there. I tell you, something in me wanted to do it. I took a long drink from the bottle, still thinking about it. I handed it to her. She held the stem of the bottle in her hand up to her mouth and said how it felt good in her hand, how she liked the way it felt in her mouth, how she wished she could get something hard in her mouth, how she would like to get something about that shape hard up inside her..." Zeke was talking low, almost a whisper. Timber had to strain to hear, leaning toward him. "I reached to take her in my arms, but then remembered why I was there. I saw Jesus *entrusting* me to do what I had to do." Zeke took a deep breath and then raised his voice, almost shouting on the bus, "'We must bow *down* before the Lord, *not* the Devil,' I told her."

He lowered his tone back to his normal speech. "I grabbed her wrists and pulled her outside. I led her down to the rock and sat her down there under the dark sky. Our eyes got adjusted to the darkness and the faint light of the stars after a bit.

"She sat on the rock in her waitress costume and I preached to her. Once I got going I couldn't stop. I told her all the things I've told you, of my childhood, my family, the banks, Jolene, my whoring in Vegas, 'bout the acid and how Jesus had come to me. I told her everything 'cept how I was going to make her a symbol to the sinful world. I didn't tell her that part. I didn't want to scare her again. We was getting along so nice. She would understand one day.

"I told her how I had fallen but the Lord had forgiven me, had given me another chance. I told her that He would do the same for her if she would repent. I told her it was never too late to be saved. I must have prayed and preached to her for about four or five hours, nonstop.

"She had listened, and although she tried to hide it, I could see she was skeptical. And she was cold, shivering in that little tight outfit. I led her back in the cave and told her to sit on the floor and wrap herself in the blanket. I relit the candle, then I propped the suitcase against the rock wall and sat on it.

"I gave her the bottle to take another drink. I took one too. Then I asked her where she was from, what her childhood was like, if she went to church when she was little. She was reluctant at first, but after a few more drinks and my continued questions, she got going.

"She said she was from Long Beach, California, near Los Angeles. Had grown up playing on the beach most every day. Her mama had grown up in California. She didn't know her father at all. He'd left when she was a baby. Had only seen photos of him. He was an Italian businessman—she didn't even know what kind of business. She had been inside a church only two or three times in her life. And that was for some type of school event.

"She told me lots of childhood stories. We was passing the bottle back and forth and I think she got a little drunk. She said she had started developing at an early age.

"The night she turned fifteen an older boyfriend took her to Vegas and busted her cherry in a hotel room at Caesar's Palace. She said she had loved him very much but she cheated on him anyway, sleeping with his best friend only six months later. Said she didn't know why she did it. She said she just loved sex. She said she always had from that very first time. She couldn't help it. Said that was how she was made. She didn't see anything wrong with it.

"And Las Vegas to her *was* sex. She said she knew that first time she was there, when that boy went deep inside her and made her scream, she knew Vegas was where it was at. When she was eighteen, she and a girlfriend moved there and got cocktail waitress jobs at the Luxor. She's been there ever since. Said it was good money.

"That's about where she ended her story. She had talked for several hours. The sun was just beginning to come up, peeking over the distant mountains.

"I knew that wasn't the end, however. I asked her how long she'd been whoring. It pissed her off. She said she wasn't a prostitute. She said she only was friends with those other two girls and sent men their way. She said if she was a whore, she would just keep the men for herself and make all the money.

"I reminded her that after I threw eight thousand in cold hard cash on the bed, that she was the first one in there to screw me. She got quiet. She twisted the corner of her mouth up, moving those groomed dark eyebrows around. Then she gave me those sexy eyes again—even in the near darkness of that cave I could see her eyes, now reflecting the candlelight—and said, 'Yeah, but I liked you. I felt something special for you…And *you* were a *good* lover. You knew how to use what the Lord gave you.'

"I know…I *know* I shoulda had better sense than to believe her. I couldn't honestly trust what she was telling me. That was the Devil talking, the Devil talking with her mouth, her body language. But a man only hears what he wants to hear, believes what he wants to believe. And like I told you, my friend, Timber, I'm a man of God, not a god of a man.

"So I started rationalizing to myself. I could wallow in her fruits of evil one last time before she died. I could let her taste the pleasure of this earth before she'd go into the great beyond. But that seemed selfish, earthly.

"And then an idea came to me. I decided I could purify her by being the last one to have her on this earth. And I know there's nothin' like it in heaven. So I would be her last one…besides, she'd never had any religion put into her. I had something I was going to put in her. I moved toward her.

"I guess she could see from the look in my eye what I had in mind. She stood and dropped the blanket. Then she reached back and unzipped that tiny little costume, slipping out of it and letting it fall. She stood there in all her glory, candlelight dancing on her curves. She was shaved bare.

"She dropped to her knees and went for my belt. She took me in her hands and then her mouth, that fast up-and-down motion that I had put out of my mind for so long but remembered so fondly, so well. After awhile, I don't know how long, she pushed me down and straddled me, wet and hot and on top of me, her big chest hanging down over my face.

"She grinded on me like a banshee. I was as close to heaven as I could get on earth, about to shoot my wad, my eyes closed, when one of the six-inch nails I'd packed in my briefcase came down into the side of my neck. Man, that hurt sumpin' fierce. I bucked her off of me and knocked her on her back. I crawled on top of her, the nail stuck in the side of my neck, and put my elbow into her throat and mashed. I could feel her throat cracking like chicken bones. I got back inside her and finished…hard. She passed out cold right as I came and her eyes rolled back in her head.

"I rolled off her and pulled the nail outta my neck. It hurt like hell. She had stuck it about an inch deep, right into the muscle," Zeke gestured to the bandage, "but it didn't get into my throat. My windpipe and esophagus was OK. I couldn't say the same for her. She was gasping like a beached whale.

"Her breath was raspy but she was alive. I rolled her over on her side. Her breathing sounded better like that, smoother, although it was still rough. She was bleeding from her nose. I covered her with the blanket. She would survive at least one more day. And I could work on saving her soul the next night…I figured she might need a little more of me inside her, to make sure she was all the way pure.

"I was beat after that, I'm telling you. I took an old sock and applied pressure to my wound. I bled pretty good for a while. Then it started to clot up. Jesus was with me to keep that thing from going into my throat. She got me right in the fat part of the neck, where the muscle is. It hurt like hell but it coulda been a lot worse.

"I lay there on the blanket most of the day, just drifting in and out of sleep. She wasn't going anywhere. But I tied her hands up and held the rope just in case. She'd surprised me twice already.

"It was hot out that day, over ninety I'd bet. Hotter than it had been all week.

It got warm in our happy little home of a cave. I dozed all day. Late that afternoon I woke up and went outside. The desert looked different under a cloud cover. A storm system had rolled in from somewhere. Maybe it just bubbled up on its own...I don't know...I ain't a meteorologist.

"Anyway, it was humid, rare for the desert. More like an August day back home in Georgia. A swift wind picked up, blowing past the cave. I sat there and listened as thunder began to rumble in the distance. I could see flashes of lightning, followed by thunder several seconds later. The rumbling came down from the mountains and echoed out into the valley where we were.

"The sun began to fade earlier that day with the heavy sky. The air was getting warmer and stickier by the second. It wasn't cooling off like it usually did when the sun went down. The sky got darker and darker at a rapid pace. The clouds were building, roiling up.

"A storm was growing inside me too. I knew what I had to do, and soon. I wasn't worried. I wasn't afraid. I was ready.

"I went back into the cave to prepare Brandi to be saved. It was dark. I lit the candle. I rolled her onto her back and pulled the blanket off her. She was buck naked. She didn't wake up.

"I'm telling you, my brother, even with a black and blue neck and blood crusted around her nostrils, she looked *fine*. I wet the T-shirt I had used as a gag on her and wiped the blood off her face. Her eyes opened up. There was fear in those eyes like you ain't never seen before. I'm talking horror. She tried to talk but couldn't get words out. It was just a groan, a gurgling kind of noise.

"I asked her, 'do you want to be saved?' She tried to speak again but only gurgling noises came. She nodded her head, grimacing in pain. I told her that she could be saved, that all she had to do was open her heart to Jesus and ask forgiveness for her sins.

"She nodded again, groaning this time. The horror in her eyes had faded some. I continued to wipe her down with the wet rag. I moved down to her chest, cleaning her off slow, delicate-like. Her body was warm from being under the blanket and the heat of the day. Her skin was smooth and firm but still soft, like a ripe garden tomato picked after a summer rain.

"I began to kiss her skin, her breasts. Her red nipples hardened under my tongue. I was overcome again with lust, the Devil's lust again. I had to get it out of me. I couldn't stop. I kissed her all over her stomach, her legs, her knees, her feet even, until I went between her legs. I tasted my own seed from the night before, still dripping down from inside her.

"I took off my clothes and turned her over...*spit*...and I lifted her up and went where I'd never been before.

"She was tight, *ferocious*, the grip of the Devil. She let out a low scream. It was a wail almost like an animal. I got a rhythm going and yelled out to her, '*Are you saved?*' on each thrust, *again* and *again* and *again*...She howled back each time, louder with each stroke...She was getting her voice back and began to answer me: *yes, unh!* and *yes, unh!* and *yes, unh!* It didn't take me long when I felt Satan pass out of her and me...the white paste of salvation."

Zeke paused. He had fallen into a trancelike state. Timber eyed him nervously, scared, wanting to run away but nowhere to go, pinned to the window seat. The bus slowed and the driver exited the highway and headed downtown. The fringes of downtown Salt Lake City were like so many bland towns Timber had known. The blue sky had given way to clouds that had moved in and cast a dark shadow over the city. A light snow began to fall.

"Outside the storm had ratcheted up," Zeke continued. "The heart of it was right over us. Lightning struck right by the cave, flashing brightly inside our dark little hole in the rock. As soon as the lightning hit, thunder as loud as I ever heard cracked, shaking the whole earth. The temperature was dropping fast from the heat of the day.

"Rain began to fall on the desert floor. I lay there on top of her back, listening to those big fat drops, a Georgia-like thunderstorm. An outburst of hail was mixed into it, cracking on the ground like glass marbles tossed down by God.

"This was holy water falling down. She had to be cleansed, prepared for the sacrifice. I needed it too. I lifted her up. She was barely conscious, weak, but she was awake, her eyes were open. And those pretty eyes had a look of joy in them.

"I carried her outside and we stood, me holding her up. The rain beat down on us, washing away the sweat, the blood and the grime, my seed dripping from inside her. It washed away our sins, washed away the Devil. That cool cleansing rain. The fires of hell can't burn in no rainstorm.

"I said a prayer. I thanked God for His forgiveness, thanked Him for the eternal bliss, the afterlife of salvation that she was about to begin.

"I ended my prayer and the storm blew over quickly. I took her back in the cave and laid her out on the blanket. I pulled her Luxor costume back on her the best I could. I wanted them to find her in that outfit. It was a message to Satan, a message to the Pharaohs of the past and all non-believers of the present that Jesus was the way and the evil ways represented by the little whore suit would be overcome.

"Her breathing was slower, still raspy. She drifted off to sleep. I didn't know if she'd wake up or not.

"I sharpened my knife again. It would split a hair, I'm tellin' you. Then I sat and read my Bible by the flickering candlelight. It was burning down near the end, barely enough wax to get me past midnight.

"I fell asleep for a while when the candle burned out…I woke up a few hours later when I heard a rooster crow. Now I've got good enough sense to know there ain't no chickens in the Mojave Desert. But I don't think I dreamt it. I heard that thing. The rooster was sent to me, to wake me up in time to do what I had to do.

"When the rooster stopped, it was dark and quiet as a tomb. The only sound was her breathing…regular but raspy. I grabbed three of the big nails from my briefcase and the flashlight. The knife and hammer I still had on my belt.

"I knew in my blood, in my bones, that it was time. My time—*her time*—had come. She was saved. I said a short prayer and began to do my business. I carried her out…the way a groom carries his bride across the threshold. She startled awake. She was confused, barely conscious, disoriented. She choked a little like she wanted water. But there was no time for that. The Earth was turning. I had to get the job done.

"The sun had not peeked over the horizon, but the first rays of light was creepin' up into the desert sky. A light blue shade was beginning to displace the dark blue over the eastern vista. It was dry…cold. The storm had blown through and cleaned out the clouds. We had all been cleansed for a new morning. I didn't need the flashlight once my eyes got adjusted.

"She started squirming around in my arms. I put her down by the trunk of the cottonwood tree. I cut a piece of rope about six feet long and tied her feet tight together.

"I lifted her upside down and tried to hold her up with one hand on her feet. I had the nails in this hand." He gestured with it to Timber. "I pinned her back against the tree by pressing my shoulders against her, mashin' against her stomach. I took the hammer in my other hand and was going to try to nail her ankles to the tree. She was more awake. She sensed something was going down. Her arms flailed at my legs…but she was weak. She wasn't strong enough to hurt me.

"But when I pressed more full into her, trying to hold her still…her back against the tree…she bit my crotch as hard as she could. *Damn*, that hurt like hell. I pulled back, letting her go. She fell to the ground, only a few feet. She landed head first, however, and it knocked her out cold. She'd bitten down hard on my pecker and my left testicle. My pecker didn't hurt that bad—it's durable—but my left nut hurt like hell. It still does. That thing is going to be sore for a while. I'm glad I had on pants or I'd be about like one of them sex-change freaks I was tellin' you about...a woman with one nut.

"I studied on the tree for a while, trying to put the nut-pain out of my mind. I was figuring how I could get her hung upside down on that tree. I planned to nail her up but didn't know how to hold her while I was doing the nailing. I got the idea to loop the rope over the branches and pull her up like I had a winch. Sort of like one of them traps you see in Tarzan movies where as soon as someone steps into it, the rope snatches around their feet and yanks them upside down, leaving them hanging there.

"That was the trick. The thin tree creaked, and the first branch I looped her over broke. But the rope slid down only a foot or so to the next branch, a sturdy hold.

"I took one of them six-inch nails and reached up and hammered it into the front of her ankle, right through the joint, and into the trunk. She moaned, awake again. I made sure I kept my crotch a safe distance from her mouth, pressing my knee against her neck. I drove a nail into the other ankle and she sobbed, a gurgling wail.

"I hung my hammer back on my belt and unsheathed my knife. I keep it sharp, like I told you."

Timber looked away, out the window. The bus was sitting at a red light on a downtown Salt Lake street, the city flat with towers of medium height, the mountains to the north snow-capped.

"So I took her left hand," Zeke continued, "and pulled it, straightening it out away from her body. I pulled hard on it, keeping her torso in place against the tree with my knee. The nails were holding her feet good. I studied on her shoulder, where I could cut through it. She had skinny arms.

"The knife sliced right through the skin. She passed out cold the minute the blade cut into her. There wasn't much muscle at all and it cut easy. Only the tendon inside the joint gave me problems. It was like cutting through a tough piece of plastic...or rubber...like a melted fan belt. I had to saw but I got through it. The arm fell loose, away from her.

"She bled like a stuck pig, deep red blood spurtin' out, a few long squirts and then a steady pour down onto her shoulders, her neck and her face. Her long blonde hair got soaked with it, matted. The sun was coming up by now, getting over the horizon. The red rocks were beginning to light up."

"I cut the other arm off. Less blood than the first, but just as much difficulty in getting through the gristle in the joint. Them tendons is tough.

"Finally, both arms were off and she was hung up like I was told to do. I held the arms up, holding the two hands together, letting the blood drain out of the upper arm. A little piece of tendon dangled loose out of her left shoulder.

"'Bout this time she stopped breathing. I held her hands and knelt to say a prayer for her.' Zeke closed his eyes and steepled his fingers together. "'Lord Jesus,' I said, 'I give you Brandi…for the Kingdom of Heaven. I have delivered her from the evil world, washed her of her sins, her many, *many* sins, to your forgiving temple in the sky. Only you, Lord, can make an honest woman out of her. You are so great, my Lord, to have mercy on her wretched soul.'"

Zeke opened his eyes, his pupils bigger than life, and dropped his hands back to his lap.

"I took one last look at her. Her face was soaked red, hanging upside down… her hair caked with blood. A deep crimson spot was puddling in the sand only a foot or two beneath her head. The sun was now more than halfway over the horizon, a mountain over near the Grand Canyon, lighting up this world we temporarily call home.

"I wiped the blood off my hands, my knife, my boots. I went into the cave and changed into my suit. Then I wrapped her arms in a blanket and put 'em in the suitcase to take with me…nobody was going to mistake *this* for the crucifixion. I put the last bottle of liquor, my knife and my Bible in my briefcase…everything else I left behind.

"I walked toward the campground. On the road near there I flagged down two good old boys, young fellas from Texas in a pickup truck. They had camped out the night before and were heading over to the Grand Canyon. They said they'd take me to where I could catch the next bus. They had been trippin' in the park all night. They were raving about the colors of the sunset and the sunrise, the cries of lonesome coyotes in the nighttime. I opened up my bottle and we passed it around. I listened to their stories. They had been having such a good time. I had to admit to myself there was a lot of wonder in the world…this big ole world."

He turned to Timber, a warm smile, as though he were speaking the final prayer in a long sermon.

"But this world ain't nothing but a rock, a speck of dust compared to where we'll be in the afterlife, my brother, you can bank on that…*Eternity*," he said, hanging on the word, "*Eternity*…is a *very* long time.

REDEMPTION

The bus idled at a traffic light one block from the Salt Lake City station marked with white plastic rectangular signs all lit up, the sleek Greyhound shape burning red on a field of white. Down the street dirty with wet snow pushed to the sides Timber could see the six granite spires of the Salt Lake Temple, basking in floodlights, and beyond it the mountains, snow covered in the distant horizon, dwarfing the downtown, deserted on a late Sunday afternoon. The day was growing darker by the minute and the bare trees cast no shadows in the dull street. Light snow continued to fall. A chap-faced man moved from where he had been standing on the corner and headed down the sidewalk, pushing a grocery cart. Zeke had stopped talking. He sat with his briefcase on his lap, looking straight ahead, his eyes serene, the scratches on his face ominous in the faint shadows of the interior bus lights.

Timber kept his head turned to the window, where his reflection was beginning to show as the light died, anxiously looking at the side streets of boarded-up downtown storefronts in snow flurry and late afternoon dimness. The stoplight turned green and the bus lurched toward the station. Timber desperately wanted to dismiss Zeke's story as pure bullshit, the insane ramblings of a burned-out acidhead, a sick religious nut whose brain had been fried like bacon on hallucinogenics and liquor and the Pentecost. He was yet another of the rambling lunatics who traveled on the bus, a class of people whose minds didn't know the distinction between fact and fiction. Timber had met crazy people almost every time he rode the bus and had in the past been able to avoid them or tune them out. He wished he had avoided Zeke, had never seen this fallen Georgia preacher.

Timber prayed, his first prayer in years: *Please Lord, let his story be a lie…please let it be a perverted tale, a fabrication of a crazy man to pass the time.* He reasoned the story might be what a deranged man would tell to satisfy that strange burning desire to impress another man. Timber had heard men lie about anything and everything to make other men believe claims of bedding the most women, the best-looking woman, of having the most money. Men wanted to be the king of the henhouse, a rooster crowing at the break of day, declaring his superiority, even if it was only king of the chickens. Men did that, lied about all manner of things, some for no good reason at all. Timber had done it plenty of times himself, sometimes even on the radio. He wasn't proud of it. It was the way he was, the way most men were. When he was young, he had believed all the stories older men told him, took them as the gospel truth, but now that he had been around, every story was taken with a grain of salt. He knew how men were and that what they said could not be trusted.

This story *had* to be the twisted braggadocio of a crazy preacher hysterical on the secular insanity that was Las Vegas. He should ignore Zeke and go about his business of getting home; he had his own problems to deal with. But what if Zeke's story were true? The murdering preacher could disappear into the vast wilderness of America, the great wide open West, and under yet another name, start his own church and recruit poor desperate souls, someone like Timber's mama, to listen to his deranged sermons. He might attack another woman, perhaps Timber's sister next time, wherever she might be, if she was even still alive.

Timber ticked off the details of the story in his mind. There seemed to be a preponderance of evidence: Zeke's scratches…the bandage on his neck…the huge pupils…the zest and consistent details and sincerity of the story. Timber believed deep down in his soft bones that Zeke had told him the truth about the girl in the desert, that there *was* an armless woman down in the Valley of Fire State Park hanging upside down from a cottonwood tree. He looked up at Zeke's suitcase in the overhead rack and fought off a shiver. The preacher's intense eyes did not lie.

The bus turned into the parking lot, the asphalt grimy and wet with snow that was starting to stick but still too new for the snowplow. A huge white sign with red lettering screamed BUSES ONLY. The Greyhound crossed over a bulging speed bump as though it were tiptoeing, the front left side tires rising first and then the right side tires.

"Well, my brother, I guess this is it," Zeke said. He thrust his hand out to Timber to shake. "I wish you Godspeed and good luck, Brother Timber."

Zeke's voice was tired, almost hoarse from talking for so long, but that didn't stop him. "Remember that Jesus died for your sins and the Lord is always with you, always watching you. Remember that He and I are counting on you."

The bus moved lethargically toward a parking space, waiting on another bus to clear the way. Timber mustered up a dead-fish handshake but did not look Zeke in the eye. The preacher's hand was dry and cold and smooth. A heavy weight pressed down on Timber like he was in a recurring dream where he was being chased but could not move his feet to run. His bad foot ached, numb, and he didn't know if he would be able to stand up and get off the bus when it stopped—he felt like he might simply sit in his seat until he died. He hated himself for not being more of a man; if he had any balls at all, he should be able to take this skinny man down easily.

The driver pulled the bus forward into a parking space near the door of the station, the air brakes whining like a tired metal horse. Zeke stood and reached up for his hard-shell blue suitcase, wedged tight in the overhead rack. He tugged it gently from side to side to get it loose. Timber watched him out of the corner of his eye. Zeke pulled the suitcase down and carried it carefully.

Zeke began to move down the aisle as the passengers filled the exit and slowly unloaded. He looked back with an ingratiating preacher's smile. The bus was more than half full, having filled up with passengers at the stop in Provo. The lights inside the bus were all turned on; outside the bus station, street lights started to flicker to life in the dusk.

Timber pulled his bag from under his seat and rose to leave, taking his time. He limped on the bad foot, stiff and sleepy due to the lack of circulation while sitting. He rested when he could with his weight on his strong foot. Two women and two children had moved into the aisle between him and Zeke, fooling with bags in the overhead rack. Timber watched through the tinted windows as Zeke stepped off the bus, carrying the black briefcase in his right hand and his suitcase in his left. A chubby policeman stood outside the door smoking a cigarette, staring at the ground. Zeke stopped and spoke to the cop, apparently asking him the time and patting him good-naturedly on the shoulder.

Timber breathed heavily as the procession off the bus slowed to a crawl. The women and children in the aisle were barely moving. The first woman was in her seventies, shuffling slowly along, complaining about the cold, her hand with a cane shaking. He could tell from her mumbled drawl that she was a Southerner, amazed at the snowfall, regarding the flurry like it was a miracle. The two children struggled with suitcases. Timber wanted to scream at them to hurry. He watched helplessly as Zeke turned and looked back to the bus before disappearing through the glass door into the station. Cold sweat was beading up under Timber's arms and on his hands.

Once the family gathered themselves together and the line finally began to move, Timber stepped off the bus, limping as fast as he could walk, and darted around the dawdling women to the fat policeman. The short white cop eyed him suspiciously, taking a long drag on his cigarette. He had a big bushy mustache that grew over his top lip into his mouth. Timber studied the crest on the dark-blue uniform more closely—he wasn't a cop, but a security guard.

"Hey! Excuse me," Timber was breathless, his voice higher and quicker than usual. "There's a man here. He killed a woman near Vegas. You've got to stop him."

The security guard acted like he didn't want to be bothered. He didn't look Timber in the eye. He raised his hand and pointed lazily down the street.

"The police department is only two blocks that way." He had a slow, emotionless voice. "You should go file a report on him."

The guard took another drag on his cigarette, exhaling the smoke from his nostrils.

"No! He'll get away," Timber said, grabbing his flabby arm and pulling him. "Come with me."

The guard, wide-eyed in Timber's grasp, followed him into the bus station lobby, a big dingy room with a brown terrazzo floor and a high ceiling and wooden benches and two windows on one end that opened to a kitchen that served coffee and sandwiches. Fluorescent light fixtures lorded above the room. About twenty people milled about or sat on the old high-backed benches, some reading newspapers, others sleeping and some just staring vacantly off into space. Timber rested his weight on his good foot. He saw Zeke standing three-people deep in the coffee line.

"*There*," Timber said, pointing to Zeke. "Over *there*. With the suitcase and briefcase. In the cowboy boots."

"Buddy, are you sure?" the guard said, panicking, his voice soft. "You want me to call the cops? I don't carry a gun. I'm *not* a cop. I'm just a night watchman. I just got here."

"Yeah...call 'em."

But the guard did not move.

Timber watched as Zeke turned and saw him standing with the guard. He smiled at Timber and nodded. Zeke left the coffee line without being served and began walking, toward the door to where two taxis waited outside in the near darkness.

Timber thought about the knife, Zeke's strong hands, the desperation and danger of the man's insanity. He thought about the dead girl hanging upside down in the desert, her arms sliced off. He thought about the suitcase Zeke carried, about what might be inside it. He looked to the faces of the people around the bus station for help or recognition, but no one responded.

Timber loosened his grip on his duffel bag and let it fall to the floor. He began moving across the room, toward Zeke, walking fast and then breaking into a run, picking up pace as he went, skipping along on his weak foot. He feared the sharp blade slashing into his gut but an adrenalin rush drove him on in the direction of the dangerous preacher. He hadn't run anywhere in a long time, years, and he started to breathe heavily with the exertion, even on the short sprint across the marble floor of the bus station lobby, the hard terrazzo hurting his bad ankle every time his foot touched down.

Zeke watched him coming with a serene expression and slowed his steps. Before he reached the exit, he stopped walking and turned, setting the hard-shell suitcase against the wall behind him. He took a position in front of a large window with a view of the waiting buses, the briefcase in his right hand. Timber lunged at him, arms outstretched, but Zeke stepped to the side, reared back his right arm and, in a motion like he might swat a fly, he struck Timber across the jaw with the corner of the metal-trimmed briefcase, making a loud *thwack*...

Timber opened his eyes to see Zeke looming over him and he could feel the flat of the knife blade pressing hard against his Adam's apple. Zeke's knee mashed firmly into his chest, pinning him supine to the floor. Timber gasped for air, his jaw throbbing. Zeke looked down at him and shook his head like Timber was a child in whom he was disappointed.

"*Son*," he said, his voice scratchy and scolding, "you oughta know better than to try to give me a *kiss*."

Timber glanced to the side and could see that the hapless security guard had recruited a bus driver for help. The driver, a ruddy-faced man, and the guard stood about fifteen feet away. The pudgy security guard was taking slow steps backward but the stocky bus driver moved forward and reached into his shiny blue Greyhound jacket and pulled out a sleek black pistol from a shoulder holster and pointed it at Zeke. Timber heard him pull back on the hammer, a bullet enter the chamber. He had both hands on the gun.

"Okay, boy, put that knife down," the bus driver said, calmly but gruffly, a deep Southern accent, the voice of a man who clearly didn't plan to take any shit. Timber turned his head and looked at the driver. He had neat, unnaturally dark hair and lines on his face from too much sun; his hands were steady holding the pistol on Zeke. The security guard cowered behind him. His voice cut through the silence of the bus station lobby.

"Toss it over here on the floor and I won't have to plug your ass. And don't think I won't do it. You wouldn't be the first one I shot. I was an Atlanta *poe-liceman* for twenty-two years."

Zeke kept the knife pressed to Timber's throat, rotating the blade in his hand so the sharp edge scraped Timber's neck. He turned his face to the bus driver as though he recognized an old friend.

"Well *I'll* be…another *Georgia* boy," he said, his voice the tone he might use at a church picnic. "But I ain't a city boy. Myself, I grew up down in Armstrong, down there near Macon, and lived in Piney, up where the mountains get started, a long time…Never did care much for *At*-lanta. Y'all city slickers was always kind of uppity."

The driver stepped forward, only about five feet from Zeke, still holding the pistol firm with both hands, aimed at Zeke's chest.

"I don't care if you are the royal *poo-bah* of Tim-buk-tu. Drop that knife 'fore I shoot your ass. We can have *old home* week later on."

Zeke looked down at Timber.

"Well boy, I guess the Lord is on *your* side this afternoon."

He stood, relieving the pressure of his knee on Timber's sternum, and took the knife from his throat. He tossed it on the floor toward the bus driver, clattering on the marble floor. Timber tried to get up but Zeke shoved his foot solidly into Timber's solar plexus, pushing him back down with his boot heel. The blow was hard, square in the stomach and Timber writhed in pain on his back. Zeke kept his boot heel on him and looked down, pointing a long bony finger. "Don't forget your *calling*, boy. *You*, my brother, are the one with the Lord's work to do now."

The bus driver charged forward and shoved Zeke, ordering him against the wall with his hands over his head. Zeke obeyed and the driver stayed behind him, with the pistol drawn. Zeke turned back as though to speak but the bus driver cut him off.

"You keep quiet," the driver said to Zeke. "You can tell it all to the police about why you had that knife on this man's throat. I ain't got time for your personal problems."

The driver then turned his head slightly to look at Timber, his voice friendlier. "You all right, son? You should stick around and talk to the law when they get here."

"Yeah, thanks," Timber said. He pulled himself to a sitting position on the floor; he was soaked in cold sweat, his jaw aching and his stomach numb. He saw the blue suitcase against the wall near where Zeke stood with his hands on the back of his head. He scrambled to his feet and went over to it and picked it up, limping and gasping as he went. The suitcase was light, as though it was empty, and he felt something long and solid shift inside when he picked it up by the handle. He sat it down flat and fought with the latches to open it.

"What are you doing?" the security guard said, lurching behind him. "What's in that thing?"

Timber clicked the latches and opened the suitcase, unleashing a sharp, rotten smell. It appeared to hold only an old blanket wadded up inside. He stared into the suitcase for a few seconds before he took the corner of the blanket where it was bunched up and pulled it back, revealing a woman's clenched hand with long red fake fingernails and shiny rings on two fingers. Her ring finger wore a silver band with green trim, almost in the shape of a cross, that eerily reflected the bus station's overhead lights.

Timber closed his eyes and hung his head. The security guard gasped. The bus driver, still holding the pistol on Zeke, stepped over to peek into the suitcase.

"Jeez-us Christ," he said, his voice deep. "Jeez-us *fucking* Christ."

Zeke turned his head to look back over his right shoulder, the lights reflecting in his huge pupils, highlighting the fiery blood-mark.

"That's right, my brother, that's right...He is the one...You got it *exactly* right...A-men."

PEACE OF MIND

Timber sat about halfway down the aisle, on the right side, close to the wall. He was one of only three people in the sanctuary, almost thirty minutes before the service, most of the congregation still in Sunday school. It was a clear Louisiana day, already quite warm in early May, the colorful azalea blooms long gone from the shrubs, a drastic change from South Dakota when he left, the trees still bare and the grass brown. Light beamed in through the big frosted glass windows, the panes turning the sunshine into an ethereal, soft but bright light, reflecting gently off the chandeliers. The church was very clean, freshly painted, an almost solid beige atmosphere. It was peaceful, tranquil, the way he remembered it when he was a little boy. He was content, happy to be sitting there, back home in Whitcomb. He felt like a child again.

He wished his mama were alive to see him. She would have been so proud of him, the new *manager* of the local religious radio station. He could hear her saying it, telling her church friends about her son. Religious programming was the only kind of radio she ever thought was any count, that and baseball games. Whitcomb had never had a full-gospel station in her day. She'd had to tune into a station in Baton Rouge or, when the weather was good and the ionosphere cooperated, she could pick up two gospel stations out of New Orleans and, very rarely, one in Mississippi. The Mississippi station was her favorite, as she was born and raised there. She had listened to these stations on a small plastic radio she kept in the kitchen, on top of the refrigerator. He remembered her humming along with the music when cooking.

He thought about how he had fallen so far short in treating his mama well. He should have given her a better radio or even a stereo. He scolded himself, thinking of how much she would have loved it. He could have sent her some gospel records, some cassettes. He probably could have gotten many of them for free from the record companies if he had just asked. She always had been so pleased at his gifts, even the smallest things he had given her had thrilled her. It would not have been too much trouble for him. But he had never bothered, had never been a thoughtful son. He'd always been out only for himself.

There were so many things he wished he'd done for her. He should have lied to her, told her that he was going to church regularly, even when he wasn't. She would never have known the difference and it would have made her so happy. For some obstinate reason, when he was younger, he had wanted to break her of her habit of religion. He had found it completely foolish. Sitting in her church, he realized that this was all she had, all she could rely upon, all that she could trust. It had been her rock. He had scoffed at her church, the one thing to which she clung. She certainly had not been able to depend on him, his father or his sister. They had all let her down, many times over.

He closed his eyes and clasped his fingers in his lap, thinking about his mama, about his good fortune to find the job back home that would pay him enough to start paying down some of his debts. He had gone four weeks without a drink since the bus ride from Vegas. He thought about his sister and how long she had been gone and how a private detective he contacted in New Orleans told him it would be almost hopeless to find her after all these years, not to mention very expensive to even try. He ran through his head projects he wanted to do on the house, the house he had grown up in, the first home he had owned since his condo in Houston more than twenty years ago. He was about to say a prayer when...

"*Tommy?*" A loud, high voice startled him and he opened his eyes and sat up straight. "Tommy Goodman? *Is that you?*"

A slim brunette about his age with glasses in a conservative blue sun dress, and two children, a lanky teenage boy with a surly expression and a chubby girl of about twelve, were taking seats in the pew in front of him. The children sat down but their mother continued to stand and face him, grinning.

"Hey...yeah, I'm Ti—uh, Tom Goodman, all right. That's me. Been a long time since I've been here."

The woman did not look the least bit familiar, but, oddly, he thought he recognized the little girl. It seemed he'd seen her somewhere a long time ago, many years. But that couldn't be—she was far too young for him to remember.

"Don't you remember me?" the woman said. She was excited and spoke loudly. He glanced quickly around the sanctuary to see that the people were beginning to file into the pews. All of them were looking at him and the woman he didn't recognize. He plumbed his memory but he could not recall her.

He began to speak, to say it had been a long time, almost thirty years, since he had lived here, that his memory wasn't so good, that he'd lived in seventeen cities and had met many people, most of them whose names he could not remember either, but she cut him off.

"I'm *Emily!* Emily Jacks. We got baptized together, *forty-two* years ago this month. Can you believe that? You remember me, don't you?"

The chubby little girl looked just like her mother had then.

"Oh, *yeah*, of course I do," he said, enthusiastically as he could, his radio voice booming in the church. "Emily. It's good to see you. How could I forget?" He leaned forward for a handshake but she spread her arms to hug him. They hugged lightly over the pew. She smelled good and had a gentle touch. He hadn't hugged anyone in a very long time.

She introduced her children to him, John, fifteen, and Jenny, twelve. Then her expression changed, her eyes stared straight at the floor.

"I've been single for about five years now," she said, her voice much lower. "I moved back here three years ago, after living in Dallas for almost twenty years." She lifted her face to look at him.

"Are you just visiting?" she asked, a happy tone again.

"No. I just moved back to town, this week. I'm going to be the new radio station manager."

"*Really?*" she said. "I heard they were bringing the old radio station back as a religious station. As a matter of fact, when I heard that, I thought about you…you and your daddy…" Her voice trailed off and her expression changed to a sad one.

"Ah, that's okay," he said, waving away her concern with his hand. "I'm back. We sign the station on the air again tomorrow."

"That's just great news," she said. "I want to have you over for dinner one night next week. To welcome you back into town. Maybe Tuesday or Thursday?"

"Yeah, Thursday would be good." He didn't tell her that was his fiftieth birthday. He felt blood rushing to his face. He was glad he had a beard.

The church organist came in and sat down and started playing, a sign that the service would begin in ten minutes.

"Let's talk after church," she said. She sat a few feet to his right, in the pew in front of him. She turned her head to smile back at him and caught him watching her. She was tall and had lost the chubbiness that she'd had as a girl. She was good looking to be in her early fifties.

He sat back. The sanctuary was filling up, a bigger crowd than Timber had remembered seeing in a long time, maybe the biggest crowd he'd ever seen here. A family and three old women, blue-gray hair and pastel dresses, had squeezed into his row.

Pastor Phil Gaskins came in from a side door down front. His hair was thinner and grayer and his face had filled out since Timber had seen him last, when he preached Mama's funeral. It had been more than ten years since Timber first met him when Mama got sick, before she went into the nursing home. The slight preacher walked up the steps to the dais and sat in his chair, checking the church program before putting a bookmark in the Bible. The choir was beginning to file in behind him and take their seats. The pastor looked out into the crowd, surveying the faces with a friendly, inquisitive expression. He saw Timber and smiled. He stood and walked down from the dais onto the floor of the sanctuary, toward Timber. He shook Timber's hand with great gusto, a strong grip for a little man.

"It's *so* good to see you here, Mr. Goodman."

"Thanks, Pastor Phil," Timber said meekly, conscious of the entire church watching the exchange.

"I heard the news just this Friday that you would be the new man at the radio station. It's so good to have one of our own…one of our own people in there. I'm a big supporter of that station. I'm thinking about buying time to put our services on the air."

Timber smiled, nodding the whole time. "Thank you, pastor. That would be great to have you."

"Tom," the pastor said, a serious tone. "I hope you don't mind if I introduce you during the service. I want to tell everybody to listen. And lots of folks read about what you did out West—catching that crazy man. We are proud of you."

"Thank you, I'd be glad for you to do that. But…Pastor…can I ask you something? Don't say anything about that, that incident. I'm…I'm kind of tired of talking about it, answering questions. It was a hard thing."

"Of course, I understand. I'll…I'll mention only the radio station. I'll catch up to you after the service. Let's go to lunch one day this week."

Timber nodded. "Yes, we should do that. I'll show you around the station."

"I'd like that. Thank you, Tom."

The pastor shook hands once more and returned to his seat up front.

The choir filed into the two rows behind the pulpit and the Reverend Gaskins began the service with a prayer. He then announced the first hymn, "Send the Light," and the church organ began. The congregation stood and began to sing, the old woman sitting next to him warbling loudly, and a man behind him with a good deep voice singing strong.

Timber zoned out in the first part of the service, pretending to listen, pretending to sing along with the hymns, thumbing pages in the book, moving his lips but only mumbling the words, like he had done thousands of times before. He'd never been a singer, even as a child. The progression of the service was very familiar even though it had been more than twenty years, excluding weddings and funerals, since he had last attended church. He bowed his head and went through the motion of praying as Pastor Phil led the congregation.

He couldn't help it but Zeke Blizzard was on his mind again. He substituted Zeke where Reverend Gaskins stood. He could see him back in that little church in Georgia, leading the hymns, saying the prayers, preaching the sermon, calling for sinners to come down and be saved before it was too late. In a strange way he couldn't hate him. He tried to hate him but he could only feel sorry for him. Timber didn't want to forgive Zeke for what he had done, but in his heart he couldn't help it. He also couldn't forget, couldn't shake Zeke's voice, his round pupils and the blood-marked eye, his story and the letter he had written him afterward.

The letter came to him at the South Dakota radio station two weeks and one day after the bus trip with Zeke, an envelope with its return address a Las Vegas jail. It was written in pencil in a crude, curling script:

Dear Brother Timber,

I hope the Lord finds you well today and shines His everlasting love down upon you.

I want you to know I am forgiving you for turning me in to the police. I want to thank you for doing so.

I chose you on the bus because I knew you were capable. I needed you to betray me just as Jesus needed Judas to betray Him.

Know that Judas loved Jesus even though he betrayed Him. Judas was weak and Jesus was strong. Our fates will be similar.

I will die here in this prison, the juice of death in my arm. You will eventually take your own life, if you have not already.

I can see it in your conflicted eyes. I can hear it in your weak heart. In spite of your strong voice, you are a weak man.

I wish I could change your fate—hellfire and damnation awaits those who take their own lives—but who am I to change God's plans?

The love Jesus had for Judas did not save the traitor's soul. His guts burst like a melon in the field of blood.

Yours in Christ,
Reverend Ezekiel Blizzard Jr.

Timber had ripped up the letter into tiny pieces and thrown it in the trash. He *had* considered taking his own life during a few dark moments in the days after Zeke's arrest. He'd gone home that night and gotten his daddy's old shotgun from under the couch. He had loaded it with a shell but never followed through with it. With Mama gone, he had reasoned, there would be no one to miss him. Ending it all was something he had thought about many times before, in the long wake of misery after Tammy disappeared. But, ultimately, he never had the guts to stick the barrel in his mouth and pull the trigger—this morning in the Whitcomb Baptist Church was the first time he was sincerely glad he hadn't gone through with it.

The night after he got Zeke's letter and had put the shotgun away, he slept deeply, dreaming he was back in his mama's house, lying on a daybed by the window in the spare bedroom. It was a sunny, windy day, and up through the window he could see the leaves of the big oak rustling in the breeze, the vine-covered limbs swaying slightly, a little blurred through the old, thick glass. From his angle—looking straight up—the drifting branches had an eerie, ghostlike quality. The smell of Mama's fried chicken and biscuits and gravy floated down the hallway to him. Mama stepped from the kitchen, wearing her apron, her voice like a chime, calling him, "*Tom*-Tom, *Tom*-Tom." He woke up in the middle of the night, desperate to go back South, back home.

The very next day he got the job offer, right out of the blue, to run the Whitcomb station. The religious broadcaster and new owner of the Whitcomb radio station—the station that had been his father's all those years ago—had tracked him down after reading the national news coverage of Zeke's arrest, stories that painted Timber as a hero for capturing the murderer and bank robber.

He tried to shake off the memory of Zeke and focus on the service. A group of ten children from ages four through eight had gone up front and sat at the feet of the assistant pastor who pulled up a chair to the edge of the dais and told them a story. The congregation smiled and a few chuckled softly at the unsteady ambles of the littlest ones looking around the church with bright eyes and innocent faces. The young preacher, who seemed but a child himself, told them the story of how Moses as a baby was left in a basket in the reeds along the river's edge because his mother wanted to save him from being killed as the Pharaoh had ordered. The preacher spoke deliberately so the children could follow, saying that Moses' mother had not wanted to abandon her baby, but it was the only thing she could do to save him. He concluded that she, like Jesus does for us, wanted to save him from evil. Jesus is always saving us, he said, even if what He might be doing does not seem like it at the time. "You've got to have faith," he said, "that whatever is happening is happening for the best. Jesus is always taking care of us." The preacher had the children hold hands in a circle and he prayed, finished with an *amen* that was echoed by many in the congregation and then he ushered the young ones off to the nursery.

After that, the Reverend Gaskins called on everyone to stand and greet their neighbors and welcome visitors. Timber shook the hands of those around him.

"Hello again, stranger," Emily said with an endearing laugh, clasping Timber's hand and wrist with both of her warm smooth hands.

As everyone began to sit down, Pastor Phil spoke up.

"I'd like to welcome a native son back to Whitcomb, Mr. Tom Goodman… Tom, would you stand?" Timber stood slowly, crossing his hands in front of his waist, his head tucked down a little, his eyes looking up to the preacher.

"Tom," the pastor continued, "after a very successful national career in radio, has returned home to revive our local radio station. It's now going to be an all-Christian station, locally produced and operated. Please be sure to tune in tomorrow to 1450 on your AM dial and support him. Tom, as I'm sure many of you know, is the son of the late Mabel Goodman.

"I'm sure," he continued, "many of you remember her if you've been coming to church here a long time. The church never had a bigger supporter. She helped the church get through some lean times with her financial support and her prayers. I don't think she missed a Sunday until she got ill. Mrs. Goodman loved her son…she loved this church…and she loved the Lord. I'm sure she is up in heaven now, happy as can be, looking down on her son, sitting in her church, preparing to carry the word of the Lord to us all. Welcome home, Tom. We are lucky to have had your mother as a member. And we are lucky to have you here now. May God bless you in leading the new radio station as you further His mission."

He smiled at Timber, lingering on him for a moment before opening his hymnal.

"Please turn to page 188 and join as we sing together that most wonderful of hymns, 'Amazing Grace.'"

Timber was lightheaded, almost faint. He could feel the eyes of all the church upon him. Emily smiled back at him, her eyes bright in the sunshine through the windows. He could feel his mama's eyes, God's eyes too, beaming lights through the frosted glass, shining on his shoulders.

He stood and picked a hymnal up and opened it, as though in a dream. The church began to sing but he stood there, in awe, for the first three verses. This was one of the few hymns he knew by heart, always his favorite. He caught up in the final verse, overcome by the urge to sing.

When we've been there ten thousand years,
Bright shining as the sun,
We've no less days to sing God's praise
Than when we'd first begun.

The organ played out the last few notes. He sat down, closed his hymnal and returned the white book to the narrow shelf on the back of the pew. The congregation shifted in their seats, in preparation for the sermon that was to come. He crossed his bad foot over his good one and leaned back, comfortable.